The voice

Emma couldn't remember a time when the voice hadn't
haunted the back of her mind. It wasn't her conscience, guilty
or otherwise. It wasn't hers at all; she'd never claimed it. Until
Eleanor burst into her life, Em had called it the Mother Voice
but Eleanor's voice had been as rich as her hair and utterly unlike the familiar voice inside Em's head.

*You should go home. Get out the books and the candles.
Take a walk through the wasteland. Tonight could be your
lucky night.*

Behind
Time

Lynn Abbey

ACE BOOKS, NEW YORK

BEHIND TIME

An Ace Book / published by arrangement with
the author

PRINTING HISTORY
Ace mass-market edition / July 2001

All rights reserved.
Copyright © 2001 by Lynn Abbey
Cover art by Phil Howe

The Penguin Putnam Inc. World Wide Web site address is
www.penguinputnam.com

Check out the ACE Science Fiction & Fantasy newsletter
and much more on the Internet at Club PPI!

ISBN: 0-441-00831-3

ACE®
Ace Books are published by The Berkley Publishing Group,
a division of Penguin Putnam Inc.,
375 Hudson Street, New York, New York 10014.
ACE and the "A" design
are trademarks belonging to Penguin Putnam Inc.

PRINTED IN THE UNITED STATES OF AMERICA

10 9 8 7 6 5 4 3 2 1

One

Sleeping Beauty had nothing on Eleanor Merrigan.
The hi-tech monitors that had surrounded her during
the first days of her hospitalization were gone now and the
many invasions of her flesh were hidden beneath a crisp,
white sheet. With her dark hair flared across the pillow
and her cheeks flushed with a sunrise glow, Eleanor was
the very image of a dormant princess albeit in the fluores-
cently sterile confines of a private hospital room rather
than a forest or castle.

Emma Merrigan sat beside Eleanor's bed in an almost-
comfortable, way-too-familiar chair. One yank on the
lever jutting from the right side-panel and the chair re-
clined into a less-than-comfortable bed. Em had spent her
fair share of the last twenty nights in the chair—more than
her fair share, considering that, as far as the hospital
knew, Eleanor was an unsuspected cousin with a passion
for Internet genealogy who'd dropped into Emma's life
without warning and promptly—mysteriously—suffered
the collapse from which she had yet to awaken.

It was a plausible tale—almost any tale could be made
plausible by inserting the magical word "Internet" into the
first sentence—but it wasn't the truth. The truth defied belief: Eleanor Merrigan, with her princess-perfect complexion, was seventy years old—at least seventy—and

Emma, who fought the indignities of the modern Middle Ages with regular exercise and semipermanent hair coloring, was Eleanor's daughter.

Eleanor *was* a stranger; that much of Em's story was truthful. Emma had lived her life knowing only one parent, her father, who'd died ten months ago in this same hospital, on this same head-trauma unit. Three weeks ago, when Emma had arrived home to find a stranger camped out on her front porch, *Mother* had been the farthest thought from her mind. Confronted with a woman who hadn't changed a whit or wrinkle since the day she posed for her wedding portrait—a woman who hadn't been there when her daughter had truly needed her—Em had reacted with anger rather than joy or even doubt. They'd had a few hours together, not nearly enough time to transform hostility into affection, before Eleanor was unconscious on the floor and Emma was on the phone with 911.

Em couldn't think of that call without wincing, and she couldn't wince without aching. No chair was comfortable after you'd spent too much time sitting in it. With her eyes closed, Em braced herself against the upholstery, determined to relax.

Fear. That was the emotion Em couldn't quite purge. It was the cold, hard lump beneath her ribs that kept her heart pounding as if she'd just run up several flights of stairs or awakened suddenly in the middle of the night. Emma knew all about waking up in the dark. Night terrors had been part of her life since early childhood. She'd conquered her fears of darkness and dreams without locking, or even finding, the door that let them in.

Since she'd met her mother, fear hijacked Emma's imagination whenever she tried to relax. The least sound—an elevator door opening, a rubber-soled footstep in the corridor, a whisper too soft for words wafting up from the nurses' station—and Em's nerves snapped to a single question:

Who's there?

Her mother came with enemies: powerful enemies, uncanny enemies, enemies that walked through time. Rogues, they were called, and they looked no different than Emma herself or her mother—unless you knew that Eleanor Merrigan should have looked much different— and a rogue was a curse in human form. Until Eleanor reappeared in her life, when Emma thought of a curse she thought of the words she was careful not to say too loudly when her office computer crashed; and a rogue was an edgy, attractive man, usually no more than half her age. Curses were still words, but they were also predatory pillars of fire roaming a desolate plain and a rogue could be anyone who'd caught a curse: a man, a woman, or the nurse hurrying down the corridor with a steel tray in her hands.

Emma stared out the door long after the nurse had vanished, too tired to close her eyes again. Em needed sleep; she needed to escape from the hospital. There was nothing she—or anyone else—could accomplish beside the bed of a woman who didn't know whether she was awake or asleep, alive or dead. Eleanor's doctors had said as much when they'd disconnected the monitors. One of them—a woman Em knew from a stint on the university's charity- oversight committee—had handed her a prewritten pre- scription for "something minor, something to get you through."

Dutifully, Emma had collected an amber-plastic vial from the pharmacy. It sat untouched in her bathroom.

Tonight—Em thought, glancing past Eleanor and lis- tening to the chatter of sleet against the night-dark win- dow. *Tonight I'll take a pill. Tomorrow I'll go straight to work and straight home. I won't come here. There's no reason . . . no need . . .*

Whenever Emma beat her fear into submission, guilt in all its nameless variations arose in its place. She couldn't abandon Eleanor as Eleanor had abandoned her. Two wrongs didn't make a right. Her father—the parent who'd stuck around to raise her—had taught her that.

Twice a day Emma visited her mother: briefly in the

morning on her way to work at the university's library,
endlessly in the evening. And when she wasn't sitting beside Eleanor's bed. Em wasn't worth the powder to blow
her to hell—

Hell.

For a person who, except for weddings, funerals, and
the occasional holiday concert, hadn't set foot in a church
for over thirty years. Emma's thoughts had turned decidedly religious, as they hadn't turned religious while her
father lay dying. Then again, Em and her father hadn't
been in hell arguing with each other moments before he
died.

Emma's eyelids sank of their own weight. She remembered those last moments with Eleanor as if they were still
happening.

Em hadn't wanted to believe in curses or the out-of-
place. out-of-time wasteland they haunted. She'd resisted
the coincidences assaulting her like a centipede dropping
ninety-nine other shoes. Night terrors weren't new to her
life. And befriending a student or two was an occupational
hazard when you worked deep in the heart of a university's library. But with the night terrors and the students
had come a box, a plain, cardboard box Eleanor Merrigan
had packed, sealed, and labeled before she marched out of
her infant daughter's life. In the box Emma had found a
letter informing her that she'd inherited a *wyrd*—
Eleanor's word for an extraordinary talent to walk
through time and the obligation to hunt curses wherever,
whenever, she found them.

Eleanor had graciously provided a guidebook beneath
her letter—a handwritten, Bible-like book with onionskin
pages and a flexible, black-leather binding. It raised more
questions than it answered. Emma clung to her skepticism
because denial remained her best defense against ignorance, but the tide of evidence flowed in favor of
Eleanor's *wyrd*, of a parched wasteland where hungry fire
could gulp down a woman's spirit and leave her living
body behind on a hospital bed.

Emma hadn't actually seen the curses swallow her mother; she'd been stretched out on that hard, dry, wasteland dirt trying to breathe. The curses and Eleanor were gone before she stood up again. What she knew about Eleanor's disappearance came from Blaise Raponde, who might be a man, a ghost, a figment of Emma's overworked imagination, or—as Eleanor had insisted—a rogue.

Raponde said he wasn't a rogue while conceding that there was no reason for either Emma or Eleanor to believe him. He also said that none of the ambushing curses was powerful enough to displace Eleanor's spirit from her body. They'd need to contest among themselves—consuming each other until the one of them had the strength to become a rogue in Eleanor's body—and that would give him time enough to rescue her.

Em hadn't argued. The alternative—the alternative Raponde rejected as he proposed it—was smothering Eleanor's real-world body: no living body, no living rogue. And Emma, who didn't want to believe in curses or rogues, didn't believe in murder either. She'd put her faith in modern medicine. After three weeks, the doctors were no closer to solving Eleanor's mystery than they'd been when Eleanor arrived in the emergency room.

In her reclining chair, Emma remembered Eleanor's screams as the flames enveloped her. For an instant Em felt hot wind swirling over her, then her memories were replaced by the rustle of cotton sheets. Eleanor had thrust her right hand through the bed's steel restraint bars. Velcro ribbons trailed from a padded cuff fastened around her wrist.

Em could call it coincidence and tell herself that there was no connection between her discarded memories and Eleanor's sudden movement, but coincidence had taken a beating lately, so call it something else—or nothing at all—but never doubt for a moment that there was a connection. And whether a curse was a pillar of fire or whether fire was dream-code for something else, its effects were real.

Emma surged out of the chair. She grasped her mother's hand loosely and whispered. "Don't surrender. I'm looking. Blaise Raponde is looking. We'll wake you up before it's too late."

The official word for Eleanor's condition was "coma." A month ago all Emma had known was that the word meant "sleep" in Greek—and she'd gleaned that knowledge from a crossword puzzle. Em had never seen anyone in a coma—not even Dad after his stroke. She'd blithely equated comas with serenely unconscious princesses. Most people looked serene as they slept.

Most people weren't in a coma.

Eleanor imitated Sleeping Beauty because of a sedation cocktail. When the drugs began to wear off—and the hospital wanted them to wear off—Eleanor was anything but Sleeping Beauty. She thrashed violently enough to have dislocated her own shoulder and broken the nose of an overconfident nurse's aide who'd thought he could handle her without using velcro restraints.

That, the doctors said, was Eleanor's coma. The word might mean sleep in Greece, but in an American hospital, coma meant a medical black hole, consciousness completely hidden behind an event horizon, but *there* nonetheless.

Emma had no doubt that her mother was profoundly *there* and not enjoying the visit. Without sedation, Eleanor's eyes were wide open but blind to the here-and-now. She didn't respond when doctors pricked her skin with needles, but contorted her arms and legs into grotesque pretzels and howled for no apparent reason.

Your cousin is aware, Dr. Saha would say whenever he and Emma met.

Saha had emerged as the head of Eleanor's medical team. A world-class brain-man, he spent more time in consultation than surgery and he didn't consult, even at his home-base hospital, until a half-dozen of his peers had declared defeat. By then, a patient's coma—Eleanor Merrigan's coma—was personal.

She's in another place, a strange and frightening place. If there's a way to that place—a road, a path, or a tunnel, I don't care which—we'll find it and we'll guide her back. Inch by inch, if we have to. Don't give up on her, Emma. I haven't; I won't.

Eleanor beat her arm between the steel rails. Emma tightened her grasp, trying to prevent either of them from getting hurt. In seconds, Eleanor's hand flushed with blood and heat. Usually Eleanor's hands were pale and cold. The change was far from reassuring.

"I'm here, Eleanor," Em whispered. "I haven't given up."

Eleanor went rigid. Her eyes popped open. She stared at her daughter without seeing her.

"No—" Em pleaded futilely as the scream began.

At first Eleanor's scream was a weak, high-pitched warble. Then she took a breath and bared her teeth. Paresis and atrophy—weakness and withering—were the companions of most comas, but not Eleanor Merrigan's, at least not yet. Her grip was painfully strong and so was her voice. Emma didn't need to reach for the call button. The whole floor knew it when Sleeping Beauty had a nightmare.

The first nurse through the door was a stout, hard-faced woman with thin, frowning lips, severely narrowed eyes, and a fierce dedication to her profession.

"Ellie," Jill crooned as she ran her hands down Eleanor's forearm and expertly, but gently, loosened those white-knuckled fingers from Emma's wrist. "Calm down, Ellie. Talk to me, Ellie."

Jill didn't believe in sedation cocktails. She took justifiable pride in her ability to calm her patients without recourse to phenobarbital and its stronger relations, but she had no better luck calming Eleanor than Emma had. After five endless, screaming minutes, Jill conceded defeat.

Another nurse brought the sedation kit and helped Jill velcro Eleanor's wrists and ankles to the bed. Emma clenched her teeth and stared out the sleet-streaked win-

dow. She didn't turn around until the second nurse left and
Jill undid the velcro ribbons.

"Ellie will come out of it, Ms. Merrigan," Jill said.
"You think it's been forever, but it's not even close. You
wouldn't believe the miracles I've seen. Three weeks—
that's no time at all. Most of the doctors here will wait
three months before discharging with a PVS diagnosis.
Dr. Saha's kept a few on the floor for a year. I'm on his
side. A year's not too long, not for Ellie."

PVS, that was med-speak for "persistent vegetative
state": the end of the line for coma patients. PVS meant
shipment to the upper reaches of a skilled nursing facility,
a gastric tube for nourishment, and a radio for company
until something killed the body the mind had abandoned.

Emma stiffened then faced Jill and the bed. She tried
not to imagine what her youthful mother would say about
her probable fate. When you were seventy—at least seventy—but looked twenty-five, you probably didn't waste
much time worrying about skilled nursing facilities.

"Ellie's not nearly PVS." Jill patted Eleanor's hand
twice before carefully tucking it under the sheet. "There's
plenty going on inside her head. She'll wake up one of
these first mornings and tell us where she's been."

Em nodded without conviction. She knew where her
mother was: trapped in hell while a horde of curses fought
for the privilege of turning her into a rogue.

"She could be hearing every word we say," Jill continued. "I've known that to happen. They wake up and say
they weren't sleeping at all, just trapped inside. They remember everything. They know who kept faith and who
didn't." She tidied Eleanor's hair. "Your cousin hasn't lost
faith, Ellie. You remember that, you hear? She's here
every day . . . twice a day. Your own mother couldn't do
more for you."

Em suppressed a grimace. She hoped she'd suppressed it.

Jill studied the paperwork hanging from the foot of

Eleanor's bed. "It's been a few days since Ellie's last episode."

"Monday, while I was at work. It was mild, like this. They stopped it with an injection and didn't have to start an IV." Em paused. "Does she need an IV?"

"No." Jill rehung the paperwork. "Not if I can help it. We've got to wean Ellie off these drugs. She can't wake up with them in her system. She's got another scan scheduled for Friday. They'll cancel it if I start an IV. You don't want that to happen. Ellie's different from all the others I've seen, and I've seen more of them than I should. No history. No damage. No accident. No history of drug abuse. No drugs in her system. She gets on a plane, flies from New York to Michigan, and twelve hours later she's here. That doesn't fit any pattern. There has to be a pattern, Ms Merrigan. There always has to be an underlying reason, the real reason. When we find it, we'll find the way to bring her back at the same time."

There is no "real" reason, an internal voice advised Emma. *None that twenty-first century technology can find. There's no "we" either. There's just you, Emma Merrigan, and you're not getting the job done.*

Emma couldn't remember a time when that voice hadn't haunted the back of her mind. It wasn't her conscience, guilty or otherwise. It wasn't hers at all; she'd never claimed it. Until Eleanor burst into her life, Em had called it the Mother Voice, but Eleanor's voice had been as rich as her hair and utterly unlike the scold in Em's head.

Go home. Get out the books and the candles. Take a walk through the wasteland. Tonight could be the night you get lucky yourself.

Em wondered if she were going insane or if she'd been insane all her life. The way Jill stared at her, the question was moot.

"I'm sorry," she confessed. "Sometimes it all seems like a dream . . . a nightmare. My—my cousin found me through the Internet—a genealogy search. I'd just met her. We didn't know each other. I don't know if we have anything in common except a handful of dead relatives. I didn't think I had any living relatives. The Merrigans are a small family—my dad and me. I thought I was the last. We're all each other has, but she's still a stranger." That much, at least, was simple truth, and Em had rehearsed it so many times that even the false parts felt true.

Jill shook her head. "You're not strangers, not after all this. The idea—"

Emma never learned Jill's idea. The beeper she wore at her waist came to life.

"You get some rest yourself, Emma. You're looking peaked," Jill advised on her way out the door. "Waiting's the easy part."

"Right," Emma agreed, too softly to be heard.

She glanced out the window, then down at her watch: seven-fifteen. She'd planned to stay until nine, the end of the hospital's unofficial visiting hours, the same as last night, the night before, and the night before that. It was easier to wrestle with guilt and anger in the mauve chair than at home, but if there were a night to cut her vigil short, this was it.

Eleanor hadn't moved since Jill removed the velcro restraints, and the odds were good that Sleeping Beauty would lie beneath her sheets like a corpse until sometime tomorrow morning. Meanwhile, the ice chatter had grown louder against the window. If Em left now, she'd be home before the streets got dangerous and before the en-route grocery store closed. She could cook herself a real-food dinner—her first since Thanksgiving—spend some quality time with her cats, hurl herself into the unknown, and still have time for eight hours of sleep.

Em looked at her coat hanging by the door, but didn't move toward it. Another half hour, she told herself. If she left the hospital at quarter to eight, she could still get to the store. Another half hour and her conscience wouldn't keep her awake.

Emma settled back in the mauve chair. She listened to the hushed but abundant noises of the hospital, from the elevators at the center of the X-shaped annex to the nurses gathered in front of it. No excitement tonight. She let her eyes close for a moment, just a moment—

"Charming."

Emma started. There was a gap in her sense of time and a man—Harry Graves, her mother's husband, her very own stepfather—standing in the doorway. Not being a vampire, Harry entered the room without an invitation.

Frantically collecting her wits, Em sputtered, "You've come back?" She sat up straight, fussed with her clothes, and wished she could see a mirror. Ordinarily, Emma wasn't the sort who worried about her appearance, but Harry had had a "your lipstick's smeared and your bra strap's showing" effect on her at their first two meetings and he was having it again.

Though he wasn't a particularly tall man, Harry Graves contrived to look down on everything and everyone. The nurses had commented on it, particularly Jill, whom he'd criticized for procedural and personal slovenliness, using those exact words, both to her face and to her supervisor. Jill must not have seen Harry walk off the elevator. She wouldn't have forgotten him and she wouldn't have let him walk her halls without an escort.

"For the night. I'll fly home again tomorrow, unless your delightful weather keeps me here longer. Contrary to what you seem to think, Eleanor *is* my wife. I have an obligation to care for her. It's an obligation I would prefer to discharge nearer to our home, but neither distance and weather, nor an inconvenient *cousin*, will stand in my way."

Emma caught the emphasis on *cousin* and ignored it. Harry knew who and what she was. In all likelihood, Harry knew more about the "what" part than Em knew herself.

If Eleanor was unnaturally youthful, then Harry Graves was unnaturally ageless. He had a rich man's face— smooth, suntanned, and about as expressive as a kidskin glove. He could have passed for thirty-five, or fifty-five, or a hundred-and-fifty-five. His hair was fashionably short; Em couldn't decide whether it was blond or silver, natural or bleached. The rest of him was lean in the way of celebrities—especially rock musicians—who'd managed to survive their youthful excesses with minds and bank accounts intact.

Especially their bank accounts.

Harry Graves exuded wealth. Emma lived comfortably enough to recognize the difference between wool and cashmere, and Harry's coat was definitely cashmere. Scorning the empty hook beside the synthetic-down coat Emma favored when Michigan's weather got nasty, Harry produced a collapsible hanger from an interior pocket and hung *his* coat in the room's open, empty closet. Beneath the coat, Harry wore garments that could be called casual, provided the modifiers *expensive*, *elegant*, and *European* were included in the description.

There was another chair in Eleanor's room, an armless, hard-upholstered model toward which Harry didn't move. Instead, he stood on the opposite side of Eleanor's bed, eyeing the hooks from which three untapped plastic IV sacks were hung.

Emma left the mauve chair to stand opposite him. The call button was within reach on her side of the bed.

"It's how you care about her that keeps me in your way, Harry."

She could meet her stepfather's pale hazel eyes without difficulty though she couldn't learn anything from them. Harry Graves wasn't a man who gave anything away. Given a choice, she'd never play poker against him, but she hadn't been given a choice.

"I didn't come here to argue with you, Emma."

"Then why did you come?"

"I am persuaded that you care deeply for your *cousin*. There's no reason we can't cooperate."

"I can think of a few."

"And I respect your wishes . . . Eleanor's wishes. I've

withdrawn my challenges to your power of attorney. You are in charge, but you are not alone."

The first time they'd met, Eleanor had been in the hospital for less than a day. Harry had taken the place by storm, giving orders to doctors and nurses alike. Emma hadn't known how to stop him. When push had come to shove in front of the nurses' station, Em had balked, unsure whether she *should* thwart Harry Graves's intentions, assuming she *could* thwart them.

Before her collapse, Eleanor hadn't said much about her husband—she hadn't said much about anything; there hadn't been time. Eleanor described Harry as a tolerable partner and the marriage as prearranged. She'd said even less about the prearrangers, only that "we used to be tribes, like gypsies; now we're a global corporation." Em imagined an unholy cross among the Mafia, Microsoft, and the NFL.

If only Eleanor had been a bit more honest . . . If she'd said *I haven't suddenly reappeared in your life just because you started hunting curses last Thursday; I'm here because my husband and I and our supersecret associates think that handsome stranger who hauled your chestnuts out of the fire while you were hunting might be a rogue. We need to work together to get to the truth,* then maybe Eleanor wouldn't be stretched out in a hospital bed. After two dud marriages, Em knew she had lousy taste in men, and despite Raponde's saving her life more than once, she also knew better than to trust any man who said he'd been born in seventeenth-century Paris.

Em would have cooperated with her mother. She was almost positive she would have. Once she accepted the inexplicable: that curses were real, then it was a short, easy, downhill step to believing that rogues were curse-hunters who'd been possessed by their prey. Emma could even see that rogues might be so dangerous that prudent curse-hunters would cut their losses by smothering the real-world husk of a friend—or wife—rather than risk anything further in a rescue attempt.

Harry Graves had the eyes of a man who could cut any loss.

Don't get in my way, he'd warned when they were alone for the first time in the hospital elevator, *or I'll have to take care of you now instead of later.*

Harry intimidated Em the way lions intimidated cheetahs on the plains of Africa, but the hospital had its own lions who resented Harry's implication that the U's resources were substandard. They'd fought the first round of Emma's fight for her: Saha himself had come straight from surgery to tell Harry that Eleanor Merrigan wasn't going anywhere until he decreed her condition stable.

When you were up against a man who might be immortal, it helped to have a man who thought he was God on your side.

Round one had ended with Harry promising lawyers. Emma had gone home and popped the locks on her mother's suitcase, hoping for a miracle. She got one.

Eleanor Merrigan had come to Bower prepared. She'd crammed her hefty suitcase with enough clothing for a month in the wilderness and still found room for three sealed envelopes. In one envelope Emma found her mother's passport and current financial statements, none of which mentioned Harry Graves. In the second, she found a copy of Eleanor's will and a durable power-of-attorney, specifically valid in Michigan and made out for the names of Archibald Merrigan, Em's father who'd died last winter, and Merle Acalia Merrigan, which was the name on Emma's birth certificate. The third envelope held a two-page autobiography that wasn't remotely truthful but dovetailed so precisely with the story Emma had already told the hospital that she wondered if prescience weren't another of Eleanor's occult talents.

According to the autobiography, Eleanor had been born twenty-seven years earlier in one of the more tumultuous African countries where her parents ran a rural medical clinic. Those mythic parents thought their work would protect them when a civil war flared up around them. Needless to say, it hadn't. Equally needless to say, Eleanor's supposed birth certificate had burned with the clinic.

Harry Graves showed up on page two as the patron whose wealth had endowed the clinic and whose generosity brought an orphan home. Eleanor wrote that she lived in Harry's house, and after graduating from an unnamed college, she'd worked at his company, but—contrary to what she'd told Emma—she didn't write that Harry was her husband.

Armed with what she'd found in Eleanor's suitcase, Emma was ready for round two in a hospital conference room. Harry had tried to trump the autobiography with a Romanian marriage certificate. He almost won: he was used to getting his way and she was a university librarian who played by the rules. But Harry's arrogance had alienated everyone, and Emma was a lifelong member of the university's family.

After studying Harry's certificate for a few moments, one of the university lawyers calmly noted that Eleanor had been significantly underage when she'd signed Harry's proof of their marriage, and Bower—an unapologetic bastion of liberal-leftist politics—was more than willing to prosecute child abuse wherever or whenever it had occurred. If Harry Graves didn't want a very public airing of his dirty linen, he'd be smart to fold his tent and go home.

The last thing Harry Graves wanted was a very public anything.

He'd handed her one of his business cards after the lawyers were gone. *Call me when you realize how big a mistake you've made.* Emma had insisted that she hadn't made a mistake, and that even if she had, she wouldn't be turning to him for help. She'd tossed the card into the garbage on her way to the car.

"Nothing's changed, Harry," Em reminded the man on the other side of Eleanor's bed. "Nothing at all. I'm still in charge and there's nothing you can do about it."

"Emma," Harry purred. "For a few days, even a week, we could all cling to our hopes, but she's been like this for three weeks."

"That's nothing for a coma—"

"Eleanor's not in a coma—" Harry stopped himself.

They both looked at the open door. The corridor was empty and quiet, but they each knew the risks of an overheard conversation.

"We shouldn't be arguing . . . especially here," Harry said. "I'm staying at the Executive Suites out by the Interstate. It's strictly professional—"

Emma cut him off with a quick "No." Rational or not, her paranoia was raging and she wasn't going anywhere with Harry Graves.

"A restaurant, then. Someplace quiet and discreet. The check's mine"—Emma shook her head—"Don't be foolish."

"Don't talk to me as if I was a child," Em retorted, though that was exactly how she felt. She had a child's knowledge of rogues, curses, and the wasteland they roamed. If Emma could have trusted Harry Graves, she had questions galore. If she'd trusted him. "Eleanor trusted me to do the right thing."

That was the crux. A woman Emma didn't like—the mother who'd walked out all those years ago—had signed her life into Emma's safekeeping and Emma wouldn't surrender it, not to Harry Graves or the shadowy "global corporation" he represented.

"Pity," Harry said, conveying the exact opposite.

Harry leaned over the bed. There was a half-inch scar over his right eyebrow; she hadn't noticed it before. Whatever he and Eleanor were, they weren't invulnerable. They could bleed and scar like everyone else. They could die, too. Blaise Raponde had been dead for a few centuries—his body had, anyway. The rest of him—his spirit, soul, or maybe his ghost—persisted in the wasteland: not dead, not alive, not a rogue . . . if Emma trusted *him*.

"Listen to me, Emma Merrigan," Harry whispered. "Your mother would rather die than become a rogue . . ."

Em held her ground with a firm grip on the bed rail. "She's not a rogue yet—you've admitted it yourself. I'm not giving up on her."

"Why, Emma? What has Eleanor Merrigan done for you that you'll risk your own life for hers? And you *are* risking it. When she wakes up a rogue, you'll be its first target. You'll know its secret. You'll be in its way. You're not ready for that. Alone, none of us is—"

Emma seized an opportunity: "She came here alone. *You* sent her here by herself."

"Not me. I spoke against sending Eleanor. None of us knew what we might find out here, her least of all. I questioned whether she could act decisively. As it happened, I was right—for the wrong reason."

"And that was?"

"Obviously, you are not a rogue."

"Obviously," Emma agreed, though she wished she knew why it was obvious.

Harry's eyes narrowed as he smiled. "You're not out of danger yet, Emma Merrigan. You've got the talent, and the instincts, but you're untrained. You've got the wisdom but you've got the habits of a lifetime—your lifetime. You'll make mistakes. You've seen what happens when mistakes are made in the Netherlands."

Without warning, he raised Eleanor's left hand to his lips and held it there in what could have been a tender, romantic gesture but was, to Emma's eyes, cold, possessive, and predatory. She fought a shudder of revulsion and said nothing until Harry had released her mother's hand.

"Eleanor trusted you. She called you on the phone to get your advice—the call showed up on my long-distance bill. She was depending on you to watch her back; *that* was her mistake. I won't be repeating it."

"But there are so many mistakes that can be made, Emma. Commit even one of them and you're lost."

"Should I be watching my back then? Today, tomorrow, or should I look for you yesterday?"

Something that might have been genuine surprise or concern made Harry Graves blink. "Stay away from your own path, Emma; *never* cross it."

"Why, Harry?" Em demanded before she could censor herself. "Why not go back and fix things? Why not be there when Eleanor needed you?"

"Time doesn't work that way, Emma. We don't change history; we remove curses."

"By changing history!"

Harry reached for her. Emma dropped her arms quickly to her sides and eluded him.

"No one blames you for your ignorance, Emma. No one blames Eleanor, for that matter. Things were hard enough for her when she came back. She admitted that she'd had a child while she was gone, but your father was mundane. There was doubt whether you'd inherit. She asked that you be left alone, and we granted her request. When the years passed and nothing happened, the matter appeared settled—and her indiscretions were forgiven. Then you left the door open. You can imagine our reaction to that."

Emma couldn't and didn't much care. She bristled, though, at the slight to her father. She swallowed her indignation, but not the plural pronoun. "We who?" she demanded. "Who, exactly, are *we*? What are *we*? A bunch of witches?"

"Witches? Is that what you think, Emma? Magic and mumbo jumbo? Sorry to disappoint. We're stewards . . . caretakers . . . *janitors*. We patch up the holes that blind, ignorant fools leave behind—"

An alarm chimed in another room and they both stepped silently away from the bed as soft-footed nurses hurried through the corridor. When Harry continued, it was in a whisper.

"Don't become one of them, Emma. You've spent your life at university. Your father taught here—engineering,

Eleanor said. Did he teach you to be open-minded? Eleanor wasn't. Once Eleanor made up her mind, nothing could change it. Don't let that be a family trait." Harry headed for the closet. "My parents endowed me with a more patient, forgiving nature." He extracted another business card and held it out. "Believe me, Emma, we're on the same side. We want the same things. I deeply regret that I threatened you when we first met—"

Emma didn't make a move for the card. With a visible sigh, Harry laid it on the shelf where Em had stashed her purse. He shrugged into his coat.

"We respect your wishes, Emma. If you want nothing to do with us after this is over, so be it, but until then—for Eleanor's sake—please reconsider your intransigence. Eleanor is a special woman. We value her dearly, despite her recklessness. *I* value her dearly because of it." Harry paused in the doorway. "I want her back, Emma."

Then he was gone.

Emma stared long and hard at the white rectangle beside her purse, half-expecting it to become something else. But it was only paper, and in the aftermath of Harry's visit, Em was too weary to throw it away. She shoved the card into her coat pocket and, as Harry had done, paused in the doorway before leaving.

Sleeping Beauty hadn't moved.

Two

The skies were lead gray above the meadow that gave the nursing home its name. Yellow stalks of grass and weeds poked above a light blanket of snow. That would change soon. January was coming and everyone from the U.S. Weather Service to the guys who measured the stripes on wooly-bear caterpillars agreed that Bower was due for a hard January.

A good blizzard or two would keep Emma holed up in her house and, maybe, loosen the ties that brought her out to Meadow View Manor each day to check on her mother. She couldn't call it a "visit." "Visit" implied interaction, and Eleanor didn't interact with the real world. Eleanor didn't know that the brain trust at the hospital had given up on her or that she'd spent the last month at the highest-rated human warehouse in Michigan.

Sleeping Beauty's face was thinner now. Her hair was shorter—Meadow View might be the best of its breed, but it didn't employ hairdressers for its comatose clients. Eleanor's shoulder-length hair had been clipped an hour after she'd arrived. A stainless-steel pole suitable for hanging an array of medical equipment rose from the bed frame. The pole was empty. Eleanor got her food and her medicine through a tube surgically attached to her stomach and hidden beneath a light blanket.

It was easier that way. Everything was easier at Meadow View except hope. When Emma stared out the window at Meadow View, her thoughts were the same color as the sky.

"She's not coming. She said we want to steal her money and we're trying to poison her with 'foreign food.' I said John was making bouillabaisse for tonight's party. She always loved his bouillabaisse."

Emma heard the words but a moment passed before she recognized the voice or made sense out of the words. The voice belonged to Nancy Amstel, Emma's friend and confidant since the first grade. *She* was Katherine Neeley, Nancy's widowed mother. In a stroke of fortune or karmic humor, Nancy and Emma had wound up moving their mothers into Meadow View on the same mid-December day. And the bouillabaisse was John Amstel's contribution to their annual New Year's Eve get-together, now in its fourth decade of existence.

By the time she'd remembered New Year's Eve, Em couldn't remember what she'd been thinking the instant before Nancy had arrived. She wondered how long she'd been holding a chocolate chip cookie in her hand, how long it would be before she found herself in an assisted-living facility like Meadow View?

"Don't take it personally," Em advised, as if shattered concentration were a normal part of her life, which lately it had been. "Your mother doesn't mean it."

"But she does," Nancy corrected, then added softly: "Mom's a different person since the chemo and the stroke."

Em put the cookie, the last of a dozen, on the plate and crumpled the box before tossing it into the trash. Guilt and exhaustion had wrought many changes in her life but they hadn't turned her into a baker. She bought cookies—or fruit or candy—each morning at the Kroger's supermarket. Years ago, a friend of her father's described leaving food by her husband's nursing home bed. It drew the staff, the friend had claimed, to the room as surely as milk and cookies drew Santa Claus to the kitchen on Christmas Eve.

There was little else to draw them. The sixth and uppermost floor of Meadow View Manor wasn't a place where anyone came by choice or chance. On its two lowest floors, Meadow View could pass for an upscale hotel with unusually wide halls and brass railings mounted along the walls. On the third, fourth, and fifth floors, where Katherine shared a room with another cantankerous, easily confused woman, the stairwell doors had locks but the rooms didn't. On the sixth floor the residents didn't move around under their own power. Up here, Katherine's antics would have been cause for celebration.

"At least Katherine's talking to you again," Emma added when Nancy didn't reply.

Em considered herself a comparative personality rather than a competitive one, and compared to Nancy, Nancy had it worse with her mother. Eleanor didn't alternate between bitter ranting and even-more-bitter silence. Eleanor was exactly as she'd been in the head trauma unit. The hospital had weaned her from the sedatives, but her condition hadn't changed when her blood was drug free, except to become boring rather than mysterious.

"Only to tell me that I've stolen her money and put her in a prison," Nancy replied flatly.

Emma touched Eleanor's hand. As usual, there was no response. She reached for her coat.

"That started before you brought her here, before you were even willing to think about a place like this."

Nancy nodded. "I know. I know it's not my fault and I know that it's not going to change, but I can't help myself. Every time I come here, I come hoping she'll be glad to see me."

Em turned toward the door as she pulled on her coat. "You made the right decision, Nance. Katherine couldn't stay in that house any longer, not by herself and not with you there taking care of her. It was Meadow View here in Bower or some other Meadow View out in California with your brother, and that would have been even harder on Katherine."

"It might have killed her," Nancy mused as they left Eleanor's room. "Would that have been worse? I hear myself ask that and I don't know if there *is* a right answer. I can't accept that my mother's life is supposed to end in a wasteland."

Emma started. Wasteland didn't mean Meadow View to her and Nancy knew it.

There wasn't much the two women didn't know about each other. Emma knew that Nancy's older daughter had had an abortion two weeks before she graduated from high school, and Nancy knew not only who Sleeping Beauty really was, but that the wasteland was the name Em gave to the barren, dreamworld place where curses lurked. Secrets had never threatened their friendship, and didn't threaten it now, but Nancy's slip of the tongue put a temporary end to conversation.

Meadow View's sixth floor wasn't a quiet place. Almost every room had a television or radio going; the staff station had two. None of the devices were uncomfortably loud, not nearly loud enough to drown the moaning, crying, and pleas for help that never stopped and couldn't be heeded. Eleanor's room was an oasis of silence—no wonder the staff came down to feast on her snacks.

Halfway to the elevator another sixth-floor visitor shattered Em's emotional armor with "Happy New Year, Emma!"

The well-wisher's name was Marsha and she spent the larger part of her days in a room identical to Eleanor's except that its occupant was a young man who'd paid a terrible price for joyriding with his buddies one winter night. Their car had spun out on a patch of black ice, gone airborne, and landed upside down in a pond a hundred feet from the road. Emma remembered reading about it in the *Bower Tribune* and suffering a parental shudder as she recognized names of her stepdaughter's high school classmates. The driver had died instantly—no water in his lungs. The two boys in the backseat had buckled their seat belts just before the speeding car hit the ice. The act saved their lives. They'd escaped from the car as it sank.

Lori, Emma's stepdaughter, had wanted to go to the funeral. Em recalled the whole tragedy because of the argument Lori's desire had sparked between herself, as Lori's advocate, and her husband, Jeff, who'd been sure the boys were at fault. Emma had won the argument—she usually did. Lori went to the funeral. Jeff fumed for a week.

It had been one of the first times Em realized her second marriage was in serious trouble.

She'd completely forgotten that there'd been a fourth boy in the car until Marsha reintroduced herself.

"I baked you some New Year's cookies," Marsha announced with forced cheeriness. She shed a lapful of newspapers surging out of her chair.

Emma caught her own urge to dash for the elevator and beat it into what she hoped was a gracious smile. With two disciplined strides she was in the doorway, ready to accept her gift, trying not to notice the bed.

Nine years had passed since rescue workers had hauled Josh out of the wreck. Temperature shock had plunged Josh into a suspended animation from which doctors had awakened him as much as they could. Like Eleanor, Josh breathed on his own. His body, like hers, was plumbed with tubes hidden beneath the sheets. After nine years of PVS, Josh had become a wraith: withered, shrunken, and twisted into postures that would have been excruciating if there'd been a mind left to perceive them.

Marsha called her son's survival a miracle, but the words were stale and her eyes belied her mouth. Em couldn't look at Josh without thinking of Eleanor. Worse, she couldn't look at Marsha without thinking about herself.

But look at Marsha she did and wracked her thoughts for something to say. Not Did you have a good holiday? or How was your Christmas? People checking in at

Meadow View didn't want to answer those questions. The changeable Great Lakes weather was a safer subject.

"We've sure had beautiful weather the last few days." Then Emma focused on opening the brightly colored cookie tin. "Raisin—my favorite. How—" she began and caught herself before she'd added *did you find the time?*

Marsha spent hours each day with her son, doing the things he couldn't do for himself and those which were beyond the mandate of the best skilled-nursing staff. She bathed him and changed him, massaged his wasted muscles, and kept up a steady monolog about the people he had once known and the interests that had made him human because—as Jill said so often at the hospital—sometimes they can hear.

Thanks to his mother's diligence, Josh had never suffered a bedsore. When Marsha first mentioned this to Em, she'd made it sound like a world-conquering accomplishment—and it was: Eleanor had acquired one after the rippled-foam pad on which she rested got twisted and her heel rubbed against the sheets for a single afternoon.

"How did you know?" Em asked instead.

Marsha smiled wanly. "Josh loves raisin-oatmeal cookies. Are you going out tonight?" she asked. "I might go downstairs for a few hours. They know me down there; I'm almost like a resident."

Marsha's marriage had fallen apart after the accident, just as Emma's had, though for far better reasons.

Emma explained that she'd be spending New Year's Eve with a friend—with Nancy, who waited silently in the hall. Em gave Marsha a hug then began her retreat to the elevator.

"You'll be here tomorrow?" Marsha asked before an arm's length separated them.

"I don't know."

She'd planned to spend tomorrow morning watching parades and the rest of the day watching football. The U's team wasn't playing for the mythical national championship, but it was the favorite in a prime-time bowl. Marsha might watch the game too, but only from her chair beside Josh's bed.

How much sacrifice was enough?

If the water had been a little warmer or the rescue team a little slower, Josh would have died. Could the last decade have been any harder on Marsha? If Katherine had gone to her son in California and the trip had killed her, would that have been worse than believing that her daughter had put her in prison? If Emma picked up the phone and called Harry Graves—?

Nancy's car waited near the lobby doors. She put it in reverse, backed it up a few feet, then applied the brakes.

"The first few times after I left, I couldn't drive," Nancy announced in a soft voice that compelled attention. "I'd sit in the car and cry my heart out. I was okay at Christmas. I thought I was over it—" Tears were flowing down her cheeks. "Mom's not Mom anymore; I can accept that—I'm learning to. We're Boomers, Em, and the odds are that every one of us is going to put a parent in a place like this; that's just the way it's going to play out. But when I look at that boy up there on the sixth floor . . . a young person shouldn't wind up here. His mother shouldn't."

Em turned away from her friend. "Marsha doesn't know that's my mother lying in that bed. She thinks I'm like her, looking out for the younger generation. She's desperate for someone who understands what she's going through. I feel it every time she looks at me."

"Like a curse?" Nancy asked, putting the car into motion again.

In Em's life, that was no longer an idle or metaphoric question. She considered it a moment before answering, "No—plain ordinary human misery and loneliness on Marsha's part and another step toward insanity on mine. I wonder how people in the witness protection program manage. I've got one secret to keep and I'm dragging a ton of bricks wherever I go."

Nancy said nothing, in part because traffic was more

chaotic than usual in the last nine hours of the year but also because the last month had been one of the quieter phases of their friendship. Nance threaded the car through Bower's tangled downtown streets, slowing as they neared the traffic light where a right-hand turn would take them to Em's townhouse in a neighborhood known as the Maisonettes.

"Without Mom to watch, I can handle getting ready for tonight. If you want to go home for a few hours, I can pick you up later."

Em hadn't considered the possibility. They'd made their plans around Katherine, and her car was already parked in the Amstel driveway. "Not unless you need some alone time."

"I thought you might. Your face has that look."

"What look is that?" Em muttered.

She'd stopped thinking about Eleanor long enough to recall that this time last year she'd been over on Teagarden Street helping Dad make his famous—infamous— Sweet Innocence *Kir.* This New Year's Eve, Em's first with her mother, was also the first without the sticky-sweet Indian dessert. She had the recipe, but hadn't found the time to round up the ingredients. Midnight would be strange without a lump of rice pudding churning in her stomach. Perhaps anticipation accounted for her expression.

"The look you get when you're thinking about your other life. I thought that you might want to do whatever you do to look for Eleanor."

"Whatever I do," Em replied with a bitter laugh, "it never works while the sun's up and it hasn't worked at all since Eleanor moved to Meadow View. When Eleanor was in the hospital, life was so surreal, it didn't seem at all strange that I was coming home and putting myself into a curse-hunting trance. But since I moved her to Meadow View, I catch myself thinking she *is* my niece . . . or cousin. I've told the lies so many times I'm starting to believe them. It has to be very late at night before I can con-

vince myself to try making magic. It's not as if I believe
in it, really, or was any good at it."

The light changed. Nancy drove straight for the Amstel home. "What about Harry? Have you heard from
him?"

"My stepfather? I told you about the card, didn't I?
Season's Greetings in gold on matte black—very classy,
very expensive. The sort of card you send to business associates. For all I know his secretary signed it."

"Harry has a secretary?"

"I'm guessing," Em admitted. "He probably signed it
himself. There was a note. Another 'please call, we need
to talk' note."

"Did you send him a card?"

Emma shook her head. "In my more paranoid moments, I assume my recent wasteland failures are the result of something he's done."

"That doesn't make sense, Em."

"Why should any part of my life these days make
sense?"

"I'm not saying you should trust him at all. But your
connection with Eleanor has to be stronger than his so it
doesn't make sense that he'd completely stop you from
looking for her."

"Harry doesn't want me looking, Nance. Harry made it
quite clear he doesn't think I can rescue Eleanor. And
maybe he's right. If I did find her, I'd find whatever swallowed her, too, and be at risk of being swallowed myself.
If I were Harry and I knew a way to make sure some amateur wasn't making a bad situation worse, damn straight
I'd make sure. He's cold-blooded, ruthless, and arrogant,
but not stupid. He'd doesn't want two potential rogues on
his hands."

"Is that a real danger, Em? I thought you had that guy
with the hat watching over you. You said he'd been wandering that wasteland for a couple of centuries and that he
wasn't a rogue."

Blaise Raponde—the guy with the hat, a peacock-feathered extravaganza straight out of *The Three Muske-teers.* Em had told Nancy about Blaise—and that she found him attractive—before she'd understood that he wasn't a figment of her imagination. If she were any good at the changing-history business, she'd have gone back and erased that conversation. "That's what he said . . . right before he said he'd say the same thing if he were a rogue. And I haven't bumped into him, either."

"So you want to come back to the house?"

Em hesitated before saying, "Yes." The truth was that she didn't care. A fog named Eleanor Merrigan had fallen over her life, and Nancy, perceptive despite her own burdens, saw through it.

"Maybe you should think about pulling back. You've got your own problems to take care of. Your mother showing up, after you'd thought she was dead all these years, that's got to have stirred all sorts of unresolved emotions—and then to have her . . . well, looking the way she does and where she is. Then throw in the holidays without your dad. I can't count the number of times I've thought about him in the last two weeks . . ." Nancy's voice trailed off as if she'd taken the wrong turn in her own thoughts. "I'm worried about you, Em. That's all."

"We worry about each other, that's the deal, isn't it?" Emma replied, a little quicker, a little sharper than she'd intended. She took a breath and tried to find a calmer tone. "Look, I agree with you, Nance. You know, I'd even gone so far as to think about which clinic I'd visit when the holidays started depressing me. But—I can't very well do that now. No sense spending good money on a shrink and then telling her the same lies I'm telling everyone else."

"That's why I thought, maybe, if you could just pull back a little. Go to Meadow View every other day. You've said it yourself: it's not as if your mother knows you're visiting her."

Emma shook her head then realized Nancy hadn't seen the gesture. "Nope. Can't do that. Not yet. I'm not *blind*, Nance. I know I'm tearing myself to pieces and I'm doing it as carefully as I can. I have thought about it—every night I think about not going back to Meadow View to-morrow but—trust me on this—it would be harder not to. I've *got* to make my daily appearance out there—for my own sanity."

"Why?" Nancy demanded as the Amstel driveway hove into sight. "So you can tell yourself that you're not abandoning her the way she abandoned you?"

"No," Emma replied calmly. "So I can tell *her*, the moment she wakes up. So I can grab her by the shoulders and tell her just what I think of the mess she's made of being my mother."

"Emma—"

"Oh, don't worry, Nance—I don't think I would or could, but that *is* my fantasy-du-jour. When push comes to shove, I'm a lot less noble about this than my stepfather. He's thinking about protecting the world from curses and rogues while I'm primarily peeved that I didn't get a chance to have the mother-of-all-tantrums with my mother."

"You're kidding?"

Em got out of the car before confessing. "Not as much as I'd like. I tell myself I'm doing things for the right reasons, but deep inside, the wrong reason won't go away. I'm feeling angry, Nance. Angry and helpless and she's the best target."

"Mothers always are," Nancy agreed.

A heady brew of aromas greeted them before Nancy opened the kitchen door. John Amstel was that rarity among husbands—one that cooked willingly, frequently, and especially for large groups. He had a pot on every burner of the stove, several more sitting on the counters, and bowls everywhere.

Nancy joked and asked, "What's for dinner?"

John replied with a list of dishes that started with bouil-labaisse. "Have a taste and tell me what you think. I wasn't expecting you back this soon. Where's Katherine?"

Emma tasted while Nancy explained. She said the

thick, steamy soup was delicious, then she slipped out of the kitchen altogether as John offered his opinion of his wife's mother's behavior. They'd never gotten along well, he and Katherine, which said something about the people Nancy let close to her—and something, possibly, about Em, too. If she'd stayed in the kitchen, she'd have said either that John had used too much garlic or that his comments weren't helping his wife. Fortunately, Em knew the house as well as she knew her own and that there was a huge jigsaw puzzle set up in the den, ready to bridge any dull moments in the evening's festivities. She was separating land and sea when Nancy joined her with two glasses of wine.

For a few hours, while John's soup permeated the house, the friends put mothers and other problems out of their minds as they fitted pieces together. Then it was time to cover the dining room table with food and prepare for guests. Emma knew everyone who'd been invited but they were John and Nancy's friends, not hers. When push came to shove, Emma Merrigan kept her own company. The people she knew were usually someone else's friends.

Still, the people who came to John and Nancy's for New Year's Eve were good people, people she looked forward to seeing once a year. Some arrived early and planned to stay until the ball came down. For others, the Amstel home was merely one stop on the journey to midnight. Emma mingled comfortably with them all—she'd grown her social skills early, standing in for her missing mother whenever her father entertained. Several guests knew she'd lost her father during the year, but none of them knew about Eleanor. Em could accept their sympathies for one without resorting to lies about the other.

The phone rang steadily as absent acquaintances touched base with the Amstel regulars. At ten-thirty, Em went upstairs and called the number of the party where her stepdaughter, Lori, said she could be found.

Last summer, Lori had suggested they spend the holidays together in Boston. Em had hesitated—she was gratified that her stepdaughter had grown up to be a compassionate young woman and hadn't wanted to turn down the invitation, but she had wanted to celebrate in Bower this year, however painful the memories. When Eleanor fell into her life, Em thought she'd found the perfect excuse. She'd made her apologies and thought that would be the end of it. She hadn't anticipated Lori's determination or her curiosity.

Lori had come home for Christmas, arriving in Bower on the twenty-first and staying until the twenty-seventh. It hadn't been one of their better visits. Lori saw through the stepniece lie without guessing the truth. In Lori's eyes, it wasn't Sleeping Beauty lying in the Meadow View bed, but the Evil Queen.

A cousin shows up, unannounced, says she's your long-lost family and now you're taking care of her? What about her real family? Doesn't she have parents someplace? Did she have proof? You know you can't believe the junk you find on the Internet.

Whenever the subject of Eleanor had arisen—and it had arisen often—Lori had wanted Emma to see a therapist for counseling, medication, and anything else that would separate her from that "leech."

Maybe it was jealousy. Lori and her brother had to share their mother with a stepfather and three half-siblings, but they'd laid claim to Emma's undivided attention. Jeff's kids meant more to Emma than ten Eleanors, awake or comatose, and she trusted Lori to keep a secret—divorce kids were good with secrets—but in the end, Emma had held on to hers.

Lori's party was noisier than the one Nancy and John were hosting. They couldn't hear each other easily and didn't talk long or about Eleanor, and Jeff Jr., whom Emma tried to call at home, wasn't there and his voice mail reported a full in-box. Emma returned to her own party feeling out-of-synch with everyone around her. If her car hadn't been blocked by a half-dozen others, she'd have begged off and gone home. But it was blocked in and

Em wasn't about to run the gauntlet of curiosity and kindness it would take to get it to the street. She poured herself another glass of wine—her third of the day—and tried to rekindle the holiday spirit.

She was still trying when Nancy signaled that it was time to break out the champagne.

"Are you okay?" Nancy asked as they arranged two-dozen glasses of various shapes for filling. "The last hour or so, every time I've looked your way, you've been staring out the window. You aren't having second thoughts?"

Em shook her head; that wasn't among questions she might have expected. "Second thoughts about what?"

"You and your dad used to come to my parents' house for New Year's Eve. After they moved down to Ohio, you and he started coming here instead. He was part of the ritual. The year can't end without John's bouillabaisse and your dad's Sweet Innocence pudding. *I* miss him; it must be so much harder for you. Maybe you should have taken Matt up on his invitation and gone to the field-house ball."

Emma was careful to set her glasses down before saying, "That was the furthest thought from my mind. I swear, I'd forgotten completely about the Midnight Ball."

Matt was the computer-systems administrator at the library and not much older than Lori. Em had shown him the ropes when he hired on and they'd struck up the kind of friendship she didn't have with anyone except Nancy and her husband at the New Year's Eve party. He'd seen what a wasteland curse could do to a townhouse living room or a living body; and he knew the truth about Eleanor.

"When he won those tickets to the Midnight Masked Ball and asked you to go with him," Nancy continued, "you should have said yes."

"Don't be ridiculous. I've got enough problems as it is without dating someone who is exactly half my age."

"It wouldn't be a problem unless you made it one. Times have changed, Emma; well, they've started to. Women can do what men have been doing for years: have a midlife crisis. Or don't call it a date. The girls don't date. Alyx insists that her boyfriends are friends first and men second, no romance, no entanglements, no commitments. You could be an example for the rest of us."

Em rolled her eyes. "You sound like the menopause edition of *Cosmopolitan*."

But she had considered going. The U had sponsored a New Year's Eve Ball for students and staff with nowhere better to go since Emma's student days. It had been hopelessly uncool then and for decades afterward, then a few years ago they'd added costumes to the mix and partnered with some high-profile local charities. Suddenly, the Midnight *Masked* Ball became a hot-ticket event.

If a man closer to her own age had suggested it—if Emma had known such a man—she'd have gone in a minute, just to see what the fuss was about. But not with Matt.

"I'd have felt too uncomfortable," she confessed.

"That's what the masks are for, and the costumes. You could have rented a costume from one of those places downtown and pretended to be someone else all night. No one would have been the wiser."

"Matt would have known . . . *I'd* have known. All right, maybe now I've got a better sense of what was going on in Jeff's head when he took off, but it was still idiotic on his part and no reason for me to go acting the same way, especially now when I'm seriously questioning my sanity. I might be lonely, Nance, but I'm not interested in a long-term relationship until I've settled this thing with Eleanor."

Nancy shuttled more glasses to the table. "You've got a point . . . about Eleanor, but not about Jeff. You've held the high ground for six years, Em; you can relax a little without losing it."

A cloak of weariness and memory descended around Emma's shoulders. "Not tonight, Nance. Okay?"

Nancy agreed by changing the subject without missing

a beat. "I think we've got enough glasses now. Let's get the champagne. It's out in the garage, in the old fridge."

They no sooner had the chilled bottles inside when a chorus summoned them to the den. The television had been turned on, and the ball above Times Square was poised for its annual descent. Another year was ready to beat its retreat into history. Everyone had a bubbling glass in hand at the appropriate moment. Those who had partners were standing beside them. Last year Emma had sat beside her father. This year found her in eye contact with an unattached man while couples embraced. Like her, Ted was a regular at the Amstels' New Year's Eve gathering, and because of that, Em knew they had nothing else in common.

Em tipped her glass in his direction but sipped her champagne alone. A moment later, John Amstel, whose instincts for equilibrium were preternaturally keen, arrived to give Emma a fraternal hug and a kiss on the cheek. She'd have been worse off alone—or at the masked ball—but that didn't stop her from wishing she were in bed and asleep.

Guests began departing before the replays of the Times Square celebration were finished. The driveway between Emma's car and the street was clear by twelve forty-five, but she stuck around to clear the party's carnage while John complained that he'd never gotten a bowl of his now-vanished bouillabaisse. He was nearest the phone when it rang, and he picked it up while Em and Nancy fell grimly silent. Emma was thinking about Meadow View; she assumed Nancy shared the thought.

"It's for you," John said, thrusting the receiver toward Em.

She mouthed *Who is it?*

He replied with a shrug. "A man. At a party. It's noisy. I can't recognize the voice."

Em counted the number of people who might call at such an hour and who'd know to call her here, not at home. She got as far as Jeff Jr. and took the phone with a shaking, bloodless hand.

It was noisy. The voice that shouted "Happy New Year, Em!" into her ear was definitely masculine, definitely unfamiliar. "You're missing an awesome party."

"What's going on?" Em demanded. "Who is this?"

The caller hesitated—which did nothing for her nerves—then shouted over the background din, "It's me, Em—Matt . . . Matt Barto." Matt wasn't drunk, but Em was sure he was fueled by more than three glasses of wine and a half-glass of champagne.

"Happy New Year's, Matt," she replied, silently, eternally grateful that she hadn't chosen the Midnight Ball over tradition. "I'm glad you're having a good time."

"Good time, Em—I'm having a great time, a spectacular time. I've met someone. Me! I've met someone and you've got to meet her. She's your type."

Matt, Em realized uncomfortably, had mistaken her for his mother. Considering what she'd almost mistaken him for, the realization sent a chill down her spine. "I'm glad for you."

"What? I can't hear you. You've got to meet her. The two of you will have lots to talk about."

Matt said her name.

"Mail?" Em repeated the sound she thought she'd heard. Maybe the girl was foreign. The masked ball might be gaining popularity, but the campus was closed until Monday and the party was undoubtedly heavy with international students and staff. More likely, Em had simply misheard. An exceedingly loud version of the macarena had started up in the background.

She was about to say that there was no point in continuing the conversation when Matt shouted:

"I can't hear you, Em. It's way loud and I've got to get back. I told her about you. She really wants to meet you."

So, Matt had made a mother out of her. Emma was old enough to play the part and used to playing it for someone else's children. She sucked up her gut and lied. "I look forward to meeting her, Matt."

"Great! I gotta go now . . . Happy New Year, Auntie Em!"

The connection died before Em could say another word.

"That was Matt?" Nancy asked, a look of astonishment on her face.

Em returned the phone to its cradle. "He seems to have met the woman of his dreams—at least until the sun comes up tomorrow."

"He needed to tell you this *here* and at two-thirty A.M.?" John cooked and even did the laundry on occasion, but had a pure masculine "my home is my castle" reaction when it came to intruders.

Her husband had scarcely finished speaking when Nancy said, "You should have gone to the ball."

Emma shook her head and loosened a tear. She wasn't crying. John had read the kitchen clock correctly. It was an hour later than she'd thought it was and the error caught up with her the instant she'd discovered it. Tears were her body's way of telling her to go to bed *now* and Nancy knew it. Or Nancy would have known it, if they weren't all so tired.

The next thing Em knew, Nance's arms were around her and an apology had been whispered into her ear. The apology wasn't necessary. The hug was.

"Stay here tonight," Nancy suggested. "The bed's made up. There's no need for you to drive home."

Any other time, Emma would have accepted the invitation—or suggested it herself. Not tonight. Tonight—what was left of it—she wanted to be home in her own bed. She ended the embrace and said so.

Nancy didn't question her decision. "But let John follow you. There's no telling where you'll have to park and I don't like to think of you walking two or three blocks by yourself. John?"

"No problem," he agreed quickly.

As late as it was and as tired as she was, Em wasn't going to stand on feminist ceremony. Parking was a chronic problem at the Maisonettes complex where she lived. None of the 1920s-vintage townhouses had garages or driveways, and though the owners' association issued parking stickers, one vehicle per residence, the streets belonged to the city and anyone could park outside Emma's home. She might get lucky, or she might wind up walking considerably more than two or three blocks.

"That's a good idea," she conceded, adding, "We should leave now."

John went to get their coats.

"How about coming over here for the game tomorrow?" Nancy asked. "There's food in the fridge."

Em shook her head again. The other eye started leaking. She blotted her cheek with her sleeve. "Why don't you and John come over to my place?"

They agreed not to make a decision until noon when whoever felt the most awake would call the other. John reappeared with an armful of coat into which Em gratefully shrugged. The streets were deserted, but the Maisonettes' curbs were bumper to bumper with unstickered cars.

Emma was on the verge of pointing her car back toward the Amstel residence when she spotted an empty patch of asphalt where there'd been a car a few minutes earlier. She could park her car in her sleep, which was very nearly what she did with John waiting patiently. Then he crept along behind her.

Anyone betting with the weatherman would have won the bet. The temperature had dropped like a stone and the wind was wicked. Em's coat wasn't keeping her warm; neither were her gloves or hat. It could have been worse: the sky was black with clouds but nothing had fallen. She tugged her sleeves down over her hands and strode quickly down the dry sidewalk.

One block. Two. Em could see the light on her front porch and picked up her pace.

A dog started barking, a big dog by the sound of its bark and a loose one. Bower had a leash law. Owners were supposed to pick up after their pets, animals weren't supposed to roam, and owners who lived at the Maisonettes weren't supposed to have any pet that weighed more than twenty pounds. No one, so far as Emma knew, did.

Fear—terror—shook her.

A dog she heard but never saw had heralded the start of her wasteland encounters back in November. She hadn't gotten a chance to ask Eleanor if there was any connection between dogs and curses. In her heart, she knew there had to be. She fumbled for her keys, as if they'd protect her.

The barking got louder, drew closer fast. It came from behind, on the other side of the street, the other side of John's car. Glancing over her shoulder, Em couldn't see anything through the glare of John's headlights. Then it was ahead of her, crossing the street, a huge, shaggy, Hound-of-the-Baskervilles beast. Em stopped in her tracks, too cold, tired, and frightened to make a run for John's car.

The dog wasn't interested in her. It ran past her home and past the corner which would have given it access to the grass-covered alley that formed the Maisonettes' spine.

"You okay, Emma?" John called through the electronically opened window on the passenger side.

"Yeah, fine." She started walking again.

Within a minute, her key was in the front door lock. Her cats, Spin and Charm, were there to greet her when the door swung open, stretching themselves awake and giving her looks that said she'd been gone so long they expected breakfast *now*. Emma gave an all's-well wave to John and sealed herself in her sanctuary.

Three

The *downstairs drapes* were open. Emma had them closed before the taillights of John's car disappeared. She turned the Christmas tree on, too, though she expected to be tucked in upstairs in fifteen minutes. An unlit tree was an emotional black hole and Em had enough trouble without one of those lurking in the living room.

She was in the kitchen popping the lid on a can of cat food when she heard a dog's howl. The sound nailed her to the floor. Spin wove impatient figure eights around her ankles, but couldn't get Em moving toward the food dish. The cat had to stand up against her leg and bat at her elbow to reclaim her attention.

Em tapped the food into the dish. Charm lapped the juices; Spin sat and stared as if she'd completely misunderstood his intentions. Sighing and sniffing back tears, Em bent down and gave Spin a scratching that started at his forehead, circled his ears, then dealt with every itchy vertebra in his spine. When the cat was satisfied—and not a moment sooner—he flicked his tail and marched to the food dish. Charm gave him a little growl and the hairy eyeball, but made room all the same. As siblings went, they got along better than Lori and Jeff Jr. ever had.

The answering-machine light was blinking. Em hit the replay button and listened to the tape rewind as she hung up her coat. The first message was Lori apologizing for calling the wrong number. The second was a former coworker who'd moved out west a decade ago but always called on New Year's Eve, and always left a message because Em was always at the Amstels'. The third call and the fourth, fifth, and sixth were breathers—gaspers, really—who wheezed until the machine cut them off.

Emma hit the rewind button with more force than was necessary and reminded herself that prank calls were a way of life in a college town. Then she checked the front and back doors, making sure that the bolts were thrown. Coming back to the living room, she noticed two of her Christmas ornaments on the rug.

"Spin! Charm! Get in here!"

Cats would come when called, if it pleased them. Emma usually rehung spilled ornaments without comment, so they weren't expecting trouble and loped into the living room, Charm first, Spin after.

"Which one of you did this?" Em pointed at the ornaments.

Spin made a dash for the cut-away corner of the basement door. Charm stuck one rear paw in the air and began grooming. Emma shook her head and laughed. Little, all-gray Charm with her air of innocence was almost certainly the guilty feline. She was the more independent of the siblings and the better liar. Spin, who was bigger and needed more food, was first in her lap when she got home after work and spent the night curled around her head on the pillow. He also accepted the blame anytime Em seemed out of sorts.

Em knelt down to rehang the ornaments and scratch the elusive place between Charm's ears. The cat rolled over and they were playing a game of tickle-the-tummy when Spin exploded out of the cat-cut. He was fluffed to the max, with eyes like black marbles, as he swung wide and raced upstairs.

Em's mood changed between heartbeats. She watched the basement door, unable to breathe, half-expecting the knob to move. When, after several long seconds, it hadn't budged, Emma's lungs let go, but she didn't relax.

Jeff had owned a handgun, a small, ugly thing of dull, gray metal and scratched, black plastic. Em had never fired it, never touched it at all until after he'd left. Then she'd opened the night-table drawer on his side of the bed, stuck a pencil in the barrel, TV-detective style, and dropped it into a plastic bag for transportation to the police station. When she'd left the station, a weight had lifted from her shoulders. Seven years later, it returned, doubled and vengeful.

Her hands were steady, though, when she wrapped her fingers around the handle of a broad-bladed chef's knife. Charm curled her tail into a question mark and followed Em to the basement door. The cat's calm curiosity bolstered Em's courage. She flipped a switch, flooding the basement with two hundred watts' worth of bravery, and opened the door.

"I'm coming downstairs," she warned and made the warning good.

There was enough light from the two overhead lamps to fill the corners, but there were man-sized places to hide behind the rumbling furnace. The spiderweb stretched between the ceiling and the handlebars of her neglected exercise bicycle was intact, but try as she might, Em couldn't recall if the pile of empty Christmas boxes in the center of the single room had been rearranged. Whether the answer were yes or no, the cardboard heap blocked her view of anything that might be lurking beneath the old dining-room table.

Em could clearly see the box that had turned her life upside down in early November. The faded cardboard bore her birth certificate name—Merle Acalia Merrigan— in India ink calligraphy and sat by itself amid the bowls, bottles, and wax-encased letters it had contained. The longer Em thought about it—and she'd been thinking off and on for nearly two months—the more seriously she considered the likelihood that Eleanor had left the box in the wasteland until the magic moment when her daughter left the here-and-now to find it.

And considering the dog, the answering-machine gaspers, and the way the short hairs on the back of her neck were tingling, Em feared that her life was about to change again. She stayed put on the stairway, reexamining the basement for another extra-special-delivery box. Everything visible was also familiar. She relaxed her death grip on the knife then descended to the cement floor. Nothing hid beneath the old table or amid the Christmas boxes. The water heater hadn't sprung a leak but there was an inches-high mound of shredded cardboard heaped around the back leg of her workbench.

Mice. The cold had driven them in and Em would need traps to get them out because her cats wouldn't hunt anything that didn't smell of catnip.

Mice.

Tension and terror drained down Em's spine. She felt unspeakably foolish standing beside the washing machine with a kitchen knife and eternally grateful that there'd been no witnesses. The rodents would keep until the sun had risen. Em made her way up to her bedroom, switching off the lights as she went. She would have taken a sleeping pill, if she hadn't thrown them out, untouched, in mid-December. With no chemicals guaranteed to put her to sleep, Em dialed the electric blanket up to a slow broil. She'd expected to fall asleep fast but couldn't get comfortable. The extra wine she'd drunk before midnight, not to mention the adrenalin she'd burnt in the basement, kept her eyes open and her thoughts drifting.

While Eleanor languished at University Hospital, Emma had had some regular success slipping from sleeplessness to the wasteland, even if she'd had no success locating her mother once she got there. She'd had no such luck since moving Eleanor to Meadow View. If she'd been thinking, she'd have taken advantage of her restlessness and tried to slide herself from one reality to the other. Of course, if she'd been thinking, she probably wouldn't have succeeded.

Em didn't notice her departure from the here-and-now, merely that her feet were no longer freezing, but the mattress was much too hard. Trying to rearrange her pillow, she grasped dry, crumbling dirt instead.

I'm there.

With that realization, all sense of her bedroom vanished. Sheets, blankets, and the *whirr* of the furnace disappeared from Em's consciousness, the cats and the window shade shadows, too. She'd returned to the mysterious place where she'd lost her mother. Levering onto an elbow, Em looked around.

The wasteland was a vast, barren realm where the sun didn't shine and neither did the moon or stars. It was dark, but not pitch dark, and Em could make it brighter by opening what Eleanor had termed her "inner eyes." Then the charcoal sky turned a lurid shade of purple and the horizon retreated a mile or maybe a year. Time was distance in the wasteland. If Em wanted to visit eleventh-century England, she had only to start walking. Direction was unimportant; she'd simply know when it was time to get down on her knees and sink into the past.

But Emma wasn't headed to the eleventh century. She was looking for her mother and she suspected that choosing a direction at random wouldn't be good enough.

The wasteland view didn't change much once Em stood up. The ground beneath her bare feet had the cracked, crumbling texture of baked mud, but the flood that had formed it was long gone. (It seemed that whether she started out in street clothes or a flannel nightshirt, Emma arrived in the wasteland barefoot and wearing a flimsy waltz-length gown more suited to ballet than hiking.) Nothing grew in the wasteland. Not one tree nor blade of grass rose to break the monotony of a landscape that had all the rise and fall of a football field.

One object erupted through the parched dirt: a waist-high black boulder, sheered off in front and polished to a mirror sheen. It reminded Em of Maya Lin's Vietnam Memorial, which might not have been coincidental. In the wasteland, where metaphor was reality, the mirror-black stone was her way home.

Her way, and hers alone. Eleanor's way home had been an upright sheet of plate glass. In one of her few moments of maternal instruction, Eleanor had told her daughter never to lose sight of the way home.

Emma had gotten a few other useful bits of advice from her mother during their short acquaintance. At the top of the list: The here-and-now they left behind in Bower was objective, empirical: subject to the scientific method and the engineering gene. The wasteland was real but subjective. Subjective truth could change, but the boulder, once it appeared, was there each time Emma arrived; she was grateful for the consistency.

Em approached her boulder. Kneeling, she pressed her palms against the polished surface. It was arrestingly cold, not stone at all, and if she thought of a bouquet of helium balloons (the image she'd used the first time she'd successfully—and consciously—made the round-trip from Bower to the wasteland) the mirror would become watery and float Em back to her bedroom as surely as the ruby slippers had gotten Dorothy back to Kansas.

She leaned back from the boulder before the watery transference could begin. Though she hadn't planned to wander the wasteland, before dawn on New Year's Day, she wouldn't waste the opportunity. Eleanor was imprisoned somewhere in this trackless desolation, somewhere that had to be at least slightly different from the rest.

The first time Emma had searched for her mother, she'd been doggedly methodical, counting her strides between right-angle turns as she paced a squared-off spiral across the sterile land. When she'd returned to continue the search, though her way-home stone remained, her carefully laid pattern was gone. The engineering gene fostered persistence in the face of failure. She recreated her search spiral five nights in succession before conceding that logic counted for nothing in a land of metaphor.

Since logic couldn't crack the nut, Em had put an image of Eleanor in the front of her mind and walked toward it like a harnessed horse pursuing a carrot. The challenge became which maternal image to chase? Eleanor as she reposed in her coma? In her wedding portrait? As a stranger waiting on the front porch or collapsed on the living room floor? Maybe Eleanor brandishing a silly, pink-crystal-topped wand that hadn't been nearly potent enough to save her from the flaming curses?

Emma had tried them all while Eleanor languished in the hospital, and although she'd lost the ability to transfer herself from Bower to the wasteland the day the ambulance moved Eleanor to Meadow View, Em suspected that the failure had nothing to do with Eleanor leaving the hospital and everything to do with her. She'd simply run out of images to chase.

It was easier to conjure up a half-dozen glimpses of darkly mysterious Blaise Raponde than a single memory of her mother. His hat with its abundance of peacock feathers was clearer than Eleanor's smile.

Em sat down on her rock. She pressed her fingertips around each eye.

Don't think about Blaise Raponde.

Don't think about an elephant.

It wasn't as if Emma hadn't already looked for Blaise Raponde. His last words to her had been a promise to find and rescue Eleanor. Find one of them, and she might find the other. So Em had searched for Blaise as diligently as she'd looked for Eleanor. With that hat, he could have been the inspiration for one of Dumas' three musketeers, so she'd searched for him as well in the library where she worked.

It turned out that she was wrong about the musketeers. After a thorough search of the library's art, history, and theatrical costume resources, Em convinced herself that—except for his hat which was, one hoped, unique—Blaise

Raponde wore clothes that were popular in the last quarter of the seventeenth century, during the reign of Louis XIV rather than Louis XIII, who'd commissioned the real musketeers some seventy years earlier. Well, Em had never been able to keep her Louis straight, or her centuries, until now when she could visit them.

Em found it easier to look for Blaise Raponde than Eleanor. The likes of Blaise Raponde were guaranteed to capture her attention one step into a crowded room. A long-departed coworker had divided men into two categories: Mr. Right and Mr. Right-Now. For Emma, Blaise Raponde—minus that hat—was Mr. Right-Now.

She could see the half-hard, half-humor glint in his dark eyes as she strode away from the rock. With a little effort she could hear his voice and remember the warmth of his hand on her arm. For a ghost, M. Raponde was remarkably tangible. And so much the better for all of them if he rescued Eleanor before she found him.

If there was one undisputed benefit of this whole wasteland intrusion into her life—and one indirect proof of its reality—it was the benefit of exercise. By accepting that she was in two places at once, Em had not only lost five pounds during the season when she usually gained weight, she'd improved her stamina and muscle tone. Three weeks of failure, Christmas cookies, and John Amstel's bouillabaisse had taken their toll on her silhouette. Still, Emma strode across the flats confident that she could walk all the way to the dawn of time, if that was where Blaise, or Eleanor, were hiding.

Em kept an eye on the shimmery magenta horizon as she marched along, spinning around every little while to make sure nothing followed her . . . nothing except her way-back stone, which shrank but never quite disappeared. The stone's pursuit was unnerving. No matter how many yards or miles Emma walked, the black rock was never more than a football field behind her. It could also be reassuring, especially when the rearward horizon lit up with sheet lightning—bright, full-sky flashes, rather than searing bolts.

In Emma's admittedly limited experience, wasteland lightning meant curses, not raindrops, were coming. And though both Blaise and Eleanor had assured her that curses liked nothing more than making a meal out of an isolated curse-hunting human, lightning didn't necessarily mean they were after her. Curses fed on one another, like young alligators, sharks, and frogs, building up their strength the easy way between misery-making visits to the here-and-now.

A curse had to be stronger than the hunter before it could transform the hunter into a rogue. Eleanor was stronger than any one of the curses who had captured her; she survived in her Meadow View bed because her captors hadn't finished their high-stakes game of King-of-the-Mountain.

Emma wasn't foolish enough to think she was more durable than her mother. She dog-trotted back to the stone, but lingered there, hoping to learn something before she plunged home to Bower. The wasteland granted her wish. The sheet flashes grew brighter and resolved themselves into a half-dozen shimmering whirlwinds chasing of single, larger vortex: a pack of wolves in pursuit of an elk, though Emma felt no sympathy for the elk when the wolf pack brought it down in an explosion of white light.

Not every law of science had been repealed in the wasteland. Light traveled faster than sound. Shockwaves traveled faster through air than through dried mud. Em started counting when the elk-curse fell. She heard thunder at the ten count and felt the ground shudder at twelve. By then, the pack was prowling again. She put her hands against the polished stone.

The transfer was painless and finished well before the curses came sniffing around her rock—if Emma's way-back rock existed when she wasn't in the wasteland to see it. She peeked at the clock, a self-given Christmas present that showed the day of the week in addition to the time of the day. It displayed "4:00 AM MON," or a bit less than an hour since she'd turned out the lights. In Michigan, ten days after the winter solstice, 4:00 A.M. meant a good four hours before sunrise. Em snuggled up in the blankets.

The next thing she knew a cat was patting down her nose with a delicate paw. She cracked one eye to distinguish Spin from Charm in the curtains-drawn bedroom, but otherwise didn't move. Spin wasn't fooled. He put his damp nose where his paw had been then yawned.

"What, in heaven's name, have I been feeding you?"

Spin's answer was an indignant yowl and an air-hammer bounce across the mattress. He could be stealth cat when he wanted to but not when he wanted his breakfast. The clock glowed nine. Em supposed the cat had a point and threw back the covers.

"It's not as if you didn't get fed last night."

The cats were unimpressed and followed her into the bathroom—privacy was a futile quest in a home where cats outnumbered humans. Emma had a one-sided conversation about parades and football while scratching behind their ears. She was still paying attention to them when she reached for her toothbrush. By chance, she glanced at the mirror.

She was in the reflection, looking a bit worse for the wear, and standing next to Blaise Raponde.

Surprise sent Emma backward into the bathroom door, demonstrating, before she'd had a chance to form the question, that Blaise was *in* the reflection, not the bathroom. It was quite a sight from the elbows up: him in his fancy seventeenth century garments—the man hadn't been poor in his own time—topped off by that ridiculous hat; her in a Bugs Bunny nightshirt. More embarrassed than frightened, Em watched herself giggle.

Blaise didn't respond with an indulgent smile or anything else. Em had to squint before she was sure he was blinking. He *should* have laughed at that, or run off in horror. He did neither. Cautiously curious, she reached behind her back. In the mirror, her hand disappeared when it met his reflection. In the bathroom, Emma found air that was palpably cold.

"Blaise?" Em exaggerated her pronunciation. If he could see her, he'd know she'd said his name.

His eyes darted before centering again. Emma concluded that he'd heard something. She pressed her hands against the mirror as she had pressed them against the way-back boulder. The mirror was colder than she'd expected it to be, but it didn't melt beneath her palms and the faraway focus of Raponde's eyes didn't change.

Blaise opened his mouth, but the words he uttered were neither his name nor hers. A moment later, he raised his hand as if to ward off the glare of a sudden light. There was a bandage wrapped around his hand. Practically the first thing Blaise had told Emma was that he had enemies and Eleanor was one of them, but until Em saw that stained bit of cloth, she hadn't considered the possibility that he bled like an ordinary man.

He lowered his arm and watched something Em couldn't see. If there were a textbook of expressions, his could have filled the pages for anxiety and wariness. Em pushed away from the sink. She stretched both arms back until they were absorbed in Blaise's voluminous coat. She felt an emptiness as cold as deepest January and the certainty that her onetime rescuer was in need of help himself.

"I can't," she whispered. "I can't get there when the sun's up. The world's too real—*this* world's too real."

Blaise cocked his head, listening perhaps. His eyelids fell. Then, with a sideways flinch, he was wide-eyed and Em was certain she saw the reflection of fire in his dilated pupils. He spun around and, with peacock feathers and coat panels flapping, ran for his life. In a moment, he was gone.

Warmth returned to the bathroom's air, and the cats—who'd been curiously absent while a stranger haunted the mirror—resumed their figure-eight orbits about Em's an-

kles. They scurried for the back room when she clapped
her hands loudly and bolted for her bed.

Maybe there was a chance—the curtains were still
drawn, the sheets still warmly rumpled.

Emma pulled them tight around her and willed herself
to the wasteland. The transference magic was subtle and
not yet hers to command. The harder Emma tried, the
more she was aware of herself in the bed. Spin didn't help
when he stomped onto the pillow. Threading his paw between the pillow and the sheet, he caressed Em's nose as
if it were a catnip mouse. What little was left of her concentration vanished.

Grousing, she pushed both Spin and the blankets aside.
"All right! I'm awake. You'll get your breakfast. There's
nothing I could have done anyway, except set myself up
as another target, right? An easier target."

Spin's reply was the question-mark curl of his tail as he
left the room.

Emma dressed haphazardly from the clothes already
heaped in the rocking chair. She fed the cats—they'd de-
voured the can she'd set out for them earlier—ground a
handful of coffee beans, and turned on the TV as fresh
French Roast dripped into the pot. The Rose Parade was
starting up, but neither it nor steaming caffeine erased
Blaise Raponde's face from her thoughts.

His wide-eyed fright was particularly hard to forget.
The last words Emma had heard from Blaise were his oath
to look for Eleanor because no one—even someone who'd
tried to do away with him—deserved to be possessed by a
curse. Echoes of Hamlet got between Em and the tele-
vised parade. *For Eleanor Merrigan! What's Eleanor to
him or he to Eleanor that he should rescue her?*

Particularly when Eleanor's daughter's attempts had
been so unsuccessful.

There were homes in Bower that weren't buttressed
with bookshelves, but Emma's wasn't among them. A
much-painted bookcase squatted in easy reach of her favorite chair. Two nearly identical black, leather-bound

books stood on the easiest-to-reach middle shelf. She retrieved the more worn of the pair and, with marching
bands and celebrity commentators for background noise,
opened her mother's guide to the wasteland—the guide
Eleanor herself used, as opposed to the sparser volume
she'd packed in the box for her daughter.

Though written in English, the neat pages—Em had
found no more than a dozen scratch-outs in the entire volume—were actually a kind of code, like law books which
yielded precise meanings to lawyers but headaches to
anyone else. Unfortunately, Em was a librarian by trade,
not a lawyer. She poured herself another cup of coffee and
plowed through page upon page of bad poetry and archaic
verbs, looking for a key that would transport her to the
wasteland by day as well as by night without drugs.

Eleanor used drugs. Emma's mother had flown from
New York to Detroit with enough illicit chemicals in her
suitcase to put them both away for a very long time. They
were gone now, flushed and reflushed down the toilet. But
Eleanor, and Em, too, had been under the influence when
the curses struck in November. Emma had let herself be
persuaded that what Eleanor called traditional methods
were worth a try. She rated that decision in her private
"top ten really stupid things I've done" list, far above the
hashish she'd sampled back in the Sixties.

She found two drug-free alternatives buried in the elegant handwriting. One suggested meditation, the other
called for opening a vein in her arm. Emma had tried meditation during her divorce from Jeff. It hadn't helped then,
but this was a new year and she was ready to try again. Em
would try meditation a thousand times before she'd slash
her wrists even once.

Her mother's book didn't supply a mantra to underlie a
curse-hunter's wasteland transfer. Emma focused her
thoughts on the usual New Age suspects, starting with
aum and working downward to *klaatu barata nictu, in-a-
gadda-da-vida,* and *ting-tang-walla-walla-bing-bang.*
She would have recited the notorious third verse of

"Louie, Louie," if she'd been able to find the lyrics on the Internet.

Frustrated and hungry, Em logged off her computer and rummaged a sandwich out of her kitchen. She was back at the beginning, sitting cross-legged and awkward on the floor, thinking *aum*, and holding her breath when the phone rang. The answering machine relayed Nancy's voice.

"Em? Emma, are you there?"

Emma's feet stung like pin cushions when she stood up. She winced over to the chair. Meditation was definitely not her thing.

"Em? Are you okay? It's nearly two—"

"I'm fine—just not paying attention to the time."

"What about Meadow View? There's time before the game starts. I could pick you up. Mom called to wish us a Happy New Year . . ."

Emma looked at the black book she'd left on the floor. She wasn't going to the wasteland; she might as well go to Meadow View, if Katherine was being civil to Nancy for a change.

"You drove yesterday, Nance. I'll pick you up in—say, twenty minutes?"

That would give Em enough time to change her clothes, but not enough to buy fresh cookies. No problem. She kept an emergency stash of chocolate chip cookies in the freezer. They were still thawing when she spread them across the empty plate on Eleanor's bed table.

Eleanor had had a quiet night and was having a quiet day, which was a relief. On the way to Nancy's, it had occurred to Em that whatever was stalking Blaise might have found Eleanor first. Perched on the edge of the bed, with Eleanor's hand between hers, Emma stared into the room's one mirror.

"Aum . . . Aum . . ."

She envisioned Blaise in the mirror and taking Eleanor's other hand. What Em got—and strictly in her imagination, not the mirror—was her ex-husband at his most sullen and scornful.

You don't really believe this shit, do you?

Em's will shattered. She'd get it back, just as she'd gotten it back when Jeff had sneered similar words during their divorce, but not for a few hours. Until then, she couldn't bear the sight of her own reflection.

Down the hall, the chair beside Josh's bed was empty. Irony of ironies: according to the desk nurse, Marsha had checked in by phone. She'd said she was feeling feverish and that she didn't want to risk passing an infection to her son. Infection was a legitimate concern, though Emma's more cynical self insisted that, for Josh, infection would be a blessing.

And for Eleanor?

Emma hadn't yet caught her annual cold. Probably she'd stay home when she did. Eleanor wasn't Josh. Eleanor wasn't brain injured, she was held captive by curses in an alternate reality . . .

You don't really believe this shit, do you?

Em retreated to the elevator corner and closed her eyes. Objectively or subjectively, which woman was more self-deluded? Her or Marsha?

In the lobby a half-hour later, after Nancy and Katherine had concluded one of their rare pleasant visits, Emma wasn't close to an answer and grateful that Nancy wanted to reminisce about her family's good times. They were running late by the time Em found a parking space four blocks from her front door. The pregame show had started, and John was camped out on the sofa with Charm curled up in his lap. The little gray cat went shameless whenever a man sat down in Emma's living room, though she really preferred men with more hair.

She'd go wild for Blaise Raponde.

Em shuddered and turned on the Christmas tree.

The game was close fought, but the right team had the lead from the first quarter and never surrendered to the opposition's threats.

"It's going to be a good year," John decreed when time ran out with the score at 31–24.

Not many would be foolish enough to prejudge an entire year based on a football team's New Year's Day performance—their team lost its bowl games more often than not—but a victory eased the transition from holidays to no holidays. John suggested they drive down to campus where a spontaneous celebration was sure to erupt despite falling temperatures and a lack of students. Students came and went; the team belonged to the town, which was used to January. Emma had exulted on far colder nights, but not this one.

"I'll pass."

John chided her for getting old, but Nancy knew better.

"You've been quiet all day. Did something happen last night? Something *odd*?"

Emma shook her head; she didn't want to talk about the bathroom mirror. Her silence, though, gave John a moment to revisit his own New Year's Eve memories.

"That dog—the one that ran down the middle of the street last night. There was something *odd* about that dog."

"It was big," Em agreed without enthusiasm.

Nancy didn't know about the dog. They had to explain. She pondered a moment then said, "Wasn't there a dog in November? Didn't you say something about a dog that chased you, or you chased it into that other place?"

"I never saw a dog around here back in November," Emma said, which wasn't a lie but neither was it accurate or true. She met Nancy's sidelong stare and held it until Nance broke away.

"Harry?" Nancy asked. "Did Harry call?"

That brought a heartfelt "No" from Emma. "No 'Happy New Year' greetings from my stepfather. And no hell hounds scratching at the back door. I'm just not up for a crowd. You two go—sing the fight song for me."

Nancy had a look that said she wasn't fooled. Probably John wasn't either, but he was better at hiding his opinions. They both stopped pressuring her, which at that moment was all Emma cared about.

"I'll talk to you tomorrow," Nancy said from the front porch. "Don't do anything rash!"

Em promised quickly and shut the door. The temperature had dropped every one of its predicted degrees, most of them since the game had started. Em doubted that the Amstels would be doing any open-air celebrating. As for doing anything rash—she didn't intend to do anything *rash*, but she was determined to get to the wasteland by midnight.

Four

There *was wine* in Emma's refrigerator, mass-market wine packaged in a Mylar sack. In a glass, it was the same color as a fine Bordeaux; and if the taste was a bit metallic, Em wouldn't complain so long as it mellowed her enough to make a smooth transition from the living room to the wasteland. After an unmellow second sip, she plopped two ice cubes in the glass.

With her Christmas tree for light, Em settled down on the carpet. The dark wine and the faint clatter of winter wind replaced the curse-hunter's black book as the focus of her attention. After fifteen minutes of effort, and hours short of her midnight deadline, she sat on the verge of frustration and failure rather than the wasteland. Emma fished the ice cubes out of the glass and squeezed them in her fists.

Em couldn't have said why. Maybe her instinct was simply, stubbornly to do the opposite of anything Eleanor had done. Eleanor had mentioned using ice cubes as a way to call a curse-hunter *back* from the wasteland, so she'd use ice cubes in an effort to get there instead.

Meltwater trickled between Emma's fingers. It dampened her socks. She needed considerable willpower to sit still as frigid droplets crept across the very ticklish soles of her feet. Many Orthodox Jews rocked back and forth as they prayed, in part because the swaying motion mimic-ked that of a camel rider and rulers in the countries of the Diaspora had forbidden Jews to ride camels, but also be-cause the motion created a self-induced distraction. Dis-traction made praying more difficult, and overcoming difficulty made prayer worthier in divine eyes. Emma wasn't praying—unless "Please, please . . . now" were a prayer—but self-induced distraction ended her string of failures.

Em floated away from the here-and-now. She held her breath and kept her thoughts fixed on the way-back stone until her lungs cried out for oxygen. With the last of her willpower, Emma gasped and curled forward until her forehead rested on her ankles, which were naked and dry.

"Madame Emma?"

She recognized the voice.

"Madame Emma—are you all right?"

Summoning the vision of her inner eyes, Emma raised her head. The lurid wasteland horizon glowed around her. Straight ahead, something new had been added: a crack-ling campfire and the silhouette of a man with an extrav-agant hat.

"Blaise Raponde? Is that you?"

"It is I, Madame Emma, or no one at all." He moved slowly, starting to rise then sinking down again.

Emma glanced to her right. The familiar way-back boulder poked through the dirt, but the ground near it was undisturbed—no footprints to say that she had walked here eighteen hours ago. The Frenchman—French ghost—remained seated on the ground, favoring his left side with a right hand tucked inside his dark, voluminous coat. However she examined it, the wasteland was never brighter than a cloudy sunset. Raponde shone with his own faint light—Em did, too—but shadows were deep and colors chancy. Her own skin was dull and pale. His was paler still.

Em recalled the bandage she'd seen in the mirror and

surmised that a battered hand was not Raponde's only injury, nor the worst of them.

"You're hurt."

"Carelessness," he countered and made himself tall as he sat. He removed his hat with a graceful flourish but didn't try to stand.

"How?" Em asked, padding to the campfire on bare feet. "Eleanor?"

A branch snapped within the flames, sending out a shower of embers. Reflexively, Emma retreated. Surprisingly, she smelled fresh pine and charcoal.

"It's a real fire," she marveled and held her hands above the flames. Real heat compelled her to pull them back after a moment. "Where did you find the wood?"

Raponde tapped his temple. "My memory hasn't failed me . . . yet."

"You *remembered* fire and it appeared here?"

"This is au-delà—the world of man's creation. Here, a man may create what he remembers, even what he imagines, but no man can create as God created the world, *ex nihilo*—from nothing."

Em sat at right angles to the ghost and the fire. "God didn't create the universe. The universe exploded in a big bang eighteen billion years ago, give or take a few billion. It's either going to keep exploding and expanding forever or it's going to shrink and start the whole cycle all over again."

Raponde stared at Emma while she silently berated herself for letting loose with her opinions at the worst possible moment.

"Forgive me," he said without blinking. "I forget. Madame Mouse does not *believe*."

Madame Mouse. That was the name he'd bestowed upon her when they first met. She was a mouse compared to the leonine curses pursuing her. By his own admission, Raponde hadn't intended to rescue a mouse, but to wipe out the rogue the lions would make of her. Em hadn't known about rogues that night, but her eyes had been wide open when the maw of a curse descended around her. She'd been swallowed as surely as Eleanor, and if a ghost hadn't chosen to help a mouse, she'd be dead now, or worse.

It was a debt she could never repay. "I live in a different world than you did," Em replied softly. She looked away, at the fire where a score of flames flickered chaotically. Another stick crumbled to ash and embers. The detail was there to the smallest spark. No one's memory was that good.

"You dwell in the same world that I remember, Madame Emma. Older and, perhaps, wiser in some things. But it is God's world, the world that He created, and it will endure until He casts judgment upon it. Time has passed, but time does not make God's world *different.*"

Em made a mental note to leave religion and science out of any future discussion with Blaise Raponde. "Did you— Were you able to find Eleanor?"

"Find her, yes. Rescue her?" He shrugged. "I was careless. I waited too long. Your mother got away from me."

"Eleanor got away? She's free? When?"

Eleanor hadn't looked free a few hours ago at Meadow View.

Raponde shook his head. That, apparently, wasn't the smartest move. He clearly winced and slumped over his right side. "Not free. I had found the trail her curses made and followed it as they fought with one another. I told you they would fight until one was strong enough? They, too, were careless. Like wolves fighting over their kill. It was possible to hunt the stragglers, and I began to think that I could winnow them sufficiently that the last one would not be stronger than I. Fool that I was, I fell into the same carelessness. My thoughts were on the curses I stalked and I didn't notice I was not alone until it was too late."

"A bigger pack?"

"A rogue," he corrected. "I'd chosen the moment of my attack never guessing that I would not be the one to reap the harvest. While I cut through the curses, the rogue carried off the prize."

"Eleanor. My mother. And you were hurt." A statement, not a question. "Which one got you? The rogue or the pack of curses?" Emma thought she should ask that question. Raponde's answer might be important somewhere down the line, though, in truth, she had no sense of what was important in the wasteland.

"I pursued the rogue; the curses pursued me. To be between them was neither good nor wise, but the rogue was strongest. I tried." He clasped his hands together in a gesture of faith and prayer. "I swear to you, Madame Emma: I did not retreat until there was no other choice before me except death."

Odd to hear a dead man speak of death. "And Eleanor? Does the rogue have my mother, or did the pack of curses reclaim her?"

"She is with the rogue. The pack is gone. A few might have escaped, but they will be hiding now."

Em shuffled her bits of knowledge. "What would a rogue want with a pack of curses? What would it want with my mother, for that matter? Would chowing down on another curse-hunter make the rogue twice as strong?"

"Not twice. Not that rogue; it was already quite strong, but it would gain another foothold. Even the poorest curse has a place in God's creation, and a rogue is, *enfin*, a curse. The more places a curse has, the more damage it can do. A rogue can move freely, but even it can only reach into a man's heart if it has a place there. Curses fight blindly, absorbing one another, but rogues collect curses. Of course, if that were all they did, we would leave them alone."

"'We,'" Em pondered. Harry and Eleanor spoke of "we." "We" roused her curiosity and distrust. "You were a curse-hunter, once—the same as Eleanor?"

"I, my father, my brothers, cousins. It is what we did." He shrugged, grimaced, and revised himself. "One of the things we did. It's a simple thing to tell the future when you walk the past. We were well paid for our talents, and well hated. When I was a boy, no one could tell me which came first: the curse or the hunter. The ability to walk au-delà is inherited, mother to daughter and father to son. If your brother walks, it's because of your father, not your mother. You must have persuaded your father that Eleanor could be found and rescued."

Emma didn't follow his logic, but there was one thing she wanted to make clear: "Harry Graves is *not* my father. He's Eleanor's husband—her second husband or, God knows, maybe her third or fourth. And I didn't persuade him of anything. I've met him. He came to the hospital in Bower twice and wanted to take Eleanor back to New York with him. But for reasons known only to herself, Eleanor left me in with power of attorney—" Em caught herself; there was no point in describing the finer points of Michigan law with someone who'd died in seventeenth-century France. "Eleanor would be dead by now. Harry would have suffocated her, or starved her, if he'd gotten her back to New York. It wouldn't be difficult. She's in a coma; she can't defend herself, can't take care of herself at all. She gets food through a tube to her stomach—modern medicine at its best. Her dearly beloved husband wouldn't have to *do* anything to kill her; he'd only have to *stop* doing it. Omission, not commission. She'd die in a few days without fluids."

A memory of Josh, wasted and writhing in his bed, flashed through Em's mind and cut short her diatribe. She didn't know exactly when the notion of a persistent vegetative state had entered the lexicon, surely, in her own life-time. In Raponde's lifetime, vegetative states couldn't persist: a person either awoke out of a coma or died a few days later. She took a breath and continued:

"Without all that 'modern' medicine, it would be over now. A month over and then some. No curses or rogues—Eleanor would be like you, wouldn't she? A dead body and a living mind trapped here in the wasteland. Another curse-hunter who'd lost her body."

"Perhaps, though I think not. More likely, your mother would indeed be dead. It is difficult—nay, impossible—to explain my own existence au-delà. I felt my death. I was drawn to it like a falling stone. Curses were not our only enemies, you understand. To our neighbors we were witches, sorcerers, the Devil himself. Among ourselves, we were that and worse. There was no easier way to be rid of a rival than to slit his throat while he walked au-delà. My persistence can only be an accident; otherwise I do not think I would be alone. Not at all." Raponde stared deeply into his fire before saying, "Harry Graves has left you out in the cold?"

Someday Em would ask Blaise about the magic that left her thinking he spoke colloquial American English, but not today. "Oh, he made the offer, all right. I refused it. Harry tried to deny that he planned to kill his wife once no one was looking, but he wasn't convincing. You and I, we're trying to save her. That doesn't leave much room for negotiation—unless you're telling me that you've given up. I've got to admit, I haven't had any luck at all in finding her."

Raponde prodded his fire with his foot. Sparks flew as burnt wood collapsed into ash. He added more fuel: sticks, broken branches, a chunk of wood the size of Emma's thigh. The wood came out of the shadow he cast on the side Emma couldn't see, or out of thin air or memory, from anywhere except a tree.

No matter how warm and comforting the fire—or how trustworthy Blaise Raponde seemed—the wasteland wasn't the here-and-now and he wasn't a man she could judge by any familiar measure.

"I went back to the place where I'd lost Eleanor—" Raponde watched the fire, not her. Emma had to lean toward her companion to catch his words. "There was a trail—call it a scent. I followed until it went into the ground. The rogue took your mother through God's creation. Not here—not where the past meets the future, but inside my own city and my own time! What luck, I thought. Where can a rogue hide a woman in *my* Paris? In the Sun King's bedchamber? I could find her even there. But luck became no luck at all. There is an important thing you must know, Madame Emma, if you are truly ignorant of au-delà: Walk where and when you will, but stay away from yourself. The rogue tricked me. Again and again it led me across my own path and I, so intent on pursuing it, didn't notice until I was lost in a maze of my own making. Before I freed myself, the rogue confronted me. You see the result."

He withdrew his hand from inside his coat. The bandage was uniformly dark.

"You were looking for me this morning." Another statement. "I was standing in my bathroom and saw you in the mirror."

"I sought you all the way from Paris, but I never saw a room. Until I looked up and saw you here in au-delà, I wasn't certain I'd come to the right place."

"No, it was this morning, for me. Your hand was bandaged when I saw you, but not bloody. I called your name—I thought you heard me. Then I saw fire reflected in your eyes and you ran."

"If that was *this* morning, then it has been a very long day for me. I would say that a week ago a curse mistook me for what I used to be. But no matter; time and place are no great matter au-delà."

Emma disagreed. "Time and place are very confusing here. Whenever I manage to get myself here, I'm always near that rock. For a while—too long—I wasn't having any success getting out of my living room, but I was here last night. I walked forever with that rock following me. I was looking for Eleanor . . . and you. If you'd been anywhere near my rock, we'd have found each other."

"A rock follows you? There are no rocks au-delà, unless you have created one. Why would you create a rock to follow you?"

Em was prepared to ask questions, not answer them. "I don't know. Eleanor showed me an upright pane of plate glass. She said it marked the door between here and where I'd come from, and that no matter where I went or how far I went, I should keep it in sight. If I didn't, I'd lose my way home. When I started coming here on my own, the glass had turned into a rock." She'd pointed toward the black rock. Raponde looked but she could tell that he didn't see. "There's no rock there for you, is there?"

"Not at all. It's your passage, not mine."

"But I could see my mother's plate glass!"

"You entered au-delà together, didn't you? You had the same passage and she is stronger, more experienced, yes? When you enter with your mother, you see a glass plate; when you come alone, you see a black stone."

Emma nodded—the wasteland was subjective. "And if I entered with you, what would I see?" she asked, because in her mind there was always another question.

"You would see nothing, Madame Emma. I have not truly left au-delà since the day I died."

"'Not truly left,'" she quoted. "What other kind of leaving is there?"

"Dreams. The dreams of a ghost. I haunt my memories."

Emma whispered, "I'm sorry," and changed the subject, "You're hurt and Eleanor's being held by a rogue instead of a gang of curses—what can I do to help either of you?"

"I need shelter," he said without a heartbeat's hesitation. He had a heart; she'd felt it beating once. "The rogue knows me now. It found the place where I have been hiding myself and trashed it. Why or how I don't know, but as I am, I can neither face the rogue nor repair my shelter. They do not know how weak a dead man can be, and I would rather they do not learn."

A cold breeze had begun to blow toward Emma as Raponde made his request. Though it failed to ruffle a hair on his head or a flame of his campfire, it filled her with an urgent need to get back to her body.

"Come back to Bower with me," she decided, reaching for his uninjured hand.

Raponde eluded Emma's grasp. "That cannot be done. I have no place in your time. I would be dead in all respects. It is shameful, but true: as a ghost, I fear death more than ever I feared it as a living man."

Em lowered her arm. The breeze had intensified. As usual, she'd arrived in the wasteland wearing a sleeveless nightgown. That the garment left little to anyone's imagination was less annoying than its complete inability to keep her warm. She chafed her arms to no effect.

"Then I can't help you," Emma said through a shiver. "As far as shelter's concerned, it's back to the real world or hide behind a rock you say you can't see."

His disappointment was as palpable as the wind. "I understand. You do not trust me."

They stared at each other with Emma growing colder by the moment. "It's not that I don't trust you, Blaise, it's that I really don't have any shelter to offer. I've let loose with lightning and fire once or twice since I started coming to the wasteland, but I can't conjure up a nice little fire like you've got there—"

"Surely—"

"Surely if I could conjure up something useful in the wasteland, I'd do a better job with how I dress!" Emma shuffled closer to the fire. "A warmer job, at least."

"It is better with rabbits? Warmer?"

"What?"

"Long ears, big eyes, gray . . . very skinny and standing upright like a mannequin, with arms like a little girl, but, yes, a rabbit." Blaise framed an oval with his fingers in front of his chest. "Here. Like this."

Em remembered the mirror: his face, her face, his outlandish clothes, and the Bugs Bunny nightshirt Lori had given her for Christmas. "Oh, dear God . . . *Wait!* You said you didn't see anything!"

"I believe I said I hadn't seen a room."

Em covered her mouth and closed her eyes. She shook

her head slowly until she appreciated the humor—absurd, embarrassing, but definitely worth a laugh—in the situation. *"Touché,"* she conceded, lowering her hand. "It's safe to come to Bower, Blaise—we don't all dress like me."

"Quel dommage," he replied and followed it with more French than she could translate.

"Whoa—my mistake. Back up. Back to English—" and it was her companion's turn to appear confused. "Okay, I get it now. You didn't see the towels hanging in my bathroom. You can't see my rock. And you don't know you're speaking English . . . American English, to be precise, of the late-twentieth-century variety."

"American English," he mused. "I met a man, once, who'd been to America. He called it primitive and very cold, but the natives spoke their own language, not English. Twentieth century. So late . . . I did not realize it had become so late."

"Very late. So late it's really the twenty-first century—a brand-new millennium."

They studied each other, sorting through new information.

"You are very clever, Madame Emma, living in the twenty-first century. It surprises me greatly that you have no shelter . . . or clothes to your liking."

She let that pass. "But it doesn't surprise you that we manage to understand each other—with you not speaking English and me not speaking more than ten words of French in the last thirty-odd years?"

Raponde considered a moment. "No, Madame Emma, it does not surprise me that we understand each other. All men spoke one language until God punished them for building the Tower at Babel. We are au-delà, Madame Emma. God's love and mercy do not reach us here, but neither do His punishments."

"That's—that's— You can't honestly believe that, Blaise. Even in the seventeenth century, you couldn't have believed, literally, in Genesis."

"You know so little, Madame Emma. The truth does not ask you to believe. The truth simply *is*. *God* simply is, whether you believe or not."

Em conceded defeat. "I think Niels Bohr said the same thing about horseshoes."

"I do not know this man. Is he a friend of Harry Graves? Or of yours?"

She was not going to argue metaphysics and quantum theory in the wasteland with a dead man, especially a wounded dead man who sounded—if her emotional radar had not lost all reliability—a tad jealous. "Never mind. It doesn't matter. Forget I said anything. The problem is that you say you need some sort of shelter and I don't have one to give you . . . and my mother's gone from being the prisoner of curses to being the prisoner of a rogue. Sorry, that's two problems. You're sure you can't hide out in Bower?"

"I'm sure I do not want to try."

Emma let her breath out in a sigh. Her adrenalin spike was fading and she felt the cold again. "What about my mother? You said something about Paris. Do I need to be buying plane tickets to Paris?"

"Will these plain tickets take you from your twenty-first century to *my* Paris? The Paris of sixteen-eighty? I do not think so."

She committed the date to memory: 168 , 1680. Score one for the library's costume plate collectio. —her closest match to the French ghost's clothes had come from a woodcut dated 1684.

She held her hands closer to the fire . . . too close. Whatever else, her nerves *believed* those flames were hot. "No, not your Paris," she admitted, pulling her hands back. "I can't just give up. There's got to be something more I can do."

"Stay close to your mother's flesh," Raponde advised. "A rogue can do what I can't: visit the place of rabbits and bowers—"

The cold wind came back, gustier than before. Em shivered from cold and embarrassment.

"Perhaps it is time to listen to Harry Graves. If the rogue takes your mother's place, many others will be in danger."

"More than before, when our problem was a pack of hungry curses?"

Raponde took her hand with his uninjured one. His was pleasantly warm; she didn't object. "Do you remember your mother asking me what I remembered?"

Emma had a notion what was coming, but she nodded anyway.

"When a curse takes a body and becomes a rogue, it loses the memories. A rogue takes both."

"Just when I think it couldn't get worse, it gets worse," Em muttered. She was pondering consequences when the right-side horizon lit up with lightning. "And now we've got company coming."

Blaise winced when he swiveled to glimpse the fading light. "Perhaps. Perhaps not. Can you still see your stone?"

Emma checked. "Right where I left it. Where it left me."

"Good. We remain on the cusp between the past and the future . . . your past and future. That will discourage them—if they have noticed us. Even the mightiest rogue would fare no better than I, if it tried to go where it had no place. And if we were their prey, they wouldn't reveal themselves at such distance."

"You're sure they're far away? They don't look any farther away than the ones that got Eleanor did when they first showed up."

"I could be wrong," he admitted. "The rogue that chased me could be watching us right now, waiting to pounce. Without shelter, there aren't many places to hide au-delà."

"Thanks. I needed that reassurance. If I go back to keep

an eye on Eleanor, what are you going to do? Stay here . . . without shelter?"

"Ask you to trust me and ask again for you to hide me."

Emma looked away. The horizon was quiet and dark. "It's not a matter of trust. My shelter is a townhouse at the Maisonettes in Bower, Michigan. Come home with me. We'll manage, rabbits and all."

"Madame Emma—" Blaise drew her attention by releasing her hand. "Madame. You have made a rock on the border between the past and present. You can make a shelter no rogue or curse can find."

"How? Shall I snap my fingers or wiggle my nose? If I were Eleanor, maybe I could—maybe she's got a timeshare around here. But creating shelters is something else she forgot to write about in that damned book she left behind. If there's an education that goes with this place, I never got it, Blaise. My mother walked out when I was an infant. She thought I'd show up on curse-hunter radar when I was a teenager and all would be forgiven. As you can see, that didn't happen."

The wasteland lit up again, no brighter—closer—than before.

"But, *enfin*, you have had a little place to yourself, yes? A little place where you hid and no one, no one at all, could find you? Inside a cabinet, perhaps, but it wasn't the inside of a cabinet. Not truly."

"When I hid, I hid in the attic or the basement, not here. Look, she gave me a name before she left—Merle Acalia. I couldn't stand it, so I called myself Emma, from my initials. Apparently that was a big mistake. I never did the things little curse-hunters do, and as a result I never showed up on their radar. I think Eleanor thought I'd died in childhood." An unsought memory surfaced: the shock on her mother's face when they first looked at each other in the light. Eleanor had never expected to have a *middle-aged* daughter.

"Among us, our parents do not *teach* us how to hide; they are the reasons we learn on our own. The making is asleep inside when we're born and awakens when we need to escape, long before we learn to walk au-delà. If you have never made shelter, then perhaps you never needed to escape, and if that is true, then you have been very lucky, indeed. I am asking to share that luck, Madame Emma. Awaken yourself and make a small place where I can be rid of my wounds, then I will return to Paris and take Eleanor back from the rogue who holds her."

If it had been possible to slip away from reality, Em would have done it. Heaven knew, she'd been a dreamy child and the exasperation of everyone except her father. But another world—a world of her own imagination, her own creation? The engineering gene rebelled at the thought, then Emma recalled the night terrors. Suppose the truth was that she'd been making places all her life, only they weren't small, private places where a child could escape her fears, her loneliness?

"Point me in the right direction. I'll give it a try. What's the first step of creation?"

He smiled triumphantly. "Why, belief, Madame Emma. Believe in yourself and the place you will make. Build it in your mind and it will be here beside my fire . . . only, don't forget a door to let yourself in and out again."

Blaise had a dangerously attractive smile. If he'd been real . . . If she'd met him at work . . .

But she hadn't and so Em closed her eyes and imagined a safe place. It was her bedroom, not the one at the Maisonettes, but the one in the house on Teagarden Street where she'd grown up, in its early-Sixties aquamarine incarnation. Beatles posters covered one wall, and despite the green trees and sunshine beyond the window, a bitter, icy gale blew across the narrow bed. Emma willed herself to ignore the blast, to remember the knickknacks she'd kept on a shelf above her desk and at least one of the prints in her grandmother's quilt. It was hard with the shivering, but she didn't quit.

"Return, Madame Emma."

Hands, one of them wrapped in stiff cloth, gripped Em's arms. She opened her eyes and for an instant he was a stranger and she was speechless.

"You're trembling."

"Shivering," Emma corrected. The wind passed through her companion to pelt her face. "I *believe* there's a cold wind blowing from where we saw the lightning flashes. What do you make of that?" She meant to laugh, but the cold had penetrated every nerve, every muscle, and her teeth chattered instead.

"You must return to your little home."

Emma started to say that the ice cubes she'd used to get herself to the wasteland were gone by now, and anyway, they hadn't called her back to Bower when Eleanor had used them in November. The argument disintegrated before it was out of her mouth. Once Raponde had planted the seed, its growth was explosive . . . imperative. She had to get back to herself.

Had to.

Freeing herself, Em clambered to her cold-numbed feet and was halfway to the black stone before she faced her ghost again.

"I'll take care of it. I'll fix whatever's wrong. It can't be much . . . maybe the phone's ringing or someone's at the door. I'll come back as soon as I'm done. I swear it. I'll come back. I'll make that shelter."

He smiled, a saddish smile rather than an annoying one. Emma couldn't wait for him to find his voice. The stone shimmered before she touched it. She fell forward, face-first then sideways.

The house was comfortably warm, the phone wasn't ringing, and no one was pounding on the door. Em had flopped onto her side while her consciousness was in the wasteland; she'd knocked over the wineglass. The carpet which swallowed cat hair without a trace forgave a few drops of wine just as easily. Her foot erupted with pins and needles when she stood up. She hobbled over to the answering machine, where the message light glowed a steady zero.

Charm poked her head out of the kitchen. The gray cat sat down as soon as her feet were on the carpet and washed her face vigorously—hardly an omen of urgency. The VCR clock read 10:30. Em had to squint to see the smaller letters spelling out PM and MON. No cause for alarm there either: she'd been gone less than two hours.

The tingling in Emma's foot subsided. She checked the front and back door, the basement and the upstairs. Spin was curled up amid the pillows heaped up on the bed in the back room. He began an all-body stretch when she turned on the light.

Em asked, "Quiet night?" and got a yawn for an answer.

Returning to the living room, she autodialed the sixth-floor desk at Meadow View Manor. A woman answered on the second ring and assured her that Eleanor was having a quiet night.

"Everybody's sleeping quiet, thank the Lord. We'd have called you, Emma, if anything was wrong. We take good care of your mother."

"I know," Em agreed. "I missed a call. I thought it might have been you, that's all." She hung up the phone. In the kitchen doorway, Spin and Charm engaged in a hissing skirmish—unusual, but not unprecedented. "I give up. I came back for a false alarm."

Or had she?

The winter wind had been as real as anything in the wasteland, and Raponde, who hadn't seemed affected by it, had been the one to send her back to Bower. Had he wanted to get her out of the wasteland before those curses he'd said weren't interested in them arrived? He'd asked for help and she hadn't delivered, so he'd sent her home?

She gave the living room a wall-by-wall once-over. A room with books and solid furniture would be a better refuge for a man than her junior-high-era bedroom. Or maybe not. What would a man who'd last seen the here-

and-now in 1680 make of a fluorescent lamp, a stereo, or the television?

"Sixteen-eighty," Emma repeated and wrote the number on the scratch pad beside the telephone before running up the stairs.

She'd had an inspiration—rather than rely on memory, she'd piggy-back on someone else's imagination. She hit the back-room light switch, climbed onto the bed, and reached for a picture that had hung opposite John, Paul, George, and Ringo in her Sixties' bedroom: Mariana, a brown-haired woman painted by one Edward Millais, a nineteenth-century British artist with a thing for languid women in pseudo-medieval settings. Millais had caught his model rising from a session at her embroidery frame. (Emma's fascination with colored thread had begun early. She'd tried to teach herself embroidery in elementary school and had fallen in love with the cheap reproduction the first time she spotted it.)

Mariana stood in sunlight, stretching the kinks out of her back. She wore a long, cobalt blue dress that was neither medieval nor Victorian in style. The room around Mariana had the same awkward timelessness, and was absolutely rife with religious symbolism—Blaise would appreciate that. There was stained glass in the windows Mariana faced and autumn leaves strewn on the floor and her unfinished embroidery. In all, the painting was typically Victorian—an overwrought, sentimental mess—which was why, though Emma cherished Mariana, she hung in the back room, not the living room. But if Em had ever needed to conjure a private place, Mariana's workroom would have been it.

She propped the frame against the sofa and, with no ice cubes this time, settled in to make the wasteland transition. It was her third transfer in the last twenty-four hours and practice was its own magic. In no time Emma drew breaths that reeked of smoke and emptiness.

A familiar voice hailed her: "Madame Emma, it is good to see you!" but the voice was strained and weary.

Emma opened her eyes, hoping to see Mariana's work-room around her. She saw the wasteland, but she was wearing a long, simple gown that appeared black in the shifty light. It was Mariana's gown, exact down to the woven belt unnecessarily slung over her hips and the touch of lace tickling her neck.

But Em would have preferred the workroom.

Blaise Raponde desperately needed the room. His fire was down to embers and so was he. He made no effort to conceal his pain.

Em dropped to her knees beside him. "What happened?" The horizon was quiet, but that could mean anything. "How long have I been gone? I thought it was minutes, at most—"

He cut her off with a sigh. "You forgot the door." Raponde's lips were as pale as his cheeks.

The artist as eavesdropper—Millais hadn't painted Mariana's entire workroom, only the portion that interested him. He hadn't included a door, and neither had Emma. Blaise had warned her; she'd forgotten. Em had a predictable reaction to her mistakes: she was both mortified and outraged. Eleanor had said the wasteland was a subjective reality. It was one miserable subjective reality, if Blaise were going to die a second, final time because she'd forgotten a door.

"A door!" Em snarled, rising to her feet. "Who made that rule?" She raised her eyes to the sunless, starless, moonless heaven and found no answers there. "All right—*I* want a door. My door. I want my door right *here.*"

Emma imagined a doorknob—a plain brass doorknob, polished by years of use . . . no, a glass knob, cool to the touch and cut into prisms. She stuck out her hand. There was nothing there, but she mimed the necessary movements anyway: a counterclockwise twist of the wrist, a shove to get the door swinging inward.

Nothing in her life—including her mother's reappearance—surprised Em half as much as the sunlight and autumnal air that surrounded her a moment later. A door that

Millais had never painted had opened to her command. The knob was glass, exactly as Em had imagined it. The door—to which she'd given no specific thought—was dark, varnished wood—another typically Victorian detail—with a flame-patterned grain that grew clearer as she concentrated on it. Beyond the door lay Mariana's embroidery nook in three dimensions, minus Mariana, but complete with dangling threads, half-glazed windows, and leaves skittering across the floor.

"Dear God," she whispered while, behind her, Blaise said—

"You do not lack for boldness, Madame Mouse."

"I guess that's one word for it."

She couldn't drive herself across the threshold—not until she'd circumnavigated the door at a safe arm's-length. Edge-on, it was a sliver of white light. From behind, there was nothing to see at all—nothing except Raponde doing a slow-motion collapse as his strength gave out. Emma's Mother Voice said *Go to him!* And she did, but not through the door she couldn't see. Instead, Em circled wide, carefully—absurdly—avoiding contact with her own creation.

Blaise had caught himself on one knee. Em put an arm around him and provided balance while he got his feet under him. Something like a giant soap bubble pressed against her face as they intruded over Mariana's threshold. Em closed her eyes and flinched as the bubble burst.

"It is . . . beautiful," Raponde said with the same tone Em herself had used to appraise her stepchildren's elementary school art.

Millais had painted a corner; Em and Blaise entered a room. Em opened her eyes and gasped as the scene completed itself around her. Flat swirls of color became walls with windows and framed pictures, soft shadows solidified into furniture—all of it fueled by her imagination. She thought of a bed. Blaise needed a bed in which to rest and heal—but not *that* bed, not the bed she'd shared with Jeff. So, it changed—and swiftly—from the well-remembered queen-sized monument to something single and utilitarian and wood, in keeping with Millais's timeless vision.

Emma imagined a lamp, and it appeared on a table beside the unfinished bed. Should she imagine a lightbulb inside the lamp shade, or make it an oil lamp instead? If she imagined electric wiring, did she have to imagine a generator? If she imagined an oil lamp, was she also imagining a fire hazard? If she imagined a fire department, would it arrive to put out the fire? And what was the sound of one hand clapping?

The dormitory bed lost form and focus. The walls dissolved. The *floor* dissolved.

Blaise squeezed her hand tightly. Despite his injuries, he had a grip like iron. "Believe, Madame Emma."

Through clenched teeth, Emma insisted: "I don't believe in God."

"Then believe in a room with open windows looking into an autumn garden, in a red bench and an unfinished tapestry. What did it portray, Madame Emma? A great victory? The king? A unicorn? Do you believe in unicorns?"

"A unicorn," Em decided. She could almost see it on the backs of her eyelids—the famous *Unicorn in Captivity* at the Cloisters Museum in New York City. The unicorn was white and framed by a rail fence. But was the background red? Or green? Or darkest blue?

"The particulars don't matter, Madame Emma. Do the beginning well, and the ending will find itself. Where does a room begin?"

"With the floor."

They needed a floor—not a specific floor, merely a solid one. And walls, plain, take-them-for-granted walls . . .

"Breathe now," Blaise advised. "I do not need much and you have given me more than that. There is no need for exhaustion."

Emma hadn't noticed, until he put the idea in her thoughts, that she was tight chested or that subjective creativity was hard work. She opened her eyes, surveyed her godlike efforts, and gave them a C-. Mariana's corner stood intact with the garden beyond it looking the way everything looked before Em tapped her contact lenses into place. The rest of the room was a dull, muddy brown filled with dust-cloud shapes that defied close examination.

"I've got a lot to learn," she concluded.

"Only patience."

Raponde sat down on, or in, a dust cloud and it became a solid chair subtly different from anything Em might have imagined. She realized they'd become partners in creation . . . and other things. With his wounds, Blaise couldn't get out of his huge, heavy coat. Before she'd finished helping him escape the tight sleeves, there was a clothes tree behind her.

Em gave the coat a once-over as she hung it on a hook that was neither wood nor brass. Blaise was a master of the imagination game. His fires were warm and his coat was complete down to the worn patches at its elbows and twisted braid along the cuffs that needed cleaning and repair. The coat's dark lining was damply aromatic with sweat . . . and blood.

Emma stared at her reddened fingertips. "Why bleed?" she asked. "Why believe that you're hurt? Why not believe that you're healthy and *be* healthy?"

"I had that very thought, but the rogue had your mother's wand and it was more convincing."

He had removed his sleeveless waistcoat. Emma's attention was diverted to his bloodstained shirt. Though she'd gotten her first-aid badge in Girl Scouts and bandaged her share of scrapes during her stepmother years, Emma had no experience with serious injuries or gore. Her gut went into free fall, but the rest of her met the challenge, removing the shirt, as gently as she could, and stifling nausea when she saw the wound. Raponde's right-side ribs were covered with a swollen, purple bruise. In the middle of the bruise there was a gouge about two inches wide and as long as her forearm. Blood seeped from only a few places; the rest had been cauterized—

Dear God . . . her mother's *magic* wand. Emma hadn't taken the cheap brass tube with its garish crystal and shiny ribbons seriously.

"This is too weird for words," she complained.

She expected Raponde to add another ironic comment, but he'd gone deathly pale.

"This is the point where the rugged, pioneer women start ripping the bedsheets into bandages," Emma said. When push came to shove, what Emma knew about emergency medicine could be summed up by the words *call nine-one-one.* "And I can try, Blaise, but you'll probably be better off if I do nothing."

"Do what you can," he whispered on his way to the mattress. "Believe in yourself."

If necessity was the mother of invention, then *need* was its father. Em *needed* water and found it in a pitcher on a dresser Millais had painted. The water was cool, not warm, but the pitcher never emptied; she wouldn't allow it to. She rinsed and wiped the sticky wound. The surrounding skin was hot, and tender, a warning that infection had already set in. Em's patient shuddered and moaned when she brushed her fingertips over the reddest part.

Buoyed by the ever-full water pitcher, Emma searched the dresser drawers for honest-to-goodness bandages. That quest proved the limits of her imagination and creativity. She found extra bedsheets, not the prepackaged sterile gauze and adhesive she'd hoped for. Still, she knew how to tear cloth and put the tapestry silks to good use sewing the torn strips together around Raponde's chest.

He was exhausted and on the edge of consciousness by the time Em tucked blankets around him. When asked if there was anything else she could do, Raponde gave a barely perceptible shake of his head.

"Go home, Madame Mouse."

"I'll stick around and keep an eye on you . . . just to make sure."

"A woman who believes nothing can be sure of nothing."

Em wouldn't argue theology with a wounded man, and in the here-and-now, the first workday of the new year had surely begun. "You'll be all right alone?"

"I've been alone longer than you've been alive, Madame Emma."

There was resignation in his tone and more than a little prickliness. Emma blamed it on her clumsy nursing. "Will you be here when I come back?"

"When might that be? We both know that time is slippery au-delà. I'll be here until I'm strong enough to challenge that rogue, then I'll be gone."

He hadn't opened his eyes or turned toward Em, but he must have guessed that she'd stopped short with surprise and disappointment.

"Never fear, Madame Emma. We will find each other again, through a mirror, if nowhere else."

"I'll start paying attention to what I wear in the bathroom," she replied and opened the door.

The fire had burnt down to ashes, but at least there were ashes and an old-fashioned door that failed to cast a shadow anywhere when curse-lightning brightened the horizon. The black stone was where it belonged. With thoughts of balloons and her own bed to guide her, Emma returned to Bower, where the Millais print leaned against the sofa in front of her and the VCR clock read "1:00AM TUES"—later than she preferred for a workday bedtime, but not too late for sleep.

Mariana's blue gown was gone. Em had expected that. Her jeans and sweatshirt combo was more comfortable, more practical for climbing the stairs when the cats were dancing around her feet. It was her house; Emma knew her way around in the dark. There was no need to turn on the lights in the back room while she returned Mariana to her place on the wall, though Em did flip the switch in the bathroom.

The mirror reflected just one face, her own, with a rusty smear across her cheek. Blood. Blaise Raponde's blood. She wondered what DNA investigators would make of it, then turned on the hot water and washed the smear away.

Five

E mma was comfortably warm when the alarm clock
went off. She knew that neither the comfort nor the
warmth would last. Both cats had joined her overnight and
both were under the blanket, something they did only
when the outside temperature dropped like a stone and the
furnace struggled to keep the ambient temperature above
sixty. Em could hear the furnace over the cats' "good-
morning, we're-*starved*" purrs. She poked her arm into
the air to tap the clock into silence and pulled it under the
blankets again.

When you lived in Michigan, you expected your Janu-
aries to be cold, dark, and precipitous; that didn't mean
you leapt for joy when Mr. Fahrenheit went negative.
Based on experience and what she remembered of the
weather forecasts broadcast during yesterday's games, Em
guessed it was about five below outside. She tugged the
covers tighter and lay still, resisting the inevitable until
the alarm clock's snooze feature brought her into the middle of the morning guy's spiel.

"Whoa, baby," he raved, "it's *cold* out there. The folks
over at the weather station say it's ten below here in the
city, but I'm telling you the big hand pointed at minus
twenty out on Monguagon Creek this morning—"

Em groaned. Minus ten wouldn't threaten any records

but it was a temperature to take seriously while scraping the windshield . . . assuming the engine turned over. What with the holidays and getting Eleanor into Meadow View, Em hadn't gotten her car in for its winter checkup. It had been running well, but the first subzero morning always claimed a few batteries. She couldn't remember how many winters had passed since she'd replaced hers.

Reaching out from the blankets a second time, Emma tapped a button that spun the tuner to the university's radio station, which was much too laid back for wake-up music but would have the most accurate information about Bower's weather and any local closings. Usually it took snow, and a lot of it, to shut down the U but sheer cold had done the trick more than once. Minus twenty might, with a good windchill behind it.

The station was in the middle of a baroque string piece. Em snuggled in until it ended and the smooth-throated announcer read a few headlines before getting to the bad news: the local temperature was minus twelve, the winds were calm, the streets were clear, and because the students weren't expected back for another two days, nothing was closed. With another groan, Emma abandoned her warm cocoon and scurried barefoot down the hall.

Several years ago Em had given her dad an electric radiator for his bathroom while swearing that she'd never use one herself. It could have gone into the estate sale after he died, but she'd brought it home instead, still swearing that *she* was tough enough to handle any winter without auxiliary heat. In her heart, Em assured herself that she hadn't softened, but the appliance was right in front of her and there was no reason not to plug it in. A moment later, she was caressing the enamel coils with her toes.

Belatedly, Em checked the mirror for company.

Mercifully, there was none.

Leaving the drapes drawn for additional insulation, Emma made her coffee and lunch by electric light—not that opening the drapes would have changed that. This far north, the January sun didn't rise until after eight and it set before four-thirty. Michiganders got their winter vitamin D on company time.

Emma needed a few extra minutes to find her super-warm gloves and boots—snowmobile gear, really, though she'd never ridden one of the noisy machines. By the time she left the house, her window for an early-morning visit to Meadow View was closing. It shut altogether when she saw the frost on her windshield. Thank heaven, the locks weren't frozen and the engine turned over on the first carefully executed crank. Em set the defroster on blast and got out to attack the frost. Her feet and fingers were numb before she'd scraped out portholes of sufficient size for safe driving.

The gate was wide open at the staff parking structure. The fancy electronic security system the U had installed last September had surrendered to January. If classes had been in session, the students would have swarmed, but classes didn't resume until Thursday, the day after tomorrow. Em found a better-than-usual spot near the bridge from the lot to the library.

Her toes had warmed from numb to crazy itching. Emma watched her step going across the bridge even though ice wasn't particularly slippery at subzero temperatures. She wasn't paying attention elsewhere until beams of red and amber light swept the cement around her.

The street and loading dock below the bridge were crawling with trucks and vans, most of them sporting bright, whirling lights. None were ambulances, which was a civilized relief, and though Em was curious, she was also cold and hurried toward the library door.

Emergency lights greeted Em in the stairwell. The parking structure gate hadn't been the only thing laid low by the thermometer; a few other circuits had popped when the temperatures fell. More than a few, judging by the lack of illumination in the elevator corridor. Em was recalling the scene beneath the bridge when someone from Buildings and Grounds came through a fire door with a flashlight in his hands.

"Is the whole building out?" Emma asked.

"Shut off at the power plant for precautions. They got water trouble at the construction site next door. Someone must've left a valve open Friday and it gushed all weekend, until last night, when it froze. Pipes popped everywhere. We got waterfalls in the stacks and ice on the roof!" He hurried past her to the bridge stairwell.

Water in the stacks! To a librarian the phrase was second only to *Fire!* in its ability to conjure disaster. About once each decade—or three times in her career—the stacks had flooded, and each time the cause had been construction. Fire, of course, was a greater danger. When the fire alarms went off, the library emptied like any other campus building. Floods were different. Waterfalls notwithstanding, people weren't at risk in a flood, but the books were and Emma hadn't spent her life in a university town without developing a serious addiction to bound paper.

Em knew where she belonged in this emergency. She raced upstairs to her dim office, dumped her outerwear, changed her shoes, then with her mind already on the rescue, stood like a fool in front of the lifeless elevator, punching the down button twice before catching her error. Grateful for the lack of witnesses, she hit the fire door and made her way down to the main floor where, as expected, damage control was already under way.

The Horace Johnson Memorial Library rose six stories above the ground, but like an iceberg, it was bigger below the surface. In the paranoid Fifties, the subterranean stacks had been the hub of Bower's bomb-shelter defense, and even now every freshman was required to learn the names of students, real and legendary, who'd entered the maze of shelves and catwalks, ramps and stairways, never to be seen again.

Emma knew the stacks' organization and landmarks. It had been twenty-five years since she'd gotten lost, but she'd never descended the open-steel stairs by flashlight or become part of a human chain moving the bulk of the

European literature and history collection out of harm's way.

After two hundred exchanges, Em's arms were lead and she stopped counting. The book rescue became as trudging as a walk through the wasteland and equally timeless. She was surprised, when the chain had emptied its section of the stacks, to check her self-illuminating watch and realize that it wasn't yet ten-thirty.

Following her coworkers, Em retreated to the lobby, where some angel of mercy had set up jugs of hot coffee, and Gene Shaunekker, the library's chief director, gave them the bad news: the plumbing was shut down along with the power, and it would be at least a day before either was operational again. Until then, the nearest restroom was in the Anthropology Building, accessible through the steam tunnels. Staff, he said, could take personal time or head upstairs to the cavernous Reference Room, where efforts to salvage the books they'd rescued were already under way.

Two months into her mother's reappearance, Emma's once-formidable hoard of personal time had been seriously depleted. She had enough for her own emergencies, not the library's, and the lure of catastrophe was hard to resist. She headed for the Reference Room.

Following the last watery disaster, the library had stockpiled plastic tablecloths and paper towels by the pallet. The sheet plastic went on the big walnut tables in the chamber where twenty-foot windows soared between the ceiling and the tallest bookshelf. A hundred and fifty years ago, when no one had electricity, the Reference Room had housed the entire library and every table got its daytime light from the sun.

The paper towels went between each and every page of the water-damaged books. Em grabbed a bundle of towels and a volume of dripping drama. The job was boring, but the conversation was good as the staff swapped tales about the other times they'd come together to save the books.

Emma realized, with equal touches of dismay and pride, that she'd become a library elder with eyewitness accounts of every disaster since the Sixties, before several of her coworkers had been born, and the hand-me-down tales she herself had learned from earlier generations in similar situations.

Noon was long gone before Em spared a thought for lunch, Eleanor, or a working restroom. While others headed out to unaffected restaurants, Emma braved the steam tunnels then returned to the sandwich in her office with hope that the telephones still worked for outgoing calls. They did, but before she picked up the receiver, Em spotted a legal pad propped against her monitor.

HELP!!! Matt Barto had written in four-inch-high letters followed by the parenthetical suggestion—*Bring waders.* She recognized, but couldn't possibly read, his signature below the plea.

Like the bomb shelter and the European collections, the library's computers dwelt in the basement. These highly connected days, the library got most of its bits-and-bytes horsepower from the university's computer fortress on the outskirts of town, but significant amounts of hardware lived in Matt's cluttered work space. In her knee-jerk rush to protect the library's more obvious assets, Em hadn't given it—or Matt—a second thought all morning.

Mothers, even estranged mothers, claimed precedence over sandwiches and the best of friends. Emma picked up the phone, heard a dial tone, and called Meadow View. Eleanor had passed a restless night. Comatose folk, Em had learned before Eleanor left the hospital, woke and slept the same as other human beings and sometimes suffered from insomnia. It was nothing medically serious, but the staff wanted Em's permission to use restraints if the restlessness persisted: comatose folk didn't necessarily know where they were or when they'd thrashed themselves out of bed.

Emma winced and told the nurse to do whatever they had to do. Still, her guilt levels soared, and come hell, high water, or twenty below, she'd get to the nursing home before she went home.

Primed for guilt, Emma abandoned her sandwich. She left word in the Reference Room then made her way to the non-stacks basement where fading emergency lights provided just enough illumination to reveal the pump hoses snaking through an inch or so of standing water. Emma owned a pair of neoprene boots that would have been ideal footwear in the flooded basement—mud was one of Michigan's five seasons, coming reliably each year between winter and spring—but she hadn't been thinking liquid water when she dressed for work this morning, and the shoes she'd changed into were too comfortable, not to mention too expensive, to ruin in cold, murky water. With a grimace, Em took them off and stepped into the unknown.

The water level in Matt's office was well below the lowest shelf of the equipment racks lining the walls, but more than enough to ruin his piles-on-the-floor filing system. Perched on an overturned wastebasket in the midst of the mess, Matt was—and had apparently been for some time—sorting his paperwork, sheet by soggy sheet. While Emma watched unobserved, he let several sheets fall back into the water, setting only one carefully atop an overburdened carton.

"That won't work." Em said from the doorway.

Matt started; she'd taken him by surprise. "Em! It's good to see you. I called the boss as soon as I got here. I told him I needed help, but once I'd said the computers were okay, I think he turned his ears off."

"Good old Gene," Em mused with a rueful shake of her head. "Did you explain to him that you were standing in an inch of water?"

"Four inches," he corrected. "Buildings and Grounds came in with pumps around ten."

"Gene didn't say a word to us upstairs and I forgot you'd be down here alone. My apologies. If this happens again, you should come up to the Reference Room. That's where everyone goes in emergencies. We could have spared a few people to give you a hand. You've got to dry your paper sheet by sheet or you'll wind up with expensive papier-mâché."

Em took a deep breath and sloshed across the threshold. It was hard to measure which of them was more foolish—Matt with his well-intentioned but futile efforts at salvage or her entering his cluttered office in her stocking feet. She scuffed her feet as she walked and still managed to step on something she wished she hadn't.

Stopping short of Matt's perch, she pointed at the carton and asked, "Are those what you're trying to save?"

Matt nodded. "Thought I'd take them home and put them in the microwave."

Em shuddered. "Only if you want to bake bricks. There's a truck filled with paper towels out at the loading dock."

"Yeah, somebody came by and told me that. I told her thanks, but the machines were dry. I figured the cutoff switches had done what they were supposed to do at the first sign of trouble. Won't know for sure until we get power back. Wasn't so lucky with my own stuff."

He gestured toward the shadows where his stash of spared and repaired hardware rose like icebergs from the dark water. Emma couldn't remember all the junk Matt had collected since taking the systems administrator job in June, but she knew he'd never met a chunk of silicon he didn't want to keep. She gave him a we're-friends clap on the shoulder.

"C'mon, we'll gather up some of those paper towels and I'll show you the old-fashioned way to dry out a book—" Em's voice froze: something had *moved* behind Matt's desk. Rational or not, her first though was sewer rats. Other people got the willies from spiders or snakes; Em's phobia—not counting an inexplicable aversion to wooden spoons—was rats. Her heart was in her throat until the movement became a face, a woman's face, pale, oval, and framed by severely straight dark hair.

"Who're you?" she asked flatly before Em could ask the same question.

Matt lurched to his feet. He pointed at Emma and said, "Emma, Mal," then crossed his arms like the Scarecrow giving directions in *The Wizard of Oz*, pointed at the stranger, and said, "Mal, Emma."

The stranger, Mal, said, "Oh, the ghost woman."

Ghost woman.

It took effort, but Em censored a slow burn. She'd asked Matt to respect the wasteland secrets she'd shared with him. He'd agreed, only to spill everything, obviously, in the early throes of love. Emma, though, could forgive Matt for falling in love; he deserved romance and all that went with it. He also deserved something better than stringy-haired Mal.

Mal. What kind of name was Mal?

Em took considerable pride in her tolerance. A true child of the Sixties, she paid her dues in Marx, Engels, and the radical rest; she *struggled* against her prejudices when they reared their ugly little heads in her class consciousness. She was determined to treat everyone the same and wouldn't allow herself to judge a person by the color of his—or her—skin, nor by the syllables of a name. Between one breath and the next, Em struggled to reverse her judgment of Matt's girlfriend.

It was, at best, a draw. Em's antipathy began with the young woman's chosen name: Mal. Em had to believe it was a self-chosen name, as Emma was her own self-chosen one. Names were like prophecies: given time and the least opportunity, they tended to become reality. Of average height and possibly average build beneath a torn, stretched-out sweatshirt and the ratty shirt hanging out below it, Mal radiated cold hostility. At rest, her lips shaped a frown and her eyes were lowered. Her shoulders sagged under the weight of her attitude.

And this was the woman who'd awakened Matt's romantic spirit, the woman who'd led him to call Emma at two-thirty on New Year's morning, telling her that she'd have so much in common with the woman he'd just met? If she'd had more time, Emma thought she might have been able to remember someone else to whom she'd taken such an instant, complete dislike. Off the top of her head there was no one.

Eleanor had been an unpleasant shock, but history, not attitude, set them at odds; if Eleanor wasn't her mother, they'd have hit it off better. Harry Graves was an arrogant bastard, but she could think of a dozen of her father's colleagues who were worse—and that was just on the engineering faculty. She'd gotten along with Dad's professorial peers—wrapped them around her little finger, if the truth were told—and if she hadn't feared that Harry would conveniently murder her mother, Emma would have gotten along with Harry Graves, too.

But Mal was different. Mal's sullen glower set Em's teeth on edge. Her instinct was to lash back at the young woman with the acid sarcasm that had served her well in the last months of her second marriage. She stifled the urge with a smile.

"Not quite a ghost, I hope. I'm glad you were around to help Matt when the rest of us were focused on books."

Em heard the falseness in her voice. If Mal had an ounce of perception in her blood, she'd know Em was forcing herself to be friendly.

"Yeah, well, I was already here. He gave me a ride in. I was going to spend the day studying. Soon as I saw the water, I figured that wasn't going to happen."

No guessing the measure of Mal's perception from that remark. "I can show you how we salvage books. Some of these are probably goners—" There wasn't much that paper towels could do for a completely saturated binding, and Em had spotted a few of those in the heap on Matt's desk. "But you'll be surprised what a hundred paper towels can do."

Mal's skepticism chilled the room, but Matt was eager. He herded the women out of his office and along the dim, damp corridor toward the loading dock. Shoes in hand,

Em took another stab at conversation, asking Mal what she would have been studying, if the library had been open for business.

"Books," was the one-word, no-eye-contact answer.

Emma simmered silently after that, telling herself that it was no skin off her back if Matt Barto's new girlfriend was an asocial loser. Matt wasn't a particularly close friend, despite the events of last November. She usually worked closely with whomever Gene hired to run the library's computers, but it was all extracurricular, not part of her own job description. She'd outlasted a dozen sysadmins; she'd outlast Matt Barto and his glowering girlfriend . . .

Every thought in Em's mind trailed the scent of sour grapes. She was thoroughly disgusted with herself when they emerged from the flood and into the brutally cold drafts of the loading dock. With many reservations, Em shoved her shoes over her feet and followed Matt and Mal outside.

The supply trailer was a pallet lighter than it had been the last time she'd seen it, but there were still brown-paper bundles for the taking. A Buildings and Grounds crew was taking a break around a portable heater on the far side of a nest of noisy pumps. Emma couldn't hear their conversation over the machinery but she could smell their burgers and fries. Her lunch was far healthier and three floors away. In a heartbeat she decided to give Matt a quick lesson in book drying then retreat to her sandwich and the more congenial Reference Room.

Em wasn't the only one who smelled fast food in the icy air. Matt and Mal both cast their glances at the heater. They conferred in whispers, giving Em time to collect several paper-towel bundles from the truck and to read their body language. Every time a cloud of words came out of her mouth, Mal moved a bit closer to Matt and he retreated from her. It might mean nothing—Matt was probably a bit older and the library was where he worked, not where he studied. Wise men didn't welcome on-the-job affection. Still, as Emma read the signs, Mal was taking possession with or without Matt's permission.

Again, Em reminded herself that she didn't care whom Matt attracted or why. She tucked two bundles tightly under her arms and announced her intention to get inside where it was warmer.

Matt countered with an irresistible offer: "You want to split some lunch? Mal says she'll make a Busters run—"

Emma's stomach stopped her mouth from saying she wasn't interested. Long before the McDonald's and Burger King fast-food invasion, Busters "Cheaper-than-food" burgers had reigned supreme in Bower. Em had eaten there regularly as a child, in high school and college, and afterward—pretty much until she got religion about cholesterol. She tried to remember the last time she'd had a Busters burger with its requisite two kinds of cheese and deep-fried mushrooms on the side. At least once since Jeff left, but not more than twice.

Taste memory was like riding a bicycle—everything came back in a heartbeat. Unfortunately, she had a perfectly good, low-fat, whole-grain sandwich waiting in the same drawer that held her purse and wallet. Matt must have seen the dilemma on her face.

"I've got you covered, Em. You can pay me back later. What do you want?"

Before Em could say thanks, Mal snapped, at a volume Em heard loud and clear, "Well, *I* don't have her covered."

Matt reached for his wallet. Em considered telling him not to bother, but surliness was contagious. "I'd like a Baby-Buster with Swiss and Cheddar, 'shrooms on the side, and a diet cola." Her taste buds were already watering, though if it really had been five years since her last Busters burger, her gut was going to be in an uproar all night. It was worth it . . . once every five years.

Matt pulled a few bills from a worn billfold; Mal crumpled them into her jeans pocket. The sulking young woman followed them back to the office to get her coat which, considering the weather, wasn't unreasonable, though Mal could have toted a bundle of towels, if she'd wanted to. Em stowed her no-longer-dry shoes beside an inert CPU and said not a word as Mal layered herself in coat, scarf, and gloves. It was impossible not to notice the not-at-all casual kiss Mal planted on Matt's lips, but Em tried—for Matt's sake. The mere lack of fluorescent lighting couldn't hide the blush on his face when Mal let go. Em felt her friend's embarrassment and busied herself clearing a rescue space on his desk.

"She's really nice," Matt said softly after he'd cooled off.

"I'll have to take your word for it. I did something to set her off." Em wasn't in the mood for lying.

"No, I don't think so. Mal's shy. She says she's un-comfortable around confident people."

Em's normal confidence level was a leaky roof in a storm—better than nothing, but not by much. And she didn't think shyness had anything to do with Mal's prob-lems, but Matt could learn that for himself. She asked, "What's the rest of her name?" instead.

"Malerie. Malerie Dunbar. She's a grad student. Psych."

That figured, in an absurdly ironic way, but Em swal-lowed those observations, too. "Mallory? As in Sir Thomas and *Le Morte d'Arthur*? I don't think I've ever met a female Mallory. She from Bower?"

"No, Malerie, as in Valerie with an M. I don't know where she's from. She hasn't said. Not around here. She's been living out in grad housing with a bunch of TAs; none of them speak English as a native language. I guess it's pretty much the pits. She's kind of been staying with me since we met."

Emma had a good idea what "kind of staying" was and she let it pass without comment. "Malerie? That's an odd one." She couldn't stifle every acid remark that raced through her head.

"No odder than Merle Acalia," Matt retorted. "I figured

if nothing else you two would have weird names in common."

Near the height of November's craziness and in a moment of shocking indiscretion, Em had revealed her birth certificate name to Matt. He was one of only a select few—not including her employer or her government—who knew that she hadn't been born Emma Merrigan. Em hadn't asked him—or Nancy, for that matter—to keep her secret. Oaths like that were bound to get compromised, but she expected discretion.

"I'd really rather you didn't go spreading that around, Matt."

"Geez, Auntie Em, I didn't," he shot back, a bit testy himself. "I'm telling you that Mal's a mutated Valerie, 'cause I figure you'll understand. I think she got a lot of grief growing up Mal."

Em sailed past the warning flags. "She could've started over when she got to Bower. Lots of people shed their nicknames when they first get to college. She could've gone by her middle name, or made something up that she liked better." Em ripped open one of the towel bundles, selected a likely manual, and alternating between the last pages and the first, began putting absorbent paper between the sheets. "The object is to get enough towels in here—with their edges right up against the binding glue—to turn a rectangular book into half a cylinder."

She demonstrated the technique. "Most of the books we hauled out of the stacks weren't nearly this soaked. You'll want to take them upstairs when we're done. This area's going to be alive with mold in another twelve hours. There's something you can spritz on the books as they dry to kill the stuff. The chemistry department was mixing up a huge drum of the stuff while we were sopping books in the Reference Room this morning."

Matt tried his hand with the paper towels. He fell behind quickly, and not just because Em had more practice. After several silent moments, he asked, "Other than not liking my girlfriend, what's bothering you, Em?"

"I don't know her well enough to like her or dislike her."

When Matt said nothing in reply, Em glanced up to find him staring skeptically.

"All right, she comes off somewhere between stand-offish and hostile. That could mean a lot of things, including that I remind her of someone she's got just cause to dislike. I don't need to know more, Matt—it's none of my business—but I'd be curious to know how she gets along with your other friends."

"You're the first. We hooked up at the Masked Ball and hit it off like gangbusters. She didn't want to watch the game with a bunch of geek guys yesterday—I didn't think anything of it and dropped her off on my way to Ben's house. Then she called about fifteen minutes after I got home and said she wanted to get together. I said sure—it's not like I had other plans. We talked pretty much all night."

Em tried being conciliatory: "Maybe she's tired."

"I think she's got a curse, like Bran."

Their eyes met. He was serious. Em put the paper towels down. "No," she said softly.

"She knows she pushes people away. She says she can't trust anyone on account of her family. Her mother's an addict with AIDS and her stepfather messed with her before he bailed. She ran away when she was fourteen—"

"Okay!" Emma interrupted. "I know the tune, I can fake the lyrics. Mal's had it rough, and if she rings your chimes, I'll be the first to say her luck is changing, but not a curse, Matt. There are just too many miserable people in this world. If they were all cursed . . ." She paused, realizing that she had no idea how to distinguish between those who harbored a curse and those who didn't. Except— There *was* a difference between Bran and Mal. "Think about it, Matt: Bran's life wasn't a tragedy. Apparently, he'd kept it together pretty well until he got to Bower, and when things started getting crazy—he talked about demons in his head, not his dysfunctional family."

Matt hesitated before saying, "Mal doesn't call them demons, but she's afraid she's going to wind up in an asylum."

"Then Mal needs to see a psychiatrist."

"Maybe she needs *you*, Emma. When she told me how she couldn't get along with people or make friends, I thought she was exaggerating— We'd clicked from word one. Then you walked in here. The Mal I met isn't the same person, she's trapped inside the person you met."

Em recoiled. "What am I supposed to do? Whatever I've got, it isn't X-ray vision. I can't just look at someone and say—sorry, kid, you've caught a curse, hold still while I pluck it out. I'm in the dark. Wouldn't know what to look for if I wanted to help her."

"There's nothing in your black book?" Matt asked, clearly incredulous.

"Nothing. Not in the one I got from Eleanor and not in the one I found in her suitcase either. If there's a test, I don't know how to administer it and—to tell you the truth, Matt—all things considered, I'm none too eager to find out. It's a miracle that nobody died. Think of Mal in the hospital or turned into a vegetable."

Maybe Matt did; at least, he broke eye contact with her, but he didn't let the subject die. "I can't stop thinking about it. Mal's miserable being herself. It's not her fault, and there's nothing I can do about it. I don't have the power."

Emma raked her hands through her hair. "Don't do this to me, Matt. Everything's on hold—and I mean everything—until I get to the bottom of the mess with my mother."

"Still no luck on that front? I kind of hoped that if there was something you could do for Mal, then that would make it easier for you to, you know, get in and out of the wasteland place. You know how when you can't find the answer when you're looking for it, it sometimes comes to you when you're working on something else?"

Matt was right, as far as computers were concerned,

and the wasteland, too. But he didn't have the latest information. "I've gotten past the getting there problem," Em admitted. "But I'm farther than ever away from finding my mother. Seems she's got a new wasteland jailor: a rogue."

"A rogue? One of those big-curse things. Damn," Matt muttered. "How'd you find out about that?"

"Ran into someone I recognized."

"The hat guy?"

Emma nodded. Nancy was her best friend, her preferred confidant, but Nancy had been in Ohio when Eleanor, curses, and rogues had wandered into her life. Matt had been at ground zero. He'd seen what curses had done to Em's living room and what they'd done when Em bungled her first attempt to uncreate a curse. He'd been her touchstone through those trying days, and in return, she'd given Matt the facts, though not necessarily full strength. Em had deliberately downplayed her interactions with Blaise Raponde. He'd become "the hat guy," the ghost Eleanor had mistaken for a rogue, nothing more or less, until Matt surprised Emma by asking—

"You think the hat guy was telling the truth? He could be with the other side, you know. Your mother could have been right. It happens sometimes; nobody's perfect. Who's to say a ghost can be a rogue out there in the wasteland. What makes you trust him?"

"He had the wounds to match his story."

"A *ghost* with wounds? What was his story?"

"That he was trying to get the jump on the curses who had Eleanor when a rogue curse got the jump on him. He tried going after the rogue, but it nearly killed him."

"He's a ghost, Em. That's what you said. A ghost can't die. If he can die, he ain't a ghost—simple as that."

"Maybe, maybe not. He can bleed and I nearly made myself sick cleaning him up. There was blood on my face when I got back from the wasteland. He was pretty upset about losing the fight."

"Okay, then: the hat guy bleeds. What if he's a rogue,

Em? What if he's *the* rogue and he got those wounds from Eleanor?"

Em started. She and Matt often analyzed things the same way—too many years wasted tracking down computer bugs, probably. Blaise had volunteered that he'd been wounded by Eleanor's magic wand which the rogue had. Emma assumed the rogue had taken the wand from Eleanor's original captors.

Was she assuming too much?

"I'll burn that bridge when I get to it, and not a moment before," Em said firmly. "So far he's all pluses, no minuses. He could be a rogue— He could be just about anything, including a figment of my imagination. But he says he's a man who lived in Paris and should have died there in sixteen-eighty—"

"Sixteen-eighty?" Matt's eyes narrowed.

She knew what he was thinking: a date, a name, a city, plus the resources of a research library, electronic and printed, could add up to an empirical proof of her wasteland experiences. They had come close in November, or Matt had. He'd taken to data mining with an enthusiasm that surprised both of them, but Bran's curse had its roots in eleventh-century England, where records were sparse compared to seventeenth-century Paris.

If Emma hadn't spent the day salvaging damp books, she would have spent part of it looking for traces of a historic Blaise Raponde. If she gave Matt the hat guy's name—and she was certain that she hadn't so far—he'd do the data mining for her, with his spooky girlfriend hanging over his shoulder. A shiver that had nothing to do with standing in cold water passed down Emma's spine. She did not want Mal prying into her very secret life—

"Somewhere around there," she corrected falsely. "I browsed through the costume and fashion books in the theater collection. His hat was in style around then."

Mission accomplished: disappointment made Matt's face relax. "Too bad. I thought you were on to something."

Emma seized the lull to change the subject. "We'll lose these manuals if we don't get back to work."

Matt followed her lead. Em had finished interleaving her first book and was halfway through her second before Mal showed up with grease-stained bags of Buster's food. For Matt's sake, Em tried to be friendly toward the girl while they ate the cooled but sinfully delicious burgers. She asked the usual where-are-you-from, what-are-you-studying questions and got nowhere. Malerie Dunbar wasn't interested in meeting and getting to know Emma Merrigan. She was willing to work, though, once Matt—not Em—showed her what to do.

Emma had just checked her watch and was starting to gear herself up for Meadow View when one of Gene Shaunekker's assistants poked his head into Matt's office with two messages: the power would be off for another twenty-four hours, and Em's presence was required at a director's meeting, ASAP.

"You're a library *director*?" Mal inquired. It was the first question she'd asked and she managed to give it a when-did-you-stop-beating-your-wife quality.

Em shrugged. "Every boat needs its ballast."

Of the fifteen directors, she and Reg Smith in Rare Books were the only two who ran one-man departments. They were both long-term employees, recognized more for their general knowledge of how the library actually worked than the importance of their official responsibilities. Reg had gotten his title back when Emma was a student, but Em owed her position to Gene and made her way to the stairs without a backward glance.

Six

As *meetings went*, the directors' meeting could have been worse. Though it seemed likely that the water main on the construction site had broken when the temperature began to drop on New Year's Day, water hadn't started pouring into the library until a few hours before it was discovered. Most of the books the staff's bucket brigade had lifted out of the lower stacks were completely undamaged or readily salvageable. A couple hundred would need rebinding. Less than a hundred, so far, had been judged hopeless. Horace Johnson's megamillion gift to the university had survived another catastrophe.

Emma, who handled all acquisitions, vowed that she would begin the search for replacements volumes as soon as the power was restored and the computers were back on-line. There'd be extra paperwork for insurance purposes, but assuming she got an accurate list of what they'd lost, the flood's aftermath wouldn't mean four months of living in her office as it had after the last flood.

When Gene Shaunekker asked her to stay after the meeting ended, Em expected that he had a question about his computer or something equally trivial. She was stunned when he told her that she was going to have an assistant to help her deal with the crisis and forever after as soon as Human Resources could find and hire one.

"I don't *need* an assistant. Everything's on the computer. It's a one-man job; we agreed to that when we reorganized four years ago. I farm out some of the research but I do the paperwork—"

"It's grow or die, Emma. We've accelerated our acquisitions every year, but it's not enough. I read that report you wrote on archives and database licensing. I couldn't agree more: data sharing is the wave of the future. We ride it or we lose ground to the competition. An assistant will give you the time to make sure that we ride and give us a measure of redundancy."

Em suspected that Gene had rehearsed this little speech. Gene was a good director in part because he was predictable. Whenever he could, he sweetened bitter medicine. Emma knew when she'd been dosed. If she had any doubts, they were dispelled when Gene dismissed her "I work better by myself. I don't need help" protest without making eye contact.

"And you'd never ask for it if you did. No one's complaining, but we all know your plate's been full this last year and you've taken on this . . ." Gene caught and censored himself. "What you're doing for your niece could be a full-time job by itself. We're giving you room to breathe, Emma. Don't argue. The money's been in the budget since the reorg. Nobody ever expected that you'd be able to run Acquisitions by yourself and certainly not for this long. It's high time you polished your management skills."

A dozen reasons why she didn't need an assistant or management skills filled Em's mind. They were all valid, all emotional, and they'd do nothing but convince Gene that he'd done the right thing. She realized, too, that she had a splitting headache.

"Try to think of this as the rest of the promotion you got when we made you a director," Gene urged. "You've had four years to get Acquisitions ready for the twenty-first century. Now it's time to share and move on. You can't let yourself get too specialized, Emma. You know what they say: there's no future in being irreplaceable."

If that remark was supposed to reconcile her to her fate, it failed miserably. "I like my job just as it is," she said in a tone that was wearier than it should have been.

The walls of Gene's office were starting to curve inward. After a day without power, the air was stagnant and stale. Emma's headache was getting worse by the heartbeat.

Gene must have noticed the change in her demeanor. He was, all things considered, a good man to work for, a good man, period. "I know the timing could have turned out better. It's been a hell of a day, but I had to tell you now; I couldn't wait any longer. We made the decision right before Christmas and the position was posted this morning. Give yourself some time to get used to the idea," he said gently. "You'll be a fine manager. You practically manage our computers as it is—and don't think the rest of us aren't grateful. If this database notion pans out, it might make sense to take Systems out of Maintenance and put it under you where it belongs."

Another day and that possibility might have balanced the equation, but not this day. Em took the easy way out: she promised to get used to the changes the library was thrusting on her. And she would. By accident and design, Emma's life had shrunk until her job was the largest island left in the ocean. Clinging to her island didn't spare Em from what her French professor had called *l'esprit de l'escalier*—the spirit of the stairwell, or the art of not finding the right words until it was too late to use them.

What bothered her most as she gathered her belongings from her nearly dark office was Gene's scarcely censored opinion that her work suffered because of the time she spent with Eleanor. Never mind that her work *did* suffer. Nobody in the Horace Johnson Memorial Library knew who Eleanor Merrigan really was. If she could have told Gene the truth, he would have gotten off her back about an assistant . . . and called for the little men in white coats.

The parking structure was nearly empty when Emma crossed the bridge. The wind whipping down the concrete spiral froze her nostrils when she inhaled. She drew her scarf up like a veil but the chill got inside her coat. She was shivering as she got into her car and praying a moment later as the ignition groaned and ground. Miraculously, the engine caught on the second try.

The portholes Em had carved through the windshield ice were unchanged. She guessed the thermometer hadn't risen above ten degrees and was falling again. While the car warmed, she attacked the windshield with the scraper and paid a price for a few extra inches of visibility: her feet, still itchy from standing in Matt's flooded office, succumbed to the fire of chilblains.

Emma scarcely felt the pedals on the way to Kroger's, where she picked up a half-dozen remaindered brownies for Eleanor's bedside and a prefabricated, low-fat chicken dinner from the deli counter for her supper. The chilblain fire was out when she got back into the car, but the itching had become agony. She'd have sold her soul for a knitting needle to slide down the inside of her boot, even though she knew—as anyone who'd ever suffered through a Bower winter knew—it wouldn't help. Stamping her feet did help a bit and she stamped into the Meadow View lobby, where the temperature never fell below seventy-eight degrees.

Em couldn't shed layers fast enough and had broken a sweat before she reached the sixth floor.

In theory, Meadow View was never closed. In practice, visits were discouraged after 9 P.M. At seven on a frigid January night, Emma had the corridors to herself. She was halfway to Eleanor's room, juggling layers and brownies and still waiting for her feet to settle down, when she realized the room next to Eleanor's was empty.

It had been occupied yesterday—hadn't it? She'd come to Meadow View yesterday—hadn't she? Yesterday had been New Year's Day. The team had won its bowl game. It seemed longer than twenty-four hours ago but the visit came back to her with the slow focus of a school projector. Em could recall how her mother had looked and that Marsha hadn't been in her customary chair, but for her life, she couldn't recall if Room 615 had been vacant or occupied. She did no better recalling the room's condition New Year's Eve, but there *had* been someone in that room on Christmas: a little old man—or maybe a little old woman. Up here on the sixth floor, as in a hospital nursery, the difference could be hard to detect. He—or she—had been strapped in a modified, vinyl recliner, head tilted back, eyes wide open and mouth wider, looking for all the world like some forlorn, featherless bird. There'd been no temptations on a plate beside his—or her—bed, no bright holiday decorations, however unappreciated, and never, to Em's knowledge, any visitors.

The room was empty now, waiting for another tragedy. If there were mercy in the universe, then the victims of Alzheimer's were truly unaware of themselves when the decline of their bodies finally caught up with the decline of their minds. Certainly death was mercy when it arrived, but to be forgotten so quickly, so easily, that Em honestly couldn't remember the last time she'd seen him—or her—alive . . . *that* was no mercy at all.

Emma's ribs tightened. She felt herself on the verge of tears, not for any one human being but for all of them, including herself: proverbial dust in the wind. Blotting her tears before they flowed, she entered Eleanor's room thinking the day couldn't get worse. She learned that she was wrong.

Meadow View's staff had restrained Eleanor by binding her to the mattress with what resembled two gigantic Ace bandages, one over her hips, the other below her shoulders. Eleanor's arms had been tucked beneath the second band, but she'd managed to free the left and was alternately striking the bed and reaching for her face. Her forearms were wrapped in gauze, her flailing hand encased in what appeared to be a fleecy pink sock. Em immediately understood why: there were raw gouges on her mother's cheeks and neck.

Em dumped her stuff in the nearest chair and went looking for explanations. The night supervisor intercepted her a few feet from Eleanor's door.

Charneal quickly explained that *her* shift began at five and she hadn't been on duty when the decision was made to truss Eleanor up like a sprained ankle. She could only relay the information she'd been given and forward complaints to the day shift. While she caught and reimprisoned Eleanor's flailing arm, Charneal described how, according to the notes the day-shift supervisor had left, Eleanor had managed to fall out of bed between the three and three-thirty room checks. Worse, she'd also managed to wedge herself beneath it.

And how many Meadow View employees had it taken to get Emma's mother back where she belonged and to keep her there? Seven. Four regular staffers to lift and hold the bed while two LPNs pulled her into the light and the shift supervisor gave her a shot of something potent. They'd tried to call Emma—that was state law whenever a nursing home resident fell—and left a message on her machine.

"I thought my work number was in the file. Was anyone else hurt?" Emma asked when Charneal had finished her recitation. Eleanor had lost considerable weight and muscle tone in the last month, but she remained inherently stronger than the rest of the sixth-floor residents.

Charneal shrugged and said she didn't think so, unless Eleanor had hurt herself when she fell. They were keeping an eye on her right wrist. If it started to swell, they'd get her to an emergency room for x-rays. Charneal examined Eleanor's right hand. Beneath the sock, everything looked normal.

Em chose not to ask what made anyone think Eleanor had fallen on her right wrist rather than any other part of her body. Her greatest dread—one of them, anyway—was that Meadow View would decide Eleanor was too hard to handle. There was only one lock-down facility in the county. Emma had visited it just before Thanksgiving. She'd take Harry up on his offer to move his wife back to New York before she'd sign Eleanor into that madhouse.

When Eleanor was tucked in again, Charneal asked Em to come down to the desk to sign an accident notification report, an emergency treatment preauthorization form, and while they were passing paper back and forth—

"I noticed there's no signature on the DNR."

Charneal slid a pen and the incomplete Do Not Resuscitate order across the worn veneer desk. Em slid it back, still unsigned. She offered her much-rehearsed excuse—

"The doctors said I shouldn't give up for at least six months."

Their eyes met as Charneal returned the form to Eleanor's folder. Em guessed that she was being measured and coming up short—another Marsha in the making, martyring herself for a niece, a step down from a son. Since she couldn't defend herself with the truth, Emma started to apologize for being an optimist.

Charneal silenced her by saying, "It's harder when they're so young. I don't think I could sign it either. That Joshua, he just lies there in his bed. Nothing bothers him. But your Eleanor, she gets so frightened. Her eyes go wide and she screams and screams. Like she's having a nightmare that never ends."

Em's breath caught in her throat. "I thought she'd been sleeping quietly since she got here."

"Oh, Eleanor's quiet, all right. Never makes a sound you can hear in the hall, or at the foot of her bed. You get your ear right close, though, and you can hear her. Not every night, but she's been plenty upset the last two. She's wearing herself out. They can do that, you know. They know it's not right. They know when their time has passed."

"Six months," Emma repeated. "If I can't find her by then, I'll sign the DNR."

She didn't believe she'd said "find," though Charneal

seemed not to have noticed the slip. Visitors routinely got tongue-tied at Meadow View; surely the staff had heard a thousand different euphemisms for dementia or death and paid little attention to any of them. After reminding Charneal of the brownies, Em returned to her mother's room. She'd already stayed longer than she'd planned, but Charneal's descriptions of Eleanor's silent nightmares wouldn't go away.

Dragging a chair close to the bed, Em unbound her mother's left hand and massaged her pale and increasingly delicate skin. Eleanor's fingernails had been trimmed down to the quick. Her cuticles were ragged and she'd rasped her knuckles during her misadventure—a sad state for a woman whose nails had been lacquered jewels when she'd walked back into her daughter's life. Em was thinking that she should arrange to have a manicurist and a hair dresser pay a visit to Meadow View. If there was any wisp of awareness left in Eleanor's body, she cared about her appearance.

Nancy had found a beautician who pampered Katherine once a week—

Without warning, Eleanor stiffened. Her eyes popped open, as did her mouth. Em guessed what was coming and had just enough time to slip the sock over her mother's hand before it closed into a fist. Getting the fist tucked under the second restraining belt was a greater challenge, but an important one—the way she thrashed, Eleanor could easily give herself a black eye. Emma wound up close enough to hear the faint screams that Charneal had described and to have a head-to-head collision with her mother's forehead as she thrashed against the restraints.

There was nothing gentle about the encounter. Em rocked back on her heels, certain she'd have a bruise, while Eleanor worked herself into a frenzy. The sixth-floor rooms didn't have buzzers—by the time residents reached the sixth floor, they didn't know when they needed assistance. Emma raced to the workstation.

Charneal and her coworkers were competent, even

compassionate, but unlike Jill at the hospital, they didn't see their patients as people who might recover, might overhear a conversation about diapers, diarrhea, and the kick of sedation. Feeling like a coward, Em made excuses about being in the way and retreated into the cold night, where her tears froze on her cheeks and her dinner had frozen on the passenger seat of her car.

"I'm losing it," she told the cats as soon as she was safe inside her home. "Gene's got every reason in the world to saddle me with an assistant. I'm lucky that he's not looking for a replacement."

The message light was blinking: two messages from Meadow View, one from a plumber she'd never heard of, offering to replace her copper pipes with "up-to-the-minute PVC," and the last from Nancy, who'd heard about the library flood and wondered how her day had been.

Em looked at her watch. It wasn't too late to return Nancy's call, but not calling would say everything she needed to say. She peeked into her dinner's carton. The chicken had sprouted ice crystals. She put it into the microwave then returned to the living room to turn on the Christmas tree. Though its magic faded in January, the tiny lights and memory-laden ornaments boosted her spirits while she opened Christmas card stragglers and holiday bills. The first of the spring garden catalogs had arrived. She read it while she ate a dinner that had the texture of plastic and the taste of mud.

Spin sniffed the remnants Emma shredded into his bowl and gave her the "God is dead" look.

In the back room, Em fired up her computer. She retrieved an ungodly number of e-mail messages, most of which could be deleted before being read. Among the real messages, two had come from her stepchildren. Jeff Jr. was off for a week at a California ski resort with friends from his new job, his third new job in the last twelve months. Emma didn't know how he afforded his many vacations. In truth, she didn't want to know. Jay-Jay took after his father in many ways, not all of them good.

Lori reported that her "big" Christmas present had arrived this morning in the form of a wholesale order from a giftware distributor which wanted five thousand ceramic cache pots by May first.

Emma shook her head at the monitor. Art was a rough business at best and Lori was in some ways fortunate to have a job doing scut work for a more established artist, but Em had never warmed to the other woman's designs. To her stepmotherly eyes, any one of Lori's slender, asymmetric vases was worth a thousand of Dana's duck-and-bunny pots. She feared for Lori's creativity—if Lori thought a big wholesale order was a worthy Christmas present—until she got to the part of the message where Lori reported that Dana had finally agreed to buy a second, larger kiln.

"There'll be enough space for my vases and we agreed that I can fire it twice a week with nothing of hers inside."

That was better. She skimmed through Lori's many paragraphs analyzing the strengths of more brands of kilns than Emma knew existed, proving that the engineering gene wasn't strictly a matter of DNA. Her thoughts had leapt ahead to the next message in her queue when she encountered Lori's postscript—

"Dad called last night. Sounds like his start-up's definitely turned into a belly-up and he's headed back to Michigan. He doesn't know where yet but he said I should tell you not to worry—he'd never come back to Bower. Be prepared—you know what that probably means."

Em did. Toward the end, Jeff had developed the habit of making unnecessary promises and breaking them shortly afterward. She didn't relish the thought of bumping into him on a street corner. It would be like meeting a ghost—

No, she'd done that. Seeing Jeff would simply be depressing, almost as depressing as realizing that Lori was well aware of her father's flaws despite Em's determination never to discuss them with his children.

She typed a short reply, wishing Lori luck in the great

kiln hunt and ignoring the postscript. Her other personal messages failed to hold her interest. She disposed of them quickly, considered visiting her favorite web sites, and shut the computer down instead.

Jeff was the icing on the day's miserable cake. The spirit of the stairwell ran amok in her memories and Emma caught herself replaying arguments she'd hoped she'd forgotten. It was one more ring than her emotional circus tent could contain. She sat in her chair, her mind twitching and her body inert. Em needed distraction before she tried going to sleep and looked for it in the backroom closet, where unfinished hobby projects lined the shelves. She selected a piece of needlepoint with a square foot of unfinished background. By eleven-thirty, after ripping out more yarn than she'd stitched in, Em gave up on self-distraction.

She ran herself a steamy bath with candles, bubble bath, decadent sea salts, *and* herbal oils in generally compatible scents. She poured white wine into a plastic glass that looked—by candlelight—like fine crystal, then eased into the tub. Em hadn't realized how cold she'd been all day until the warmth began percolating through her skin. She'd sunk down until the bubbles were a wreath beneath her chin and was thinking about taking a sip of wine when—surprise, surprise—the phone rang.

There was no need, Emma told herself, to leap into her robe and answer the phone, dripping wet and certain to freeze. The answering machine was on and quite capable of handling late-night calls. She'd begun letting it screen her calls not long after Jeff left, when she'd become the target of a midnight breather. But when the machine began to play through her prerecorded message, Eleanor, not crank calls, was foremost in Em's mind.

Making a one-handed grab for her robe and narrowly missing both the wineglass and a candle, Emma raced downstairs. She'd curled up in her chair before the machine switched from message replay to record.

"Harry Graves here. Pick up your phone, Emma. I know you're home."

She glowered at the blinking record light. Of course she was home. It was—she squinted across the room to the illuminated numbers on the VCR—nearly midnight and she had to go to work tomorrow morning.

"Emma Merrigan! Pick up the phone. We must talk. You're not alone, Emma."

So much for Harry's powers of extrasensory perception.

"Emma Merrigan, the situation is deteriorating. I don't care if you're stark naked and sopping wet, pick up the phone!"

Shocked into obedience, Em seized the receiver.

"Make it quick before I freeze!"

"Did I roust you from the shower?" he asked in his invariably polite, supremely indifferent way.

"The bath. Make it quick. I'm not kidding."

"When you didn't call after Christmas, I began to worry about you. We have reason to believe you're no longer alone."

"I'm divorced and over fifty, Harry. Alone is my natural state, unless you count my cats."

"Not your cats, Emma. There was a Netherlands disturbance New Year's Eve—around four o'clock in the afternoon, I should think. Your time."

Bower time was the same as New York time, thank you very much Henry Ford and General Motors. "I didn't notice anything." Unless she counted returning to the wasteland about twelve hours later; and Em saw no reason to share that with Harry Graves.

"Possibly you wouldn't. We're still regressing the intruder's path, but we're confident that the breach occurred at about that time and, more to the point for you, into your fair city."

Emma thought fast. "Who's 'we'?" she asked. "What's regressing? Who intruded and what makes you think whoever it was intruded into Bower?"

Harry's end of the line was silent a moment longer than was necessary. "We are the curia, the Atlantis curia into whose purview your activities fall. Regressing is tracing the path of a curse or rogue through time and the Netherlands so we can answer your last question."

Had Harry actually said "Atlantis"—as in the drowned home of crackpot spiritualism? Emma expected better of her mother's impeccably arrogant husband. She assumed she'd misunderstood and pursued the answer he hadn't provided. "My last question was, how do you know Bower is involved?"

"The door was left ajar and the door led into Bower . . . *your* Bower, the Bower where you live."

Was there another Bower? Emma thought, then she recalled Malerie and Matt's assertion that his girlfriend— the girlfriend he'd met New Year's Eve—was cursed. "So, there's another curse loose in town?"

"Nothing less than a curse," Harry agreed. "May I presume that my wife is still in Bower, and that her condition has not changed either for the better or the worse?"

With a valid power of attorney locked up in her safe-deposit box, Emma had been under no obligation to inform Harry Graves where Eleanor wound up after the hospital discharged her. So she'd left him in the dark and eased her conscience with the belief that Harry could have found his wife himself, if he'd truly wanted to.

"I saw her not more than six hours ago. She's—" Emma swallowed the lie she'd been about to tell. "She had a restless night, a worse day. She's had worse, though, and there's been no real change since the day she entered the hospital—" Charneal said Eleanor had screamed her silent screams for two nights running, but was that a change? Em didn't want to confess to Harry Graves, but she felt uncomfortable lying. "Eleanor thrashed herself out of bed this afternoon, but she was fine New Year's Eve. They tell me these things happen sometimes with coma patients."

"She's not with you, is she?"

Em's feet were freezing. She twisted her robe around them and kept on twisting. "No, there's no way I could take care of her. She's completely dependent; she can't do anything for herself. I've got her in a skilled-care facility. My friend's got her mother there, too. It's one of the best in the state." Why, Em asked herself, was she justifying her choices to Harry?

"I expected nothing less of you, but is this mysterious 'skilled-care facility' also a secure facility?"

"They've got locks on the stairwells and cameras at the entrances to keep the inmates from leaving the asylum. Harry, Eleanor's been bed-ridden for nearly two months. She gets a little physical therapy, but it hasn't stopped the atrophy. She can thrash herself out of bed and sprain her wrist in the fall, but if she woke up tomorrow morning, she wouldn't be able to sit on her own, much less stand or walk. She's lost most of her muscle tone and her tendons have shrunk. Her feet point like a ballerina's and her hands are starting to contract, too. It's not like the movies."

"Nothing is, is it, Emma? I wasn't asking about Eleanor's security, per se, but about guest security, visitor security. Can anyone just walk into this depressing place where my wife is withering away?"

"You'd have to sign in at the front desk."

"I wasn't planning to visit her. Eleanor is inclined to vanity; she'd never forgive me. No, what I want to know about is strangers, complete strangers—someone no one's seen before. Could a complete stranger wander into Eleanor's room?"

Emma didn't like the direction the conversation was skewing. "Complete strangers don't visit nursing homes and they'd be noticed quickly, if one did show up."

"But not turned away. Not *prevented* from going to Eleanor's room," Harry said. His words weren't questions.

Em thought a moment. "No." She sighed. "They're set up for old people—Alzheimer's victims. To get the kind of security that would keep a rogue out—if I understand what you're saying—I'd have to transfer her to a psychiatric facility. Now that's *really* depressing. Maybe if you could tell me a bit more about rogues. Are we talking an ordinary human being, or something . . ." Emma sought a word that wouldn't be embarrassing. The best she could do was— "Weirder?"

"No weirder than you or I."

That was supposed to be reassuring? "No telltale trait sets rogues apart? No scars . . . tattoos . . . maybe a pinkie finger that doesn't bend?"

"No."

"Pod people, eh?" Em's attempt at humor reaped silence. "What do you mean you don't *know* who's intruded into Bower?" she demanded. "If rogues are curse-hunters who've been co-opted by curses, how many rogues can there be? How many curse-hunters are there to begin with? Don't you maintain a missing curse-hunters list?"

"That's a good question, Emma. I'm pleased that you're finally asking good questions. You won't like the answers. The most dangerous rogue is the rogue forged when a curse takes hold of a hunter in the Netherlands, but there are other ways to make a rogue. As you so bluntly remarked, if all rogues were turned hunters, then, even if we did not know them all, we could at least believe we outnumbered them. We don't."

"And just how many hunters are there?"

"Hundreds. Several hundreds known directly to the curiae. Four or five times that number throughout the world. It is only recently that we have begun to work together with our counterparts—relatively recently. As the world got smaller, we began to bump into one another. I wouldn't say curses are natural, Emma, but they're everywhere that people are, and so are we."

We used to be tribes, Eleanor had said. *Now we're more like a global corporation.* Or the Mafia, the Gang of Four, OPEC, and the World Trade Organization.

"That discovery must have come as quite a shock to your European sensibilities."

"Actually, we were looking for them. We were all looking. Demographics, my dear Emma: world population. People being born, people dying, people raising curses, thousands of curses every day. The percentage remains constant—at least *I* think it does—but the sheer number rises."

Eleanor had also said that Harry would answer her questions because Harry was the Einstein of the Netherlands.

"Sounds like you're losing the war."

"You mean, *we're* losing the war. You're one of us, Emma Merrigan. Hunting's in your blood. You need to be taught, but the instinct is there from the start. Myself, I prefer to think that we've adapted. Most curses wither. They're too specific to find a here-and-now host, or they overreach and, in effect, kill their host. We watch our CNN and keep an eye on the hot spots—Cambodia, Rwanda, the Horn of Africa, the Balkans—*always* the Balkans. We stomp out the embers before they become conflagrations."

"You missed some. I had to rearrange a bit of the eleventh century to stop the curse I was hunting with Eleanor. One English curse had been hanging around hating the Normans for nearly a thousand years."

"In which case, it had to be broader than one Englishman cursing a Norman. The whole notion of 'Normanness' disappeared within a few generations. The root of your curse was something more basic to human nature, else it couldn't have survived. But yes, we miss some. They hide, they stalk, they prey on their victims, and they get stronger every time they do. We shall never run out of work, Emma, but *most* of our work is mooting them as they arise from the here-and-now. It's more tedious than dangerous and does not require any particular empathy. Eleanor said you had extraordinary empathy with the old ones. Talent like that can change a bit of the past, if necessary."

Eleanor hadn't given Emma any reason to think that what she'd done in the eleventh century might have been something not every curse-hunter could do. Emma also recalled that her mother had made a long-distance call that November night. Em had been in the room at the time. Her body had been. Her mind—her consciousness of subjective reality—had been in the wasteland with Blaise Raponde, whose existence Eleanor had suspected and whose nature was presumed to be roguish. But had Eleanor taken that moment to tell Harry that her daughter was uncommonly talented?

"Don't bother, Harry. I'm not interested. All my so-called talent has gotten me is a taste of death served on the edge of sword. I don't have the stomach for a full-course dinner."

"You've gone too far to turn back, Emma," Harry said after a pause.

"Watch me, Harry. I'm not enlisting in your army. One way or the other, when this thing with Eleanor is resolved, I'm getting back to my own life."

"Why resolve it at all, Emma? Why not walk away? Eleanor did."

Emma found herself speechless.

"Accept it. You haven't come between me and my wife because of the love you bear for your mother. You got a taste of heroism as well as death when you mooted that curse and you liked it well enough. What part of your own life can equal the thrill of correcting the past or saving a woman from a fate worse than death? Your children are grown. You work in a *library*. Tell me that's not worse than the edge of a sword."

His words were neither bitter nor triumphant; but they were close to the truth, however little Emma wanted to admit it. The noose had already been around her neck when Matt revealed that he thought his girlfriend was cursed. Em had put it there herself. She could still remove it, if she were willing to pay the price in her conscience.

"Are you still there, Emma Merrigan?"

Harry didn't know everything. He was a curse-hunter, not a seer.

"I'm not going to argue with you. I learned that much getting out of two marriages: my logic circuits shut down at midnight. Are you coming out here? Is that why you called—to tell me that the professionals are on their way?"

"We *professionals* haven't made up our minds. I called to tell you what we think you're up against—and until and unless I'm more persuasive than I've been, that you're alone against it."

She wondered if Harry's position wasn't a bit like hers on the library's board of directors. A talent for empathy could be a curse, too.

Charm had oozed into her lap. Warmer than a heating pad and many times softer, the gray cat turned her motor on when Emma stroked her fur.

"All right—tell me about the rogue. Would she be someone I take an instant dislike to?" A memory of Malerie had drifted into her mind's eye. If she did have a talent for empathy, then its absence should be significant.

But Harry dashed those hopes. "More likely the opposite. And more likely a man, at least in outward appearance. Some curses are particular as to gender, but rogues are pure polymorphous perversity. Have you fallen in love in the past few days?"

Malerie became Blaise.

"No," Em answered, but she truly wasn't at her best after midnight and the word lacked conviction. "I'm too old to fall in love at first sight."

"Be very careful, Emma. You cannot moot a curse on this side of the line—you'll have to drive it back into the Netherlands or kill it in the flesh. That's untidy . . . legally untidy. First-degree-murder untidy. You're one of us by blood, but not otherwise. The curia's going to keep its distance. *I* have to keep a distance. No one will stop you and no one will help you, either. You *are* alone, Emma Merrigan."

Few things were more unnerving than the retreat of a presumed enemy. "Let me guess—you're not expecting me to beat this thing, are you?"

"Personally?"

"There's a difference?"

"You are your mother's daughter, Emma. That counts for something, usually something unexpected. You're also your father's daughter. The *wyrd* can surface anywhere, but once it's up, well, let's admit that we have to worry about inbreeding. To my knowledge, there've only been a handful of half-breeds . . . only a handful that survived. The curia knows what to do with curses and rogues. They don't know what to do with a half-breed. Without Eleanor to goad them, they're content to sit on their hands, hoping the problem will resolve itself."

"Meaning I'll be dead."

"For what it's worth, Emma, I think the curia's making a mistake."

"So, you've called to give me a heads-up? Excuse me, Harry, but my extraordinary empathy tells me that you haven't hardly begun to put your cards on the table."

"I've told you what I know," he grumbled. "I've answered your questions." But he didn't say she was wrong.

Emma scooped Charm close against her heart. The cat objected to her treatment and writhed. Her hind claws raked Em's arm on her way to the floor. The scratches stung. "Why should I trust you?" Em snapped.

"Because you have no reason not to, and no one else who can answer your questions."

He didn't know about Blaise Raponde. Of course, Em had the same doubt about Raponde. For a moment she was tempted to bare all, but she'd learned the hard way that post-midnight confessions were worse than post-midnight arguments.

"If I were to call you, say, tomorrow afternoon"—

when she'd have her wits about her, as much as she'd had them since Eleanor's return—"would you take the call?"

"Call anytime you wish. If I'm not here, leave a message, brief and not too specific. Do you have e-mail?"

She did, but hadn't considered that Harry might as well. "If I invited you to meet me—"

Harry cut her off. "Don't waste time with ifs and maybes. I can't foretell the future."

His ability to leave Emma feeling awkward and ignorant was intact. By the faint light drifting down from the bathroom, she scribbled down Harry's e-mail address and let the conversation end. She'd been on the phone less than ten minutes but that was long enough for her bath to cool. Em pulled the plug, blew out the candles, and pushed Spin off her pillow. The sheets were ice, but Emma immediately launched herself at the wasteland and didn't feel them for long.

The wasteland was . . . *different*. Making a room had left an enduring mark, albeit not the mark she'd expected. Her door no longer stood upright on the parched dirt, visible from the front, invisible from the sides and behind. It had sunk into the rind wall of an orange-section crater some ten feet high and twice that from end to end. The way-back stone sat beside it like a doorstop.

Beyond the crater the wasteland was unchanged, and from twenty feet away, the crater was just another shadow in the shifty, lurid twilight. Em would have congratulated herself on the camouflage, if she thought she'd been responsible for it.

The door opened inward. She knew the room was empty before she entered it.

"Blaise?" she called in a voice that wouldn't span her living room.

He'd finished her room before leaving. All the Mariana details were intact. The rest was nothing she'd seen before. The wall opposite the door had been given over to a fireplace. The ashes were cold and where the chimney went Em wouldn't hazard a guess, except she hadn't seen it when she'd stood outside the crater. A bucket of water and two dented pots hung inside the fireplace. Within the room, the cot where she'd tended Blaise's wound had become a solider piece of furniture with coarse linens tucked over a lumpy mattress—at least he was a man who made his bed.

Raponde had added a heavy, upholstered chair with a high back, wings, and a matching footstool. It looked no more comfortable than the bed. A wooden gate-leg table stood behind the chair. Once Em noticed the leather-bound book atop it, nothing else mattered.

She opened the cover hoping for revelations and got Genesis instead. Blaise had left her a Bible, printed in French, in Paris, in 1665. Fighting frustration and anger, Em held it by the binding and shook it over the table. Two dried leaves, a lock of light brown hair, and a bit of lace landed on the table. The Bible came through the abuse unscathed. And why not? It wasn't an antique, not to the man who'd left it behind.

Seven

Emma *walked herself* weary chasing Blaise Raponde. He'd left an arrow-straight trail a lapsed Girl Scout could follow and set a pace Em couldn't match, much less beat. Judging by marks his boot heels had left in the dirt, he hadn't been slowed down by lingering injuries. After several hours and several miles, she gave up.

The way-back stone was a couple football fields behind Em when she stopped, the orange-slice hollow, Mariana's room, and the Bible, too. She thumbed through its pages, looking for clues she'd missed the first time. Verses, not many, were set off by black ink dots in the margin. Here and there a word had been crossed out or underlined. They might have formed a code or a religious philosophy—either way, they were more than she could translate with her rusty French.

Em considered hauling the Bible to Bower. Blaise's blood had stuck to her cheek. Mariana's blue dress had vanished, but she'd been wearing it when she raised her head beside the way-back stone a few hours ago, even though she'd given no thought to her clothing before launching herself toward the wasteland. Maybe the Bible was like blood. Maybe it was like cloth. Maybe it would disappear altogether.

She gathered loose threads from Mariana's unfinished

embroidery and wound them around her fingers. They were gone when she turned on her bed-table lamp. She didn't understand the rules of subjective reality.

"There's not a problem that wasn't born with a solution as its twin—that's what Dad used to say whenever things got out of hand . . ."

The blue-green numbers on the clock radio showed a few minutes after 2AM WED, or two hours since she'd closed her eyes. Her aching calf muscles knew she'd been gone longer. Time flowed differently in the wasteland. It kept Eleanor and Harry young even as it turned weekdays into thirty-hour marathons.

After quenching her thirst and restoring her faith in clocks, Emma settled in for what she hoped would be five hours of dreamless sleep. She could function on five hours, not as well as she had twenty years ago, but well enough for a day without electricity.

There was a sour, familiar taste in Em's mouth when the chorus of "Born in the USA" awakened her and its name was Jeff Trask. Her life was burdened with curses rogues, a kidnaped mother, and a missing Frenchman, but eight years after their divorce, her ex-husband still had the old magic. Walking the wasteland was a walk in the park compared to the breakdown of their marriage, especially in the crazy-house imagery of dreams.

The weather had cratered overnight—a full five degrees colder than yesterday compounded by a steady wind from the northwest. A sane person would have pushed a few buttons and gone back to sleep . . . and risked another rehash of battles she'd rather forget. Em swaddled her feet in a second pair of socks and fixed herself a thermos of coffee before braving the elements.

It was an ill-wind that blew no good, and the one blowing down from Canada was no exception. Not only was the air too cold and dry for snow, it was too cold and dry for frost. Emma made quick work of the thin crust that had formed overnight on the inside of the windshield while the motor warmed.

The parking structure's electronic security was still kaput and most of the stalls were empty. Em found a spot on the south side of the elevator shaft. Another bitter night without power had taken a toll on the library's comfort zones. Half the emergency lights had expired and the air was stale. In the Reference Room, where Emma spent the morning replacing damp paper towels with dry ones, a keen ear could practically hear the mold growing.

A good number of Emma's coworkers had decided to take the day off. Yesterday's den of foxhole comrades was reduced to a dozen heads-down salvagers, each working alone. Em could swap paper towels in her sleep and nearly did. When she wasn't drowsing, her thoughts, like her dreams, skidded down the well-worn mental spiral that bore her and Jeff's names.

One message from Lori and she was replaying acid arguments as if nothing had changed when, in truth, everything had changed. Nancy insisted she looked better since the split—younger, fitter. And Em had made a campaign out of getting back into shape when she moved into the Maisonettes. Eating sensibly, walking to work, shedding the pounds she'd gained on the battlefield. Her goal had been simple: pick up the pieces of her life. She'd had reason to expect success: she'd taken her first divorce without breaking stride.

But Emma's second marriage had been longer, harder, and fraught with children. When it was over, a whole new generation had staked their claim to cultural center-stage and their only rival was the spectre of AIDS. It was hardly a good time for a woman in the middle stages of adulthood to go looking for excitement. Snug in her Maisonettes townhouse, Em assigned and resigned herself to the roles of daughter and friend.

It was a good life. She was active, informed, respected, even *liked*. She was also isolated and withering slowly away. Slaying curses—mooting them, as Eleanor and Harry called it—had brought more excitement, more meaning, into her life than she'd had in years.

Em blotted her eyes with a paper towel. The weepies were nothing new. She'd had them from the day Jeff left to the day after their divorce became final, and again last year when Dad died. Lately, Emma cried when she was happy and when she was sad. She cried over anything and nothing. No sobs, just tears with little warning.

My cup runneth over.

Maybe Nancy was free for lunch? Em remembered the weather and dismissed that idea. She retreated to her office where enough light filtered through the half-glass walls to enable some long-neglected filing. A cup of coffee from her thermos burnt Em's tongue and brightened her spirits. Taking up a bulging folder, she settled on the floor to sort the year-old sheets into keepers and discards. She'd winnowed the pile down to manageable size when Betty, the administrative assistant—formerly secretary— she shared with four other library veterans poked her head through the doorway.

After the usual pleasantries and comments about catastrophes, weather, and the team's New Year's victory, Betty got down to business.

"So, it's true—you are getting an assistant."

Gene had warned her. "So I hear. The condemned are always the last to know."

"Where are they going to put her? There's not a lot of room back here."

They both looked around, confirming the obvious. Emma imagined her office with another desk, another body. The Maisonettes was home, but the library had become the center of her life. If she lost her job satisfaction, there wouldn't be much left . . . except the wasteland.

"Maybe they'll move us both," Em mused.

It had taken twenty years to work her way up to a private office with a door that locked and walls that went all the way to the ceiling, even if three of them were mostly glass. The fourth was brick, scarred by a century of Michigan weather and the ivy that had covered the library before the great building boom of the Sixties. Her office spanned the past, present, and future. She didn't want to give it up—especially for the dubious privilege of an assistant.

Em's tear ducts filled. She pinched the bridge of her nose, hoping that would stop the flood, hoping Betty wouldn't notice.

"Maybe they won't find anyone," Betty countered. "They're asking for five years' experience *and* a master's. That cuts me out. You'll probably wind up with some hotshot fresh out of school."

Betty was pleasant and competent enough when it came to dealing with bureaucracy, but the thought of her as an assistant . . . Em tried not to blanch. "I had no idea you were interested in acquisitions."

"I'm not, really, but I could use the money they're offering. Are you making recommendations?"

Emma froze. There wasn't anyone who sprang instantly to mind, but that wasn't important. Important was that she hadn't asked Gene if she could—or should—submit a name or two. Most important was that she hadn't asked if she had any say in the final decision. Between the unions—of which she was not a member—and antidiscrimination laws, giving someone a university job could be as tricky as taking it away, but surely the other directors controlled their staff?

She should talk to Gene again. She should take a look at the job posting. At the very least she should say something to Betty, who was starting to stare.

"It wasn't my idea," she admitted.

Betty nodded, leaving Em to wonder how many people thought she was losing it and whether they might be right. "If you change your mind, Em—I know your style. We could work together well."

Em said she'd keep the suggestion in mind and waited for Betty to leave. She waited a few minutes longer before heading off for Human Resources. Betty said nothing as Em walked past her desk. Neither of them were particularly good liars even when they kept their mouths shut.

Frigid weather was nothing new in Michigan—the state's unofficial motto was WATER WINTER WONDERLAND, and it referred to the sidewalks in January. When the university had begun building its current campus, the first thing the engineers did was dig a network of tunnels beneath their stately brick-and-granite buildings. Generations of students, faculty, and staff referred to the passages as the steam tunnels, which was a misnomer. The tunnels only provided access to the huge steam ducts that heated the central campus, and since a student had gotten scalded to death back in the Seventies, the access doors had been replaced with steel plates and double locks.

As a matter of principle, Em preferred fresh air to the tunnels with their dingy green walls and locker room smell, but not when she'd spend more time bundling up than she would between buildings.

There were a half-dozen routes from Em's office to the tunnels. The shortest brought her face-to-face with workers in overalls emblazoned with the words KATASTROPHE KLEAN-UP. They seemed to know what they were doing with their pumps and hoses, buckets and brooms. Emma decided not to interrupt them. She backtracked to a different stairwell and a path that took her past Matt's office.

The door was closed, locked. Matt must have decided there was no point in showing up until the power came on. He had a decidedly low-tech way of keeping in touch with visitors: two feet of string thumbtacked to his door. One end was tied to a pencil, the other to a small, spiral notepad. Em left him a message hoping that the system came up uneventfully and telling him to give her a call if it didn't.

Human Resources in the Administration Building was noticeably brighter, noticeably warmer than the library. Em took her time getting to the Employment Office and the Plexiglas-covered bulletin board where every opening had to be posted before it could be filled. She found the card she was looking well to one side of the board—not Acquisitions Assistant or Assistant to the Director (which was different than Assistant Director), but "Researcher, Acquisitions; new position, salaried."

The offering salary was decent; the prerequisites were a bit stiff—Em had taken ten years to get her master's and didn't find it particularly useful, but she appreciated the efforts Gene was making to get her a qualified assistant. A couple of languages would have been more useful, Japanese for a start, or Arabic. She'd make room for an assistant who could read both Japanese and Arabic.

When Emma asked the desk clerk if anyone had asked about the Researcher, Acquisitions opening, he handed her an application. When she explained that she merely wanted to know if anyone had applied for the job or if there were any qualifications not listed on the card, he said that information was confidential but, confidentially, no one had applied yet and no one probably would because it was a dead-end position.

"No escalator. The library's full of dead-end jobs. Maybe one posting in ten from them has a built-in escalator. You'd think they'd get their heads out of their books and figure out which century we're living in. Nobody in their right mind wants to do the same thing for the rest of their lives. People want change; they want to know they're on time and on track."

Em thanked him and left without applying for the fast-track positions he suggested. She supposed she should feel grateful that a horde of would-be researchers wasn't massing in the corridors. Instead, she felt like a dinosaur, an insulted dinosaur who no longer valued change for its own sake. It occurred to Emma that she was starting to see events in their worst light and that it wouldn't be the end of the world if she made an appointment to get herself some antidepressants.

The challenge would be finding a doctor who could see her before February.

She was weighing her options as she walked the tunnels back to the library and leaning toward a phone call—if she could find someone who'd be content with dispensing a prescription without asking for hours of confession. The last thing she wanted was talk therapy. Fifty minutes describing the life she was living without mentioning Eleanor, curses, or the wasteland would be closer to punishment than cure, but if she was still weepy and pessimistic come February, Emma promised herself that she'd make the call.

Someone—maybe Pavlov—had said that men can be relied upon to do anything, provided the alternative was worse. If the alternative was another trip down therapy lane, Em would manage to lift her spirits before the month ended. Maybe a vacation with palm trees and sunshine . . . She didn't have to visit Meadow View every day . . . She wasn't Marsha.

Emma's conscience reared its ugliest head.

Get to the high ground. Keep to the high ground. Abandon Eleanor and you become *Eleanor.*

Em had cracked her own moral code. She wasn't the nonconformist she wanted to be. In the pit of her fears she had a superego the size of the Rock of Gibralter and a dread of disapproval. What was surprising was that the weight of her conscience felt exactly like a confrontation with a wasteland curse. Recognizing that, Emma realized she'd been slipping into the wasteland since she was a little girl and calling the visits night terrors.

Em's memories sighed as they rearranged. Things that had never made sense, suddenly did. If she could convince herself to trust him, she might learn more from a few fifty-minute sessions with Harry Graves than with any ten therapists. She was thinking about trust and change and halfway up the library stairs to her office when she noticed that the power was back.

Lightbulbs had never looked so good.

The computers were back, too . . . after a fashion. The beige box beside Em's desk whirred and clicked, then ground to a halt with the monitor displaying the university's battle flag rippling in an electronic breeze. Matt was going to regret taking the day off, but Em wouldn't be among those looking for the young man's head. Digging deep in a drawer, she found *her* emergency stash of hardware. A screwdriver, a flashlight, and ten minutes crawling around on the floor detached Emma's computer from the university network; a length of silver plastic cord got it ready to phone home. She had to check her notes before she restarted the machine, but the floppy disk she slipped into the drive and an illegal modem successfully awakened her home computer.

Newspapers were full of scary stores about teenaged boys wreaking havoc from the family PC. The uninitiated tended to think that no one over the age of twenty-five really understood how computers worked; the truth was simpler. The laws of natural selection ruled the information highway as they'd ruled the primal jungle and the open sky. There were bold hackers and there were old hackers, but very few old, bold hackers. Emma wasn't interested in bringing down the network; she just wanted her e-mail.

Tapping keys, she knocked politely on the network's front door—no need to break in if she could convince the butler she was a member of the family. The system took her account and password, then left Em hanging. Em grew a little anxious as the wait-time seconds piled up. The guys over in central computing were constantly improving their firewalls and security. They didn't always tell Matt when they upgraded—and he didn't always tell her. Her hand was moving toward the reset button when the screen cleared and she faced her office e-mail options.

Only a hundred messages since Friday, but it had been a holiday weekend. Emma started at the front end of the queue. She was still disposing of messages at four o'clock, when she broke the connection, dismantled her jury-rigged hardware, and returned to the Reference Room for paper-towel shuffling before heading out to Meadow View.

As soon as the power returned, they'd brought out the drying fans, huge, noisy three-foot-wide beasts on five-foot-high pedestals. They circulated air safely above the wounded books, not on them, and turned the cavernous room into a noisy airplane hangar. Em learned the current tally—forty volumes beyond salvage, a hundred headed for rebinding, three hundred and change drying out on the tables. Not too bad, as catastrophes went: worse than the '88 flood, but mere dribbles compared to '79 and '92.

The sky was low and leaden when Emma left work. It smelled of snow, which meant the temperature had risen ten or fifteen degrees and the clouds would lock the heat—such as it was—in for the night. The cold snap was over; they might get a thaw or three feet of snow. She set the car radio on scan, hoping for a weather report on the way to Meadow View. The Detroit stations were all broadcasting traffic reports while Bower's local stations were counterprograming with canned commentary and music.

Eleanor's restlessness had ended. She lay quietly in the bed, unrestrained, unmedicated. Her face seemed paler, grayer, and more gaunt. The slurry they put in the gastric feeding tube kept Eleanor alive but it couldn't maintain her weight, not when she thrashed and spasmed. When the light was right, Eleanor had begun to look older. Emma thought about the wasteland, but there were better explanations. Down the hall, Josh was shrunken, twisted, skeletal. If, by some miracle, he woke up, he'd never walk again.

Eleanor could win her battle and lose the war. Or she could lose it and the rogue who replaced her would find herself trapped in a body crippled by bone loss and atrophy.

Em's fiber-arts group met the first Wednesday of the month. When she'd left the house this morning, she'd planned on skipping it the way she'd skipped December's holiday gathering. Whether at the hospital or here at Meadow View, her daughter's vigil had seemed more important. *Keep to the high ground.* But she'd seen her future in the tunnels a few hours ago and martyrdom didn't

suit her. She squeezed Eleanor's hand gently after arrang-
ing a dozen cookies in the bed-table dish, then left.

Or tried to. She'd missed Marsha on her way in, but not
on her way out.

"Have you got a minute, Emma?"

She didn't, if she hoped to eat dinner before the fiber-
arts group met. Their last Christmas together Jeff had
bought her a sweatshirt that proclaimed, "Stress is what
happens when your mouth says Yes, but your tummy says
No." He'd known her well . . . well enough for permanent
wounds. Em smiled and crossed the threshold into Josh's
room.

Marsha had heard about Eleanor's thrashing. She'd
also heard about an experimental drug therapy that relaxed frozen joints, quelled tremors, and encouraged
weight gain. For a mother in Marsha's position, the therapy promised miracles. Emma wasn't in that position yet
and vowed silently that she never would be even as she
accepted the stapled paper.

"Between Josh and Eleanor, they might be willing to
give it a try."

Em kept smiling as she retreated to the elevator. She
took the article into a fast-foodery where she nibbled a
wilted salad with chalky, no-fat dressing. The article was
one step short of voodoo and her smart-heart dinner only
guaranteed that she'd be starving when she got home.

But the fiber-arts group redeemed the whole day. From
the moment Emma walked into the wood-paneled vestry
of a church almost as well endowed as the university, her
spirits lifted. Nancy was a closer friend than any of the
women in the group. Maybe too close: Nancy knew Em's
life story as well as she knew it herself. The two dozen
thread-benders in the vestry had little in common besides
the need to complete themselves with a variety of needles.
When the group first came together some thirty-five years
ago—a good twenty years before Emma discovered it—
they'd called themselves the Ladies Home Sewing and
Terrorist Circle, memorializing the campus anarchy of the

Sixties and the older notion that nothing made a community stronger or faster than a quilting bee. Times had changed—they'd voted to abandon their too-cute name in favor of the staid Fiber Arts Guild not long after Em joined—but the camaraderie endured.

Emma wasn't prepared for the evening's program: a demonstration of how to shape roses from wired ribbon. But like most of her thread-bending companions, she never traveled without a bit of unfinished stitching in her purse. One never knew when one would suddenly be faced with a one- or two-hour wait. Her traveling piece was Hardanger, an old Scandinavian technique that relied on counting, symmetry, and a single color of thread to create patterns almost certainly inspired by winter-frosted windows. She'd started it while Eleanor was in the hospital and there was no danger she'd finish it tonight.

Relaxed, restored, and hungry, Em returned home at ten-thirty. By the time she'd indulged herself with a slab of homemade bread layered with cheese, tomatoes, and crumbled bacon, it was past eleven and too late for anything more than a cursory look at her home-account e-mail wherein Lori continued her analysis of ceramic kilns and was mercifully silent about her father.

In keeping with her resolve to take care of herself first, Em thought about fishing boats anchored in a postcard harbor when she snugged up beneath the blankets. If thinking about the wasteland helped her get there, then thinking about not going anywhere might keep her home.

The strategy worked. Em awoke to a weather report. The temperature was on the plus side of zero, it hadn't snowed, and the only face she saw in the bathroom mirror was her own. It was going to be a good day, the first real day of the new year—yesterday and Tuesday had been dry-runs, experimental errors. The engineering gene understood experimental errors.

The library corridors were awash in fluorescent light. Her computer, and the library network, rose from the dead when she pushed the appropriate button. Matt must have gotten the word in time. Emma picked up the phone to congratulate him. She was leaving a message when he walked into her office.

"Have I got some old news for you!"

"Old news?" Em expected to hear how he'd resurrected the network or even that he knew she'd tapped her account through tainted channels.

"If you're looking for a rogue, Paris, France, in sixteen-eighty wouldn't be a bad place to start looking."

She shouldn't have been so surprised that she'd bolted down a mouthful of hot coffee trying not to gasp. "How so?" she asked with her eyes watering.

"The city was a hot bed of sorcerers and magicians. Fortune telling, love potions, Black Masses—you name it and Parisians were selling it. These guys did a big business in abortions and miscarriages and poisons. Especially poisons . . . and antidotes for poison. They played both sides of the street. Hey, I want to poison my husband! I've got just the thing, madame. Ten dollars please. Hey, I think my wife's putting poison in my food! I've got just the thing for you, too, monsieur. Ten dollars please. It was incredible. Then somebody fingered the king's mistress for slipping love potions into the king's pudding—"

Emma shook her head. She'd gotten some impression of the era while paging through the costume books. "I don't think anyone ever had to put a love potion into Louis the Fourteen's pudding. He wasn't exactly renowned for his fidelity."

"That was half of the scandal. Ol' Louis got daily reports from police and threw them on the fire when the trail got too close. A whole bunch were tried and executed between sixteen-eighty and sixteen-eighty-two and a bunch more got sent to prison—dungeons—for life."

"The *police*?" Em said when Matt paused for breath. "Isn't sixteen-eighty a bit early for *police*? Unless I've slipped a few years, that's about the time we were burning witches in Salem—without the help of the Salem police.

Somehow, in France, I imagine the Inquisition handled anyone who got involved with Black Masses."

Matt grinned triumphantly. "No! That's what's so great about this. Louis turned the investigation over to some guy—" He flashed a sheaf of papers Em hadn't noticed before and began flipping through them. "I got it here— Nicholas De La Reynie, who was the first real, honest-to-God, Chief of Police in Paris. It was a criminal case from the git-go. Bits of treason and fraud, but mostly murder— especially the murder of husbands and unwanted children. You wouldn't believe the glop they sold women to poison their husbands or cause miscarriages, but if I read right, they did surgical abortions, too, and weren't above killing—or sacrificing—a baby. There was a big demand for aborted fetuses—*yuk!* And the ones who were midwives, too, weren't above *stealing* from their customers— if you get my drift. But no heresy, not even any witchcraft. The Black Masses just added to the scandal and I guess they were crimes—sort of like indecent exposure and ob- scenity—but the scandal was known as the Affair of the Poisons, not the Affair of the Black Masses. The Catholic Church was never involved—I guess it had something to do with the king of France not taking orders from some Italian guy living in Rome. There were trials . . . with court reports who wrote everything down. The evidence standards were pretty low. A voluntary confession wasn't worth the paper it was written on, even Reynie figured that people wouldn't tell the truth *unless* they were tor- tured—but voluntary accusations seemed to be okay. Lots of people denounced their neighbors as sorcerers and you've got to figure that not all of them were—"

Emma interrupted: "*None* of them were." She would have said more about ignorance and superstition, if her memory hadn't served up Blaise saying that in the eyes of his neighbors his family was filled with witches and sor- cerers.

Matt continued, "This Reynie guy—he was pretty good, considering that nobody had ever done what he was doing. He took notes, like any good cop, and kept track of his suspects. He analyzed motives and where it was all leading, which was straight to the king's mistress. But best of all—Reynie didn't turn his notes over when his boss got cold feet. He kept 'em secret until he died, but he kept 'em all the same, so there's documentation of the stuff Louis burned.

"Auntie Em," he said, meeting her eyes directly, "this isn't like the last time when all we had was a couple of words you'd overheard and the idea that it had to be after William the Bastard conquered England. We've got a police record. A *searchable* police record, if the library wants to acquisition a copy of it, but plenty of translated excerpts to start with."

Did she want to start an investigation? Did she want to find out that Blaise Raponde had been a criminal, maybe even a murderer? Did she have any choice?

Em was weighing her options at breakneck speed when the mental process came to a dead halt. Another thought streaked through her mind: Eleanor, Blaise, and even Harry Graves implied that curse-hunters weren't united in one happy family.

"Paris might be a good place to start," she conceded, "but you're still talking a needle in a haystack as far as my rogue's concerned."

"You got a name? Any name? Most of the time Reynie refers to the bad guys as La This or Le That—it gets confusing: our La Reynie's a guy but La Voisin isn't and she was the prime suspect for providing 'goodies' and Black Masses for the king's mistress. Everybody had a nickname like La Vigoureux and La Bosse. But there are real names, first and last names, for most of them. How about Le Sage? The Wise. He was definitely a guy, a piece of work and a half. They tried chaining him to a galley bench, but he got loose so they chained him to the floor of a dungeon and he lasted there for years."

Emma hesitated then shook her head. All her blood had retreated into her heart, which pounded while her hands and feet grew cold, but she needed information more than trust. "Raponde, Blaise Raponde. I asked him. I looked for it myself. I didn't find anything. It could be just a name he made up."

"No kidding. This guy Le Sage, he had aliases all over Paris. Drove Reynie crazy."

Matt ruffled his papers again. Em saw that they were annotated printouts.

"Can I see?" She held out her hand.

"Nothing like Raponde," he replied, not sharing the papers. "What about Romani? Here's a Romani. Somebody called him 'the man of a thousand disguises.' He delivered the poisons. Reynie wrote down that other witnesses described this Romani guy as charming and handsome."

Blaise Raponde was that, but he came across too gentlemanly to be the sort who'd made his living as a drug courier. Or maybe he had. The most successful criminals played against type and expectations. The Blaise Raponde she knew could well have charmed himself into the king's mistress's private quarters. He'd had three wasteland centuries to perfect his act . . . or repent his sins.

"Em? Em, are you all right?"

She shivered out of her reverie with the worn explanation, "Sometimes I still can't believe all this is happening. And Romani—that's not a name. Gypsies call themselves the 'rom' and Romani is what other people would call the gypsies—when they weren't calling them something worse."

Could Blaise have been a gypsy? He had the dark eyes and black hair.

"Let me see those, please?" She grasped the papers, and after a fleeting hesitation, Matt let go. There was no order to what she saw—names, dates, and bibliographic references were jumbled and obscured by handwritten notes. "How long did it take you to put this together?"

"Not long," Matt grinned. "A couple hours of data mining on the Internet to get the basics. Then Mal and I hit the stacks for backup details. We've got more references to check out, but to tell you the truth, it gets repetitious. I wish I could get my eyeballs on Reynie's notes and knew enough French to read them. Mal and I, we'd each be looking at something, and it was for sure based on the same page of Reynie's notes, but the translations were different, and so was the interpretation."

"Welcome to the world of research." Matt was learning the ropes and the pitfalls quickly, but what really held Emma's attention had nothing to do with the seventeenth century. "You're saying that you and Mal did this?" With a second glance she could distinguish two distinct handwriting styles on the sheets. "I tried to tell you the other day—I'm really not comfortable getting other people involved in this."

That was an understatement. Despite her resolve to reopen her mind about Matt's girlfriend, hearing her name filled Em with instant anger.

"Don't get upset, Em—I said I was helping a cousin do some genealogy research. We were looking for a Barto who'd died in Paris in sixteen-eighty. B-A-R-T-E-U-X—" He spelled it out. "Pretty cool, huh?"

"Pretty cool," Em agreed, though it sounded pretty flimsy. But if they were in the electromagnetic phase of their romance, she could imagine Malerie faking research delight; she'd faked a few things herself when she was that age and for years afterward. "Why don't you let me handle it from here?"

She didn't even try to be subtle, and Matt, who had a full quota of perception, understood immediately. "I talked to Mal about how you and she didn't hit it off the other day. She got upset—she didn't mean to snarl, it was just . . . just . . . well . . ."

"Her curse?" Emma finished for him.

"Yeah, that's what she said. She thinks you're really cool—being a library director and all. I told her you could run me out of my job here anytime you chose."

"I'm not sure that was a good idea, Matt—even if it were true, which it isn't, in more ways than I can count.

Reg and I are ballast, not directors. Our function isn't even to rearrange the deck chairs on the *Titanic*—we just polish them."

Matt ignored her. "Okay, Mal suggested we all get together, maybe a movie or a meal. I think she'd like to cook something, but that would mean cleaning up my place—"

"Hokkaido," Em suggested. She'd conquer her prejudice, simply because it was prejudice. "We could all meet for lunch one day next week?" But she wasn't in a big hurry.

"How about dinner, tonight?"

Before she'd had a chance to study the papers she held? "Tomorrow?" She, Nancy, and John frequently got together for Friday dinner, but they hadn't made plans for this week.

"Great! You won't regret it, Em—and neither will Mal."

Em didn't share his confidence. "Can I keep these? Maybe something will jog my memory." She flourished the papers.

"Sure, I made a copy before I brought 'em up here. Maybe we'll bump into each other in the stacks after work?"

Maybe she'd skip the stacks. "I head out to Meadow View after work to visit Eleanor."

"How is she?" Matt asked, instantly sobered.

"Withering," Em answered with abrupt honesty. "Every day she's a little frailer. She could get sick and die no matter what I do."

"If we just knew what we were looking for. If you see the hat guy again, ask him about Le Sage and La Voisin and the other names you've got there. If one of them is our rogue, we could track him down. Mal found an actual street map of Paris from 1683. The book was too big to put on the copier, so we filed a duplication request at the charge desk. We don't know where La Voisin and her cronies lived, but we know where they died—tied to stakes and bonfires in something called the Gravy Plaza. You could start there and follow them backward the way you did with the eleventh century."

Em shuddered. She'd experienced some pretty grue-some moments in November and didn't relish the thought of invading the thoughts of anyone facing a certain, fiery death. On the other hand, Matt had given her several ideas which—to her shame—she didn't want to share with him. They talked a bit about safer topics. He told her that he knew she'd picked up her e-mail and asked her not to breach his security again. Emma made no promises.

Not long after he left, she went down to the duplication office and, exercising a director's unofficial privilege, re-moved the bulky Parisian atlas from the shelves and the li-brary.

Eight

Snow fell with a vengeance. Emma stuck her arm over the wall in front of her car and collected flakes on her glove. Sparkling gold in the amber-colored streetlight, they were the real thing: spikes, crystals, and perfect hexagons—the sort of flakes that mounted up fast and played games with sound as they fell. The temperature had risen to about twenty, but thanks to the last forty-eight hours, Bower was hard frozen. Every surface in the city, from power lines to streets, had become a welcome mat for winter.

A snow plow scraped a street Em couldn't see from the structure and snagged her attention. Bower didn't usually send out its plows until the white blanket was four inches thick, unless the weather service was willing to swear on its collective grandmother's grave that there'd be a foot on the ground before the skies cleared. Applying her experienced, if not expert, eye to the situation, Em guessed that about three inches had fallen already. She checked the tallest trees she could see from the parking structure and found them swaying in a wind that didn't reach the ground . . . yet.

This wouldn't be the first time a cold snap had gone straight into a blizzard. Usually Em paid better attention to weather forecasts. She was paying the price of distraction in countless small ways.

Emma turned right at the foot of the ramp, toward the Maisonettes, the prudent place to be when January got ugly. But her conscience was an implacable pair of four-hundred-pound gorillas, joined at the hip. The one on the right was guilt; the one on the left was obligation. She could walk the wasteland regardless of the local weather but she couldn't do anything without visiting Meadow View first.

Em had been driving on snow since she turned sixteen. She could navigate three inches of crunchy, Styrofoam snow in her sleep. At the first traffic light—already switched into its flashing-red storm mode—Em reversed directions.

She asked the Meadow View receptionist, "How much are we supposed to get?" and nearly lost the answer— "Fifteen inches"—when she spotted Nancy in a lobby chair engrossed in a magazine.

"Problems?" she asked when she was close enough to speak softly.

Nance lowered the magazine with a start. "No," she answered quickly. "Katherine's fine—complaining as always. John had a conference meeting in Detroit and decided to get a hotel room rather than chance I-94, so I'm on my own for the night. I tried calling you at work. Betty said you'd just left. I thought I'd catch you here. Can I interest you in dinner after you check on Eleanor? I'd thawed some ravioli before John called."

Em considered the map book she'd smuggled out of the stacks, the notes Matt had given her, and her plans to poke around seventeenth-century Paris. Her natural inclination was for a solo expedition and Emma was a heartbeat away from resenting her friend for intruding when she recalled Eleanor saying that curse-hunters worked best in pairs: one roaming through the wasteland and history while the other stayed put in the here-and-now, ready to pull the plug in an emergency. Once Emma had thought of emergencies, Nancy's suggestion seemed fortuitous.

"You can interest me, but let's say we pass on the ravioli and go back to my place instead. I was going to dig up a few things from the past. You can help."

Nancy's eyebrows rose, as Emma expected they would. "I'd love to help. I can swing by the house and pick up the ravioli. It's already to go in the oven. We'd save time."

Em hadn't given much thought to dinner. Ravioli—especially ravioli heated the old-fashioned way in the oven—sounded much more appetizing than anything she could nuke in the microwave, for all that the microwave was the only kitchen appliance she truly could not do without.

"You win. We'll save even more time if I meet you back at your house and you leave your car in your driveway. There won't be two parking spaces in my neighborhood now that we've got to leave room for snow."

With bright, schoolgirl eyes, Nancy agreed to return home while Emma checked on Eleanor and refilled the bedside dish with enough cellophane-wrapped mints to keep the staff in sweets until Saturday—just in case they did get a foot of snow in the meantime. She was waiting at the front door, wreathed in what proved to be a tomato-sauce-scented cloud, when Em's car crunched to a stop at the end of the Amstel driveway.

"So, tell me what you're up to!" Nance appealed as they pulled away from the snow-covered curb. "What sort of spells and magic have you got planned?"

"Technically, I don't think I cast spells, and unless I'm mistaken, the wasteland's an alternate reality—subjective, rather than objective and empirical, like the one we're used to, but not magical."

"What sort of *subjective phenomena*, then?"

Emma chuckled at her own resistance to the notion of magic and slowed down to negotiate a corner where the snow was already hubcap deep. "I'll let you look at my notes when we get there—and the book I've subjectively 'borrowed' from the stacks—but what it boils down to is that there's a chance I can pick up the scent of the rogue who's taken Eleanor to Paris . . . seventeenth-century Paris."

"You can do that—pick up scents like a bloodhound?"

"I don't think it will literally be a *scent*, but I'm going to try to backtrack a person's life. What I've read and heard implies that backtracking is what people like Eleanor and Harry do. I don't know what *I* can or can't do in the wasteland, but it's worth a try. I made myself a sitting room the other night—turned that Millais print I've had forever into three-dimensional space, complete with windows and a garden."

Nancy said nothing, which reminded Emma that no matter what labels she resisted, her life had gone places where her closest friend could not follow.

"Eleanor said I'd need an anchor—someone to keep an eye on me when I walked the wasteland. Someone who can pull me back when things start getting squirrelly. I want someone I trust."

"Just tell me what I have to do, Em."

Parking could have been worse. Emma found a spot two blocks from the front door where the plows were unlikely to wall her in. The association president was out with his brand-new snowblower. He'd blown his sidewalk down to the cement and done the same for old Mrs. Borster, who lived on the other side of Em's townhouse. Em offered him the going rate if he'd blow the snow off hers as well.

"Don't worry about the money, Em," he replied and cleared a path to the front door.

The cats were not pleased to have company. No doubt they associated Nancy with the noisy blower and cold puddles that surrounded their food-bearer's feet. They retreated to the carpeted living room, where they sat licking their paws with backs to Emma and Nancy alike. Em reached past Spin to turn on the Christmas tree and the television. A series of electronic squawks came through the speakers, sending the cats down to the basement while a weather advisory crawled across the bottom of the screen.

"They're still saying fifteen inches," Nancy read aloud as Em left the living room for the kitchen. "Are you sure it's a good idea to be out walking?"

Emma quipped, "There's no weather in the waste-land—it's like California," then thought about her ulti-mate destination: February 23, 1680, the day the poisoner known to history as La Voisin had been burnt at the stake. Matt and Malerie's notes related the details of the woman's execution—her white robe, her drunkenness as the tumbrel carried her through Paris to the Place de Grève (not Gravy), her refusal to make a final confession. Their notes even mentioned the hour—five in the after-noon—when the pyre was lit but the notes were silent about the weather.

Em hadn't felt the weather when she'd visited the eleventh century in November, but she remembered that the sky had been blue and the trees, green. Perhaps there hadn't been any weather worth noticing. That might not be true in a Parisian February. Unless she were mistaken, 1680 was a year near the end of what historians called the "Little Ice Age." If she was smart, she'd be thinking about boots and gloves as she made the transition.

Nancy looked over Matt's notes while Em put dinner together.

"Two people contributed to this," she observed. "And neither of them was you."

"Didn't I mention that Matt's acquired a girlfriend? I must have. That was what he called about New Year's Eve. He met her at the Masked Ball."

"And three days later he's told her what's been going on in your life? That's a bit much."

"He swears he hasn't told the truth—"

"Swearing that you haven't told the truth. That's pretty close to an oxymoron, Em."

"But he swears it just the same—he came up with some story about researching his family tree. *I* believed him . . . almost. And Mal probably did, too—they're at the stage where everything is mutually fascinating."

Nance waited until Em carried the ravioli out of the kitchen to ask, "Do I detect a whiff of hostility?"

"More than a bit," Em admitted. "She's sullen and mousy—in the traditional way and because when she doesn't look like she's afraid of being eaten, she looks like she's about to steal something. I keep telling myself it's none of my business, but she sets my teeth on edge and I can't help but think that Matt could do better."

"Hostility and jealousy?"

Em laid down her spoon. "I've asked myself that, but really—it's out of the question. If opportunity knocked, I wouldn't open the door."

"Not you! *Her!* What did you say her name was? Malaria? Does *she* know that you're not interested in Matt?"

For the first time in years, Emma felt herself blushing. "I think Matt does. He's pretty perceptive—very perceptive when it comes to not asking too many questions about the 'hat guy.' "

"Hat guy?" Nance asked, then answered her own question—"Oh, you mean Blaise. Does he have any part in this?"

Em sobered. "That's what I want to find out tonight. The other night he said that his body died in Paris in sixteen-eighty. Before that, I didn't have a solid date to connect him with. I mentioned it to Matt, 'cause he was pressing and I didn't think it would do too much harm. He was a big help back in November doing research. After reading what he came up with—he and Malerie . . . Well, if I were a rogue and into motiveless malignity, then I'd be doing exactly what Raponde's doing: being ten kinds of sincere and helpful to beginners who don't know their ass from their elbows. He's been the perfect gentleman. You know, I might even get myself wounded, for credibility's sake, if the stakes were high enough. And I don't really know what the stakes are, Nance. That puts me at a huge disadvantage.

"In the back of my mind I see Br'er Rabbit and he's saying 'Please, please, whatever you do, don't throw me in that mean ol' briar patch,' and you know that's exactly where he wants to be, 'cause once he's in the briar patch, he's invulnerable."

"So, in short, Eleanor might have been right about your boyfriend?"

"The operative word there is 'might' . . . and he's *not* a boyfriend."

"And the part about letting yourself get wounded? What brought that image to mind?"

They finished dinner while Emma sketched in the ups and downs of the last forty-eight hours, including bandaging Blaise's magic-wand wounds, her conversation with Harry Graves, and Harry's warning to be wary of love at first sight.

"A bit late for that," Nancy commented drily.

"I gotta tell you, Nance—the whole romantic vampire seduction thing looks a *lot* different when you're not curled up in bed reading about it. If Blaise were a man— an ordinary man—yeah, I'd be flattered and interested, but the only thing I'm sure of is that he's not ordinary. I'm aware of the sparks, but there's no fire."

"Forgive my prurient thoughts," Nancy muttered without sarcasm. "Harry and Blaise—what a combination. You aren't going to tell them about each other?"

"I've told Blaise that Eleanor had—or has—a husband named Harry Graves. The name didn't trigger a reaction. I haven't told Harry. I came close . . . and I might go through with it, depending on what I learn tonight. We sort of left it that I might call him sometime at a more reasonable hour. He probably guesses there's someone. Remember: Eleanor came out here to set me up. She wasn't interested in the curse I'd found. Somehow she knew— and Harry Graves knew—that I'd had help on more than one occasion and that could only mean that I was consorting with a rogue. When she lost me in the wasteland, she came back to this living room and she called Harry on my phone. It was a fifteen-minute phone call—I got the bill."

"You'd think she'd have at least used a credit card," Nancy mused. "On some level, she must have wanted you to know—people make mistakes like that when they're conflicted. Harry Graves is the only living, able-bodied person who might be able to help if something were to go wrong tonight."

Emma met her friend's eyes. She held Nancy's stare a moment, then looked away. "I've got his phone number, but only as a last resort."

"The very last," Nancy agreed. "Nothing ever goes according to plan, right? So, plan for the absolute worst and it won't happen. That's what you always say, isn't it?"

Em flashed a grim, lopsided smile just before the lights flickered. The wind had come down from the tree tops in the last hour or so. Her home was in the middle of a long row of townhouses. It would take a hurricane or tornado—neither of which was common in Michigan or January—to shake its foundations, but the power lines were vulnerable. She collected candles and flashlights and tried not to think of omens.

The lights had dimmed twice more when Em poured two glasses of wine and set them on a tray in the middle of the living room floor.

"We're going to perform a witchy ritual?" Nancy asked with thinly concealed hope from the sofa.

"No, we're going to—*I'm* going to sit on the floor because then, when I fall over, I won't hurt myself." It was a practical strategy for an absurd situation, and watching Nancy's wide-eyed reaction almost made Em decide to turn on the television instead.

"You're going to fall over?"

"I'm going to try to have an OBE—an out-of-body experience." She lit two of the candles. "Frankly, it works best when I'm lying down in bed, but when I've started from other places and positions, I've tended to wake up on the floor. You can stay up there—"

Nance slid down to the carpet and folded her legs into a perfect lotus position, something Emma had never been able to achieve.

"I got back into my yoga and transcendental meditation while I was staying with Mom down in Ohio last year. It hurt like heck for the first few months, but even the pain helped me relax, so I kept at it. Now it's part of my life again."

Em shook her head. "Always said you were better at the Eastern philosophies than me." She opened her borrowed book to a map of Paris that had been drawn in the year 1683—or so the unnamed cartographer had written in the lower-right-hand corner. The map, she supposed, was intended for seventeenth-century tourists. It showed the locations of the city's major churches and palaces as well as the Bastille fortress-prison and the Place de Grève, where public executions were held. Grève was marked with a gibbet, a nasty-looking sword, and a flaming pyre, each of them larger than Notre Dame.

Nancy interrupted Emma's reverie regarding the evolution of tourist entertainment and civic self-promotion.

"Don't slouch; sit up straight, *then* let your arms and legs find a comfortable position. Close your eyes. Breathe stress out; breathe peace in—hold it, then repeat. And resist distraction."

"I know *how* it's done, Nance. It just doesn't work for me."

"It works for everyone, if you do it right. It works better, though, if you do believe."

"Not belief again. I'm sadly deficient in belief. How about hope?" Em asked, ever the negotiator. "Will it work if I *hope* it works?"

Nancy laughed. "It'll work once you stop making excuses!"

Emma tried. She straightened her spine—that was a

distressingly uncomfortable process by itself—and then let her limbs relax. To her surprise, she *was* comfortable. She took a deep breath and felt very foolish, knowing that Nancy was in the room with her. A few breaths later, Em began to let go of the foolishness and, without the aid of a bouquet of imaginary balloons, let go of her body as well.

The wasteland soil was hard, dry, and almost familiar when Emma rolled over on it—someday she'd figure out how to arrive on her feet rather than her face. She wore Mariana's dark blue gown and her own fleece-lined boots. The way-back stone was missing—that gave Em a serious fright until she found it beside the storm-cellar door at the bottom of the orange-slice hollow.

Mariana's workroom was dark until she imagined a lamp and lit it with a thought. Blaise hadn't returned—or if he had, he hadn't moved anything. His Bible lay where she'd left it. The loose threads she'd removed from the embroidery frame hadn't reappeared. At least Em thought they hadn't. She hadn't been careful enough when she'd selected her experimental samples. To satisfy the engineering gene, she'd have to remove all the dark greens or all the golds, but later, not when she'd just realized it was nighttime in the garden beyond Mariana's window.

Emma had recreated the garden and without sparing a thought for the scientific problem of bringing bright, autumn sunlight to a place where sky was thick with swirling magenta clouds. Now that sunlight was gone. Straining her eyes, Em thought she could make out the shapes of trees and walls but she couldn't be sure, not with her new imaginary lamp shining behind her.

The window directly in front of Em was open. She could have leaned over the embroidery frame, stuck her head outside, and checked for stars overhead. Her nerve failed in mid-lean when she imagined her body *here* and her head somewhere completely different.

Emma left the room and the hole it hid in. She was trying to decide in which direction the seventeenth century might be found when the Mother Voice—a nagging phenomena noticeably absent from her life the last month and a half—urged her to go back inside and climb out the window instead. Em resisted the urge. Her real mother had informed her that walking was the rule of the wasteland, walking forever until you found yourself where you wanted to be. Em picked a chunk of horizon and, with the wood-block map of Paris and an imaginary calendar page with a circle around February 23, 1680, as firmly in mind as she could keep them, started walking.

The Mother Voice attacked Emma's concentration. *Use the window,* it urged. *You could walk all night and you'd still have to pick your way through the streets of Paris. Climb through the window and you'll put your feet down in the Place de Grève. You can get there the moment that La Voisin woman dies and see if she gives rise to a curse. You can check around the crowd for Blaise Raponde . . .*

Emma had her head down and was pounding across the dirt the way she did when she was getting ready for one of the charity walk-a-thons she did throughout the year, but she'd lost sight of the Place de Grève and the twenty-third of February. The horizon hadn't changed but heaven only knew where she'd been headed the last little while. With a self-disgusted sigh, she stopped short and buried her face in her hands.

When she looked up again, Em half-expected to see Blaise standing there laughing at her . . . or a circle of blazing curses. Instead, she was looking down the slope of the orange slice, straight at the storm-cellar door.

Use the window, Merle, her Mother Voice repeated, sounding nothing like Eleanor but very much like a Shakespearian actor of the distinguished British variety.

In an odd—very odd—way, climbing through a window to another century made more sense to Emma than walking until instincts she didn't trust told her she'd come to the right spot. She took the voice's advice and opened the storm-cellar door. The embroidery frame was heavier than she'd expected it would be when she pulled it away from the window, and squeezing through the window felt a lot like wedging a round peg into a somewhat smaller square hole, but Em persevered and was rewarded with a four-foot drop onto paving stones Edward Millais had never painted.

Night reigned in the City of Light; fog, too. Paris was blanketed with a fog that London in its heyday might have envied. Emma couldn't see three feet in front of her fingertips, but she could hear men shouting at one another. They were complaining about something and they were doing it in French that Em could recognize but scarcely understand. The thrill of success dulled the ache of the ankle she'd wrenched while landing.

The cobblestones of Paris, she thought as she tested the ankle. For the first time since November, Emma perceived advantages to a curse-hunter's life. No more crowded buses and tour guides waving their umbrellas to marshall a hurried herd from one landmark to the next. If a curse-hunter wanted to tour the capitals of Europe, she needed only inspiration and an ace bandage.

Em was eager to begin her explorations— How good had her aim been? Was this the right place, the right year, the right day? For starters, the time seemed wrong. Matt's notes indicated that La Voisin had been brought to the square for a 5 P.M. execution—gallows by day, but pyres by night? It felt later than 5 P.M., or earlier, or perhaps Matt's notes were wrong. Were the men complaining about erecting a stake and pyre, or were they taking it down?

She had so many questions that she could ignore the most personal ones: Would she faint when the pyre was lit? Could she look at a charred corpse without getting sick? And the most important one— Could the death of a self-professed poisoner and abortionist give rise to a rogue curse?

So many questions, but before Emma sought the answer to any of them, she carefully examined the wall behind her. The window she'd used was shuttered on its seventeenth-century Parisian side. She pressed her palms against the wall beneath the window, trying to convince herself that it was another way-back stone. No luck. The stones she touched were cold, damp, and relentlessly solid. Returning to the here-and-now might be a challenge.

Emma told herself that she'd burn that bridge when she got to it . . . and avoid all *burning* metaphors until then.

Three strides into the fog, Emma found herself in the path of a raggedy woman who limped and swore as she hurried along. They passed so close that their skirts brushed together and Em could smell the filth clinging to the woman's clothes. Proletarian costume evolved far slower than aristocratic fashion. Emma couldn't guess whether the crone dwelt in the eleventh century or the seventeenth, but she wasn't from the twentieth.

Em had been invisible in the eleventh century—as invisible to herself as she'd been to the Normans and English around her. This time—whenever that time was—Emma could see herself glowing softly the way she did when she walked the wasteland. It made walking easier, even at night through a fog, but if the Parisians could see her? The gown Millais had painted was a Victorian fantasy, as out of place in 1680 as it would have been in here-and-now Bower. Em's heart skipped a beat while she considered how bad things could get, but the doddering woman went on her way toward the middle of the square.

Reassured, Emma pressed on in the same direction, pausing once to let a horse-drawn wagon rumble past— definitely *not* a modern horse or wagon. The wagon was loaded with wood. She knew then that she'd arrived early: the men she heard through the fog were building La Voisin's execution pyre. Another few steps and she saw their torches haloed in mist and two dark hulks, one man-high, rectangular, and raked with what appeared to be benches. The other—where the men were working and cursing—was shaped like a pyramid.

Like a pyre.

A woman would die horribly today. Never mind that "today" had happened more than three centuries ago or that by all accounts the woman had aided and abetted in dozens of equally horrible deaths. A human being would die horribly today. A few human beings—the cream of seventeenth-century Paris, no doubt, would watch from elevated seats while less exalted folk were laying claim to front-row cobblestones: the limping woman crossed Emma's path again, dragging a log which she positioned midway between the platform and the pyre.

Em hadn't recognized the woman without her knitting: the many-times-great-grandmother of Dicken's Madame Defarge.

The juxtaposition of fact and fiction, past and present, subjective and objective was more than Emma could handle. The wine she'd had drunk in Bower soured in Paris. Her stomach contracted and she crouched low, resting her forehead against her knees and her fingertips on the cobblestones. The sinking nausea passed. Em could breathe, then swallow and finally raise her head. The crone had swiveled her head around like an owl and was staring at her.

She can't see me. I can see myself, but no one can see me. I'm not here. I'm not here.

Nothing Emma said to herself changed her perception. The crone stared directly at her, mouthing words that Emma couldn't hear, raising her hand, extending a finger. When a fist of wind wrapped around Em, lifting her and hurling her backward, she assumed the absolute worst and was astonished beyond words when she blinked and found herself looking at Nancy instead.

"Are you all right?" Nance demanded. She had a hold of Emma's wrists and gave them a gentle shake. "Talk to me, Emma! Nod your head. Blink. Do something!"

Em managed a blink, followed by a dry-throat gulp that hurt like hell but gave her back her voice.

"I'm fine. You pulled me back. What happened? How did you know—?"

"How did I know? How did I know! You got pale as a ghost and sweaty—like you were going to be ill. When you started to wobble and mutter, I forgot about the ice cubes and just grabbed you. *What* happened? Did you get to the wasteland? To Paris? Did you find Eleanor or the rogue or Blaise?"

"I got to the wasteland and Paris—" The Place de Grève was a memory now, but a potent one. Em grasped her wineglass with both hands and took an unsteady sip.

"What about Paris?"

"I try to convince myself it's not real, because when I'm there in the eleventh century or, now, in Paris, I know it's real as can be. It was nighttime and foggy, and workmen were building a pyre, Nance, a *pyre* . . . for a public execution. The audience had begun to gather."

Nancy looked a little ill herself. "You saw it?"

"Saw it, heard it, smelled it." Em took another sip of wine then rubbed her hand over her closed eyes, as if that would erase the memory. "If what I'm doing *isn't* visiting the real past, then, I tell you, Nance, I've got a frightening imagination for details that I've never encountered in my own, real life."

Without a word, Nancy took the glass from Em's hand, set it safely aside, and gave her a hug. "For what it's worth," she whispered in Emma's ear, "you've convinced me that what you're doing is real . . . and dangerous. When I grabbed you, you were saying 'I'm not here,' 'I'm not here.' Maybe I shouldn't say this, but I could feel the fear pouring out of you."

Em freed herself. "I guess it's good—or just interesting—to know that there's some connection. I didn't find anyone that I was looking for, but there was a woman—I hate to say this, an old, ugly woman—who saw me. Not the first time. We passed once and I'm sure she didn't see me. Then I watched her set up a front-row seat for the burning. Something about her doing that just got to me. I started to feel sick and faint. And just when I thought I was getting myself back under control, I realized she could see me. She said something—I couldn't hear—then she pointed her finger at me like a gun. And the fear, like you say, started to gush."

"Was she the rogue? Another curse-hunter?"

"I don't know. She must have been something." Em sipped her wine. "I honestly don't know. But you got me home. That's the best news I've had in a month. Eleanor told the truth: it's safer with a guide, with an anchor. You know when I'm in trouble and you can get me the hell out of wherever I am. I've found a way to get to Paris and you've got the way to get me back."

"Em . . . Emma—you're not thinking of going *back*?"

She hadn't, until Nancy asked the question, and then she already knew the answer. "I've got to have answers. About Eleanor and about Blaise Raponde."

"You could get hurt, Em. *Killed!*"

Em thought a moment. "No, I don't think I can be killed—not while you're here watching over my body. Eleanor hasn't died. And Blaise is dead because his *body's* dead. He didn't die in the wasteland—"

"He got *hurt* in the wasteland, didn't he?"

"Maybe. That's how it looked. And a day later, my here-and-now time, he was gone. If I find him, I've got questions for him—more than I've got for Eleanor. And I'm going to find him, Nance . . . or find some answers."

Nancy got quiet and thoughtful. "You're changing, Em. This thing—this curse-hunting thing has already changed you. You can't walk away from it."

"Eleanor—"

"Not Eleanor, Em. You. You should look in a mirror right now. Two minutes ago, you were scared spitless, now you're rarin' to go back."

Nance had the truth of it. "Instant addiction."

"Not to mention the power to do something that every human being who's ever lived has dreamt of doing. I'm jealous, Em. I don't want you to go because you say it's dangerous and you might get hurt, but that's only part of it. I don't want you to go because you can and I can't."

Emma appreciated Nancy's honesty, but she couldn't hold her friend's eyes. She shouldn't have told either Nancy or Matt. The risks were too great, and the temptation. "It's not fair. I'll find another way—"

"You won't! Who else would be your anchor? Harry Graves? Don't think for a moment that you're doing this without an anchor!"

Nance was joking, and dead serious. And visiting the past was far safer with Nancy standing guard in Bower. Emma filled a bowl with ice cubes and set it on the floor between them. She'd started herself on what was becoming a familiar path, but stopped before she reached her destination.

"What's changed your mind?" Nancy demanded.

"I don't want to go to Paris empty-handed."

Em climbed the stairs to her bedroom, complaining about her sore ankle. She opened the top drawer of her dresser where, in a velvet-lined box, she kept the most precious things she'd brought out of the Teagarden house. Chief among them was the ebony-handled pocket knife, about three inches long with the blade folded into the handle, that had never been far from her father's pocket. It was a utilitarian blade, a tool for opening packages, cutting flowers, and whittling bits of wood. Dad had never needed a weapon; Emma did. Let Eleanor have her silly-looking wand and Blaise his sword, Emma's weapon of choice would be her father's pocket knife, smooth, warm, and comforting in her hand.

And what if she lost it? What if, like her here-and-now clothing, it didn't translate into the wasteland or from there into Paris? And what if it got that far, but disappeared on the return to Bower? The knife was a tangible connection to her father and her history. She *believed* it would become a powerful weapon in the subjective realm—but not until the engineering gene tested her over-all strategy with a less significant object—like the three-bladed Swiss Army knife she'd used as a Girl Scout, also in the dresser drawer, its plastic lanyard wound tight over the red case which was marred by a black ellipse where it had followed a hamburger onto the grill during her first overnight camping trip.

Halfway down the stairs, Nancy greeted Em with— "If we're considering instant replay, I'd like to have the number that Harry Graves gave you."

It was a reasonable, even wise, request, and Emma's initial reaction was cold, quiet fury. If Nancy had said even a single word in support of her request, Em would never have backed down. But Nancy knew her better than anyone alive—far better than Jeff—and waited silently until Emma simmered down and pulled one of the black books off the shelf. Harry's business card was inside the cover, along with all the paper Em had removed from Eleanor's suitcase.

Nancy looked at it quickly then handed the book back to Em. "I won't use it, Em, except in a real emergency."

"I trust you." She returned the book to the shelf. "If it comes down to choosing between the frying pan and the fire, Harry's your man."

With the lanyard double-looped around her wrist and the knife clutched between her hands, Emma settled into the straight-backed meditation posture.

"Don't pose," Nance suggested. "Forget I'm here and *relax.*"

That was easier said than done, but it was done. Practice had produced a ritual, like starting the car on a cold morning—tap the gas, count to three, turn the key, pray. Emma arrived in the wasteland wearing the blue dress, comfortable shoes, and clutching the knife. There were no surprises: the horizon was quiet, Blaise was still missing-in-action, and it was night outside Mariana's window. The same night. Once a curse-hunter found a useful moment in time, getting back there was as easy as getting to the wasteland itself.

Em slipped the lanyard around her neck—hardly the best place to store a weapon, but she needed both hands for balance when it came to wriggling out the window.

This time Emma was prepared for the drop. She hit the cobblestones and started walking through the fog. For caution's sake, she didn't try to retrace her steps—she didn't want to run into the crone again. The knife was a comfort around her neck, but only if she didn't have to use it.

She circled the inner square. Everything seemed familiar—the workmen, the horse-drawn, wood-filled wagons, the ice lurking between the cobblestones that threatened to wrench her ankle again with each step. Emma had hunkered down to tighten her shoelaces when the crone limped out of the fog. She had an animated conversation with one of the workmen and wound up giving him something—probably a coin—in exchange for the block of wood she dragged into position between the pyre and the platform. Another few moments passed and the crone turned and stared into the fog behind her.

Three centuries ago, when the here-and-now had swept across the Place de Grève, that woman hadn't turned around. An hour ago, from Emma's perspective, she'd done something to attract the woman's attention and changed a bit of the past forever. Tomorrow—the twenty-fourth of February, 1680—the crone might tell her friends: *I had the strangest feeling yesterday as I waited for La Voisin to burn . . .*

Eleanor said time was resilient. The adjustments that curse-hunters made to stop a curse from rising might change the past, but they didn't change history. Emma hoped Eleanor had gotten that part right.

The crone turned back toward the pyre and the workmen whom she hailed with words that left a few laughing, others scowling. She had a whole day to kill, and so did Emma, a wealth of time for the cold and damp to do their work. The crone had a jug to keep her warm. Em kept moving, looking for someone other than the crone whose thoughts she could invade, whose memories and knowledge she could ransack for images of Blaise Raponde, though the old woman was exactly what Em had come to

Paris to find. She had an interest in the criminal and an apparent sensitivity to curse-hunters.

The old woman might be a hunter herself!

Emma suppressed a shiver. The three curse-hunters she'd met—Eleanor, Harry, and Blaise—were, above all else, healthy specimens of the human race; she wasn't prepared for a doddering crone. It might not be possible, and certainly wouldn't be wise, to bond with another curse-hunter, with a person who knew the rules of the curse-hunters' game better than Emma herself. And the crone was drunk, to boot; her memory couldn't be trusted.

Good reasons all, but mostly Em stayed away from the crone because she was repelled by the idea that the crone might be far more typical of her seventeenth-century breed than Blaise Raponde.

There were others in the Place de Grève—revelers making their unsteady way home, tradesmen and women going about their business. Either the city never slept or the hour was closer to dawn than midnight. A chestnut vendor made his way across the square. Emma recognized his wares by their aroma. She'd never been fond of roasted chestnuts until she thought of holding the warm, little morsels in her increasingly chilled hands. She considered sampling his thoughts—he'd know Paris, lots of people, and his sacks of steaming chestnuts were keeping him warm.

It was a foolish notion, but Em didn't reject it entirely until she spotted another man lurking in a doorway. His cloak was dark and heavy with a hood drawn up for warmth and concealment. He stood in the shadows without leaning against the convenient walls. For a moment Emma thought the man was Blaise, minus the peacock-feathered hat. A second glance said no, this man was broader in the shoulders, shorter in the arms, but definitely keeping an eye on the Place de Grève. A criminal, she thought, rejecting the notions of a waiting lover or tradesman. Or he might be a cop—Matt's notes were largely based on the report of a cop.

A torch-lit wagon rolled by as Emma approached and a beam of light penetrated the hood. If it illuminated the face of Nicholas de la Reynie, then Europe's first chief of police had been a hard, implacable man. Emma reconsidered her plan to wade into the memories of those who took an interest in La Voisin's death—and considered it again, for Eleanor's sake.

Emma knew two ways to get inside the head of a long-dead human being: one was sheer accident, the other was to get to kissing distance and wait until something attracted their mutual attention. She learned a third when her target strode out of the shadow, headed toward her while she was still weighing possibilities. Indecision kept her nailed to the cobblestones; invisibility guaranteed a collision. Between breaths Emma was transported to the most subjective reality of all: the thoughts of another human being.

Her host's mind was every bit as unsavory as Em had feared, though quieter than expected—as if he were a man who habitually kept his private thoughts under lock and key. Emma made herself small as he prowled the Place de Grève. He knew the sights, sounds, and odors of a burning by heart and took pleasure from them, but he wasn't in the Place de Grève to witness an execution. Like Emma herself, the dark-minded man was looking for someone.

He scanned the workmen, recognizing a few, rejecting them all. He knew the crone and despised her. The pot calling the kettle black. But he was wary of the old woman, too, taking considerable care not to stand where she could see him. Prickly with frustration and annoyance, the man returned to the doorway shadows where Emma had first spotted him.

She waited until his mind was calm then loosed her mother's face into the slow-moving thoughts. It swirled a moment, as if he'd asked himself *Where did that come from?* then faded. Em was disappointed, but not surprised. She had higher hopes for the second name she released: La Voisin.

Derisive laughter and less respect than he'd given the crone on her stump echoed briefly in the man's otherwise quiet mind. He knew La Voisin. Of course he knew her—he was here, in the Place de Grève where she would die. Like bugs scuttling in a darkened kitchen, idle thoughts emerged from the man's memories: a loud, vainglorious woman—not half so clever as she believed herself to be and drunk more often than not, yet not without skill in her trade . . . Corpses—infants and the occasional adult male—rained through his thoughts. He knew La Voisin, all right. He knew her crimes . . . and, to Emma's astonishment, her flesh: the last flash before his mind went silent again was cold, yet unmistakable passion, favors given for favors received with no way for Emma Merrigan to distinguish one from the other.

Em almost withheld her third name, not wanting to learn that Blaise Raponde been part of the sordid world she'd discovered in her host's mind. But she'd come too far and needed the truth, or another version of it. Emma loosed the name and a face more detailed than her mother's had been. She waited, not long, for a reaction.

Derision and wariness were small disturbances compared to the contempt that swept down to swallow the face Emma had released. She became aware of the sword on her host's hip, the knife tucked into his boot, and the tense curl of his fingers as Raponde's face returned, cruel, but distorted—swollen, dark—*strangled*.

Had she stumbled into the mind of the man—the rival curse-hunter—who had or would murder him? Could she intervene to save Blaise's life? Should she? And if she did, what would happen to her, or Eleanor, one November three centuries removed from the Place de Grève?

Emma hadn't begun to sort through her questions when something drew her host's attention. Staring with his eyes, listening with his ears, Em perceived nothing, until he blinked slowly—

Open your other *eyes*, Eleanor had said the first time she'd escorted her daughter to the wasteland. *Your inner eyes.* If she'd had the sense God gave an ant, Em would have tested that inner vision the moment her feet hit the cobblestones of the Place de Grève, and if she had, she might have figured out that she was not at all invisible to the likes of her host.

With *his* inner vision—Emma saw a slack-jawed woman shimmering faintly in a long, blue dress. (Thank heaven for tiny blessings.) Fortunately for her, the cloaked man was as astonished as she was. Doubly fortunate, she caught his astonishment like the perfect wave and rode it back to her own consciousness. The last masculine thoughts Em perceived as she left were his self-disgust that she was escaping and his confidence that she wouldn't remain free for long.

Now, Nance. Now would be a real good time to haul me back to Bower.

But two shots of good fortune were Em's limit for the night. Space and time did not collapse around her. The Place de Grève stayed real beneath her feet. She was going to have to get back to the living room on her own and to do that she was going to have to get out of the square. Em started running before she decided where she'd run to and lost ground changing direction. She made it up out near the center of the Place, weaving through the workmen, who didn't notice her but took note of her pursuer.

While the workman shouted their incomprehensible French, Emma circled the pyre. She meant to hide in the deep shadows there and think her way back to Bower, but the crone—the drunk, second-sighted crone in her front-row seat—had her head up and was watching Em the way cats watched mice. Emma wrenched her ankle a second time pivoting away from the crone. Wincing with every stride, she ran toward the perimeter where, God willing, she'd find a street that led somewhere other than a dead end.

Inner vision didn't help much with the fog. Emma was forced to slow down when she got into the deeper shadows at the edge of the Place de Grève. She followed the first cobblestones that led away from the square and hurried past a half-dozen possible boltholes: pitch-black doorways or alleys where a panicked visitor from the future might collect her wits.

She pushed ahead until the street presented her with three choices: straight ahead, turn right into a narrow alley, or turn left and climb the wide steps to what appeared through the fog to be a church. Em chose the church without remembering Eleanor's warning that doors were a problem for an out-of-time curse-hunter. She threw herself against the unyielding panels once, twice, three times before accepting defeat. By then she could hear footfalls on the cobblestones between the church and the square.

Cursing silently, Em ran down the steps and along what would have been the straight-ahead street. The fog reeked of sewage and the cobblestones sloped downward to a mid-street gutter. Slowing down for safety's sake, she kept one hand on the wall as the street became a downhill slope. Soon, she told herself. Soon either Nancy would haul her back to Bower or she'd come to another alley or entrance where she could hunker down and compose the balloon-filled thoughts that would lift her out of Paris.

Emma found her doorway, though not before her ankle was screaming in protest. Balancing on her good foot, she wasted precious time with guilt and recriminations. She'd barely focused her thoughts on aspirin-shaped, helium-filled balloons when she heard not one but two footfall patterns, one in pursuit, the other ahead. She tested her foot. It held her weight and she pushed off into new territory.

The second set of footfalls *had* to be coincidence, Em told herself. Granting that the cloaked man was another curse-hunter, that he knew Paris, and that he had an accomplice or two squirreled around the city, there was no rational way she could be limping *toward* danger.

As if reason and logic ruled much in her life anymore.

Emma came to an intersection, dithered a moment, trying to outsmart herself, then turned right—and up the hill she'd just limped down. A streamlet too foul to freeze burbled through the treacherous cobblestones. She listened for footfalls and, hearing none, thought she was safe. Then she looked up and saw a familiar cloaked silhouette scarcely twenty feet ahead.

Fight or flight—the primal question—loomed in Em's mind. She had her Girl Scout knife; he had a sword. The answer seemed obvious. Emma spun on her good foot.

She expected to fall; she did not expect something huge and heavy to lunge out of a wall she would have sworn to heaven was solid. It wrapped ape arms around her and carried her toward the opposite wall. Fight instantly replaced flight as Emma's guiding principle. There was a chance she'd broken the ape's forearm squeezing it between her ribs and the wall they crashed into. For certain, Em had broken a rib but that didn't keep her from stomping her good heel down on the gorilla's instep. When its viselike grip loosened, she lashed out with her elbows and let out a scream.

The ape made a very human sound and clamped a gloved hand over her mouth. Em fought for air and found herself with her right arm wrenched brutally against her spine and her neck pressed backward to the snapping point. Even so, she didn't stop struggling.

"Quiet!" the ape warned—in masculine English— torquing her arm a bit closer to fracture.

Reluctantly Em obeyed because she could hear the cloaked man's footfalls on the other side of a door that wasn't open now and hadn't been open a moment earlier when—apparently—she'd passed clean through it.

Someone had come to her rescue—maybe. If it was Harry Graves and if he'd let go of her as soon as the danger had passed, Em would have swallowed her pain and outrage to thank him. But he didn't relax a whit so she stomped him again and bit down hard on the leather pressed against her mouth. In an instant Emma was face-down on rough wooden planks and listening to the *hiss* of steel as a sword left its scabbard.

Not Harry, she realized as she spun onto her back, but Blaise Raponde—minus his ridiculous hat—illuminated by lamplight from the top of a stairway. He had his sword pointed at her throat and looked every bit as cruel as he had in the cloaked man's mind. A woman shouted down the stairs; Em's French was good enough to translate— "Who goes there? Is anyone downstairs?"

They could see each other, she and Blaise Raponde, but it seemed that the woman of the house couldn't see either of them. Blaise laid the index finger of his off-weapon hand across his lip. Em caught his meaning and didn't twitch until they were surrounded by darkness. Indeed, she hadn't twitched at all when Raponde seized her shoulder and yanked her upright.

At least this time he opened the door before shoving her out into the street.

Nine

Emma stayed upright as she lurched across the street, propelled by an obviously—and perhaps understandably—angry ghost. She had a half-dozen questions lined up on her tongue, but wasn't about to ask them—or say anything at all—until he had sheathed that sword. The street was so narrow that the sword would have pierced her throat if Raponde completely straightened the arm that held it between them. Rather than lower the weapon, he sidestepped along the opposite wall until he had the right distance for a steady threat.

"You will explain yourself, Madame Emma."

She matched him, snarl and growl. "I'm looking for my mother."

"Your mother is not here."

"You'll excuse me if I'm not satisfied by the word of a man who's got a sword pointed at my neck." When it came to anger, Emma's had been tempered in the heat of divorce. She *was* terrified, but she'd be damned, literally, before she'd let anyone see her fear.

His wrist twitched. The sword tip swung ten degrees and came back. "Why seek your mother *here*, in this place, in this time?"

"Because you as much as said she was here when you

said the rogue had taken Eleanor to *your* Paris. This is your Paris, isn't it? I'm only following you."

"My city is vast and time is vaster, still. You did not follow me, Madame Emma; you *could* not. Yet you came *here*. Not merely to Paris, but to this moment of Paris, this place within Paris. What brought you *here*?"

His shoulder dropped and the sword inched closer to Em's vulnerable neck. She couldn't see the tip, but felt it catch and pull on the white-lace trim of Mariana's gown. Would Blaise kill her? *Could* he kill her? Were either of them, standing in the Parisian fog speaking, to her ears, a credible version of American English, real enough to die?

Belief, Raponde had said. Belief was everything. He had believed in Eleanor's wand and his own wound. Would Emma believe in her own death? When she swallowed hard, Em felt cold metal against her skin. She wasn't religious, but she believed in death.

"*I* brought me. Remember that window in that room I made—the room where you got your shelter? You left your Bible behind, by the way, when you lit out. I don't have it with me. I climbed out the window of that room and found myself—" Em stopped herself. She wouldn't tell Raponde anything he didn't already know and she wouldn't mangle Parisian geography with her Midwestern accent—no sense in alienating him worse than he already was. "I found myself in your Paris because I figured, frankly, that if I could find you, I'd probably find Eleanor because I'm starting to think—I'm damned near convinced at this very moment—that you're *exactly* what she thought you were."

That was a lie. Emma couldn't parse the reasons why Blaise had her pinned against the wall, but a roguish nature wasn't among them. She would stake her life on that. She was staking it and she won her bet—maybe—when the sword flashed and pointed at its scabbard rather than her throat.

"I am not a rogue," Blaise insisted. The blade slid home with a hiss and clack that Em would never forget.

"A rogue would not tell you to go home before you sink further into affairs you do not understand—or get me killed."

"Can you die, Blaise Raponde? Were you hurt the last time I saw you—whenever that really was—or was that just for show? I'm living my life in a straight line. Maybe I'm here, now, but I know where I was yesterday and where I'll be tomorrow, I hope. And it will be a week, an honest week of the Earth spinning on its axis as it spins around the sun before my ankle stops hurting—"

Blaise's expression tightened. The two of them weren't headed for another religion-versus-science debate, were they? Well-dressed people in late-seventeenth-century Paris *knew* that the Earth went around the sun and not the other way around? This wasn't the time or place for debate.

"You are truly Madame Mouse," he said with little of the anger that had tinged all his previous words. "You don't understand yourself and you can't, you truly can't, perceive the difference between one who hunts curses and one who is himself—or herself—a curse."

Momentarily speechless, Emma simply shook her head in disbelief. "Good lord, Blaise—I *told* you that the first time you hauled my chestnuts out of the frying pan. I'm getting better, though—if I keep on surviving mistakes, there's no telling how much of this craziness I'll manage to piece together. I've figured out that I'm not always invisible when my mind's here and my body's back in Bower. You can see me. An old woman in the square back there saw. And the guy who was chasing me, he could see me very clearly. I got inside *his* head; that's how I knew. I saw myself—not a pretty sight, I must confess—"

"Emma—"

For the first time, Blaise dropped the "Madame." He reached out, but Em eluded him easily.

"What?" she demanded irately. "Yes, I'm winging it. I'm making it up as I go, I'm risking God knows what for a woman I don't know and probably don't like. I'd rather not be winging under these circumstances. I'd really like to have someone I trust teach me what I need to know. But hey, I looked in the course catalog and no one's offering Curse-Hunting 101 this semester. And if there's one thing I *have* figured out, it's that the only thing worse than winging it is tying on to the wrong mentor."

"Have you considered the man, your father—Harry Graves."

"Harry Graves is *not* my father. But yes—he's offered, sort of, and I've considered his offer, sort of. You know, one of the few really useful things my mother did manage to tell me went something like 'We used to be tribes, now we're a global corporation.' Harry Graves sits on the board of that corporation." Em took a breath and cast her earlier caution into the fog. "He's part of something called the Atlantis curia—does *that* name mean anything to you?"

"No," Blaise replied without a heartbeat's hesitation. "Never heard of it."

Too fast, too glib, Em thought. She'd asked the wrong question. "Maybe not the Atlantis Curia, then, but you've heard of the curia before."

"Curiae, councils, and unholy orders. Every generation someone takes the idea to be lord over the hunters. The idea, but nothing more. There are no hunter *tribes* in my Paris, Madame Mouse. Families, perhaps—but families do not last. Trust comes hard among people who walk. Your family is important because you share a path . . . for a while. It is hard to change a shared path. Hard, but not impossible. In time, even a father and his son follow a different path. *Enfin*, the man you trust the least is the one who shares your blood."

He had the sad, sour look of a man who knew exactly whereof he spoke and, once again, the manners of the man who had saved Emma from curses on more than one occasion. She had no doubt that she would have been in for a very uncomfortable time had the cloaked man gotten ahold of her, but did the fact that Blaise Raponde was once again his gentlemanly self mean that he was any less dangerous?

Em measured her options, staring at a worried man and being stared at in return. She was, she reminded herself, a mystery to him, and he didn't have the resources of a university library to fall back upon. However unwisely, Emma was leaning toward reconciliation when Blaise cleared his throat.

"Go home, Madame Emma. Go back to your own place and time before you make a knot no one can untie."

She shook her head, never mind that she'd been desperate to return to Bower before Blaise grabbed her. That was then; this was a new now. "Don't tell me what to do. Eleanor's my mother and I'm going to pursue her for my own reasons. I don't know why, but I'd rather not lie or deceive you, which is what I'd be doing if I said I'd go home. I know this time and place. I can return, and I will . . . until I find what I'm looking for."

"You were two strides out of the grasp of a man who would use you like a beast before he sold you to your enemies."

"I'll stay out of his way next time . . . out of his head, too."

Blaise slashed his hand through the air. "You know *nothing*, Madame Mouse. You can change the past, but you can never undo what you have done. Jean le Peu—"

(Or was that Jean le Peau? A little bit of John or John the Skin? Even at the height of her linguistic powers, Em could read French far better than she heard it. Either way, Skinny John and Blaise were known to each other.)

"—will remember you. He remembers you now and he will recognize you should you return to this night. If the bridge is swaying and you run across it without falling into the river, do you believe you can run across it again and again without danger? You have used up your luck on the first crossing. Do not risk the second! And above all else, do *not* cross your own path."

"I'll come back tomorrow, on the twenty-fourth of February. If I don't find what I'm looking for then, I'll sneak a peek at one of the other executions. My notes say there were about three dozen of them."

Her companion started when Em rattled off that information. He'd seemed especially surprised that she knew the date. She expected a question but heard a familiar request instead.

"Go home, Madame Emma. Please, go home. I don't want to see you harmed."

An odd choice of words that, always assuming Em heard any of his words correctly, but she'd take advantage of them all the same. "If you don't want to see me harmed, then teach me what I need to know to survive here and show me what I've come to see. You said Eleanor was 'behind' Paris. Where's that?"

"*I?* You want me to be your teacher?" Blaise backed into the wall trying to escape Emma's questions. "*Pardieu*, Madame Emma, I am no teacher. I have no patience. I travel alone, always alone."

"You've already taught me more than anyone else which, granted, isn't saying much. You did a pretty good job with the shelter—convincing me that I could create it, and holding my hand when it started to fall apart."

"No. It is impossible. Go back to your home. Tend to your mother's body while I seek her soul and spirit. You have had my word from the beginning. Let that be enough, Madame Emma, and return to your own time and place."

"I'll come back, Blaise; I swear it. I don't care about knots or tangles. Better you show me where she is."

"I should disgrace myself if I took you to that depth. You are too young, Madame Emma. Too innocent."

Of all the reasons he could hide behind, those were among the least effective. "I'm not young but I am a fast learner. I'll pay real close attention to whatever you say, so long as I'm learning something."

"This is foolishness," Blaise complained, but Em knew then that she had him. "You must swear to me. You must give me your *parole*—your word as one of us—that you will do whatever I tell you to do, whenever, wherever I tell you to."

Emma hesitated. She didn't want to lie to him, but off the top of her head she could think of a dozen situations in which she'd willfully break her *parole* like so many eggs in an omelette. She was bound to disappoint him, but she said—

"You have my word," even knowing that she played a dangerous game with a man who believed that honor required—no, honor *demanded* a physical defense.

Raponde hesitated. The man who'd died in the late seventeenth century, then survived another three centuries in the wasteland, seemed to have some suspicion of her honesty, some notion of the pragmatism that marked her culture. Emma kept an eye on his right hand, the hand that would reach for his sword. It remained at his side.

"Come, then. We have some walking before us."

Some walking! If Paris were Bower, Em would have sworn they walked from the Maisonettes to the library and back again. Between the fog and the narrow, twisting streets, she was totally lost and completely dependent on her companion's sense of direction. She suspected him of trying to exhaust and discourage her, but she'd dreamt up a pair of walking shoes as good as anything Nike or Reebok had ever produced for this trip to Paris and kept up despite her sore ankle.

A chilly predawn breeze tore apart the fog and brightened the sky. The streets of Paris grew lively. Ordinary people seemed to see and avoid Blaise Raponde. He had, Em guessed, a place in the city where he'd lived. Emma was a tourist without a place; she dodged as best she could and endured waves of nausea when there was no room and some stranger walked through her like a shadow. With furtive glances, Em knew Blaise was watching her, grinning smugly each time her stomach heaved, but she refused to concede defeat.

"Meet their eyes," Blaise whispered while she reeled

from a particularly unpleasant encounter with a man toting two jugs of what *had* to be urine. "Make them get out of your way."

"Make people see me!" Em snarled. "Isn't that what I'm *not* supposed to do?"

Another sly smile. "It is one thing to be invisible, another to be seen, and another still to be noticed but not remembered. On a crowded street, you wish to be seen, but not remembered. It is very simple, simpler than making a shelter."

Emma gave Blaise a scowl she hoped he would remember and tried to face down the next pedestrian. The attempt backfired: the woman walked right into her and for an instant Emma was awash in laundry and the price of soap. Blaise caught her arm before she fell.

"The idea, Madame Mouse, is to make them avoid you, not defy them to walk—"

Without warning, he spun Em back-first into a doorway where he trapped her in a strong-armed embrace.

"Damn you! Let go of me!"

Blaise had a demand of his own. "Don't fight against me!"

Astonished and outraged, Emma tried to escape, but Blaise anticipated her moves, even her attempt to grind her heel into his instep. In a matter of seconds, she'd succeeded only in bruising her nose against his jaw and wedging herself more thoroughly into a corner.

"If you cherish your life, kiss me. Help us both."

"Help you do *what*?" Emma hissed with all the malice she could summon.

"Fool the rogue walking this way," Blaise replied and stifled her protests with his lips.

If he was lying, Em thought as she let herself cooperate. *If* he was lying— Blaise Raponde *was* everything she found attractive in a man. The last time she'd kissed an attractive man, she'd wound up marrying him and come to regret it. She'd sworn off attractive men when she asked Jeff for a divorce. The risks far outweighed the rewards.

But he wasn't lying, at least not lying about a rogue. There was a presence in the air around them: cold, yet electric, as if lightning might strike with ice rather than fire. It was unlike anything Em had encountered before and nothing she'd forget.

"Emma . . ."

Em uncurled her fists and let her hands roam beneath his open coat. She was rusty, perhaps, but not without experience, not ignorant of what she enjoyed, nor incapable of communicating her desires. And all the while they touched and talked in a language that required no words, Emma told herself that it was a deception meant for a mutual enemy, an act without meaning for the actors involved.

She knew she was lying.

If Blaise was lying—

The icy presence intensified, then faded. Emma didn't need anyone to tell her the outside danger had passed. If Blaise was ready to end the charade, so was she. She lowered her arms. He wasn't, and unsure when in any time or place the next opportunity might arise, Em didn't insist.

"It's gone," he whispered when at least another minute had passed.

"I know. I told you I was a fast learner."

Soft laughter surrounded Emma, then a final, gentler kiss, and at last she was standing on her feet again. There wasn't much light in the doorway. Em could contemplate Blaise's face without seeing too much and be studied in return without feeling too wretchedly self-conscious.

"I didn't understand what you meant, at first," she confessed.

"Neither did I."

He held out his hand. Emma took it without saying anything. Double meanings were the plague of passion and there was nothing, really, to say that hadn't been said. There was a bed back in Mariana's room. It was a bit narrow for two people, unless they let nothing come between them; and they wouldn't, if it came to that.

Blaise set a faster pace. Em didn't slow him down with questions. They'd escaped a rogue, the sun was up, and the streets were getting busier—any of which were good reasons to move quickly. If there were other reasons, she didn't want to know.

People got out of their way, parting like the Red Sea and never seeming to wonder why. That was Blaise's doing. With sunlight filling Paris, Em had succumbed to the tourist disease, her attention drawn by every new or different thing she passed. It was easier to gawk than think about what had happened in the doorway.

They came to an unbroken wall, a churchyard, Em guessed by the roofs she saw on the other side. She expected a garden, but when Blaise led her through the gate, she found herself in a muddy field the likes of which she'd never imagined.

There were no graves or gravestones, only mounds of dirt and open pits ten feet square. Priests, mourners, and a white-robed choir gathered on the perimeter of the largest pit. While they sang, wept, and prayed, workmen used ropes to sling shroud-wrapped corpses over the edge, one right after the other, four in all. There were more where the four had come from. A dozen or more corpses were stacked like logs, trussed up in pale sheets, with ropes already attached around their necks and ankles.

That was not, however, the sight which stopped Emma in her tracks and gave her the dry heaves. No, that honor went to the unfinished pit near the center of the yard where a gang of masked workmen wielded their shovels and tossed up a steady stream of dirt, bone, and chunks of rotting flesh. When she turned away, her eyes fell on rats and more bones—*human* bones she thought, until she spotted the bloated carcass of a pig. A flock of ravens swooped in, challenging the rats for the pig.

When one of the birds rose up with a foot-long tangle of vaguely blond hair trailing from its beak, Em had seen enough. Light-headed and weak in the knees, she didn't want to collapse in the mud, but she didn't have the

strength to stop it from happening. The boneyard faded as
Emma fell, replaced by the colors and textures of her living room.

"Emma!"

That voice was Nancy's.

"Madame Emma!"

That voice came from Blaise, who caught Em before
she splattered in the mud. He carried her to a damp, stone
slab where he set her down gently. The morbid smell set
off another round of heaves—and that despite knowing
that she'd smelled nothing at full strength since she'd
climbed out of Mariana's window. Bending forward, trying to get the blood flowing back toward her brain, Emma
spotted a broken, mud-caked skull at her feet: an infant's
skull—no bigger than her two fists clenched together. Em
raised her head in time to see a dog run away from the
half-dug pit with an arm in its mouth.

"Oh, no—" she complained as the world began to tilt.
Maybe this time she'd make it all the way home. "Nancy?"

Blaise grabbed Emma's shoulders before she fell off
the inverted sarcophagus—she recognized its function
now. He stood in front of her, blocking her view.

"You have never set foot in a cemetery?"

"This is *not* a cemetery."

"This is the holiest ground in Paris, Madame Emma—
the Cemetery of the Innocents. This is a sacred place. No
soil consumes flesh faster than the soil of the Innocents. If
you believed in God, you'd not be frightened."

"I'm not frightened. I'm—" Em rested her forehead
against Blaise's coat. "It's different, that's all. Different."
She took another deep breath. This time she was prepared
for the stench, and the sounds, and the sights when she
stood up. "My mother's here someplace, with the
corpses?"

Considering Eleanor's condition in Meadow View, that
seemed a plausible assumption.

"Not here, Madame Emma. Not *in* Paris at all, but behind it—*beyond* it. Au-delà. Are you able to walk? We do not have much time."

Blaise offered his hand and they set out for a wide-open door in the church wall. As soft as the ground was and as grateful as Em was to have someone to lean on while she tried to walk and keep the blue dress out of the mud simultaneously, she couldn't help but note that they left no footprints behind them as they walked.

Em pointed the discrepancy out to Blaise when they reached the door and asked, "What would happen if some-one did notice and called the authorities, whoever they are?"

"Nothing." He squeezed her hand. "We would each melt away—you *can* do that much, can't you, Madame Emma? You can retreat au-delà?"

She shrugged. "I've done it, sort of. I was kind of try-ing to do that when you grabbed me on the street back there and again when you caught me on my way to the mud."

Blaise scowled. "It is as easy to leave as it is to arrive, Madame Emma. I do not understand why you find one more difficult than the other. But we must be careful, then. And quick." Blaise squinted at the sky where the sun had just become visible above the rooftops.

"What are you looking for?" Em asked. "Is sunlight a problem?" It hadn't been when she'd explored the eleventh century. Neither curse-hunters nor curses nor, she assumed, rogues were subject to vampire rules.

"I'm marking the time until midday. There is enough." He stepped over the sill into the church sanctuary.

"Enough time for what?"

"To show you where the rogue holds your mother and to get you out again. I wouldn't want to leave you sud-denly."

Emma grabbed his sleeve and stayed outside the church. "I don't like the sound of that."

"While I lived, I was in the habit of rising no earlier than noon, now I haunt my own dreams. When my living self awakens, the dreams end and I return au-delà. It would be some time before I could rejoin you—very much time before I could rejoin you here-and-now. I will see you safe in your little house before that happens."

"I hope you didn't have any early-morning appointments scheduled for February twenty-third, then."

Blaise gave Em the same narrow look he'd given her before when she'd mentioned the date, then held out his hand to help her over the sill. They had the sanctuary to themselves, which was fine until they came to the iron-work door fitted into the floor behind the altar. According to Blaise, the door to the crypt wasn't supposed to be closed, much less locked, but on February 23, 1680, it had been both.

"Wait here," he told Em. "I'll return with someone who has the keys, and a lantern, too."

"What *is* the problem with doors? You crashed both of us through that one when that Jean-guy was closing in on me, and you *opened* it, no trouble at all, when we left."

"Opening a door is hard, tiring work, crashing through—as you call it, Madame Emma—is worse. I've already done it twice in one night, I'd rather not try it a third time—not knowing that you may need help leaving the place where I am—foolishly—leading you. Far easier to take advantage of someone who can wield the keys and a lantern for us. I'll return as soon as I find him."

Em nodded absently, already determined to test her own cleverness against the lock. She missed him closing in for a parting kiss, a quick reminder of business left unfinished in the Paris streets. After a silent, one-handed bound over the altar rail, Blaise disappeared in the sanctuary shadows. Emma lost a few seconds to daydreams then forced her curiosity back to the wrought-iron door.

It was appropriately solid. Her arm fit through the herringbone ironwork; her body did not magically glide around or through the gaps. Yet when Emma tried to grasp one of those black metal slats, the metal proved elusive, as though she were a drunken fool. And when, on the fourth or fifth try, Em managed to wrap her fingers around a bit of ironwork, the texture was indescribably *wrong*, and try as she might, she couldn't make the door rattle on its hinges.

The door, she concluded, was real enough to affect her; she wasn't real enough to affect it. Blaise, who had lived here and who continued, in some sense, to live in Paris, was realer than she was, which accounted, perhaps, for how he'd opened the door, but not for how he'd managed to crash through it without damaging it or them.

Grimly, Em named the lessons she'd missed growing up motherless in Bower: *Doors 101, Rogue-Spotting,* and *Do-It-Yourself Shelters*—not to mention the elective course in chronologically incorrect relationships.

Footsteps put an end to Emma's distraction. A solitary man—a priest of some sort by his loose, flapping robe—charged up the aisle. Em ducked for cover but the priest, with a lantern in one hand and a key ring jangling in the other, had only one thing on his mind: unlock the crypt door.

Quite a coincidence, Em thought from her hiding place between two rows of high-backed, pew-type benches. *When Blaise gets back*—

The door clanked open. The priest turned around, looking for something. His mouth opened. Emma read her name on his lips and gagged down a dose of idiocy. Blaise had said he'd return with someone who could open the door. She was the fool for assuming that meant he'd come back with a companion.

"Sorry," Em mumbled on her way to the open door.

The priest—Blaise—said nothing, but swept his lantern toward the crypt, indicating that Emma should descend first. The flickering light did nothing to improve Em's view of the steep, narrow, and treacherously uneven stairs. She longed for a handrail or simply a hand, but as neither was available, she took the steps one at a time, never relying on her twisted ankle for strength or balance.

The crypt itself was a claustrophobic, rectangular box,

black as hell, and pocked with bone-filled niches. Two
stone sarcophagi took up most of the floor, and a life-size
crucifix, heavy on Christ's agony, dominated the short
wall opposite the stairway. The air was twitchy with soot
and stale incense. Emma tried breathing through her
mouth, but it was too late. Once she started sneezing, she
couldn't stop, not until the young priest had let out a
shriek of terror and raced up the stairs, taking the lantern
with him and slamming the iron door like a gong.

"Madame? Are you—?"

Raponde didn't know what to say. Emma couldn't
blame him. She sat on a sarcophagus wishing for a handkerchief. "Where I come from, we have *laws* against air
like this." Silence of the sort that comedians complained
about followed Em's witless attempt at humor. She wondered how many other ways she'd find to embarrass herself before this adventure came to an end. "Are you still
here or have I driven you off like that priest?"

A faintly luminous and familiar face popped into view.
"I am here, madame, and if you're able, we can continue."

Sniffling—because she refused to wipe her nose on her
sleeve—Emma felt her way across the crypt. She found
Blaise on his knees between the second sarcophagus and
the wall. There was, he claimed, another way out of the
crypt, the way to a rogue's subjective reality.

Em strained her eyes. "I see a trapdoor—an open trapdoor that I'd swear on my mother's grave wasn't there
when I came down the stairs. Please tell me I don't have
to leap into that hole."

Ten

"I'll go first, Madame Mouse, and catch you before you fall." He gave her another of his cryptic looks. "Your mother is not dead, even if she is in a grave. So long as she draws breath in the world God created, she is very much alive. She belongs to Him, as you belong to Him, regardless of what you believe."

While Emma considered futility and theology—again—Blaise lowered himself through the hole, which was not so deep that his hands didn't show above the crypt floor when he reached up for her. Em took a deep breath and swung her legs over the edge. He caught her at the waist, but did not immediately lower her to the floor.

"If you would pull the door shut—?"

Emma had read enough mystery novels—not to mention having lived through the Watergate break-in—to believe it was wise to close the doors behind you when you were skulking about. She wasn't terribly surprised that the door moved when she tugged on the edges—it truly hadn't been there before and couldn't be any realer than she was. What was surprising was that she didn't catch her fingers when the heavy planks slammed down and that the noise didn't summon every curse in the wasteland.

"This way," Blaise said, leading Em around one of two

stone coffins and up a steep, narrow, and treacherous flight of stairs.

"The crypt in reverse. I should have guessed. Au-delà. Beyond. On the far side of. I looked it up in the dictionary, but I didn't *think*." Emma knew she was babbling, but she couldn't stop herself. "Behind Paris, you said: Eleanor's behind Paris. That's what I was searching for, the other side of Paris, Paris in a looking glass. I suppose Lewis Carroll was one of us and a white rabbit's going to be running up to say we're late for tea with the Red Queen. We're not in a wasteland, we're in goddamned *Wonderland*—"

Blaise hissed at her to be quiet. Em whispered a quick apology and swallowed her budding hysteria.

"Stay close to me. Don't argue. Don't fight. Don't talk at all. Do you understand?"

There was an unspoken *"or else"* tacked on to the question. Emma had a knee-jerk habit of rejecting ultimatums, but she kept a grip on her temper and her hysteria. That didn't leave much energy for rational thought.

"Good. We are here to see if this is, *enfin*, where the rogue has hidden your mother. When we find her—*if* we find her—we will leave the way we have come. If anything is amiss— If *I* decide that anything is amiss, we leave and *you* do not try at all to return. Is this clear? Remember, madame, you gave me your *parole*."

Em nodded a second time. Silence spared her another round of embarrassment: she was wrong about what she'd see at the top of the crypt stairs. They hadn't emerged into a mirrored version of the 1680 Parisian church they'd left behind, though it was a close cousin. Reflexively, Emma looked around for inverted crucifixes and other black-magic paraphernalia and was relieved when she found none. Whatever else Eleanor's rogue captor might be, it wasn't a Satanist.

Blaise suddenly lost his silvery glow, leaving Em like the full moon at midnight, bathing him in reflected light. He was staring, obviously waiting for her to stifle her glow. She tried—she'd done it once before, with Eleanor—but the trick was beyond her now. Blaise made a small gesture, rather like flicking away a bit of dust. Em felt nothing, but the light which had surrounded her was gone.

"How—?" she began.

Blaise touched his finger to her lips, reminding her that she'd agreed to be quiet. With a sigh and a scowl, Em obeyed.

There was some ambient light in the sanctuary—the wasteland's shifty, purplish light. The object that stood in place of the Parisian altar was dark, plain stone—unnaturally plain stone that left Emma thinking about the generic objects in her version of Mariana's workroom, until Blaise took her by the elbow. He'd drawn his sword; Em hadn't heard it slide free of the scabbard. The crystal set into its pommel glowed with an amber light. She felt no inclination to talk or bare her little Girl Scout knife.

They stayed in the shadows against the wall, creeping slowly toward the door which, in Paris, would have opened onto the cemetery and the jagged teeth of the city's rooftops. In the wasteland the skyline scene had the shapes and size of Paris but with an abandoned, unfinished air, as if whoever had imitated God here had run out of creative juices partway through.

The sky was wasteland magenta, and the Parisian mud had been transformed into familiar dry, crumbling dirt. Blaise kept them close to the wall where the ground was soft enough for footprints and they left theirs behind. Not all the yard was so impressionable. A spiderweb of hardened lines connected the wasteland grave pits, one of which seethed with flames, and fair copies of the Innocents' boneyard statues. Paths, Em realized and stopped short, considering the implications.

Blaise tugged at her sleeve. Their eyes met. His were narrow and calculating. If trusting Blaise Raponde was a mistake, then the odds were good that the piper was headed Em's way right now with his hand out for cash.

Blaise tugged again, brandishing the sword at the flaming pit. Emma caught sight of the crystal pommel against his wrist, shining brighter now and darker, like the flames themselves, and pulled herself free.

Eleanor Merrigan was in the pit, in the flames. Emma knew it beyond doubt, the same way she knew that if she thought about making a fist, her right hand would close. The rogue had brought Eleanor here. The question was, as it had been from the beginning: was Blaise the rogue?

Emma was ready to face a rogue. It was the shame of being wrong about Blaise, of poor judgment when it came to the men in her life, that nailed her feet to the ground.

Three strikes and you're out, Em thought when Blaise grabbed for her wrist. She leaned backward and made him miss, then strode forward of her own free will, expecting to march up the brink to look down on what had become of Eleanor and—quite possibly—join her.

But Blaise kept to the shadows, following the wall until a mound of dirt was between them and the flaming pit and the pit was between them and the church. The gate which in the Paris of 1680 had separated the cemetery from the city stood open, revealing a desolated square lined with buildings that looked solid enough at first glance. Emma didn't give them a second glance. Once she noticed the imitation streets, the imitation buildings no longer mattered. The streets ended in familiar, flat emptiness.

Better the frying pan than the fire?

Emma hadn't decided when Blaise scabbarded his sword and, hunched over like any soldier in enemy territory, belly-crawled up the mound of dirt. There wouldn't be a better time to run . . . if she could leave before she'd looked into that pit. Em got two steps toward the gate, stopped, turned around, and joined Blaise on the mound. Stretched out on the dirt, Em felt more exposed than safe and she learned nothing when she stuck her head over the top. The angle was wrong for seeing the bottom of the pit, and light from the flames hurt her eyes.

Minding her promises, Emma tapped Blaise's shoulder. She pointed at the pit and was reminded that she'd never been good at charades.

"Curses," Blaise replied to whatever question he thought she'd asked. "By the dozen and shrunk down to their very essence."

He spoke in a normal voice; Em wouldn't have heard a whisper. A steady hum, rather like a hive of baritone bees, rose from the pit to drown out lesser sounds. If Blaise could speak, then she could too—

"Eleanor? Is that her prison?"

"Your guess is as good as mine. Time is short—" He picked up a dirt clod—another difference between here and Paris: no bones, no corpses, no stink of death. "Let's stir the pot and see what boils out."

In a night marked by bad ideas, questionable judgment, and unpleasant surprises, that had to be the worst. Emma rose up, lunging for his hand, and caught his cuff before he could hurl the clod into the pit.

"There's *got* to be a better way—"

Blaise stiffened. Emma couldn't have moved him if she'd hung all her weight from his wrist. For two painful heartbeats, she thought she'd committed her last error, but Blaise was content to give her another calculated glower before lowering his arm.

"So we wait. How long, Madame Emma? How long can you remain au-delà?"

It was a trick question, and for her life, Em didn't know the answer, so she told the truth: "I don't know." That wasn't the right answer. His eyes narrowed to unreadable slits. "I'm not alone," she said quickly, unable to recall if she'd mentioned Nancy before. "I've got a friend sitting with me—with my body—to pull me back, if something happens to me while I'm here."

"Wise."

Raponde dropped the clod. It broke into pieces when it hit the ground. Emma released his cuff and, with neither thought nor reason, cradled her arm beneath her breast.

The pit with its tangle of curses was undoubtedly dangerous, but her companion's mood swings were more disturbing. If Blaise Raponde assaulted her, she hadn't a
prayer. Strength and speed, though, didn't always go together. She could hitch up Mariana's gown and make a
run for the open wasteland. Nancy might notice the
change in her breathing and haul her out—

"I wouldn't," Blaise warned.

Had he read her mind or simply noticed that she was
staring out through the gate? Emma chose to believe in her
own foolishness rather than another paranormal power.
She crouched down in the dirt again, dividing her attention
between the pit and her companion, waiting for something
to react to. She didn't have to wait long. Light flickered in
the sanctuary. Raponde noticed it too. He didn't have to
remind Em to be quiet; she could barely breathe for the
tension.

Four people and one will-o'-the-wisp curse emerged
through the door they'd used. Once in the yard, the quartet formed a square around the curse. Then together and
without ceremony they walked a path that led to the
seething pit. The surrounded curse was a poor, spindly
representative of its kind, a narrow whirl of red-orange
flame no more than twelve feet high. It couldn't hold a
candle to the monsters that had swept up Eleanor, unless
it had been weakened prior to emerging from the sanctuary.

As for the escort itself, they were refugees from the
Paris that Em and Blaise had left behind. Each was
wrapped in the faint silvery light Blaise had quenched. Although Blaise, Eleanor, and Harry Graves referred to
rogues as sexless, the four approaching the pit were
evenly divided between men and women. The women
bracketed the social ladder. One of them was tall, blond,
and dressed to meet the king in yards upon yards of pale
satin and lace, tightly fitted above the waist and scarcely
covering her breasts at all, while the other woman wore
the drab, shapeless layers of the working poor. The aristo-

crat marched in the second rank while the worker marched up front beside a short-haired man with a dark complexion and a monkish robe. The second man in the second rank was a lithe, adolescent with curled hair that framed his face and tumbled onto his shoulders. Em might have pegged him for a woman had he not been dressed in matching striped knee breeches and greatcoat. He, more than the others, looked like a rake as well as a rogue. His hat (a tamer combination of felt and feathers than the oddity that Blaise usually wore) sat at a steep angle among his curls, and his coat hung open to reveal a loose-fitting shirt and a casually knotted neck cloth.

Emma cast a sidelong glance Blaise's way. *His* attention was focused on the blonde aristocrat, and his expression—if Em dared to trust her judgment where Blaise Raponde was concerned—conveyed deep worry and shock.

The procession halted some ten feet short of the pit, some forty feet away from the mound where Emma and Blaise lay in the dirt like flounder fish. The monk left his place in the left front corner and approached the edge of the pit alone. He clapped his hands once. The sound echoed and hung in the air, commanding attention, though nothing happened.

Emma thought she saw anxiety forming on the rogues' faces. She assumed they were rogues. They might be curse-hunters for all she knew; she'd been wrong about so many things. The monk clapped his hands a second time in a staccato burst, and still, nothing happened. She turned again to Blaise. His attention hadn't shifted. His eyes were on the blonde and his fingers dug the loose dirt like claws.

Who is she? Em wanted to ask. *What makes her special? Is she the one who wounded you?* Em looked to see if the woman carried her mother's tacky wand. She couldn't spot it amid the yards of satin, which proved or disproved nothing. Emma hadn't realized Eleanor was carrying a weapon until it had appeared in her hand.

Frustration was a momentarily more powerful emotion than fear. Emma hovered on the verge of asking her questions, then the pit went silent and the seething flames began to rise, hauled out of the ground on an invisible line, like so much seaweed dangling from a lobsterman's trap. No, like so many *eels*, because they writhed while they burnt. And they sang; all the locusts of Moses couldn't drown that droning song. The escorted curse arched upward, joining the others. For a heartbeat there was silence, then there was a scream and many things became perfectly, horribly clear to Em.

The scream had come from her mother as yet another curse fastened itself to her. It was the sound which had echoed off the university hospital walls in November and faintly in Meadow View the other evening. Em didn't have to know exactly how the curses were consuming her mother; it was enough to know they were weakening her until the magic moment when her defenses cracked.

It was metaphysical rape. Her mind's eye filled with memories of science films and sperm swarming an unfertilized egg. The image pushed Emma over the edge of reason. Trembling, she rose to her knees. If she couldn't free her mother—and no madness could blind Emma to *that* impossibility—then she could put an end to the torture. One of the first lessons she'd learned in the wasteland— before she knew how ignorant and outclassed she was— was how to transform her rage into a stream of fire. It might not be enough . . . Almost certainly it wouldn't be enough, but Em wasn't thinking about consequences as she rose from her knees to her feet and began a slow descent toward the pit.

The rogues noticed Emma. They focused their attention on her and she could see them clearly, especially the drab woman in front who spoke directly into Em's consciousness.

You're pathetic, Emma, a wimp and a loser. You should have stayed in the library where you belonged. I'm going to take everything from you. Everything you ever imag-

ined and more. And then I will come for you, Emma Merrigan.

I'll deal with you first, Emma replied, hoping the rogue would hear and understand. Then she threw the intruder out of her thoughts—her skills were sharper when her instincts ran rampant—and summoning her rage, began a headlong charge to the pit.

Em never got there. An irresistible force on the order of a truck or a train struck her from behind. It lifted her off her feet and spun her through nothingness until, inevitably, she collided with an immovable object: parched and hardened dirt.

"You gave me your word! But what does truth or honor mean to one such as you? *Pardieu*, you have made me your fool, Madame Mouse, but you will not win. Not this time."

Pulling herself out of a stunned shock, Emma found herself in the wasteland barrens. She recognized Blaise's voice, recognized him and the sword he held pointed at her throat. He had been the force hauling her away from Eleanor and vengeance. Em levered herself upright.

"The hell I won't," she said and let fly as she knelt. She had rage inside and the will to set the world on fire.

But Blaise was a rogue and rogues combined the powers of curses and curse-hunters. He spun the sword around and caught Emma's flames on the jeweled pommel. Her rage remained, but her power was gone.

"What do you want from me?" she asked. "Or are you just evil incarnate, destroying what you can because you can?"

"I, Madame? *I* am evil incarnate? Better I should ask the same question. What are you? You blunder and stumble, pretending to know nothing at all about what you do, then you open your heart and threaten to destroy us all."

"Only rogues and curses."

"Yourself, your mother, *me.*"

Emma shrugged; there wasn't a muscle in her body that wasn't stressed and aching. "I was willing to take that

risk to get rid of you and the other rogues. It's the least I
could do. God knows how much long-term harm I've
done by trusting you."

"God? Now, *enfin*, you bring Almighty God into your
arguments? I repeat, *what* are you, Madame? Who made
you and turned you loose au-delà?"

"No one *made* me and you can blame yourself for turning me loose. If you hadn't rescued me last November, I'd
probably be a rogue myself right now."

That quieted Raponde. He raked his hair and turned
away from Em, giving her a moment to look around.
When Eleanor had brought her to the wasteland, Emma
had asked, in all sincerity, if they could fly once they'd
left their bodies behind. Eleanor had said no, walking was
the only way to travel across the parched wasteland. But
Blaise Raponde knew tricks Eleanor hadn't known, or
hadn't shared. Em didn't know if they'd flown away from
the rump Paris, or how far away they actually were, but
the rooftops were gone, and needless to say, neither her
storm shelter nor the way-back stone was in sight.

Nancy? Em cast a prayerful thought to the here-and-
now, wherever it was. *Have you lost me for good, Nance?
I don't think I can get home without you.*

"Who were they, Blaise?" Em asked when the silence
lengthened. She'd get a few answers, if nothing else.
"Friends of yours?" He looked her way, a blank expression on his face. "La Voisin? The authorities were building her pyre when I arrived. How about La Bosse? Or Le
Sage? Or Belot and La Filstre?" Em rattled off the names
she'd memorized from Matt's notes. "How about Romani? I wondered if you might not be Romani, but he
could have been the guy dressed up like a priest—"

Raponde surged toward Em like a madman with his
hands cocked to squeeze the life out of her throat. She'd
meant to hold her ground, but retreated at the last moment. Her two steps wouldn't have protected her, if he
hadn't stopped himself.

"How do you know those names?" he demanded, waving his fists but not touching her. "Who are you? Show me the face that you're hiding. Give me *that* small honor. I've earned it, keeping you amused."

Dawn broke over the universe at last: "You think I'm a rogue," Emma marveled aloud. "All this time—*you've* thought that I'm the rogue." The idea was so patently absurd it had never entered her mind.

"I wasn't sure. At times, it did not seem possible that you were the merest hunter, then it was impossible for you to be other than a rogue. I changed my thinking more times than I can remember. I wanted to believe you, Madame Emma, more than you'll know, but those names—you have no place in my Paris, no place at all—yet you know those names and Grisette recognized you. When she called, you came running!"

Grisette? Em translated: the little gray girl? The rogue in the dumpy clothes who'd known Em's name and that she worked in a library? Pieces came together, and for the first time in months, Em thought she might have the upper hand.

"If I'm a rogue, Blaise, why did you bring me here—wherever *here* is? Why not let me run down that hill to Grisette while you saved your own rear end?"

He raked his hair a few more times. "I don't know," he admitted, then corrected himself. "No, this is between us, you and me. You have beaten me with your guile-disguised-as-ignorance. You could never have been as simple as you seemed. No one born a hunter could fail to know what you have pretended not to know. I let myself be blinded. Say that I have been alone too long. This time I choose my death at a woman's hands."

It would have been unconscionably rude to burst out laughing, so instead Emma said: "Consider this, Blaise Raponde—*neither* of us is a rogue. We're both aberrations—a curse-hunting man who didn't die when he was supposed to and a woman who, as God is my witness, doesn't know what's going on around here. I was so busy worrying that *you* were a rogue that it never dawned on me that you might think *I* was."

Raponde relaxed then stiffened himself up again. "But those *names*," he protested. "How could you know them if you were not one with the rogues? I know them, *pardieu*. Fate threw us together. In the belly of Paris, we worked together, but we did not trust them at all. They knew we were different. What they called their magic was fraud and artifice while our magic—which we would never call magic—was steady as the sun. They coveted our secrets, and though we'd sell one another, we would not sell our secrets. Yet here you come, off the edge of time itself, claiming innocence and ignorance and knowing those names. Show me your true face, Madame, that I may recognize you before I die."

He had his hand on his sword but did not draw it. Emma didn't think he would.

"You're looking at it, Blaise, and if you're not, there's really not anything I can do about it. For the record, I never claimed to be innocent, but the ignorance is real enough, at least where it comes to all this. On the other hand, I know these names you're so worried about because they're part of history. They were all part of the *Poisons Affair*, you've heard of that?"

Blaise started, as if he'd caught a whiff of something acrid. "I lived through it, Madame—died in it. You claim it has been three centuries between my worldly death and your birth, and yet you know these names. I submit either you are a rogue who dwelt in my Paris or you have given yourself to a rogue who did."

"Books, Blaise. Where and when I come from, we have books about everything, books by the millions and books to tell you what's in the other books. Once I decided that Paris in sixteen-eighty would be a good place to look for rogues and curses, it wasn't long before I'd read about La Voisin—" Never mind she hadn't learned about La Voisin that way. Blaise had left her a Bible—he was literate and he cared enough about books to own one. She wasn't going to confuse him with computer databases or the Internet. "I figured the day she died would be a good place to start—even if she wasn't a rogue to begin with, or didn't bring down the mother of all curses when they burnt her at the stake, there was a chance I'd spot someone interesting in the crowd . . . maybe even you."

"On the edge of time, there is a *book* about Marguerite Montvoisin?" he asked, both incredulous and sad.

"Several."

Em almost blathered on about Nicholas de la Reynie's notes and his suspicion of conspiracy stretching from La Voisin to the bedroom of the Sun King himself, but the king had burnt his copy of la Reynie's notes precisely to keep men like Blaise Raponde from suspecting that his mistresses dosed him with love potions. If she revealed too much, she'd succeed only in rekindling his suspicions which, just then, were fading. Raponde's hand had drooped away from the sword and the anger was gone from his eyes.

"Is there a book about me?"

She shook her head, more of a shiver than a shake—a cold wind had blown out of nowhere. It was time to be headed home—if she could find the way.

"La Voisin is remembered . . . there were better people. Three centuries and such things are remembered! While I lived, I remembered nothing so ancient—"

"Try the Crusades. Eleanor of Aquitaine," Emma interrupted, because her mind sifted facts regardless of how tired or cold the rest of her felt. "Eleven-twenty-two to twelve-oh-four. That's more than three centuries. Crecy and Agincourt."

Blaise grimaced. He *did* remember. Unfortunately, Emma knew her English history far better than she knew her French and every event she'd mentioned was at best an embarrassment for the French.

"How—?" Blaise began, all suspicious again; then he calmed himself. "No. No. If you are not a rogue, Madame Emma, at the least you must be older than you appear."

She laughed between shivers. "I know I look older than Eleanor, but I'm not nearly nine hundred."

"I was not comparing you to your mother. You, yourself, appear quite young, Madame. You have the figure of a maiden. You must be older than you look."

Emma wanted to chide him for unnecessary flattery but she couldn't control her shivering. "It's happening again. I belong back in Bower. My friend—"

She meant Nancy, but Blaise put his arms around her. He was warm, and Em didn't hesitate before weaving her arms beneath his huge coat, but wool couldn't stop the wind, not when the wind blew through her heart.

"I'm nowhere near the edge of time. I don't know where to find my way-back stone—" Em hung on the verge of tears. "I'll wind up like my mother."

"Go easy," Blaise advised. "Nothing holds you au-delà. I wouldn't, if I could. Close your eyes. Think of the place where you wish to be."

"Eleanor—" Emma muttered, even as she took his advice. "The rogues—the rogues!" She pulled away from him and stood unsteadily on her own feet. "That one— Grisette—she *did* know me, Blaise. I've seen her. She's living in my time, hanging out with people I know—dear God, she's the one who put me on the track to La Voisin." *That* was a careless remark, considering what she'd already said, but Blaise didn't seem to notice. "She'll find out about Eleanor. What have I told her? I can't remember. Matt knows. Matt knows everything; she'll get it out of him."

Emma lost her bearings completely; Blaise caught her before she collapsed. Later, when she recovered—*if* she recovered, Em swore she'd be appalled by her swooning behavior. At that moment, she was grateful for the support.

"Madame . . . *Emma* . . . This cold you feel, is there more than cold?" Blaise paused. His hands tightened over her shoulders. "Is there pain, Emma? Do you feel a great pain in your heart?"

She knew immediately what he was asking: Are you dead, Emma? Has Malerie Dunbar sneaked into your living room and put a knife in your back? In Nancy's back? But: "No, just cold. Very cold." And damn near suffocated by Blaise's sudden, vigorous embrace.

"Can we trust each other—we who are *aberrations*? Do you believe that I am not a rogue?"

Emma nodded against his coat.

"Then close your eyes. Try to sleep. Dreams will take you where you wish to go and once you are there, *stay* there. Guard yourself."

She didn't need anyone to tell her that. "It's not enough. I've got to guard Eleanor, too—"

"Guard her body until she recovers or dies, but leave Paris to me."

There was a grimness to Blaise's voice that made Em stand straight again and look him in the eye. "Who are they, Blaise? You know them. Grisette. The tall blonde."

"Yes. Yes, I know them. Each of them, I will take and destroy them. Each of them. You have my word, my *parole*. I ask you to stay away from Paris and au-delà. It is too dangerous for you and too dangerous for me, if I must worry about you."

"Who was she, Blaise—your lover?"

He nodded a half inch. "Though she loved what I was more than she loved me. She feared for her beauty, and when I could not save that, she found those who could. I should have known. I should have known that she would take me as I slept. I did not die alone, Madame Emma."

"What?" Emma demanded, but it was too late.

Shock proved as good as falling asleep when it came to making a rapid exit from the wasteland. She sat bolt upright in bed— "Where the hell am I this time?"

Eleven

A *phone rang* beyond the bedroom where Emma had awakened. Nancy answered it on the second ring. Not that Emma was eavesdropping. Once she'd recovered from the surprise of opening her eyes in a room where she didn't remember closing them, she'd instantly recognized the Amstel guest room and her friend's voice.

By the light streaming through the east-facing window, Em knew that it was morning—as bright a morning as January had to offer—but she didn't know whether it was Friday morning or Saturday. Recalling her visits to the Place de Grève, her encounter with Blaise Raponde, and the four rogues they'd found behind Raponde's seventeenth-century Paris, Em calculated that she'd done enough to have lost a day or two in the process.

If she had missed Friday, it would be one more embarrassment in a growing string of them, but she had long since learned that embarrassment wasn't fatal. It would have been far harder on Nancy. Em threw back the blankets, grimly aware that her new life as a confused curse-hunter was straining her most cherished friendship.

It was putting a strain on Emma's body, as well. Pain shot up her leg when she stood. Looking down, she saw that her ankle was red and swollen. Eleanor had warned Em that injuries in the wasteland were real and that her here-and-now body would reflect them. She could walk without limping, but every step would be a reminder of her night in Paris . . . seventeenth-century Paris.

The Amstels kept their home warmer than Emma kept hers. She could have made her way comfortably down the hall past Katy and Alyx's hermetically preserved bedrooms wearing only the university-logo sweatshirt she didn't remember borrowing. For decency's sake and politeness, she pulled on the matching sweatpants she found at the foot of her bed. Her own clothes—the clothes she'd worn Thursday—were folded neatly on the cushion of a florally upholstered chair.

The heard, but not overheard, conversation had ended, replaced by the *clank* of plates, pans, and silverware: Nancy unloading the dishwasher. For a few seconds Emma considered calling out *I'm alive* or some similar reassurance, then she closed the bathroom door. Once she turned the faucet, the eighty-year-old house would tell Nance everything she needed to know.

Viewed through storm windows, January had done itself proud. A bitter night had given way to cloudless blue and a blanket of snow too pristinely white to be more than a few hours old. The weather service had gotten it right: a true Alberta Clipper that blew a foot and a half of white froth against the sides of everything while leaving the elms and maples bare against the sky.

Nancy had already blown the snow off their pavement. Bower had a twelve-hour clean sidewalk ordinance and last October the city council had sworn that this year mailmen would be empowered to enforce it. Em would have to go home and clear hers, if she wanted mail delivery without a summons attached—

Sidewalks and mail delivery! Emma marveled at her own thoughts. As if clearing a path for the mailman were the biggest problem facing her. Never underestimate the human need for habit. At the very least she was late for work and, like a child, found herself hoping that the university had declared a snow emergency day.

Lacking a toothbrush, Em made do with hot water and a swig of minted mouthwash. Nance heard her coming and thrust a cup of steaming coffee in her hands as she crossed the kitchen threshold.

"Sorry about last night," Em apologized.

"You scared me," Nancy replied. "But—well—first things first. According to the radio, the U's not officially open until noon, so you've got time to get there. I would have called them, but it's just as well I won't have to."

Emma blew across her cup with an unforced sigh. Trust Nancy to have her priorities straight—steady employment *did* come before curses and rogues. She glanced at the wall clock: 10:15. She had time for coffee and explanations. "Thanks, I need to keep my secrets." She shook her head and sipped. "It's scary, Nance; real scary. I don't remember a thing about last night."

"Nothing at all? And here I was expecting all kinds of stories! I even baked some blueberry muffins for the occasion." Nancy's grin was sincere, though it didn't completely hide her concern.

"I'm sorry, Nance. For whatever I've put you through, I truly am sorry . . . and I remember all the things that couldn't really have happened. I just don't remember leaving my house and coming here. What did you have to do? Drag me up the stairs?"

"No, you walked. You weren't unconscious, Em." Nancy's voice took a turn to the serious. "You weren't yourself. Not drunk or anything, just not all there. Kind of dazed, like Mom's roommate out at Meadow View. You have to tell Marge to eat her lunch, even though it's sitting in front of her."

Em joked, "Worse than curses—I'm coming down with early-onset Alzheimer's," and realized, as she heard her own words, that she wasn't joking.

"Oh, nothing like that. I couldn't let you drive, though— That was the hardest part: getting here in your car. When are you going to get a grown-up's car, Emma?

Do you have any idea how long it's been since I drove a stick shift?"

"I *like* driving a stick," Em defended herself. "I feel like I'm watching television when I drive an automatic. You didn't have to fight with my car. You could have left me on the floor and slept in my bed. The cats would have kept you company."

Nancy shook her head, slowly, deliberately, profoundly. "I believe you now, Em. I believe everything—"

"Oh." She took a sip of coffee. "What happened?"

"It wasn't *Poltergeist* or *The Exorcist*. You weren't speaking in tongues and things weren't flying around the room, but it wasn't right in your living room. There was like a fog or a mist in the room with us—not a real one. I couldn't see anything—I mean, I could see everything just the way it was supposed to be. Everything *looked* normal, but I *felt* a fog." Nancy hugged herself tight before adding: "Emma, I called Harry. I didn't know what else to do. You weren't yourself and the air was strange. I didn't know what else to do. I asked you if you minded and you said no, but I knew you weren't yourself. You didn't understand the question; you didn't know who I was talking about . . . not really."

Em stifled a heartbeat of anger. She'd given Nancy the number and the authority. She'd have done the same thing, were their positions reversed. "What did he have to say?"

"He was worried—I was expecting, oh, someone stuffier and above-it-all, and of course, he didn't know me from Adam and here I was talking about all this top-secret stuff. I thought he might *do* something, or threaten to *do* something or refuse to help at all, but he was very nice, very pleasant and patient—"

"Pleasant people, Nance—you know they're the worst kind. Harry's not a ogre—I'm sorry if I mislead you there. He'd fit in just fine in the English department." English was renowned as the university's most politicized department; its last very-public tenure dispute had progressed all the way to the state supreme court before being settled. "What did Harry say when you told him I wasn't myself?"

"He asked if you were shivering. I told him yes, and that seemed to be the right answer. I think he would have been more worried if you'd been sweating. He told me to bundle you up and get you out of your house. Something about how you'd find your way back no matter what, but it wouldn't do to advertize your condition—he actually said that: 'It wouldn't do to advertize.' I could hear the Z instead of an S. You didn't tell me Harry was English."

"I don't know that he is. What sort of accent do you suppose Benjamin Franklin had, or George Washington?"

Nancy's eyes widened. "Did he tell you he was *that* old?"

"No, Nance. Harry Graves looks to be about our age. Eleanor looks twenty-five and we know she's got to be at least seventy. You do the math. And no, I wouldn't want to try to guess whose side he would have taken if he had been here for the Revolution."

Nancy reined in her curiosity. "Well, he's on your side now and he's coming here as soon as he can." She broke eye contact with Emma. "He called a few minutes ago—just before you got up, in fact. He's got a two P.M. plane reservation. He was leaving for the airport as soon as he hung up."

Em shouldn't have been surprised that Nancy so obviously wanted to meet Harry Graves. There was no way Nance could meet Blaise Raponde so she focused on Harry. Em could only blame herself. She could have kept her mouth shut . . . and driven herself crazy along the way. Instead, she'd tried to keep her independence and have a confidant, too. Now her confidants were confiding to each other, her independence was history, and what Emma felt as caffeine percolated through her system was mostly relief.

"What time does his plane get in? Is he coming here—to your house—where he expects to find me asleep and shivering?"

Nancy blushed, faintly but noticeably. "I told him he could stay here—we've got the room—but he's taking a hotel room out by the Interstate. He'll be here by dinnertime, if all goes well. That storm we had last night's still moving east. The Weather Channel shows it picking up moisture from the Atlantic and doing a number on the East Coast from D.C. to Boston. Harry said he thought he'd get to the airport okay, but there were no guarantees that he'd get on a plane."

Em repressed the urge to snipe *He could always use his broomstick.* Harry wasn't evil incarnate. She'd looked into the eyes of that a few hours ago—

"Omigod." Emma set the coffee cup down before it sloshed onto the floor. "Omigod."

"Emma? Are you all right?"

"The rogue, Nancy. I saw the rogue—"

"That crazy woman—La Voisin? The one they burned. You saw her?"

"Not her. She's got nothing to do with it." Or did she? Could she really say that none of Nicholas de la Reynie's prisoners were rogues or hunters? "Matt's new girlfriend, the one named Malerie, I saw her in the past . . . behind the past. We'd found Eleanor, Nance, Blaise and I— mostly—no, entirely, thanks to Blaise. We were sizing up the situation when four rogues put in an appearance. One of them looked right at me and did the 'talking inside my head' thing—the opposite of reading my thoughts. She was drab and sullen and she knew what Malerie knows . . . and I'm supposed to have supper with her and Matt tonight."

"You'll cancel," Nance said without an eye blink of hesitation. "Oh, Em—you've found Eleanor! Where? How did you find her? Tell me everything."

Em didn't know where to start. Now that caffeine was circulating through her brain, she was thinking about several things at once, though all of them eventually came back to the mousy young woman keeping company with Matt Barto.

Nancy plied Emma with aromatic blueberry muffins warm enough to melt butter. She was good with questions, better at waiting for Em to build her answers, and able to add a few gems of information to the mix.

"Harry mentioned that there's a rogue in Bower when I talked to him a few minutes ago. He said he'd stayed up all night retracing it. It's older than he expected and not alone. That really seemed to bother him, Em, that it wasn't alone. And he never said 'she,' I'm sure of that. When he needed a pronoun for a rogue, Harry used 'it,' not 'he' or 'she.' Maybe this Malerie's not a rogue at all but someone like Brian, who caught a curse."

"Bran, not Brian." Emma supplied the proper name of the student she'd uncursed in November. She tried putting Malerie into a Bran-shaped part of her mind, but the sullen woman didn't fit the mold. "I saw four rogues behind Paris—two men, two women. I don't know why Harry refers to them as 'it.' Eleanor did, too, and so does Blaise, for that matter—though he's not as consistent as they are. It's some kind of defense, probably—making sure you don't have empathy for your enemy. But Mal's a rogue; I'm sure of it. A rogue or a rogue's avatar."

Nancy cocked her head. She hadn't spent her professional life reading the title and synopsis of every book that came into the Horace Johnson Memorial Library. Emma had to explain her choice of words.

"Hindu gods make themselves known by choosing avatars to represent them in mortal society."

"Like saints?" Nance asked doubtfully.

"More like demons."

"Then you'll stay away from her—at least until Harry gets here?"

Emma considered. "No," she decided. "I'm going to work and then I'm going to dinner with Matt and a wasteland rogue."

"Em—be serious! This isn't a game anymore."

"It never was, Nance—never was a game." Em finished her second cup of coffee.

"But you're safe here. We don't know Matt or his girlfriend and they don't know us."

"You can't be so sure. Matt called here on New Year's and I didn't give him the number. No, I'll be safe at the library, too, and at Hokkaido afterward. Malerie Dunbar's not going to come after me with a gun."

"How do you know, Em? How can you know what she's going to do? Wait until Harry gets here."

Nancy had thirty years of a successful marriage under her belt. She was in the habit of relying on other people, especially men. Emma was in the habit of relying on herself.

"Look, when Harry gets here, he and I can talk, but these are my problems, not his, and I'm not going to curl up in a corner hiding from them. That rogue's got my goddamned mother in a hole filled with ectoplasmic leeches and I'm not going to stand for it."

The two women stared at each other. Nancy broke first, as Emma knew she would. When it came to a show of willpower, Em rarely lost, not against her ex-husbands and certainly not against her friends. In elementary school, she'd been called Snake-eyes for her relentless glare. Her classmates had seen something in her that Em had needed another four decades to discover.

"I think we should call Harry—"

Emma narrowed her eyes.

"*You* should, then. I told him I'd call when you woke up or if you took a turn for the worse. I've got his cell number."

"A witch with a cell phone," Em mused. "Whatever is the world coming to?"

But she followed Nancy into the den and tapped in the number her friend had written down. It rang until a computer-generated voice cut in to say that the number she'd dialed was temporarily unavailable. She went upstairs, ignoring her ankle as she did, to get his home number from her wallet—and threw on her clothes at the same time. The house number rang ten times before the answering machine cut in to say that Harry was unavailable and wouldn't be returning calls before Monday.

"So much for revolutionary technology," Emma concluded. Nancy, she realized, had been hoping Harry could convince her to sit tight until reinforcements arrived. That had never been in the cards. "I'm not going to do anything stupid, Nance," she explained gently. "It goes against my nature to sit around waiting. I'm just a take-the-bull-by-the-horns kind of—" Em hesitated, catching herself, as she'd caught herself a thousand times before, on the verge of describing herself in sexist terms. "Person."

"You are, you know."

"I am what?"

"A take-the-bull-by-the-horns sort of guy. I can remember Mom saying in first grade that you were more like a boy than a girl."

"Good grief, Nance—when I was in first grade, I had a ponytail that hung down to my waist, and if Almighty God had ever wanted me to catch a ball, he should have had the decency to web my fingers. The only time I wasn't the last person chosen for a team in gym class was if some other kid was on crutches. I was the most untomboy kid I've ever known."

Nancy let the subject slide. "What should I tell Harry when he checks in? He's got this number. He's going to call here. John will be home by then. I've told John, Em—I had to."

Em nodded, a bit unhappy, but unsurprised. The problem with allies and confidants was that once she had them, she had to make good use of them and she didn't have the time for elegant plans.

"Here's an idea: why don't you and John bring Harry to Hokkaido? Harry can get a good look at Matt and Malerie while I pretend that none of you are there. He should like that. You know where it is, don't you? A little basement place near campus."

"That sounds good," Nancy agreed. "We haven't been there in years. Will that be enough? What about your mother? I'm going out to see Mom. I could check on her . . . make sure that no one gets into her room who shouldn't be there. Harry said—"

Emma short-stopped Nancy's explanation with a sour look.

"He asked, Em. We hadn't discussed what I should tell him, so I told him the truth. It seemed like the right thing to do, with you sitting on the floor staring and shivering and me feeling like I was in an invisible fog."

"It was the right thing to do," Emma agreed. She didn't like hearing it or admitting it, but Nancy was right to be worried about Eleanor's body out at Meadow View. "If you don't mind keeping an eye on Eleanor, that would be appreciated."

She started for the stairs and the bedroom where she'd left her purse and all-important contact lenses. Nancy followed.

"I can pack a book and spend the afternoon with her, if you think that would help. The phone here can be set to forward messages to the cell. If Harry calls, I can tell him what's happened—"

With her lenses in, Em could read a clock across a room. She measured the minutes and the odds of getting to work on time if she went home for a change of clothes. "Do what you need to do, Nance. I trust you . . . and I'm going to be late for work."

"You're not thinking of going home first?" Nancy asked, clearly incredulous. "You'll never find parking. Just borrow a dress—I'm sure mine will fit you. I know just the one—"

Nance surged ahead on the stairs and led the way to the airy room she shared with John. Her closet was hung with a dozen or more of the ankle-length flowing dresses— mostly floral prints and dainty foulards in dusty pastel colors—that gave Nancy Amstel a style that veered away from Emma's tailored, shades-of-black-and-navy comfort zone. Still, Emma couldn't argue with the idea of borrowing her friend's clothes: snow wreaked havoc on her neighborhood's already car-clogged streets. About one Maisonettes parking space in four disappeared after a substantial snowfall, and that said nothing about the drifts that might have piled up at her front door. She laid hands on the darkest fabric in sight: teal, pink, and purple paisleys swirled across charcoal gray.

"I knew you'd pick that one."

Em nodded without comment and headed for the guest bedroom. She left the Amstels' house a half-hour later favoring an ankle and feeling as undressed as she'd felt wandering the wasteland in a waltz-length nightgown.

The library reeked of whatever the chemistry department had cooked up to stop the rampant mold and mildew. Em started sneezing as soon as she left the stairwell. Making a swift retreat to her office, she shut the door and dug through her desk for last season's allergy tablets. The ones she found in a bottom drawer were one month past expiration. She took them anyway, hoping for the best, and fired up her computer. Between e-mail and the paper in her in-box, Em crafted an afternoon that would neither cheat the ghost of Horace Johnson as it prowled his library nor tax her drugged, distracted brain. While databases on both coasts crunched her requests, Em tried Harry's phone numbers, and when they failed to connect her with her stepfather, she dove into a travelers' aid Internet site.

The Alberta Clipper storm which had turned Bower into a winter fairyland had joined forces with warmer, wetter air over the Atlantic and the nation's air-travel grid, which had barely recovered from the overnight snowfall in the Midwest, was falling apart before Emma's eyes. By the looks of things, Pittsburgh had already surrendered and Buffalo was besieged. A handful of flights at the New York City airports promised to leave on time, including one nonstop to Detroit that was due to depart in fifteen minutes, but if Harry wasn't already sitting on that plane, he was facing the real possibility of an airport stranding.

Em couldn't imagine Harry Graves weaving himself

across airport chairs in search of a night's sleep, not in his cashmere coat and designer sweaters. He'd buy his way into a hotel—

Her monitor flashed and rolled up a message:

"Come down to the basement, Auntie Em—we're having a celebration!"

Matt Barto was the only person who called her Auntie Em and who had the ability to commandeer her computer. That gave her a pretty good idea who "we" were. One of the elevators was out of service—POST-FLOOD REPAIRS, the sign read. When the other didn't show up after five minutes, Emma took the stairs. The competing scents of burgeoning mildew and its nemesis left her nose tingling while the stairwell itself reminded her of the Parisian crypt.

"I don't have the wherewithal to deal with any of this," she muttered out loud as she opened the door onto a corridor shorn of its carpet and reeking of stagnant water.

Matt's door was closed—a prudent but largely ineffective precaution against the toxic air in his corridor. Emma knocked then entered. Matt sat at his desk surrounded by paper and hardware, no different from any other day. Malerie sat curled up in his side chair. She shot a big smile Em's way.

"I got the callback. They made me an offer. Everything's settled. I got the job."

The young woman's smile raised the short hairs at the back of Em's neck, and Matt's grin was worse. The lights were on but no one seemed to be home. He didn't even offer an Auntie Em wisecrack about her borrowed dress.

"What job?" Em asked, guessing she wouldn't like the answer.

"Your job!" Matt replied, bouncing slightly in his chair. "Mal applied. The interview went great and she's going to be your research assistant. Isn't that awesome?"

The world slowed as Emma wrapped her mind around Matt's statement. "The degree," she protested. "The degree. You said you had a bachelor's in psych. You said you're studying for your master's in psych, not library science. You don't have the experience. You don't have the degree."

Both Matt and Mal looked at Em as if she'd grown another head or started babbling in Aramaic.

"Psychology? Where'd you get that idea?" Malerie asked, and before Emma could manage an answer, Matt chimed in with—

"Mal got her degree in Information Resources from Wisconsin. She's had almost as much database exposure as I got—the two of you will make a great team."

"What about experience? The position requires five years' library experience. I *saw* the posting."

"Well, there was nothing about experience when I went in to apply." Malerie said, looking like the cat that ate the canary. "You must've been looking at the wrong card, Auntie Em."

Em despised that nickname. She tolerated it from Matt because she knew he meant no harm. Malerie was different. Very different. *Don't cross your own path,* Blaise had told her, Harry, too. *We don't change the past, we moot curses. Time is resilient. History preserves itself—but never cross your own path.* She hadn't crossed her path or changed her past, but a rogue had. A rogue had sneaked into Human Resources and mooted Gene Shaunekker's authorization for an Acquisitions Researcher.

It was last night in the counter-Paris graveyard all over again—staring into a rogue's malice-filled eyes and feeling hopelessly outclassed. If life were a movie, the camera would pull back and let special effects handle the final defeat of an amateur curse-hunter who'd mistakenly thought she could outwit a rogue.

Fortunately—or unfortunately—life wasn't a movie and Emma didn't burst into flames or dissolve into a puddle of blood. She held her ground because she was too numb to move and held Malerie's stare because habit was stronger than terror.

Neuron by neuron, synapse by synapse, the paralyzing

shock drained from Em's mind, releasing a prayer-like thought: *Oh, Harry Graves, I hope you got on that plane*— Then Emma was on her own. "I guess, after all the years I've been here, I should know better. Administration is nothing but a parcel of rogues."

Malerie blinked before saying, "Yeah, can't trust a rogue."

"We'll just have to trust each other, won't we? I didn't know Wisconsin had a library science program," Emma lied—she knew every department in the country by reputation and most of the senior faculty by title, if not by their first name. "So, which town do you like better, Madison or Bower?"

Another blink. "Matt's not in Madison."

Malerie Dunbar—or Grisette or some altogether different name—improvised well, but she hadn't finished her homework. Mal didn't know that Wisconsin's library science program was based in Milwaukee, a good ninety miles down the Interstate from Madison.

"So, you plan to stick around as long as Matt does?" Em asked, pushing hard to see what kind of a reaction she'd get.

Matt blushed spectacularly. Malerie nodded. Emma felt sick to her stomach, and owed an unexpected debt of gratitude to her ex-husband Jeff. It was worse, by far, to realize that time and truth were subject to change but those confrontations with Jeff, when venomous words alternating with acid silence had left Emma with the strength to ignore her own panic. (Never let him see the pain he caused; never let him figure out which barbs merely stung and which were mortal wounds.) She could face a rogue without flinching.

"Well, we'll have things to talk about over dinner," she said calmly, offering her hand to the younger woman. "Congratulations. I've never been anyone's boss before . . . this will be a learning experience for both of us."

Em was prepared for any number of sensations—hot, cold, scales, or slime—when Malerie grasped her hand.

What she got was ordinary flesh. Then again, she got the same when she embraced Blaise. She held on to her dignity and her sanity until she was back in the stairwell, where she raced up one flight before succumbing to light-headed palpitations.

The engineering gene clung to a belief in the fundamental one-way direction of chronology: you could always jump back in the river, but it wasn't—it absolutely *wasn't*—the same river it had been a moment ago. No matter what Emma *thought* she'd done back in eleventh-century England or the streets of seventeenth-century Paris, the past couldn't be subject to change. There *had* to be other explanations. Hypnosis. Hysteria. Drugs. Brainwashing.

Propped against the stairwell wall, Emma sliced a fine line between what she could believe and what she wouldn't. Malerie Dunbar could be a rogue, or a rogue's here-and-now avatar, but she could not have rewritten history. What Malerie *could* have done—and the only thing she could have done, though it was sufficient to rouse a Don Quixote outrage in Emma's judgment—was brainwash Matt into believing that she'd gotten a job as Em's assistant. Malerie had motive. If Matt had been reluctant to share what he knew about Eleanor or Em's forays into the wasteland, the belief that they were going to be working together might well loosen his tongue.

Malerie *had* to realize that her time was limited. She didn't have a library sciences degree, bachelor's or master's, from Wisconsin or anyplace else. Probably the woman didn't have a psych degree, either. She hadn't interviewed for the Acquisitions job, she hadn't been hired, and she wouldn't be showing up for work. Matt would realize he'd been scammed, and their entirely inappropriate relationship would come to a crashing end.

Malerie *had* to be gambling that she could pick Matt's brain clean before he caught on to her deception, *had* to figure that Emma herself—neophyte and bumbling curse-hunter that she was—wouldn't catch on until it was too late.

But Em had caught on. Her heart no longer raced; she had a plan, simple and elegant. She'd pay a visit to Human Resources and bring a copy of the job posting to dinner. Returning to the basement via a different stairwell, Em traveled the steam tunnels to the Administration Building and the Plexiglas-covered bulletin board, where a quick glance informed her that the posting was gone.

The room was crowded with students who'd come back to school needing a job. Emma got on line and waited ten minutes before it was her turn to ask the clerk—

"There was a library job posted—something about an Acquisitions Researcher?"

"If it's not on the board, it's been filled or it doesn't exist. Sorry."

"Could you check, please?" Em braced her arms on the counter to convey that she wasn't leaving without the answer she wanted. "I'm sure it was there yesterday."

She was twice the age of everyone else in the room and didn't know if that were an advantage or not until the clerk heaved a sigh and fetched a folder from a desk near the window.

"Here, have a look." She thrust the folder across the counter. "Give it back when you're done or I'm toast."

Grateful—and confident that she could finagle a copy of the posting card once she got her hands on it—Emma eased out of the line's way. The folder contained a dozen or so cards stapled to their backup paperwork. Hers was about halfway down the pile and stamped diagonally with FILLED in big, red letters which did not obscure the original text. The degree requirement was there, reduced to a bachelor's, and the line next to EXPERIENCE held the words WILL TRAIN.

Emma's nausea returned, stronger than before. Her fingers were numb when she flipped the card aside to read the paperwork. There she found what *she* remembered: Gene Shaunekker's signature above a hiring authorization for a position that required, in addition to a master's degree, five years' experience with a university library. She reexamined the posting card. There was nothing at all to suggest it wasn't the genuine article—no erasures or cross-outs. The corners had been pierced by thumbtacks that left pressure rings on the paper.

"Can you tell me who got this job?" she asked, barely able to get her voice above a whisper. "Or who did the interview?"

The clerk shook her head and reclaimed the folder. "That's confidential. I shouldn't've let you look at this. You can try over at the library . . . or downstairs at Compliance and Enforcement. You can file a complaint with C and E, if you think you've been discriminated against."

Emma hadn't been discriminated against; she'd lost her hold on her own history. She could complain to Gene—as lord of the library, he'd take action against Human Resources: they were trying to fill a job that wasn't the one he'd authorized. But if Malerie could forge a posting card, she could undo anything else that Gene did.

How in heaven was a curse-hunter supposed to protect her history?

Em returned to her office in a quaking daze.

Twelve

Emma summoned up the Internet site which claimed to know not only whether a plane had taken off and when it would arrive at its destination but also its air speed and approximate distance from the nearest major airport. The 2:05 P.M. Detroit flight out of LaGuardia had pushed back from its gate forty minutes late and was still on the ground, a half-mile east of the control tower, waiting patiently and hopefully to take off.

There was no point in trying Harry's cell phone. Em left a message on his home phone instead—

"I'll meet you whenever you get in, wherever you want. I'm ready to surrender. There is a rogue—in fact, there are *four* of them holding Eleanor prisoner in a cemetery in the wasteland behind Paris and things aren't any better in the here-and-now. Events that happened yesterday turned out not to have happened today."

That ought to get Harry's attention, and in odd-numbered seconds, it was the plain truth. In even-numbered seconds, Em reminded herself to breathe.

Concentration eluded her. To complete the sense of absurdity, she recalled a long-ago conversation with her dad who'd been with Patton's Fifth Army when it raced across Germany at the end of the Second World War.

In the war's final months, the Allies had bombed Germany without mercy. Dad said that nothing whole was standing in some of the cities the Allies liberated, not a building or a wall, yet war-weary Germans appeared every morning with ragged brooms to sweep the cracked steps in front of homes that existed only in their imagination. The Germans were insane, she'd told her father; they'd lost their minds when they'd lost their homes. Dad said no, the Germans weren't insane, not the ordinary Germans, but their world had gone mad and they fought that madness by clinging to the habits that made them human.

Emma hadn't argued—Dad had been there and he had a rarely heard tone to his voice that meant he was remembering things he could neither describe nor forget, but she hadn't truly understood until she began obsessing about her unshoveled sidewalks. If she went out to Meadow View before meeting Matt and Malerie for dinner—and Em wanted not only to see her mother but talk to Nancy as well—there'd be no time to go home and clear off her sidewalks. The postman wouldn't deliver her mail. Her neighbors would complain. The Bower police might give her a ticket.

Her life was unraveling back to front and all she really cared about was getting her sidewalks cleared. It was embarrassing, even shameful, but at least it was a problem she could solve. Her hands were steady when she dug out the Maisonettes' residents' directory and called the association president at work.

"Hi, Alan. Emma Merrigan here. I've run into a problem with my sidewalks. I couldn't get home last night and I'm going to be working late tonight, too. Do you happen to have the name and number of that lawn service that wanted a contract to clean our walks?"

Alan didn't have the phone number; he had something better. "Jack said he'd blown yours off last night when there were only a few inches on the ground. He and I went out again this morning with our blowers. We double-teamed the whole lot, only took a half hour. I noticed yours was covered and figured you were sleeping in, so I made a pass up the walk, too. It was all powder—no weight to it at all. We were shooting rooster tails eight feet high."

Emma imagined the sight: dueling snowblowers by dawn's early light. "I owe you one, Alan."

"I'm having a problem with e-mail on my computer at home. My wife keeps losing messages from her sister."

She took down the details and promised to drop by on Sunday—assuming she didn't forget who she was between now and then. Relief, though, faded quickly. Within moments of hanging up the phone Emma was staring at the screen saver patterns and wondering if curses could cause Alzheimer's. Em tried an old standby for organizing her thoughts: listing knowns and unknowns on a sheet of paper. She'd gotten as far as connecting Harry and Blaise with an ornate, overdrawn figure-eight when Betty poked her head in.

"You're looking all feminine today. What's the special occasion?"

Telling the full truth was out of the question so Em said, "No special occasion, just going out for dinner after work."

"Got a date?"

Emma shook her head. "No, just friends."

"Too bad," Betty sighed, then continued: "Thought you might like to know that I've gotten paperwork from Human Resources. They've got your assistant. Some kid a couple of years out of school. You want to read the interview write-up?"

Morbid curiosity extended Em's arm in Betty's direction. She put the file on the desk in front of her but didn't open it.

"From what HR's got to say, this girl walks on water. She sounds like a real go-getter," Betty continued. "If you've got veto power, you might want to consider exercising it or keep a close watch on your back. She's not going to be content with being someone's assistant. If you're lucky, she'll draw a bead on someone else."

It occurred to Em that Betty, who'd wanted the assistant's job for herself, didn't particularly like her. Was that something new—a by-product of Malerie's meddling—or was it something older? She'd always thought they got along well enough, for office comrades, but maybe she came across too aloof to be friends with a woman whose life revolved around her children and her church. Maybe when Betty looked at her, she saw a Harry Graves clone: too much culture, too self-satisfied and self-centered.

"Do you need this back?" she asked of the unopened folder.

Betty nodded. "They're pushing this. Gene's going to say yes or no this afternoon. I think they're hoping she'll start work next week." She cast her eyes around Em's office. "Who knew there was someone with a Library Science degree hiding out off-campus waiting for the chance to work here?"

Did Betty remember what Matt had forgotten? And if she did, did she think Emma had authorized the change? Em opened the folder. A copy of the posting card sat atop the file: bachelor's degree, zero experience, will train. Betty must have seen it, but did she remember something different?

"I don't know, Betty. I'm with you—I thought it would take more time to come up with someone qualified. If it were up to me, I'd count experience higher than any degree. I wanted five years' experience and I thought Gene agreed with me."

She watched the other woman's face closely as Betty said, "Something must have changed his mind at the last minute."

Emma thought she saw prior knowledge in Betty's eyes. With a little effort, Em could see herself at the center of any number of malicious conspiracies. She opted not to expend that effort. Whatever else might be going on, Malerie Dunbar was the root cause. It was *personal* between her and Malerie and it was time to declare war . . . even if she didn't know where or when or how to find, much less fight, the enemy.

A good place to start was by doing what she did best. After glancing through the personnel file and returning it to Betty's desk, Em moved a day's worth of paper off her desk in the final two hours of Friday afternoon. At 5 P.M., after learning that Harry Graves' one chance for arriving in Bower before Saturday was in the air and bucking the jet stream five miles above Lake Erie, she shut down her computer and headed out to Meadow View.

Night had fallen, and any snow that hadn't melted during the day was safe until sunrise. Bower's road crews had gotten the main streets scraped and salted down to the pavement. Side streets were another story, with every shadow hiding a potentially treacherous patch of ice. And whoever Meadow View hired to clear their parking lot had decided to turn it into a skating rink instead. The low sections were slick with frozen meltwater while a four-foot-high berm ran uninterrupted around the perimeter.

A handful of visitors—Nancy Amstel among them— had scattered their cars haphazardly through the lot. Emma aimed for an empty section along the berm where snow-covered pavement promised better traction when it came time to leave. She scaled the berm by stepping in the holes someone else had made earlier in the day—a good way to break an already sprained ankle. Inside the lobby, the desk clerk apologized while Emma shook snow out of Nancy's dress.

"The contractor's plow broke down before he could get here. He says he'll have it cleared tomorrow or Sunday."

They'd need a jackhammer to chip through the crust if they waited until Sunday.

Em pushed the button and entered the waiting elevator. Luck smiled down on Emma for a few moments. She got past the staff station and Josh's room without drawing attention and found Nancy reading a book in Eleanor's room.

"I almost didn't recognize you," Nance laughed.

"That's what everyone's been saying. I might have to try varying my wardrobe—but not on a day when we've just had fifteen inches of snow. How's she been? Any problems? Restlessness?"

"Calm and quiet all afternoon. No excitement at all. To tell you the truth, I fell asleep myself for a little while."

Emma guessed Nancy hadn't gotten a lot of sleep last night, and Nance might get less after Em told her about her new assistant. She closed the door to Eleanor's room. Nance wore a worried look when Em faced her again.

"What's wrong?"

"Brace yourself—this isn't going to make a whole lot of sense at first. Did I mention that in the midst of the great flood Gene told me that he'd decided I needed help doing my job?"

Nancy shook her head and Em began at the beginning with her post-flood conversation with Gene in his office and ending in front of the job board in Human Resources.

"The card had been changed—not erased. It was a completely new card. I'm wondering if Malerie Dunbar actually interviewed for the job or if she simply wrote up the evaluations—the interviewer had written that she was outgoing, dynamic, inventive, and—oh, yes—ambitious. I don't care whether she's a time-twisting rogue—no human being could possibly meet Malerie Dunbar and think she was outgoing, dynamic, inventive, or ambitious."

"I don't know—she sounds pretty innovative and ambitious to me," Nancy joked, though neither of them cracked a smile. "Did you see who did the interview? You could track him or her down."

Em thought a moment and shook her head. "Waste of time. I *know* she's done it, Nance, because it's the same thing that I did to those people living in the eleventh century, except I didn't go back to gloat over it. Malerie Dunbar changed the past—my past—and she sat there in

Matt's office smiling like the Cheshire Cat. I swear she thinks I haven't got a clue."

"You'd think a rogue would know more about what would or wouldn't work against someone like you and wouldn't make a mistake like that."

"You're right," Em said slowly; she hadn't considered that angle. "Maybe I'm odd—for a curse-hunter."

Emma expected Nancy to rib her about being all-around odd, but Nance's mind was moving in other directions.

"Or she's trying to isolate you. If you remember things one way and everyone remembers them another way . . . eventually you won't seem odd, you'll seem insane, or worse."

Nancy stared out the window. From this angle Meadow View truly did overlook a meadow, at least until someone planted a strip mall or apartment complex in what had been prime farm land not ten years ago.

"Worse?" Em asked cautiously.

"You say you know that Matt's head's been turned around, and maybe Betty's, but how would *I* know, Emma?" Nancy asked, still staring into night's darkness. "Do I rely on you to tell me when my memories have been tampered with? Who do I believe? Right now, I believe you, but—maybe—that could change. How would I know? What's the limit? Could I 'forget' about John or Katy or Alyx? This is George Orwell come to life, Emma: 1984, Big Brother, and Harry Smith—"

"Ah—that's Harry Graves and Winston Smith, Nance."

Nancy gave Emma an *I don't care* look and said, "Whoever he was, he worked in a library rewriting history. He was a librarian, because librarians have unquestioned access to original sources."

"You've got a point. That might account for Malerie's interest in working at the libe, but I'm not going into the business of rewriting history, I promise you." Emma looked into the eyes of her oldest friend and saw nothing there that resembled confidence. "Look—write things down. Whatever Malerie did to the past, she *didn't* change all the paperwork in the Human Resources job folder. She couldn't fake Gene's signature and she wouldn't be able to fake your handwriting, either, so write things down. Keep an old-fashioned diary."

"That's a good idea," Nance agreed cautiously. "I know my own handwriting."

It wouldn't work. A rogue—or a curse-hunter—didn't rearrange someone else's memories. A rogue—or a curse-hunter—treated someone else's present like a length of video tape and ran it through a real-time editor. Blaise Raponde had commandeered a priest and then marched him around the altar to unlock the Innocents' crypt. Surely he could have made the man rewrite his diary.

But Nancy didn't need to know that.

"Use permanent ink—nothing that can be erased without a trace—and you'll be safe." Emma could feel her isolation like a noose tightening around her neck.

"I'll look pretty silly writing down what I order for dinner tonight, but I'll do it, if that's what it takes."

"Maybe you shouldn't come to dinner." Em took a deep breath. "I've dragged you in too deep already, Nance. This is getting nasty and dangerous and I don't want someone I care about getting hurt in ways neither of us can imagine."

"No way. I'm coming. We're coming. If you say writing things down will do the trick, then that's good enough for me. If I have to write down everything I eat, I'll lose those five pounds I put on last month. We're both coming. John's home right now taking a nap. He's going to get to Hokkaido at seven; I'll join him there. We've got it all planned out: I'll stay here until about ten after seven. If I haven't heard from you by then—because you'll call me if they don't show up—I'll head up to campus. Otherwise I'll stay here with Eleanor. We won't leave her exposed to the Forces of Evil."

Little as she wanted to expose her friends to danger, Em recognized decent tactics when she heard them—except for one detail: "How am I going to call you, Nance? Assuming I can use a phone at Hokkaido, there's none here." She pointed to the bed table where sat no phone and an empty plate.

With a sinking heart, Em realized she'd forgotten to bring the daily bribe for the Meadow View staff. It was just cookies, but her "perfect attendance" had lasted less than a month.

While Emma wallowed, Nancy said: "I've got my cell phone with me. You're going to have to get a cell, Em. No more excuses. We need reliable communication."

"Can I borrow it right now?" she asked sheepishly. "Harry's plane should be on the ground—if he got the last plane out of LaGuardia."

Nancy proudly fished the device out of her purse. Emma took one look at the profusion of buttons and shook her head in defeat.

"All right . . . what do I do to get a dial tone? Does it *have* a dial tone?"

After Nance gave Em a primer lesson, she tapped Harry's number across the buttons and then couldn't decide whether to hold the beast next to her ear or in front of her mouth. In the end, it didn't matter: Harry wasn't answering.

"Try the Executive Inn out by the Interstate," Nancy suggested. "He said he'd get a room there."

"I don't know the number."

"Call Information."

"Not for a local number, Nance. That's a waste of money."

"Cellular's about convenience, not money. Call Information."

"You sound like an advertisement," Emma muttered, but she followed orders and got the number.

A clerk confirmed that Harry had made a reservation. "He hasn't checked in but his room's guaranteed. It won't do him any good to call in and cancel. You want to leave a message?"

Em did, and left yet another message at Harry's New York home, telling him that she was off to have dinner with a rogue. If he got to Bower, he could have the hotel call him a cab and join the Amstels at the restaurant, or wait until she got home afterward. She pressed the buttons that ended the conversation and returned the device to Nancy, who accepted it with another question.

"What about your friend, Blaise Raponde? Can you do anything to bring him on board?"

"He can't come to Bower, if that's what you mean. He's a ghost, Nance."

"Isn't there something he can be doing in that other place?"

Em shook her head.

"How can you be so sure? Shouldn't you do that out-of-body magic thing and talk to him?"

"I don't think so. My gut's telling me to stay in the here-and-now and he told me the same thing, a bit more emphatically. Remember, I'm dealing with someone whose cultural evolution stopped in the seventeenth century. Blaise is a gentleman; he's courteous, not liberated. He thinks he's running the show. He doesn't want me underfoot. If I knew what I was doing, I might argue with him—I *would* argue with him. But I don't so, at least for now, I'm not. Things could change, but for now, I gave him my word that I'd stay out of the wasteland."

Nancy started to say something and thought better of it. She looked at her watch and announced that it was twenty after six. A journey from Meadow View to campus shouldn't take more than twenty minutes, but if Em didn't want to be late, she'd be wise to leave now.

"You've got my cell number?"

Em recited it.

"Okay—I'll stay here until ten after seven. Then, if I haven't heard from you, I'll assume that you're settled in at Hokkaido. I'll meet John there and we'll all pretend we don't know one another. What could be simpler than that?"

Em didn't know if Nancy was joking or not. She agreed that she'd call if Matt and Malerie stood her up. The television was on in Josh's room and Marsha was reading the sports section aloud. Emma put her head down and got past that obstacle but broke concentration in front of the elevator. She wasted five precious minutes talking to Charneal about how much better Eleanor had been since they'd removed the restraints.

The city had two snow crews out grooming the campus area, bulldozing piles of snow into trucks. When they were finished, the streets would have their full complement of parking spaces again. Until then, Em had to choose between parking for free in the library structure and racing along icy sidewalks to the restaurant—or paying to park in a municipal garage across the street from it. She chose the municipal garage, thinking it would be faster, and wound up spiraling past every car in Bower before squeezing between two snow drifts on the roof. After waiting too long for an elevator that never showed up, she raced down the stairs and arrived breathlessly on time.

Matt and Malerie, looking cold and impatient, hovered in the doorway. Matt said "hi" the way he would at work, but Malerie wanted to perform the whole social hugs-and-kisses ritual. Emma had seen too many bad horror and science fiction movies to be comfortable pressing flesh with a rogue who had designs on her life.

Friday was sushi day at Hokkaido, with the owner standing behind the counter rolling bits of seafood in rice and seaweed instead of taking orders or manning the cash register so the line moved at half speed. Though Emma was tempted by the sushi, Matt was so plainly appalled by the thought of merely *watching* someone eat raw fish that she ordered an innocuous plate of rice, chicken, and stir-fried veggies. Malerie ordered the same exact thing, while Matt, selecting from the entrees pictured on the wall, ordered the nearest thing to a hamburger an Oriental-style kitchen could serve.

"I'm a geek, not a gourmet," he explained when Emma

and Malerie, in an unanticipated show of solidarity, chided him for his absent spirit of adventure.

That solidarity dissolved when they sat down and Malerie fired a shot across Emma's bow.

"I think you can help me," the young woman said. "I'm at the mercy of something I can't control, but I think you can. People don't like me—*you* don't like me, don't pretend that you do. I can tell. I'm great at telling. You look at me and you can't keep your eyes in focus. Call it a nightmare, a demon, or a curse, I'm always on the outside looking in . . . until now. Matt told me about Bran Montgomery. Maybe I don't have all his symptoms—his demons and his creeping crud—but I've got something that needs fixing. And you can do it. You're *supposed* to do it."

Malerie was right about one thing: Em couldn't meet and hold the rogue's eyes at an across-the-table distance. She looked down at a dinner she probably wouldn't eat. "You've jumped to a lot of conclusions, Malerie."

"Are any of them wrong?"

"For starters, you're assuming I know what you're talking about and that I believe, in my heart of hearts, that Bran Montgomery harbored a curse. Any number of things could have caused or contributed to his condition."

"Name one," Malerie challenged.

"A tropical disease. Maybe a fungus. People come to Bower from all over the world—and not just the civilized parts of the world. It's a standing joke around here—people show up at University Hospital with illnesses that occur in only two places on earth: some remote jungle, swamp, or mountain valley and here in good old Bower, Michigan. We've even got a Type-A flu named for us."

"I don't have the flu. The flu doesn't last a lifetime. I've got a curse, Emma Merrigan, and you know it. Just look at me!"

Reluctantly, Emma accepted the challenge. Suppose the girl was right? Curses invaded bodies like viruses. So, in a way, did curse-hunters. What did rogues do? Was Malerie an innocent woman playing host to a rogue, an alien?

Em broke away from the stare. She watched Nancy come through the front door and realized that John was already at a deep corner table with an array of empty sushi dishes in front of him. The man was a natural-born spy. Even Nancy had to look hard to find him.

"I've spent *years* studying myself, Emma. You don't think Matt and I could have collected all that information about seventeenth-century Paris in such a short time if I hadn't already spend a whole lot of time compiling my sources? I dream about Paris almost every night—seventeenth-century Paris. I've haunted the city from top to bottom and I've seen things—I've *done* things that would curl your hair."

"Maybe," Em hedged, though she believed almost everything Malerie had said. The very best deceptions were those that were most nearly true. "But dreaming about Paris doesn't mean you're cursed."

"Doesn't it? I know the people who go with the names we gave you and more besides. I've even dreamt about a man named Blaise Raponde. In my dreams I know *him* very well."

Emma was glad to be seated when Malerie said that, glad her mouth and lungs were both empty. Even so, she didn't think she could fool Malerie with a denial and quickly decided not to try. "Then, in your dreams you know Blaise Raponde's a dead man and a dead end."

The rogue didn't flinch. "Help me, Emma. Free me from a dead man. Go back to Paris and free me from this—this *thing* that twists inside my thoughts. I'm ready, Emma. You say the word and we'll go back to your place right now and you can moot the rogue that curses me."

Mooting a curse—that was what Eleanor called the uncursing process. Harry, too. Em couldn't remember if she'd ever spoken those words to Matt, who sat between her and Malerie at the square table, eating his beef tempura as if he were all alone. How heavy a conscience was he hauling around?

Could Malerie be telling the truth? ·

"I need time, Mal. This business of dealing with curses—if there *are* curses snaking from one generation to the next. Whatever Matt may have told you—I don't really know what happened or how. Really, I'd say it was a dream except—" Em caught herself on the verge of mentioning Eleanor and Meadow View. Was that a simple slip of the tongue or a rogue's meddling? Heaven knew, Matt could have told Malerie about Eleanor, and if Malerie and the behind-Paris rogue, Grisette, were the same creature, she already knew. But there was no need to give anything away for free. "I stumbled into Bran Mongomery's dreams. I haven't stumbled into yours."

"Matt and I have given you everything you need, Emma: the names, the dates, the places. He can hypnotize you."

Emma felt the blood draining from her face. She tried not to blame Matt for a breach of confidence—he might not have had anything to do with the revelation. Malerie could have walked the past until she found that moment in November when Emma had counted backward from 100 and found herself on the verge of the eleventh century.

"Hypnosis won't be necessary. We didn't know what we were dealing with in November. This time, as you say: I have your notes. I'll think about them, study them, and maybe I'll dream about the seventeenth century. I'll let you know if I dream anything interesting."

"I *need* your help, Emma Merrigan. I know what you are. You have to help me. I've been cursed. You can't let me suffer. You'll suffer worse yourself if you do."

That was something to discuss with Harry, when he showed up, which he hadn't. He must not have been on that last plane—he'd have gotten to the restaurant somehow, Em was as sure of that as she was of anything right now. His absence left her on her own until sometime tomorrow, at the earliest.

Thirteen

E mma *trudged four* long, cold blocks from a street outside the Maisonettes proper to her front porch. Her ankle hurt and she clutched her skirt like some Victorian lady of the night. About a third of the sidewalks were un-shoveled—some people obviously had no fear of citations or weren't eager to get their mail. Emma's mailbox held another garden catalog and bulk mail from a fly-by-night loan company that offered, no doubt, usurious assistance with her holiday bills. She stuffed the envelopes in her coat pocket, opened the storm door, and thrust her key into the heavy-duty, solid-metal lock.

Em was prepared for the worst when the door needed an extra shove. Something had gotten into her house last November, hurling books from their shelves, defacing her parents' wedding portrait, and wedging an antique bent-wood chair against the front door in such a way that one of the legs had broken like gunfire when she opened it.

Actually, Emma hadn't opened the door that time. Bran had—Bran the football player with a neck as thick as her thigh. She wouldn't have minded having a football player at her back right now.

The door swung uneventfully open. With her breath held and her teeth clenched, Emma reached into darkness for the light switch. The coat closet door was open. It shouldn't have been—the cats had chewed one of her best boots to bits a few years ago and there was no sense in heating a coat closet—but Em didn't remember putting her coat on before she left last night and Nancy had had more important things to worry about than closing a closet door.

She stepped across the threshold and summoned the cats. Spin came running; Charm didn't. Em closed the outside doors and reset the locks before moving deeper into her home, turning on all the lights as she did. A single unbreakable Christmas ornament lay in the middle of the rug, near the library's historical atlas, still open to the map of seventeenth-century Paris. Spin walked between the objects as if to say—*See what we didn't do even though you left us without breakfast?*

He yowled when Em chose to hang up her coat before doing the right thing by her starving cats. (She didn't dare close the closet door until she found Charm.) When Em bent down to scratch behind Spin's ears, he marched out of reach and yowled again.

"All right. Food before affection."

Charm appeared when Emma popped a food can lid. She hissed at her brother when he dared approach *her* dish. Em took pity on her bigger, politer cat and emptied a second gourmet-sized can onto a saucer. They were both eating loudly when she left the kitchen.

Traditionally Emma took her holiday decorations down on Twelfth Night, which would be tomorrow. That made tonight the tree's last night for this season and, for her, a traditional moment for reflection. She held the fallen ornament for an extra moment before returning it to the tree. It wasn't one of her treasures—those were hung on catproof branches—but it held memories of Jeff, Lori, Jay-Jay, and the years when they'd been a family; and it triggered a bout of the weepies.

Emma found a handkerchief. She rubbed her eyes and blew her nose until it hurt and the weepies had ended, then she noticed that the answering-machine message light was blinking.

While the machine rewound its tape, a computer-chip voice said she'd received six messages. The first was a reminder that she had a dentist's appointment at seven-thirty Monday morning. The second was a hang-up and the third had barely begun when the phone rang. Em hesitated before picking it up, but the machine couldn't screen calls in mid-replay.

"Hello?"

"Emma?" Em recognized Nancy's voice. "You're okay? You got home okay? You sound kind of *distant*."

"I'm home okay."

"We left a few minutes after you did and tried calling as soon as we got home ourselves. You didn't pick up."

"Parking was awful. I got home okay, it just took a while."

"So? What happened? I couldn't see her face clearly, just round shoulders and long, dirty hair—like she was a refugee from the Sixties and the SDS. Your friend Matt looked like he was in another world and you had your game face on."

It was embarrassing to talk about curses, rogues, and subjective realities, and it got worse once Emma realized that John was on an extension phone. He was a good listener, and that was part of the problem—John Amstel would listen for hours, take a deep breath, and deliver a thirty-second opinion that cut to the bone. Em's bones were tender just then. She defended herself with honesty.

"I can take only so much of this metaphysical cloak-and-dagger stuff before I succumb to systems overload. It's all 'seems' and 'feels.' Malerie seems and feels strange to me. Everything she said could be coincidence—or something she got from Matt. Or she could be exactly as cold and calculating as she seemed and felt. My brain wants something solid to hold on to. Too many shadows and it goes into denial."

"The girl's a strange one, Emma," John pronounced

from his extension. "If I saw her coming down the street, I'd get out of the way. If I had to shake her hand, I'd count my fingers afterward."

John's opinion gave Em more relief than she wanted to admit. She began a more detailed description of her meal with Matt and Malerie.

"Malerie took the lead. I didn't challenge her all that much—I wanted to hear what she'd have to say for herself. She didn't hide much."

"She probably thinks you're not as smart as she is and that she runs rings around you," John said. "I seem to remember doing that with my parents when I was her age."

Of course, if Malerie were a rogue, the three of them together weren't nearly her age.

Nancy added her thoughts: "And we were wrong about what our parents did or didn't know most of the time. Sometimes they couldn't stop us, but that didn't mean they didn't know what we were doing, and sometimes they didn't need to, because they knew how things *had* to turn out."

"I hope that's not the case with Malerie," Emma cut in before John and Nancy got too far into their own discussion. "What bothers me most is that she made a plausible case for being a victim. I couldn't vote to convict. I've got reasonable doubts."

She adjusted the playback volume on her answering machine and tapped the pause button to resume the tape while John and Nancy discussed the reasonableness of doubts. The interrupted third message was from a Maisonettes neighbor asking if she knew anyone with a blower who'd clear it for her. The walk had been clear when Em walked home. She didn't need to return the call.

The fourth message started—a woman's voice, clipped and edgy. "Ms Merrigan? Emma? Are you home? This is Charneal Andres-Black. I'm calling from Meadow View Manor. Your cousin's taken a fall out of her bed. We've arranged for an ambulance to take her to University Hospital. Emma? Ms Merrigan, please call as soon as you get home."

Em's first thought was—*What did she have to do to get them to call her at work when an emergency arose?* Then the computer-chip voice recited the time stamp it had appended to the message. Eleanor hadn't fallen during work hours. Charneal worked the night shift and had called at eight o'clock, when she, John, and Nancy were each and all keeping an eye on Malerie.

"Guys—" Em pushed the pause button. "Guys—I've got to get off the phone. That noise you heard in the background—that was my message tape. Eleanor's fallen at Meadow View. I've got to find out what's happened."

Nancy gasped. "She was—"

"The message was time-stamped at eight. I've got to hang up."

"Call us when you're done—before you do anything or go anyplace," John said. "Nance filled me in on what you told her—this whole time-travel angle. You shouldn't be alone."

Emma sensed that John didn't believe a word his wife had said. He thought she was losing her mind and needed 24/7 observation. She was regretting that she'd ever confided anything in either of them as she hung up and hit the autodialer for Meadow View. Charneal herself picked up the phone.

"So what happened?" Em asked at the earliest opportunity.

"Eleanor had a seizure. She was still seizing when we got into the room—the same thing must have happened the last time, but we got there too late. Doctor Nabliss ordered an ambulance. We bundled her up and sent her to the emergency room at University. That was before I called you. She's still there, Emma. I can't tell you anything more. I've been calling every half hour since she left here and no one's telling me anything—not if she's stable, or coming back here, or if they've admitted her. I won't be surprised to learn she broke her wrist in the fall. Her hand was twisted pretty bad when we found her and she registered pain when we touched it."

Emma absorbed the information in a silence that made Charneal uncomfortable.

"I would have gone to the ER with her, Emma, but we're short staffed tonight. Two of the aides didn't show up at all. I'm the only physician assistant in the building. I couldn't leave. I would have; believe me, I would have ridden in the ambulance myself."

Em couldn't tell how sincere Charneal's protests were and there wasn't sense in finding out. Her path was clear: gear up for the hike to her car and plan to spend the night ensuring that her comatose mother's body got the care it needed while at the same time trying not to think about what might be happening to the rest of her in the wasteland.

She honored John and Nancy's request, juggling the phone as she wrestled with boot zippers.

"Meadow View says Eleanor had a seizure," Em told Nancy, who was the Amstel who picked up the phone. "They sent her to the University Emergency Room—"

"Harry didn't make it."

Em let go of the zipper. "What?"

"He didn't check into his hotel. I called. I figured you'd want to know, but wouldn't take the time to check yourself, so I called. The East Coast was socked in until closing time. It'll be a madhouse tomorrow morning when they start moving planes again. He might not get here until Sunday."

Nancy was right. Em was interested in the information and she wouldn't have taken the time to get it herself, but that didn't sweeten her thank-you. She begged off additional conversation and left the house with her coat half-buttoned. She'd buttoned it all the way and wished for another layer or two by the time she got to her car.

If the airports would be madhouses in the morning, University Hospital's Emergency Room was a madhouse at 10 P.M. Em stood at a cluttered counter, biding her time, while a pair of bloodier emergencies got the attention they deserved.

"You're looking for *who*?" a harried clerk finally asked when the chaos had ebbed to manageable levels.

"My cousin, Eleanor Merrigan she was transported by ambulance from Meadow View Manor around eight this evening? I think she may have been admitted."

The clerk began flipping through a clipboard file. "Is that with one or two Rs?"

"Two."

"Not admitted," he read from his forms. "Broken right wrist. Dehydration. Cast. IV drip. Not admitted. Requested transportation back to Meadow View at eight-fifty." The clerk looked up. "We've been short transportation all night. Gotta be a full moon behind those clouds. We didn't get your cousin out of here until"—the clerk looked at his watch—"twenty minutes ago. Meadow View should have her tucked now. Sorry."

"My fault," Em said without conviction. "I should've called here first."

She returned to the parking lot, fighting tears. Frustration could cause a weepie attack as easily as mournful memories did. Clouds weren't covering the moon, which wasn't nearly full but was surrounded by three shimmering rings—a virtual guarantee of more snow in the next twenty-four hours.

The Meadow View lot was empty when Em pulled in. The front door was locked, too. She leaned on the bell several times and, over her ankle's protests, was ready to trudge around to the loading dock when an annoyed-looking supervisor let her in. They had a terse conversation about visiting hours and emergencies that fell just short of threats on both sides. Em was shaking inside her coat when she got into the elevator.

Charneal was waiting for her when the doors opened.

"I tried calling you, Ms Merrigan, but you'd already left. We just got your cousin bedded down. She's asleep or resting—"

There was a difference, although it couldn't be detected without a CAT scan.

"I just want to see her."

Em started toward the room. Charneal kept pace.

"I told you about her wrist. They've put a cast on it."

The way Charneal drew her attention back to Eleanor's wrist time and time again Em had to wonder if it had broken tonight or an earlier fall. She wanted to tell Charneal not to worry, but there was no way to say that without raising the very suspicions she was trying to allay. Even with nothing more than the corridor lights for illumination, Emma could see that her mother had taken new damage since 6 P.M.

A palm-sized rectangular bandage clung to Eleanor's forehead. "She cut her head, too. Stitches?"

"Staples, I think. We haven't changed the bandage yet. There was quite a lot of blood. She'll need a new gown—unless you won't mind the stains."

"I'll order one, maybe two." There was a site on the Internet that sold snap-together clothing for invalids. There might be more than one but Emma hadn't felt the need to do any comparison shopping for breakaway nightgowns. "Can I go in?"

"No reason not to."

Both women approached the bed. Em wasn't surprised that Eleanor was wrapped in the wide elastic restraints. The cast on Eleanor's right wrist appeared to be made from bubble wrap, but Em didn't doubt that Eleanor could do herself significant harm with it. Emma hadn't expected to see an IV running clear fluid into Eleanor's left arm. Her mother hadn't had an IV since she had the surgery that put a feeding tube in her stomach.

"What's running?" she asked Charneal.

"It's a precaution. She was a little dehydrated—they almost always are, you know. ER didn't find any obvious cause for the seizure. It's possible it could have been brought on by dehydration. Doctor Nabliss saw her in the ER and changed her protocol to get more fluids into her."

Em usually avoided touching the arm that had the IV in it, but with Eleanor's other arm locked up in a cast, she'd lost her choice. Maybe it was dehydration that cratered her cheeks and left her eyelids looking like crepe paper, but Eleanor had fallen below the Sleeping Beauty threshold. She looked *old* for the first time.

"Time's running out," she murmured, unaware that she'd spoken aloud until Charneal assured her that it wasn't.

"Her heart's good and her lungs and liver. She's plenty strong yet."

Emma didn't know if that was a blessing or—literally—a curse. Charneal left Emma sitting beside Eleanor's bed, holding her hand and wondering if, when she went home, she should disregard Blaise's requests and warnings to pay another visit behind Paris. From what he'd said at the end, Blaise had plenty of motive to destroy the rogues holding Eleanor prisoner, but it was also hard to interpret Eleanor's current condition as a sign that his campaign against them was going well.

She tried Harry's hotel when she got home—*five* blocks this time!—but Harry wasn't there and he wasn't at home either. Em left a less-than-coherent message about Eleanor's injury on his home-based answering machine. She'd turned out the lights when she recalled that she'd never played the message tape to its end. It rewound to the beginning and eventually got to the fifth message, which was from Harry Graves.

"The absolute present's against us, Emma. I'm battened down in a hotel near the airport—" He recited the particulars and Em dutifully transcribed them to scrap paper. "I've got a reservation for a six A.M. flight—the earliest anyone seems to think that anything's going to fly. I got your messages after I checked in. Since you're not picking up the phone, I'm going to assume that no news is good news—or at least no worse than the news you've already passed along. Don't hesitate to call me if I'm wrong in my assumption. Betwixt you and your friend, I'm not

making much sense of the situation there in Bower. Mind
you—I'm not saying that either of you aren't telling the
truth—I'm saying the truth doesn't fit any known patterns. Rogues do not cooperate. Be careful, Emma, and let
me repeat that: as far back as anyone has gone, rogues
have never been seen to cooperate with one another."

There was a hiss-y silence during which Emma could
almost hear Harry saying the words he hadn't actually
said: until quite recently, curse-hunters hadn't been much
on cooperation either.

Em peered across the room, squinting to read the VCR
clock without her contact lenses. It read somewhere between 1AM and 2AM. Despite his assurances and much
as she wanted to talk to him, Emma decided against calling Harry—conversation at this hour would only guarantee that neither of them would get enough sleep to face
tomorrow.

Emma turned off the lights and climbed the stairs to
her bedroom one weary, in-the-dark step at a time. Her
ankle throbbed without her boots to support it. She shed
her borrowed dress in the bathroom and belatedly checked
the mirror for spies. Hers was the only face in the mirror
and it looked a lot worse than Eleanor's. She slathered her
skin in moisturizer and crawled into bed, where she found
herself wide-eyed and nervously awake.

Em considered getting up, getting dressed, and getting
herself back out to Meadow View. She thought she'd feel
safer beside her mother's bed—the old "put all your eggs
in one basket and watch it very, very carefully" gambit. In
the end, she stayed put in the Maisonettes. A half-century
of more-or-less proper behavior had taken its toll on
Emma's non-conformist instincts—she *cared* what
Charneal Andres-Black thought and didn't want her thinking that Emma Merrigan was some sort of nut case.

Belting her warmest robe over her nightshirt, Em settled in her favorite chair. She pulled the two black-leather
books—the sparse one Eleanor had written for her and the
fuller one she'd written for herself—from their shelves

and thumbed through the more complete one in search of peace and protection.

Curse-hunters had a thing about poison—easily half of the recipes Eleanor had written down called for mercury, or wormwood, or something else that no sane person would keep in her house. Em found one recipe for warding windows and doors that started with ordinary table salt and progressed to garlic and olive oil. Add oregano and wine vinegar and it might have made a decent salad dressing, but Emma couldn't take it seriously as protection against the likes of Malerie Dunbar and the other behind-Paris rogues. She returned the books to the shelf and sat staring at the darkened Christmas tree.

This, the Mother Voice whispered, *is the part of the movie where the camera pulls back to show the audience what the actors don't know: The villain lurking in the closet with the whites of his eyes and the edge of his knife glinting in the spotlight. The actor closes her eyes, never to awaken again except in terror and death.*

Mired in the irrational logic of dread and exhaustion, Emma resolved to remain awake all night, protecting her precious memories. Of course, her determination to stay awake was a near-perfect soporific. She was staring into dark shadows one moment and looking at dawn-fingers the next. In the stillness of that second moment, before she'd moved a hand or foot, Emma recalled a dream—

She'd visited the wasteland, her own little corner of the wasteland where Mariana's workroom hid underground and yet was warm with autumn sunshine. She'd been stitching on the unfinished embroidery, but the dream wasn't about embroidery. In the dream she set her threads and needles aside and drifted—the way one did in a dream—to the table where Blaise had left his Bible. A stack of smooth paper sat beside the worn book, and a feather quill. She'd written a letter with that quill, never once needing an inkwell or a blotter. It was a short letter—less than one side of one sheet of paper—and she'd folded it carefully to keep the contents private.

That was all. The dream ended with the folding. Emma had no idea what confidences her dream self had chosen to share and had no time, either, to dwell on the mystery. The phone rang, and without thinking, she lifted the handset before the answering machine intercepted the call.

It was Harry Graves, freshly arrived at Detroit Metro Airport and waiting for his rental car. Emma resolved to be polite.

"I haven't seen this much snow in—" Harry paused. "At least ten years."

Emma sat up in the chair. She was stiff all over, but at least she'd left the footrest extended and her ankle wasn't throbbing. She shivered, not from cold but the realization that a curse-hunter's memory could become a liability over time and that both Harry and Eleanor censored themselves reflexively.

"I have my map here in front of me," Harry continued. "We can meet anywhere you choose, Emma. Hotel, restaurant, park bench, or living room. It's your choice, but someplace private would be better, considering what we've got to do. Can you lead me to this counter-Paris you've discovered?"

"I think so," Em stalled. Blaise told her not to follow him. Would he feel the same way if she was bringing the same cavalry that hadn't shown up to save Eleanor? "Maybe. If I can find the church. Did you get my last message? I didn't want to disturb you at your hotel; I left it on your home machine around one this morning."

"No—May I assume there's been a change in circumstances?"

"Yes, and for the worse. Eleanor fell out of bed again. She cut her forehead and broke her wrist. I saw her last night. She's going to be all right—medically, I mean. I'm worried, though, very worried. I had a very interesting dinner last night—listening to a woman I truly believe is a rogue tell me, in so many words, how she was cursed and how it was my obligation to uncurse her. She said I would suffer if I didn't; I wasn't sure if that was a threat from her personally or a statement of fact about curse-hunters in general. She skated a fine line, Harry, and I was talking to her when Eleanor fell."

"And now you don't know what to believe? I can assure you the words were a threat, but you're wondering if you're dealing with the real thing or a pawn?"

"Exactly."

"And you're wondering if it's coincidence that your mother fell out of bed or if she had help? And if she had help, from whence did it come?"

"I'm trying hard not to leap to any conclusions, but yeah—those questions have crossed my mind since midnight. There were four rogues behind Paris—you got *that* message, didn't you. They were cooperating, Harry, I'd stake my life on it. The four of them walked up to the pit where they're keeping Eleanor and tossed another curse in. They're fastened to her, feeding on her like leeches."

"You have a gift for words, Emma. Indeed, I listened to your message several times. I daresay I've committed it to memory."

"Well, you said a *rogue* had come to Bower—that leaves three unaccounted for. I'm starting to feel seriously outnumbered. One of them must have gotten into Meadow View after I left last night. Honestly, I think we should meet out there. They discourage visitors before noon—before one, really—but they make exceptions. They'll make an exception for us. I've decided to trust you, Harry—heaven help you if I've made the wrong decision—but together there's still only two of us. We're going to be outnumbered no matter what, but if we're with her, then none of us are alone."

"I'll take your trust as a compliment, Emma—and your warning as unnecessary. I'd still prefer to meet you privately and not at a nursing home. If you've decided to trust me, there are precautions that can be taken, for you and Eleanor both. I presume the good folk of Meadow View Manor have your phone number and will call you, if needs be?"

"They should. They always call my home number, but that's where I am right now."

"Then they'll call you again, if needs be. We can look in on Eleanor after one; that's easily done, but let us meet first somewhere where you feel comfortable. I assume that would be inside your own home. You're not some tree worshiper who lives under the open sky?"

Emma's gut fought gravity the way one did when a roller coaster had climbed to the top of its first and steepest drop. There was one moment when the universe was perfectly balanced, then everything went downhill and it was time to scream. "No. Here is the best place." Em recited the route; it had been years since she'd lost a visitor. "It's really simple until it comes to parking. This neighborhood's a nightmare for parking. Worse because of the snow. And you don't dare double-park. They'll tow your car in a New York minute."

"Another unnecessary warning," Harry assured her. "I'll manage the parking, once someone here finds me a car. It's what? Eight-fifty—no time change, right? Give me an hour to find you. We'll have a few hours to talk before Meadow View Manor unrolls its red carpet. We'll set your mind at ease and then get down to the business behind Paris."

Emma rubbed her forehead. Even if Harry Graves could solve all her problems with a wave of *his* magic wand, this was still going to be a long, difficult day. "Did you get breakfast on the plane?" she asked, determined to remain polite and friendly.

"You jest. Surely you jest, Emma Merrigan."

She guessed that was Harry-humor and managed a halfhearted chuckle. "I'll round up brunch, then. What would you like?"

"Surprise me— Ah, the marching moron has returned, bearing a key in its paw. My carriage awaits. I shall be with you anon, Emma."

They ended their conversation. Emma remained a moment in her chair, trying to imagine Harry and Eleanor as man and wife, sharing the same bed. It wasn't a pretty picture.

Emma could make the airport run in under an hour, but she didn't have to sign for and drive a rental car along unfamiliar roads or check into a hotel. She doubled Harry's estimate and, since her ankle seemed willing to bear her weight, left the house in search of brunch. Surprising Harry wouldn't be as difficult as pleasing him, but she had an ally. The best delicatessen in Bower—by some counts the best deli between New York and Chicago—hung its shingle a mere half mile from Em's front door.

In better weather she often stopped at the Outpost to undo the good effects of walking for exercise. In winter she usually waited for spring, but for Harry Graves, Em braved the cold and the icy sidewalks. After fifty minutes of walking, browsing, and waiting on line, she returned to the Maisonettes with more food than she'd eat in a week. She was rinsing dust off wedding presents that hadn't been off the top shelves of her kitchen cabinets since she put them there seven years ago when the brass knocker clanged against the front door.

A glance at her watch convinced Em that Harry had an unerring sense of direction, unconscionable luck when it came to parking his car, and couldn't possibly have registered at his hotel. It also implied that he was taking her situation very seriously—but then, she'd known that from the moment he'd made overnight plane reservations.

There was a moment of awkwardness at the front door—not quite a vampiritic awkwardness that required an explicit invitation before crossing a threshold, but a sense that there was something significant about one curse-hunter entering the home of another. Thinking back, Em hadn't felt anything unusual when Eleanor arrived—but Eleanor's arrival had been so extraordinary by itself that she wouldn't have noticed anything subtle.

Em stepped back and let the door swing wide. "Come on in, Harry." If an invitation were necessary, she'd do it in style: "My house is your house. Make yourself at home."

"May it be forever safe from harm."

A blast of frigid January air followed Harry into the hall. Emma quickly shut the doors. When she turned around, Harry offered her a brown-paper shopping bag.

"A token," he called it, and Em was certain it had some significance beyond old-school manners.

By the weight and balance it was a bottle of wine, which she set on the hall table while she hung Harry's cashmere coat on the best hanger in the house, freed from its usual duty of supporting her best coat. Then, bag in hand, she led him into the living room, where the cats, having heard a man's voice, were ready to give him the once-over. Harry didn't reach down to scratch their itchy foreheads. Probably he was worried about getting Charm's silver-gray hair on his jet-black pants.

Or maybe he was allergic. Emma had forgotten to ask and she wasn't, by any stretch of the imagination, a fanatical housekeeper.

She lifted the bottle out of the bag and peeled back the tissue paper wrapping. From the label, she knew it was French and from the shape of the bottle she knew it was a Bordeaux. Beyond that she didn't know vintage from vinegar, though she suspected Harry had given her a vastly better wine than she usually drank.

"Thank you. Thank you very much." Ten A.M. was a bit early for wine. "I'll save it for a special occasion—unless it's for dinner." Emma hoped she hadn't just committed herself to cooking a fancy meal.

"No, not tonight's dinner. Let it rest awhile. Maybe later this year. The bottle should have recovered from its journey by, say, September."

Good grief—what kind of life did Harry think she led? Em tightened her grip on the bottle. There was a wine rack built into the cabinet where she kept the wedding china. The wine would have to slum there next to a screw-top bottle of white zinfandel until something *very* special came up. Harry inventoried her books and artwork, saying nothing while she got down on her knees to settle the bottle in its new home.

Em interrupted his appraisal to ask: "Would you like some coffee?" Her coffee, at least, could stand up to the most rigorous inspection.

"Black and regular. No decaf. There's something else in the bag. You did notice?"

She hadn't, but covered by saying—on her way into the kitchen— "I wanted to get you some coffee first."

The shelf above the coffee maker held eight of Lori's ceramic mugs. No two were alike, and all of them were special to Lori's stepmother. If Harry Graves couldn't appreciate Lori's art, then there was no hope. But Harry noticed the glaze and the S-shaped handle that was as easy to hold as it was elegant to behold.

"So, you were married, once upon a time?" he asked after Emma had explained that her stepdaughter had made the mug. "Children as well as stepchildren?"

Emma avoided his eyes by fishing a black-leather-bound book out of the paper sack. "No children except stepchildren. I married twice," she admitted, and wondered what had prompted her to volunteer the extra information.

"But you're not now?"

"And never again—unless my mind starts to go and I forget why I got divorced."

"Ah—" said Harry, and they both fell silent while Em thumbed through the book.

Like the others in her growing collection of black, leather-bound books, Harry's gift was handwritten. The boldly scripted pages were marred by scratch-outs and squiggled insertions. Em recognized some of the recitations and recipes, but it was the many unfamiliar pages that caught and held her attention. Harry's black book was more like a journal than a grimoire—densely written, impossible to read at a glance. Em paused at a random page—

*I asked myself—how can that be? Is the absolute
present a true absolute or simply another illusion?
Could I ever visit tomorrow as easily as I visit yesterday? The answer, I'm convinced is No . . .*

"I hope you find it interesting."

Em nodded. "I'd already guessed the books I inherited
from Eleanor are incomplete. I'm glad—"

"No, I'm sure the book Eleanor wrote for you is complete in every traditional way. Mine is, dare I say—over-
written? But you're an educated woman. I presumed
you'd appreciate another point of reference."

Once again, Emma heard the words that her visitor didn't
say: his curse-hunting peers, including his wife, weren't im-
pressed by Harry's efforts to create wasteland science. He
wanted a student, or at least a fresh audience. Em took a step
backward, framing his reflection in the glass over one of her
pictures. She saw an intimidating man of indeterminate
years, but what did people who knew Harry Graves best see
when they looked at him? A man of insight and precision? Or
a blow-hard who had to think highly of himself because no
one else did?

"I look forward to reading it, Harry—honestly, I do."
Emma tucked it on the shelf between the other two volumes. "We can talk while we're eating. You said to surprise you, so I got enough food to feed a small army.
Would you like to start with lox and bagels or a Greek
croissant?"

"What, pray tell, is a Greek croissant?"

"An Outpost specialty," Em explained, going into the
kitchen to arrange the honey-and-nut rolls on a plate.
"Somewhere between a regular croissant and baklava—
except in calories. It's got all the calories of baklava and
the croissant together."

As she set the plate on the table, Harry said, "You don't
take after your mother much."

The statement caught Em with her mouth open. "Why
should I?" she stammered. "I don't know her. If I take

after her at all, it's the triumph of nature over nurture, genes over experience."

"Yet, you'll risk everything to reunite her body and spirit?"

"That's not taking after Eleanor," Em said in a tone she hoped would put an end to the discussion, even though Harry's initial remark had left her aching with curiosity. "And anyway, it's gotten personal. They're rearranging my past and it's starting to have consequences in my real life. The rogue that's here in Bower has managed to get the library to hire her as my assistant! She looped through time itself to change the prerequisites and I'm the only one who knows it. That's the reason I'm trusting you, Harry. I want this settled. I want my life back."

Harry swallowed a mouthful of sticky croissant, then gulped down coffee. "Hunting is your life now, Emma. You won't go through withdrawal if you stop walking, not physical withdrawal. You'll start to grow old again, of course, but once you've done what you can do, nothing else can make you feel alive." He paused, seeming to expect her to agree or argue. Em did neither, and after another awkward moment he continued. "You're sure there are four rogues? Four of them together? Could you possibly be mistaken?"

"No. I think I know a rogue when I'm face to face with one. I've learned that much on my own."

"That's not good at all, Emma. The rogue I traced to Bower—the only one I *could* trace—*isn't* rooted in the seventeen century or in Paris. It has other places. A lot of places, but not Paris and not the sixteen-hundreds."

"Whoa. Wait a minute. If we're going to do this, let's do it right. I know what I saw, Harry—I was *in* Paris and the year was sixteen-eighty, but what, exactly, do you mean by *place*, Harry? Maybe that's where I'm confused and where I'm confusing you. Is *place* a physical location in the real world, past or present? Is it a human mind susceptible to infection by a particular curse? Is the wasteland a *place*? Or is the answer D: all of the above?"

"Place is place, Emma." Harry sat back in his chair. "Everything to do with curses is subjective. Eleanor must have told you that. Therefore 'place' means whatever you think it means." He folded his arms over his negligible gut while Em battled the urge to throw something at him, then he leaned forward. "Or do you want the *full* explanation?"

Em saw doom looming before her, but she nodded her head all the same.

Fourteen

There was justice in the world. What went around did come around . . . and sat on the far side of Emma Merrigan's table, providing her with answers more detailed than she either needed or wanted. Only a few years ago, when Em and Lori had been driving home from the airport and neither of them could see the other's face, Lori had confided how she and her older brother used to huddle in their bedrooms, asking each other—

Do we want to know the answer bad enough to sit through the full *explanation?*

For Emma, who'd been driving at the time, it was the closest she'd come to dying from embarrassment. Lori assured her stepmother that her answers were always interesting, always informative, and usually *did* answer the original question. Eventually. But they'd learned not to come to her for a quick answer.

Ever since that night, Em had tried to keep her answers short but short didn't come naturally to a professor's daughter and short didn't come at all to Harry Graves. Though he didn't quite puff up like a preening pigeon, it was plain to Emma that *place* was something to which Harry had given a lot of thought.

In essence, *place* was where some thing or person belonged. For ordinary people and things, *place* was simply a real-world location in space and time. Locations in space could change; locations in time invariably did, but the links were direct and unbroken. Most important: ordinary people and things didn't wind up in the wasteland. For people and things that weren't ordinary—hunters, rogues, and curses—*place* was more complicated, though it retained its essential meaning.

Em *belonged* in Bower; her root was there and her curse-hunting talents were strongest there. If she moved somewhere else, her talents would wither until she put down roots again. Once she had new roots, she'd have *place* and her talents would rebloom. Em didn't usually think of herself as a potted plant but the concept of *place* was clearer after Harry's full explanation.

The curiae were divided as to whether the curse hunters living and working along the edge of time (or as Harry called it, the absolute present) should spend as much their lives as possible in one geographic location, putting down one mighty root and *place*, or whether they should move around, developing many roots, many places. Either way, their theories about *place* and everything else were due for a test once they came face to face with Merle Acalia Merrigan, better known as Emma.

When Harry had finished his sermon about Em's uniqueness, he began to talk about curses and rogues. She looked at the clock. It was nearly eleven. There might be time for another answer.

Curses had no *place* when they were spawned on the edge of time. They withered, some faster than others, if they couldn't find a victim whose mind was fallow and whose circumstances were similar to those in which they had been spawned. Harry didn't know how a wasteland curse located a victim across the edge of time or if the infection was invariably successful once the victim had been located. He did know that curses, although they roamed the ever-increasing breadth of the wasteland, could leave it only at the edge. When a curse had corrupted and consumed its victim, it returned to the wasteland, stronger than it had been when it departed, but no wiser.

"Your cats learn more in a day than a curse learns in decades. I think of them as malignant vegetables. You're not a vegetarian, are you?"

Emma shook her head and Harry began his discourse on rogues.

Rogues were mutant curses: curses spawned with an iota of intellect and the capacity to remember and learn. They were more selective in their victimizations, seeking variety rather than similarity—

Em interrupted: "Until they stumble across a wasteland-walking curse-hunter?"

"That's one way," Harry grumbled, miffed that she'd stolen his punchline. "But as you once pointed out to me—if that were the only way to make a rogue, there wouldn't be very many of them. Deviating a hunter may be the most spectacular way for a curse to become a rogue, but I very much doubt it is the easiest way or the most common. No, I think that sometimes a victim welcomes the curse and what began as infection becomes partnership. At the end of a mortal lifetime, instead of a death there's a new rogue in the Netherlands." He paused and selected another Greek croissant. "I assume this won't bother you, but the consensus is that curse-hunters don't have souls. The story goes that we surrendered them in return for the ability to walk through time. I think it's all nonsense, but you'll find those who take it very seriously indeed."

Emma did not need another theological conversation. "You're right. I'm not bothered. Back to the important questions. So, Malerie Dunbar could be an ordinary woman who caught a curse, but instead of fighting it, she welcomed it and became a rogue?"

"Possibly. Have you heard of Occam's Razor?"

Em nodded. "Otherwise known as 'Keep It Simple, Stupid.'"

"Then the simple explanation is that this Malerie was a

rogue long before it precipitated itself here and it's here because *you're* here."

"Me? Your razor needs sharpening, Harry. If a rogue's quest is to expand its horizons, then I don't see where I'm all that attractive. Except for two years in New York City, I've never lived anywhere but Bower, and as a curse-hunter, I don't know my ass from my elbow, Harry. When I *do* successfully transfer myself from here to the waste-land, I wind up with my nose in the dirt."

"But you get up, Emma. You get up and you do what must be done. Your instincts and your empathy guide you. You mooted an old and potent curse. You've made a *place* for yourself in the Netherlands."

Emma set her coffee mug down. "Who told you that?"

"You didn't have to. It lit up like a beacon at midnight. If nothing else, the curiae have gotten the watches organized—think of the watches as a DEW line: distant-early-warning radar for our cold war against curses and rogues. I'll admit, not all the changes of the past century have been for the good, but the watches have made a tremendous difference. We don't know *where* in the Netherlands, but after the watchmen compare notes—*I* developed the formulas that allow us to calculate *where* in geographic terms the deed was done. If someone reshapes a chunk of the Netherlands, we know it happened."

"You've been spying on me."

"That's a harsh word, Emma."

"But an accurate one."

"An incomplete one. Knowing that something has happened in the Netherlands is a far cry from knowing where and when it happened. That's why Eleanor came out here in the first place: to see who you were, in absolute terms, and who was helping you, since you obviously had help and no one knew where you were getting it."

"Blaise Raponde."

"Who?"

"His name is Blaise Raponde. All this trouble started

because Eleanor was convinced he's a rogue. He's not. Blaise Raponde is a ghost."

Harry tucked his chin against his chest before saying, disdainfully: "There are no such things, Emma."

"Blaise has been dead for centuries. He doesn't have any *place* except in the wasteland. He says he haunts his own dreams. What does that make him if not a ghost?"

Harry shrugged. "There are no ghosts. There are only curses, hunters, and rogues. Before Eleanor left, the consensus was that you were dallying with a rogue."

"Dallying?" Emma arched her eyebrows. "I'm not *dallying* with anyone. Blaise isn't a rogue, Harry. Maybe 'ghost' isn't the right word. I've been over it and over it— he's not a rogue."

"I agree. Blaise Raponde is not a rogue."

"That's it? No argument?" Emma grappled with anticlimax. "You agree? Eleanor tried to destroy him. What changed your mind? Had you already changed it when we got ambushed? Weren't you part of the great consensus? She expected *you* to show up with the cavalry and the marines to help her."

"A point of clarification, Emma: Eleanor hears what she wants to hear. What I told my wife was, 'Don't do anything until I can round up witnesses.' How that became cavalry or marines is a question you'll have to ask her. At the time, yes, I assumed we were dealing with a rogue. Might I have changed that assumption had I arrived in the nick of time? Possibly. Since then, you've come and gone from the Netherlands many times and he has neither opposed you nor followed you. I, for one, am convinced he *can't* follow you into the absolute present, and if he can't do that, then *ipso facto* he's not a rogue." Harry cocked his head then added, "He's not a ghost, either. There are no such things as ghosts."

"Blaise says that he is—that he was—a curse-hunter. He lived in Paris and died there in sixteen-eighty."

"'Is.' If you've heard Monsieur Raponde say he was a hunter, then he *is* a hunter, I see no reason to argue the point. If you did indeed see four rogues together, we need all the allies we can get. *Four!* In all the time that I've hunted—and as you may have guessed, that is a substantial amount of time I have seen curses form packs, but never rogues. Never. Isolation is the essence of a rogue, isolation and power. Replace the isolation with cooperation, without lessening the power—" Harry shook his head. "As a hunter, Monsieur Raponde most assuredly knows what that means."

"He might but *I* sure don't."

"Forming the curiae gave us an advantage over the rogues. Prior to that, we were scarcely less isolated than the rogues and curses we hunted. Now when a rogue is spotted, we can mass resources against it. It's been a good century for hunting, whatever you might think from the newspapers and history books. But if the rogues have begun to emulate us, our advantage is gone. Individually, rogues are more powerful than we are. Even now, the average rogue is ancient compared to the average hunter. The fringe benefits of hunting curses were of limited use when infection was a death sentence. No one has benefitted more from the rise of scientific medicine than we. The last century has been our golden age. Scores of the old terrors have been mooted. Some members of the curiae believed we were winning the war against the old rogues—and not a moment too soon, considering how many new curses six billion people spawn each and every day."

Emma was unimpressed. "If rogues are so clever, I'm surprised it's taken them a century to adopt their enemy's tactic. I'm even more surprised that it's a surprise to the curiae. Hasn't anyone been paying attention to the stories about antibiotic-resistant bacteria? The analogy should have been clear."

They locked stares a moment before Harry admitted, "There have been attempts to enlighten them, but there's been no proof. Without proof, the curiae see no need to listen."

"So, if you come back with proof of four rogues working together, then the powers-that-be might pay attention to you?"

He hesitated before saying, "I can hope."

Emma glanced at her watch. It was after noon. She began collecting plates. "Meadow View's open for business. I want to go out there. We can hunt rogues after we've seen Eleanor. You do want to see her, don't you?"

She was at the kitchen sink before Harry answered. "You want to see her; that's reason enough." A minute passed, maybe more, before Harry spoke again. "It has happened before, Emma. You needn't be self-conscious about it."

"What?" Em called, not certain she'd heard him correctly. "Self-conscious about what? Turning fifty before I discovered how to turn on the tap at the Fountain of Youth? I'm not self-conscious about looking a generation older than my mother, who is almost certainly older than my father ever imagined."

"About your partnership with Monsieur Raponde. Now that the watches are well established, it's not unusual for hunters to meet first in the Netherlands. Common shelters have become—well, almost *common.* Of course, no one has shared a Netherlands shelter with a *dead* hunter. In the usual course of events, when a hunter dies, both parts— the part that lives and the part that hunts—are gone. There's no looping back for a last kiss or quarrel—even if it weren't dangerous to cross your own path. But that's not quite your situation, is it? Monsieur Raponde has died by halves. It's an inconvenience if you can meet only in the Netherlands, but not an insurmountable inconvenience. Who's to say—there might even be advantages."

Emma stood in the doorway, a plastic-wrapped slab of lox in her hand. "Harry Graves—do you, or did you, *know* Blaise Raponde?"

She didn't know what she'd do if he said yes. Fortunately, he said—

"No, I didn't get to France much in those days. When

opportunity arose to sail west—well before sixteen-eighty, I might add—I leapt at the chance. When choices had to be made, I made mine to stay. I didn't get back to France until, oh, the early seventeen-eighties."

"Are you telling me you were here for the Revolution?"

"I hunt rogues and curses, Emma, and it's counterproductive for a hunter to leave his mark on history. But I did take sides—and risks—for the Continentals. Does that surprise you?"

Em stammered and said "No," but it was a lie—how could she not be surprised to find herself talking to someone claiming firsthand knowledge of the American Revolution?

"The wall crumbles at last. I never had any intention of smothering my wife, Emma."

He wasn't a villain, but Harry could be effortlessly overbearing when he chose—perhaps even when he didn't choose—and he wasn't telling the truth about Eleanor. "You would have. You'd do it today—if you thought it was that or watching Eleanor turn into a rogue like Malerie Dunbar."

"It won't come to that, Emma. We're not going to let it happen—you, me, *and* Monsieur Blaise Raponde. He's the one who found her, isn't he? He knows the way to that Parisian church you mentioned and behind it, too, I'll wager. He probably had a hand in forging it. I can make inquiries about Monsieur Blaise Raponde, if you'd like. There are those who might well remember him. Was he a priest? The cloth has always been good cover, and celibacy was never a problem—"

Emma backed out of the doorway. "Drop it, Harry. We're not counting on Blaise. Sometimes I see him in the wasteland, sometimes I don't, and when I don't, I haven't got a clue where to find him. We're not business partners and we're certainly not more than business partners. I can get to the Place de Grève and I've got a contemporary map from the seventeenth century that will get us the rest of the way to the Cemetery of the Innocents. So, drop it."

But Harry persisted, following Em into her kitchen. She stood at the sink with her back to her unwelcome guest, slicing the croissant remnants to take to Meadow View.

"I would hope that you are partners, and more than 'business' partners, Emma. It wasn't that the curia objected to you dallying with a stranger, it was *what* they thought that stranger was. Ours is a lonely life. The greatest danger we face isn't a rogue, or a quartet of them. It's suicide. Suicide and the sort of loneliness that drove your mother into your father's arms—"

"Don't you dare—" Em spun around, knife in hand.

"I'm not criticizing your father, Emma—but *think* about it." Harry wasn't fazed. "I didn't know your mother well before she ran away, but we've been partners since she reappeared in nineteen-fifty-two—"

Emma blinked—she couldn't help herself. Eleanor had left Bower in 1949, not 1952. The FBI had traced her to New York City. When, in November, Eleanor said she and Harry lived near the city, Emma had applied Occam's Razor and assumed her mother had gone straight back to the curse-hunting Atlantis Curia. Where had she been for the three missing years? And what had finally driven her back to Harry Graves' Atlantis curia?

Harry kept hammering—"She'd thought she could escape the inevitable. She'd thought if she turned her back on hunting and the Netherlands, she would have an ordinary life, with an ordinary husband and ordinary children. Eleanor wanted to grow old with your father, Emma, and she *didn't* want you following in her footsteps. When she realized that she could never be ordinary—and what would happen to you and your father if her secrets were exposed—she left . . . without her heart.

"We can destroy curses and rogues because they are the enemy, but what are we to do with our ordinary friends? You *will* have to abandon this Nancy and her husband *and* your stepdaughter. Don't deceive yourself. Telling them your secrets won't prevent it, only make it more difficult when the time comes—"

Em was trembling, and she could feel a flood of tears swelling behind her eyes. She dropped the knife on the counter. Her voice was thick in her throat as she said: "If I've got to walk away from the people I love, I'll do it *when the time comes,* and not one moment earlier."

A normal person would have backed away. Even Jeff would have gotten out of the kitchen, but not Harry. Harry didn't retreat an inch. Emma turned the faucets on, hot and cold together, full blast.

"You can't wait that long." Harry made himself heard over the water's white noise. "If you want to control the end, you must control the beginning. Cultivate this Blaise Raponde—you're going to need him down the road and not simply to find a crypt in a church. Tie a lifeline to someone who won't die a lifetime before you do."

Emma turned the water off with enough force to clatter the plumbing. "Stop pushing me. You're trying to help— I'm going to believe that, Harry, but you're going about it all wrong. I'm going upstairs now, and you're *not* going to follow me. Do you understand that, Harry? When I come back down, we'll go to see Eleanor, then we'll go out to your hotel room and I'll do my level best to get the two of us to that churchyard behind Paris. If Blaise is there, fine, we'll join forces. If he's not, that's better."

"Emma—"

"Harry, I don't want to talk about it. You don't know me well enough to lecture me about lifelines. Is that clear?"

Harry didn't say that it was. He didn't say anything at all, which was fine with Emma. Leading with her shoulder, she slipped between Harry and the doorway and made it to the bathroom before the waterworks started. For one horrible moment Em thought she had company, but there was only her own reflection in the mirror. The steady application of cool water against her cheeks had her emotions stabilized before Spin clawed his way in.

Harry was reading the paper when she descended the stairs again, dressed as she would have dressed for work in tailored slacks and a sweater.

"We can take my car—if you don't mind walking five blocks."

Harry looked up, neutral and unperturbed, as if they hadn't been at the brink of an argument a quarter hour earlier. "Mine's closer—across the street. Someone was pulling out. I leapt at the opportunity."

"Beginner's luck," Emma said as she handed Harry his coat. "What I really should do is go get mine and sneak in behind you—"

"Whatever you wish."

Em cringed, recognizing the determinedly pleasant voice of a man stuck with an irrational woman. It was embarrassing, but not far from the truth.

"That was a joke, Harry." She shrugged into her coat.

He smiled politely and held the door. It had started snowing, big, lazy flakes that hadn't yet amounted to anything. They took his car. Emma directed them out of the neighborhood. When they were on the avenue that would take them to Meadow View's driveway, she asked Harry about the precautions he'd mentioned on the phone.

"Nothing much. No great magic. Just a few grains of salt and drops of oil to renew our claims—things a rogue or curse would notice."

"No mercury or arsenic or tincture of poppy?"

Harry laughed outright. "Not anymore—those *will* work, Emma, if they don't get you killed—or arrested."

"You said 'no magic.'"

"No great magic—nothing like the good old days, but a few things that can't quite be explained by high school science or quantum physics. Mind you, I haven't given up completely. There are some aspects of string theory that might allow for the distribution of time throughout space . . ."

Emma listened with half an ear. Harry was kidding himself. String theory wouldn't explain curses or the wasteland and didn't need to. It was there, like the horse-shoe over Niels Bohr's front door, regardless of belief or explanation.

They drove through the last green light between the Maisonettes and Meadow View. "We're here. Turn right at the driveway, then left, into the visitors' lot."

Harry followed directions. Conditions in the lot hadn't improved since yesterday. Emma was about to suggest he park the car by itself at the back of the lot when she noticed an old Ford Escort, equal parts blue paint and rusted steel, with a frame of duct tape around its right rear tail-light. Another look revealed a university parking sticker, valid for the Horace Johnson lot, in the rear window and a peeling bumper sticker that equated the fans of Ohio State University with that state's notoriously useless offi-cial nut, the buckeye.

It was possible that there were two such Escorts in Bower. Possible, but unlikely.

"Matt's here," Em said softly. "That's got to mean that Malerie's here, too."

"Malerie, as in the rogue calling itself Malerie Dun-bar?"

When Emma nodded, Harry cut the steering wheel sharply and nosed into the nearest parking space.

"You've sensed her through walls! Your empathy *is* ex-traordinary, Emma."

"No—nothing like that. Matt's car is over there. If he's here, she's here."

Harry reached across Em's lap as she unclasped her seat belt and removed a small leather case from the glove compartment. It had the wrong dimensions for a gun, at least Emma thought it did, but there was no doubt that Harry Graves was preparing for battle.

"Guard your thoughts, Emma," Harry advised as he led the way to Meadow View Manor's front door. "Don't give yourself away."

She thought of the doorway where she'd hidden with Blaise. "I'm not sure I know how to do that here."

"Then never mind. The rogue will recognize you anyway. Describe her to me, and this Matt as well."

They entered the lobby. Saturday was a busy day at Meadow View—not as busy as Sunday—but there were easily twenty people in the lobby, young and old, none of them Matt or Malerie. There were two staffers handling questions at the desk. Neither noticed two more people waiting for the elevator. Emma pushed the button. There was easily ten feet between them and the next person and enough background noise to cover soft conversation. Em finished her description of Matt.

"—I guess you'd say he looks like someone who spends all his time with computers and doesn't have much of a social life. Mal's messed with his head, that's a given, but—can you tell me that I'm not a complete idiot for hoping that's all she's done? I'd be real upset if she's set him up to become a rogue."

"There's no law against hoping. If there were only one rogue involved, I'd say you were home free. The rogue's taken Malerie Dunbar, it can't take Matt as well. But you say there's more than one rogue."

The doors opened. They got in and were alone.

"You'll be able to tell for sure when you see him, won't you?" Emma asked.

"Perhaps. The broad answer is yes, but a rogue can pretend not to be a rogue and sometimes it will succeed. You've got a better chance than I have, Emma. You know Matt and you've at least seen the rogues behind Paris."

The elevator reached the sixth floor. As soon as the doors opened, they were engulfed in moans and pleas and the astringent aroma of industrial-strength disinfectant. Em was accustomed to it, but Harry recoiled.

"I had no idea. Eleanor is *here*?"

"Word of honor, Harry: This is one of the good places. In the bad ones, they're screaming and all you smell is urine."

"I shall accept your word without needing proof."

On the sixth floor, Saturday was pretty much the same as any other day. Most of the residents were alone, the staff was huddled in the work area opposite the elevator watching television, and Marsha was sitting beside her son. Marsha must have heard Emma's voice because she was looking out the door when Em and Harry walked past.

"Emma! I've missed you. I heard about Eleanor."

Eye contact was established, and much as Emma wanted to get to her mother's room, she had to stop for pleasantries. Harry—astute observer that he was—hung back, refusing to get near, much less cross, the threshold into Josh's room.

"Yeah, she's had a rough week. They had her up at University Hospital Emergency Room last night."

"Maybe she's coming out." Marsha smiled a painful, ambivalent smile. "Maybe she's going to wake up."

"We can hope."

"She's having a busy day. Lots of visitors."

"Just a friend," Emma said quickly, and regretted her choice of words almost before they were out of her mouth. If Eleanor looked like Em's daughter, then Harry looked like her date. "An old friend of the family." She tried to motion Harry closer, but he'd drifted toward Eleanor's room.

"And the two young people her own age—"

Emma's heart froze between beats.

"They were here a little while ago. They left just a few minutes ago. I'm surprised you didn't bump into them. Josh's friends still visit when they're in town."

"Emma!" Harry's voice, not yet a shout but easily heard. "Emma."

"I've got to go, Marsha." Em backed out of the room.

"Emma," Harry called. "Emma, you said Eleanor fell."

There was accusation in Harry's tone and she couldn't blame him. The Eleanor Merrigan that Em had seen last night looked nothing like the Eleanor Merrigan lying in the bed. Today's Eleanor had a face that was dark with bruises and swollen so badly that she could scarcely breathe.

"They've been here. Marsha saw them," she whispered. Braced against the doorway, Em lowered her head and took deep breaths until her strength returned. "I'll get someone."

Harry lunged for Em's arm and kept her from leaving the room. "Not so quickly."

Every last one of Emma's suspicions flared back to life with doubled intensity, especially when Harry opened his little leather case. It was filled with vials and squares of folded aluminum foil and several plastic-wrapped syringes.

"Look around."

"For what?" she demanded.

"I don't know. You know this room. Look for something out of place. Anything the rogue might have left behind."

Em couldn't look at anything but the syringes, though Harry left them in the case, choosing two of the liquid-filled vials instead. He shook a few drops from each other into the palm of his left hand and began mixing them together with his right index finger.

"What are you doing?"

"Precautions."

"It's a little late for precautions, wouldn't you say?"

"Eleanor's still alive, Emma," Harry said, drawing circles around Eleanor's eyes with his moistened fingertip. "It will have to come back to finish what it started."

Em retreated until her back was against the window. "Malerie tried to kill Eleanor? Why would she do that? I thought the whole point was to turn her into a rogue?"

Moving away from Eleanor's eyes, Harry traced lines across his wife's cheekbones and along the underside of her jaw. "I haven't the slightest idea. Cutting losses, I should think. We can ask it that question when we catch up with it."

Emma blinked and looked again—the lines were definitely glowing with faint, golden light. She watched in silence as Harry shook out a few more drops, mixed them together, and went to work drawing lines down Eleanor's weakened arms. Someone from the staff was going to walk by, see what Harry was doing, and they'd be lucky if they weren't both arrested.

Harry certainly didn't look like a husband tending to his wife. Emma couldn't put words to it, but there was something oddly detached about the way Harry dragged his finger over Eleanor's flesh. Em couldn't have touched Jeff, even after all the pain they'd caused each other, without feeling something. There were too many memories locked in Jeff's flesh. Harry could have been painting a FOR SALE sign for all the emotion his face revealed.

He looked up, saw her staring, so Emma looked away. She looked at the mirror, then at the floor.

"Harry, there's something by your foot."

Fifteen

It *was another* syringe with the plunger fully extended and it hadn't fallen from Harry's leather case. He stepped carefully around it.

"Give me your hand, Emma." Without thinking, she extended her right hand. "No, your other hand."

Suddenly suspicious, she kept both hands at her sides. "What for?"

"Precautions. A stronger bond between you and your mother."

A bond with Eleanor couldn't hurt. Emma extended her left hand. Harry reached with his left hand, then sealed the clasp with his right, holding their palms together as the oil grew hot and paralyzing pain shot from Emma's wrist to her elbow. Instinct pulled Em away but long moments passed before Harry released her. Once freed, she could do nothing more than stagger backward until she felt a chair against her legs. She landed heavily on the cushion and cradled her arm beneath her breasts. It felt as if it were on fire, though looking down, she could see that it was not.

"What have you done?"

"I forged a bond between you and Eleanor. I had no idea."

The pain had begun to fade, but so had her resistance.

She rocked back and forth, stifling sobs. "Don't lie to me, Harry."

"I swear, I had no idea. There's a tingle, not even that most of the time. Your empathy is extraordinary, Emma. The curia—"

Em was about to tell Harry what he and the Atlantis curia could do with their curiosity when the burning pain reintensified. She slipped to the edge of unconsciousness then, as suddenly as it had started, the agony ended. She flexed each finger and found them all functional.

"Better now?" Harry asked.

He offered his hand to help her out of the chair. Emma pointedly ignored his assistance. The syringe still lay on the floor. Harry got there first.

"Don't touch it!" Em snarled. "It's evidence against Malerie."

"Or your friend Matt."

The syringe was filled to the last calibration line with a transparent, faintly red liquid. The temptation was to say there'd been no injection, but they couldn't be certain. The barrel could have been overfilled, or the one they'd found might have been a backup.

There was a small bathroom attached to each sixth-floor room, for the convenience of the staff and visitors. Harry stepped up to the metal sink and pointed the needle at the drain.

"You can't do that!" Emma reached for Harry's arm a moment too late. He depressed the plunger and the liquid was gone. "We needed that! Eleanor needed that. The emergency room needed that to figure out what Malerie shot into her."

"It hadn't been used." Harry turned the water on full bore and began dismantling the syringe.

"You can't be sure."

"It hadn't been used," he repeated. "I feel nothing. You feel nothing. No harm was done."

"I felt like my arm was burning up."

"You'd feel far worse if our rogue had poisoned your

mother." He broke the needle off and slipped it into the barrel. "If she's harmed; you'll know it. Among other things."

Emma rubbed her arm. "What other things?"

"Call it warding—a shield against malicious intent. The wards I erected in November were intact, but they're focused. A rogue will get a shock if it touches her. It won't be stopped—not if it's determined, or if it's using your friend as a cat's-paw. That's why I added the bond. Between the two, we'll get a warning with enough time for intervention."

"The rogue tried to strangle her." Emma indicated the most massive of Eleanor's bruises. "Will your wards stop that?"

"Not if it's determined or using someone."

"Then we've got to stay here." She picked up Eleanor's right hand and tucked it beneath the restraint band. "We can't leave her alone."

"Agreed—not until we're certain the rogue and your misguided friend have left the building. I'll stay here while you reconnoiter."

"I'll stay," Emma countered. She wasn't yet comfortable with the idea of leaving Harry alone with Eleanor.

"Emma—may I point out that you know the rogue? You'll recognize it at a greater distance and you'll recognize your friend. Plus, you know the building layout. I assure you, I can hold Eleanor's hand as ably as you, and between the bond and your innate empathy, you'll know if there's trouble."

Though Emma could have recited a half-dozen reasons why Harry should be the one to go wandering, she chose not to argue and took the elevator to the lobby, where she hoped to find Matt's car missing. It, however, was still in the lot, collecting snow.

One person couldn't hope to do a thorough sweep of Meadow View Manor. There were three stairwells, two elevators, and more ways than Em could count for Matt and Malerie to elude pursuit. On the plus side, residents got lost regularly and no one thought twice when she poked her head into each room on the first and second floor looking for signs of trouble. Nancy's mother roomed on the third floor. Emma approached that room with greater reservations—not because she expected to find Malerie hiding in the corner, but because Katherine might recognize her.

It didn't occur to Em that Nancy might be visiting her mother—Matt's car was the only familiar vehicle in the lot. She was surprised to find the two of them together looking at Christmas pictures.

"I—I had no idea you were here," Em stammered. She would have told Nancy the truth—Nance would guess most of it anyway—but not with Katherine scowling at her. "I didn't see your car outside."

"John dropped me off. The garbage disposal's on its last legs. He'll pick me up after he's gotten us a disposal fit for the twenty-first century. Did Harry get in okay?"

Em nodded. She didn't want to be talking to Nancy right now any more than she would have wanted to chat with Katherine.

Nancy ignored Em's restlessness. "I was just thinking about you two. You won't believe this, Emma, but I saw someone one who looked like that girl—what's her name? Melanie?—walk down the corridor not a half hour ago. She walked right past the room. I got up to check, but she was gone by the time I got to the door. Visiting someone else, I guess—it couldn't have been that girl. That would be too much of a coincidence, don't you think?"

Emma nodded. Coincidence seemed to be the norm when you were dealing with people—rogues—who ran roughshod through time. "Was she alone, Nance?"

"Alone? I didn't see anyone else—I didn't really see her. You think it could have been her?"

"Eleanor's been attacked."

"Eleanor?" Katherine demanded. "Who's Eleanor? Isn't that Emma Merrigan? Her mother was named Eleanor before she ran off with that foreigner."

Nancy cringed then asked, "And you think—?"

"Not much doubt now. Matt's beat-up, old car is in the lot. It adds up, doesn't it? Eleanor's neck is badly bruised and we found a syringe on the floor—"

"Drugs?"

"Who knows," Em said bitterly. "Harry squirted whatever it held into the sink before I could stop him. He's up there now—I *think* that's an okay idea. I'm doing a fast pass through the corridors. Heaven knows what I'll do if I bump into them, or once I get back upstairs."

"Oh, Em—this is horrible. What can I do to help? I'll look for her—I'd recognize her, I'm sure. She was wearing something that looked like a football jersey. Or—I could go upstairs."

Katherine scolded Nancy for ignoring her while Emma considered the offer versus its risks. She hadn't reached a conclusion when another blinding wave of pain crashed over her. This time the pain wasn't confined to her left forearm. She barely made it to a chair before her knees gave out.

"What's the matter with her?" Katherine demanded.

Nancy wanted an answer to the same question, though Nance was more tactful: "Are you going to be okay, Em?"

The pain hadn't lasted but a heartbeat and was already a memory—a powerful, frightening memory. "I've got to get back upstairs, Nance. Harry did something so I'd know if there was trouble. Don't ask—" Emma took a deep breath and stood up.

"There's trouble," Nancy decided.

Em nodded and started for the door. Ignoring her mother's protests, Nance stuck with her.

"I'll be fine. You can stay with your mom."

"Nonsense. If you have another collapse like that, you're the one who could get hurt."

Em took one more try at discouragement: "There's no telling what's happening up there. It could put Hollywood special effects out of business."

Nancy pressed the up button. "I'll manage."

Watched pots never boiled and waited-for elevators took forever to arrive. The stairs would have been faster, if all the third-floor access doors weren't blocked with alarms. The elevator emptied when it arrived—Emma and Nancy had it to themselves. Em leaned back into a corner as the car rose, collecting her thoughts and telling herself that she, too, could manage.

Emma took the lead when they reached the sixth floor. She hadn't gone ten feet when Harry's "precautions" struck for a third time. Nancy caught her before she fell though, like the attack in Katherine's room, this one was over in a heartbeat, but not before they'd heard a noise from Eleanor's room that sounded like something heavy hitting the floor hard. The women exchanged worried glances and started walking again.

Marsha emerged from Josh's room. "I heard something fall."

Emma left Nancy to deal with Marsha. It took her brain a moment to make sense of what her eyes recorded when she got to the door: That was Malerie Dunbar standing next to Eleanor's bed, eyes wide with surprise and rage, her arms frozen awkwardly in front of her. That was Harry on the floor near the window. And he was on the floor, curled up protecting his gut and face, because Matt—*Matt Barto!*—was stomping the stuffing out of him.

Harry would have to take care of himself because Em had taken another look at Malerie and realized that the rogue looked awkward because one hand held a syringe and the other held Eleanor's IV bag.

A surge of adrenalin quickened Emma's nerves. She had the strength—and the will—to tear Malerie Dunbar in half once she got her hands on her—and she'd have her hands around the rogue's neck as soon as she could lunge across the six or seven feet that separated them.

Malerie read Emma's intentions. The rogue hurled the syringe at Em's face. Em easily dodged the clumsy missile. She extended her arms, anticipating the feel of flesh beneath clenched fingers, and forgot Harry's warning that

rogues were generally more experienced and more powerful than their enemies. Mal made a sweeping gesture, and
without knowing why or how, Em lurched sideways, col-
liding with a chest of drawers. She caught her balance, but
she couldn't catch Malerie as she surged toward the corridor and freedom.

Nancy picked that exact moment to enter Eleanor's
room. She didn't so much confront the rogue as block her
path. Malerie seized Nancy by the forearms and shoved
her at Emma. If Em had had a moment to think, she would
have dodged Nancy and gone after Malerie, but the habits
of friendship took precidence: she steadied her friend and
lost another stride on the rogue.

Malerie was in the corridor and accelerating when she
collided with Marsha. Marsha went down with a shout,
and for an instant it seemed that Malerie might land on top
of her, then the rogue bent low, kept her feet beneath her,
and took off down the corridor. With more bravada and
confidence than she'd imagined she possessed, Emma
leapt over Marsha like a log.

The rogue didn't bother with the elevator. She raced
past the staff station and hit the stairwell door at a dead
run. The alarm blared loud enough to wake the dead;
someone shouted "Stop!" Both Malerie and Em ignored
the order. Emma caught the heavy door as it closed and
shouldered into the stairwell in time to see Malerie's head
vanish around the downstairs landing. Without hesitation,
she plunged after her.

Emma didn't count floors or steps; she kept her concentration fixed on the middle of the rogue's back, and
while she didn't gain on her enemy, she didn't lose ground
either. She was the same stride-and-a-half behind when
they reached the bottom of the stairwell as she'd been at
the top.

Emma was the cop, not the robber. She didn't have to
decide where to run next. That decision was Malerie's,
and while she was making it, Emma pounced. She
grabbed a random fist of hair and cloth and tried, with all

her strength, tried to spin the rogue into the concrete-block wall.

Malerie whirled around, all fists and elbows. The rogue struck Emma in the chin and stomach. Stunned, Emma lost her grip. Staggering backward, she tripped over her own feet and struck her forehead against the steel newel post at the bottom of the stairwell. The jolt knocked the sense out of her skull, but not for long: the stairwell exit door hadn't swung shut when Emma flung it open and followed Malerie onto the loading dock.

"Give it up!" she shouted as the rogue leapt into the truck pit and started running up the driveway.

No amount of adrenalin could propel Emma off a four-foot ledge. She spotted a handrail and raced toward it instead. By the time Emma had emerged from the dock, she was a good twenty feet behind Malerie Dunbar but sublimely confident that she'd make up the lost ground even though she'd never, in her entire life, won a footrace.

The driveway down to Meadow View's loading dock was steep, curved, and slick with new-fallen snow. Emma wasn't cautious, but the gap between her and Malerie continued to widen. She swerved to the side of the driveway, where Thursday night's snow had crusted over and the footing was a little more treacherous but the path, if she didn't fall, was shorter. Malerie stayed in the middle of the asphalt.

A delivery van appeared at the top of the curve. Its driver leaned on the horn and the brakes. The van's wheels locked and it started to skid, out of control and unstoppable, down the driveway. Self-protection was Emma's strongest instinct; she clambered up the snow-plow berm to safety, expecting that Malerie would do the same. The rogue had enough time to get out of the way . . . or she should have had.

From her knees atop the berm, Emma watched Malerie sidestep *into* the van's path then dive forward, almost aiming for its front wheel. The rogue was on the ground before the van rolled over her—Em was certain of that much—and not moving once the rear wheels had finished crunching over her hips.

Emma opened her mouth to scream, but if she made a sound, her ears did not hear it. Liquid seeped over the asphalt pavement, absorbing the snow as it fell. The puddle was large and growing fast.

She's dead, Emma heard her Mother Voice say. *You should be relieved. You should be satisfied. Justice has been done.* Em was numb instead. She'd expected magic. She hadn't expected Malerie to die in such an ordinary, yet horrific way.

The van stopped against the concrete steps Em had used to reach the driveway. Its young and panicked driver burst out the passenger door.

"I couldn't stop!" he shouted at Em. "I tried. Did you see it? She looked at me and then she went down!"

They approached Malerie together, each taking the shortest path. Emma stopped when she could see Malerie's wide-open, empty eyes. The driver went a little closer but he, too, stopped short of tracking through the blood puddle.

"Oh, God—she's not moving. I think she's gotta be dead," he said, wringing his hands in helpless anguish.

Emma nodded and said, "I'm sorry," because she was, without knowing why.

By then they were no longer alone. A handful of visitors and staff had followed Emma and Malerie down the stairwell. Em was aware of them not as people, but as objects in motion: swarming, shouting, blocking her view of Malerie's body. Hands touched her arms and shoulders. They turned her around and guided her out of the falling snow. She wasn't aware of moving her feet.

"You're bleeding, Emma."

"Nancy?"

Em blinked and slowly recognized her friend.

"You're hurt, Em. Your hand's bleeding and your head. What happened?"

"Suicide."

"I can't hear you. You're whispering. Did the truck hit you, too?"

"No." Emma shook her head and made herself dizzy. "Not even close. She had time, Nance. Malerie had the time but she just stood there in front of the truck, then she went down."

"She panicked? Froze up?"

Em clung to Nancy's arm and shook her head again. There were sirens in the distance, growing louder quickly. The sirens fell suddenly silent. An ambulance appeared at the top of the loading dock driveway. For a moment it seemed history might repeat itself, but the driver got his vehicle stopped before the accident compounded itself. A trio of med-techs scattered the crowd around Malerie.

"Eleanor? Is she—?"

Nancy shrugged. "I followed you."

"That's *her* ambulance," Emma decided. "They should be taking care of Eleanor." She stood up—she didn't remember sitting down on the loading dock steps—and took a few steps before Nancy stopped her.

"Be careful what you do and say, Emma. You can't go up there talking about curses and rogues."

The warning cleared Emma's mind, and just in time. A pair of police patrol cars, their lights flashing, stopped behind the ambulance.

"Do you want to talk to them?" Nancy asked.

"Eleanor. Harry. They need treatment. Malerie's dead. She killed herself. That kid's going to get in trouble and it wasn't nearly his fault."

"Emma, there's a cop coming this way. Do you want to talk to her now or later? I can say you're hurt and that we need another ambulance—"

"I can talk to them. Get it over with. Go find Eleanor and Harry." Like a switch being thrown, Em remembered there'd been a third person in Eleanor's room. "Matt, too. Keep an eye on Matt. He could be in trouble, or he could be trouble itself." The cop was about twelve feet away then. "I can handle this, Nance. Go see what's happening upstairs."

The adrenalin rush had ended. Emma felt every body part she'd abused in the stairwell—especially her left hand—which was bleeding from a gash across the knuckles that she didn't recall receiving—and her forehead—which she'd split open when she'd collided with the newel post. She was shivering from shock and probably had a mild concussion, too, but her mind stayed clear when the cop took out a notebook and asked her for her name.

Emma told as much of the truth as she dared. Yes, she knew the dead woman, Malerie Dunbar, but not well or long, although that would have changed had Malerie lived to become her assistant at the Horace Johnson Library. She acknowledged that Malerie had been involved with a library coworker since New Year's Eve. No, she hadn't warmed to the woman, not at all, but Ms Dunbar was (Emma took a deep breath) *precisely* qualified for a research assistant's job and Em had been prepared to make the best of it. She certainly hadn't held a grudge or been chasing the Ms Dunbar out of spite or malice. In fact, she would never have expected to see Ms Dunbar at Meadow View Manor. So far as Em knew, Ms Dunbar had no connection with Meadow View, but the nursing home (Emma took another deep breath) *was* home for her own cousin— her twenty-five-year-old cousin, Eleanor Merrigan—who had become seriously ill and fallen into a coma during a pre-Thanksgiving visit. No, surprise didn't begin to describe Emma's reaction when she saw Ms Dunbar in her cousin's sixth-floor room—the young woman had had a syringe in one hand and the other on Eleanor's IV line.

"Did your cousin and Ms Dunbar know each other?" the cop asked. "Did they have any history that might provide a motive? Boyfriends or anything like that?"

Em watched the snow fall a moment, marveling at the simplicity of the policewoman's assumptions. She considered possibilities, considered lies before saying, "No, none that I'm aware of. Eleanor's from New York. When she came here in November, it was her first visit to Bower. We didn't know we were relatives until she'd found a connection on the Internet. We'd barely met when she got sick. You'll want to talk to Dr. Abraham Saha—" She spelled it out. "He was Eleanor's doctor when she was at University Hospital. The whole thing was pretty much a mystery to everyone."

"First, I'll go upstairs and talk to your cousin—"

"No, you can't do that—" The cop's demeanor hardened instantly; Emma explained herself quickly. "Eleanor doesn't talk. She's in a *coma*, Officer, you know, like Sleeping Beauty?" A deeply disturbing thought flashed through Em's mind. "Unless she's dead now, too. I don't know what was in that syringe or whether I interrupted the rogue before or after she shot her junk into my cousin's IV." Em cringed when she heard herself describe Malerie with the wrong word.

"What makes you think drugs were involved?" the cop asked.

Emma began to shiver again. The shakes weren't a complete fraud—she was outdoors in January and coatless—but she could have fought them off. When that didn't work, she complained of dizziness and got escorted into the employee lounge, where the staff doctor (Meadow View boasted that it kept a physician on the premises seven days a week, twenty-four hours a day) told her that she could have ridden in the ambulance with her cousin, but that it had just left and she'd be better off going to an urgent-care facility.

"They'll put a couple of stitches in your hand. Your forehead's fine with a Band-Aid—unless you get dizzy or nauseated, then get to the emergency room."

"Do I *need* stitches in my hand?" The cop was gone by then and, for someone whose hobby was embroidery, Em would do just about anything to avoid getting sewn up.

The unfamiliar doctor smiled benignly. "No, not unless

you plan to do anything strenuous for the next little while."

"Nothing strenuous," Emma promised and held still while the doctor painted her cuts with stinging antiseptic and covered them with Band-Aids.

Nancy was waiting outside the lounge with a rapid debriefing: "Eleanor's at University Hospital, with the syringe and the IV—no longer attached to Eleanor, of course. The syringe was still half-full. Malerie hadn't finished shooting it into the IV bag when we showed up. There's a good chance whatever was in it never got into Eleanor, but I think they'll keep her there overnight, just to give everyone else a rest. Harry looks like he lost a fight with a heavyweight boxer. The med-techs wanted to transport him, too. He refused—I see what you mean, by the way, about Harry. Before he was done explaining why he didn't want to go to the emergency room, I don't think they'd have let him on the ambulance anyway. Matt's in bad shape—not physically, but mentally. And John's still looking for the world's best garbage disposal. I tried calling him, but he's got his phone turned off."

The elevator opened and carried them up to the sixth floor, where Emma had become an instant celebrity and Harry sat on Eleanor's empty bed holding a plastic bag filled with ice against the right side of his face. The bag completely covered his eye, but not all the bruises, and the hand holding the bag could have used some ice itself. Harry's fingers looked like stiff, red sausages.

Emma greeted him with—"You should have gone to the emergency room."

Harry's scowl was potent with discomfort. "Close the door, if you would."

Nancy obliged and leaned against it afterward for extra measure.

"What happened? Did the rogue seem to die?"

"She didn't *seem* to die, Harry. She's *dead*. A delivery van showed up—I overheard someone say it was delivering linens that weren't delivered yesterday on account of the snow, so I really think it was all coincidence. But Malerie saw it coming and instead of getting out of the way, she threw herself down in front of it and it rolled over her."

Memories replayed themselves. Emma covered her eyes, which only made the stop-motion vignettes stronger. She'd heard a series of cracks as the wheels rolled over Malerie—the sound of bones breaking.

She lowered her hand and steadied herself against the dresser. Em got her first good look at Matt at the same time. He was in his own private torment, hunched over in the room's one chair with his forehead nearly touching his knees and his shoulders quaking. The sight of his misery was a good antidote against the driveway memories.

"She chose to end her game with a suicide. It's over. Matt—are you listening? It's over."

"If the van had hit the rogue, and hit it so it lost consciousness before it died, then there's a chance you'd be right, Emma. But if the rogue lay down—if it had even an instant of consciousness *before* impact, then you're not talking suicide. It returned to the Netherlands. A body died, a young woman whose nature we shall never know died, but not the rogue. I've already explained that to your friends, since you've taken it upon yourself to tell them everything else. Unless a rogue is imprisoned in flesh, it can't be slain in the absolute present. Your work's not done. You've got to go to the Netherlands to finish it . . . and, Emma, you'll have to go alone."

Emma opened her mouth to protest and shut it again before she'd said a word. Harry had lowered his hand. She could see what Matt's boots had done to his face. His eye was swollen shut and nearly black while his cheek looked as if it had been stretched over a red and purple tennis ball. He really should have gone to the emergency room.

"What about the curia? Shouldn't you call your associates back in New York and tell them that things have gotten just a little bit out of hand out here?"

"I should think they already know—which is all the

more reason for you to find this rogue and finish it. Approach the curia with a problem and you'll be in their debt. Approach them with a solution, and they'll be in yours. I think you can figure out which is the better way to keep faith with the curia. I've given Nancy the keys to my rental car. Return home and do what must be done. Young Matthew, here, will take me to the hospital. It will give us time to talk. You can see that he needs to talk?"

Emma agreed about Matt—though she wasn't optimistic that a single conversation in a busy emergency room would do more than scratch the surface of his despair. She had more pressing concerns, though, than Matt's mental health.

"I hate to admit this, Harry, but I've never managed to transfer myself between here and there while the sun's up. I'm strictly a nocturnal hunter and, well—remember that behind Paris there are *four* rogues holed-up together. Unless they're suicidal, I don't think I'm up to taking them on single-handed."

Harry set the ice bag on the bed and attempted to remove a black-onyx pinkie ring from his banged-up hand. Em told him not to bother, that she'd manage, but he persisted and with a final groan got it over the swollen knuckle.

"If rogues threaten you, use this to focus your wrath. Do you notice the tiny chip that's missing from the surface cut? That's the *front* of the stone. Be certain it is *toward* the rogues, not you, when you envision whatever you need. It may not be enough to destroy them; it will hold them at bay while you reconnoiter."

Emma had small fingers. Harry's ring fit loosely around her thumb. "What about Eleanor?" She looked at the empty bed.

"If you can free Eleanor from captivity, then by all means free her. Pull enough of those curses off her and she might be able to free herself. But we must assume that there have been changes behind Paris. Do the rogues continue to cooperate, or do the attacks on Eleanor's present life represent something else? That's what we need to know. That will put the curia in your debt. I conceive that their experiment has failed and they have turned on one another. The rogue who holds Eleanor's spirit behind Paris may not be the rogue, or rogues, who tried to kill her here. Rivalry might make it easier to free her or it might make it impossible. You'll have to use your own judgment. If you cannot win, be careful not to lose."

"Assuming I can do anything at all. Will this ring help me get behind Paris?"

Harry motioned Emma closer and whispered a few words in her ear.

She stood straight and incredulous. "You can't expect me to believe *that*?"

"It never fails. Never." Harry stood up slowly—his ribs had taken a pounding, too—and fished coins out of his pocket. He selected a large, silver one, worn nearly smooth with use, and offered it to her. "Trust me, Emma."

"You're sure?"

"Take it. Take it, go home, and get to work."

Grimly, Emma took the coin—it wasn't a silver dollar; it wasn't anything she recognized—dropped it into her pocket, then gathered up her gear.

"So what did he tell you when he whispered in your ear?" Nancy asked when they'd reached the open privacy of the parking lot. "Or can't you tell me?"

"He said to flip a coin. Heads is here. Tails is there. And I'm to just keep flipping it until I call it right." She marched to the driver's side door and stood there in silence until Nancy handed her Harry's keys.

"Do you think it will work?" Nance asked from the passenger seat.

"Yeah," Em said slowly. Her hand throbbed when she gripped the steering wheel, but the Band-Aids held. "Yeah, I think it will work. It's no crazier, really, than anything else: curses, rogues, the whole wasteland. Why shouldn't flipping a coin work?"

Snow continued to fall—about an inch so far—but

Bower had been in the deep freeze all week so every flake stuck to the roads and sidewalks. Em drove slowly in the unfamiliar car and used up a month's worth of luck finding a parking space abutting the fire hydrant nearest her front door. She'd sooner face all the rogues in the wasteland than parallel-park a car that was at least two feet longer than her own when the streets were snow-slick.

Sixteen

Nancy made cocoa while Emma practiced flipping the silver coin. Throwing and catching weren't among the skills Em had acquired in childhood. She was pretty sure she'd managed to avoid all opportunities for actually tossing a coin into the air, catching it, then slapping it onto the back of her hand. For her it had always been easier to go second than risk losing control of a moving object. In the privacy of her living room, with only Nancy for a witness, Em chased Harry's coin under the sofa, under a chair, and out into the hall. Once the heavy bit of metal struck the staring gray eye of her television and she feared momentarily for the picture tube.

When the cocoa was steaming and Emma was catching the coin at least once for every three tosses, she sat on the carpet with her back to the darkened Christmas tree. Harry's ring, with the chip pointed away from the nail, was on her thumb and she concentrated on memories of Malerie Dunbar with the syringe in her hand.

Emma missed what she termed her final practice toss. The coin struck her bandaged knuckles and headed for her cocoa. Nancy lunged from the sofa to catch it before it landed in the steaming mug.

"I'm constitutionally incapable of catching anything smaller than a basketball."

Nancy returned the coin. "If you waited another half hour, it would be dark and you could meditate your way there."

"If I'm still sitting here in a half-hour, that's just what I'll do. Maybe if I *believed* I could catch small, moving objects. . . ." Emma flipped the coin again . . . and caught it, barely, but she'd forgotten to call heads or tails.

"Do you want me to try to pull you out at the first sign of trouble?"

"No, the first sign is apt to be too early. You'd better wait until you're really worried."

"I've got my ice cube." Nancy tapped the cube-filled bowl beside her. "And a safety pin. Harry said the whole idea is physical shock. He had a lot to say while you were talking to the cops and getting your Band-Aids."

"Did he tell you where to stick the pin?"

"As a matter of fact he did—and that I shouldn't tell you."

"Wonderful."

Emma flipped the coin, caught it, and stayed put because she'd called "tails" and it had come up heads. She tried again and got lucky catching the coin for the third time in a row, but once again, it showed heads. "One more time and we'll be pushing the laws of probability." Em flipped it for the fourth time and called "Tails" as it spun.

The coin spun away from her, as it so often did. Em lunged, as Nance had lunged, and snatched it successfully. She slapped it on the back of her left hand. The spot was getting tender—she'd have a callus there eventually, if Harry's trick worked. She lifted her right hand, but before her eyes registered the coin, the rest of her senses were in transition to the wasteland.

Her fall was short, the landing hard, and the welcoming committee greeted her with sheets of orange fire. A blanket of air some six inches thick held the flames at bay. Emma would bake before she broiled, but at least she'd come to the right place. Between the flames, Emma could

see dank walls, sarcophagi, and a stairway, but no crucifix: she was fighting for breath in the crypt behind Paris.

In desperation, Emma raised her arms and sighted
across Harry's chipped onyx ring. She thought *fire* and
imagined the conical, blue flame of a very large blowtorch. The ring response was nothing short of miraculous.
Blue flame pierced the orange envelope. An instant later
Emma confronted her enemy: the sullen, self-luminous
rogue she knew as Malerie Dunbar and Blaise had named
Grisette.

"You haven't won yet," Malerie snarled as her half of
the crypt plunged into darkness.

Em stifled her own luminance with a thought—not that
light really mattered. The crypt was only about ten feet
square, not large enough for secrets. Emma's empathy
warned her that Malerie's second attack would be *edges*.
She envisioned a shield shaped like the prow of a boat and
thanked Harry for his gift as bits of metallic magic
streamed around her.

She tried a riposte—another blast of blowtorch flame.
Malerie laughed as the hot, blue cone fizzled and lightning arced across the two sarcophagi. Harry's ring was
equal to that challenge and the ones that followed it.
Emma foresaw that wasteland duels could easily become
stalemates, so she took a chance with a physical assault,
bounding onto a sarcophagus and leaping at her enemy
like the star of a Hong Kong martial arts movie.

Though Jeff had been into karate throughout their marriage, Emma's martial arts training had never gone beyond bits of colored tape wrapping the ends of a pristinely
white belt. She'd never thrown a punch outside the dojo
classroom but she remembered the theory well enough:
keep your fist flat and aim *inside* the target. Her thumb
hurt—no self-respecting *karateka* wore rings when throwing punches—but Malerie's lungs emptied with a gasp
and Emma was able to stiff-arm the rogue into a stone-
walled corner before pummeling her again and again with
her free fist.

The rogue flailed back, but Emma's arms were a little longer and Malerie didn't know how to throw an effective punch. Em would have some nasty bruises along her ribs, but she'd survive. Malerie wouldn't.

Malerie wouldn't . . .

Emma—who'd never killed anything larger than a cockroach—became distracted by her conscience—

I'm killing her—murdering her!—with my bare, naked hands!

The balance shifted toward the rogue, but not for long.

I'm not murdering a woman. I'm destroying a rogue, mooting a curse. I'm doing what I was born to do.

Emma fastened both hands around the rogue's throat and began to squeeze.

Suddenly, there was light in the crypt and Emma saw her mother's face above her strangling hands. The struggling, gasping image tugged at Emma's conscience but didn't loosen her hands. She knew what she was doing and squeezed tighter until, with an explosive shriek, the crypt went dark and her hands were empty. Emma envisioned light and became self-luminant. She couldn't light up the crypt as Malerie had—Em still had a lot to learn about wasteland science—but she convinced herself that Malerie Dunbar was gone.

Had she destroyed the rogue, or merely driven it out of another body? Was it time to celebrate? To go back to Bower? Or should she go upstairs and check out Eleanor's fiery pit?

After eliminating the questions she couldn't answer, Emma climbed the narrow, uneven stairs. The door to the sanctuary was open. Em hesitated before going through it. The wasteland sky—visible through the open roof—was a web of lightning and the ground trembled beneath an endless peal of thunder which—oddly—had been inaudible in the crypt. Her skin tingled and her hair shed sparks in the gusting wind.

Having survived one ambush, Emma took care to avoid a second. She crouched in the doorway, waiting for her eyes to adjust to the eerie shadows. When they had, she made a dash for the nearest wall and nearly tripped over the legs of a corpse. It had no head, nor shoulders, nor arms, nor blood—its fatal wound had been completely cauterized and shone like glass in the ever-shifting, brilliant light.

For one awful moment Emma thought she'd found Blaise Raponde for the last time, then memory assured her that Blaise was brawnier and favored dark, woolen breeches, not light-colored linen. The foppish rogue, she recalled, had worn pale breeches. Em allowed herself to hope that Raponde had eliminated one of the rogues. And though that was a satisfying thought, it also hinted that Malerie had escaped.

Emma looked back toward the crypt, half-expecting her enemy to rise out of its depth, but there was no light, no movement behind her. She squared her shoulders and crept along the wall toward the door that led into the courtyard. The rogue priest's corpse sprawled across the threshold. It, too, had been partially vaporized by a force that had taken a crescent-shaped chunk out of the sanctuary wall. A wooden staff lay just inside the sanctuary. A disembodied hand lay beneath the staff.

Emma reflected on the nature of the weapon that had mangled two rogues and a wall. If that was the measure of force that curse-hunters deemed necessary to destroy a rogue, then Blaise Raponde's God had not abandoned the wasteland and He'd watched over an unbelieving fool who'd attacked Malerie Dunbar with her hands. Em eased past the remains.

A broad pillar of milky light stood in the center of the courtyard, the source—or perhaps the result—of the lightning. Within the pillar, a duel was in progress. One of the duelists was a tall, blond woman in a sweeping gown; the other was Blaise Raponde. Blaise held his sword as he'd held it during his confrontation with Eleanor: hilt up, in both hands. The lump of amber in its pommel shone like the setting sun. His opponent—the rogue he'd named his lover and his murderer—held something in the palm of her outstretched hand. A ring or possibly a hand mirror, it was smaller, but brighter than Blaise's amber.

Blaise and the rogue circled each other within the light. They leaned toward each other with their hair and garments streaming behind them, as though a gale-force wind blew outward from the center of the pillar. While Emma watched, an arch of shadows blossomed between them. She guessed it was an attack, but couldn't discern who had begun it. Either way, it dissipated without harming either duelist.

Even without Harry's warning that it was more important to gather information than to vanquish a rogue, Emma wasn't tempted to intervene. Though Raponde's duel was the most eye-catching activity in the courtyard, it was not the only activity. Something that looked for all the world like a burning log lay beside the pit where Eleanor had been imprisoned. Emma approached it cautiously, confirming her suspicions. The flames were curses and her mother was the log. It was hard for Em to understand why she felt none of Eleanor's pain when she'd shared it so acutely back in Bower. But almost everything about the wasteland was hard to understand.

Harry's warnings evaporated from Emma's mind. She reached among the writhing curses, seizing the first one that came within her grasp. Though she would have sworn that nothing could make itself heard above the din of Raponde's lightning-shrouded duel, the curse let out a vibrating howl that echoed off the walls and rattled her arms. Em's grip never faltered, and after yanking it away from the others, she cracked the loose end against the ground.

That was a mistake—or at least not the best way to destroy a feeding curse. The curse stiffened, then curled back on itself: a yawning, black emptiness aimed at her own face. It struck—and Emma batted it aside, astonishing herself with her speed and precision. She got her other hand on it, a few inches short of the maw. Taking inspira-

tion from myths about snakes eating their tails, Em
brought her hands together, feeding the curse to itself. It
resisted, but myth had power in the wasteland, and when
the curse had reduced itself to the size of a softball, Emma
let it fall and seized another from her mother's body.

By the fourth curse, Emma had found a rhythm: grab,
bend, feed, wait a moment, then drop and start over. She
couldn't be sure she was actually making a difference—
that the plague of curses attached to her mother weren't
like the Hydra, sprouting two for every one that she removed, but she was determined to keep at it until she did
know. Determined, that is, until the circling duels and
their lightning pillar orbited in her direction then the risk
of getting swept up in a confrontation where her only contribution was likely to be disaster became intolerably
great and Em abandoned her efforts.

She lay low by the courtyard wall until the pillar spun
past and she thought it was safe to creep back to Eleanor.
Em had begun feeding the next curse to itself when an
ominous silence surrounded her. She knew before she
turned around that she'd drawn the rogue's attention and
that she'd only tested the waters of rogue-born danger in
her confrontation with Malerie Dunbar.

Emma understood, as well, why Harry and Eleanor
never used gendered pronouns when speaking of rogues.
There was nothing male or female in the black eyes that
stared at her from the depths of the lightning pillar, nothing remotely human, either.

That bit of insight might well have been the last logi-
cal connection Emma's brain created. A globe of light
some six feet in diameter hatched from the side of the pillar. It moved slowly, but it moved toward Em no matter
where she ran, and the stream of fire she summoned out
of Harry's ring affected it not at all.

Nancy? I'm in a whole lot of trouble now, Nance.

Emma?

Pull me out of here!

Gentle pressure circled Emma's wrists and the familiar

shapes of her living room shimmered around her. Nancy knelt beside her, as Em had knelt beside her mother, whispering her name. Em felt safe. Then the rogue's black eyes burst through Nancy's face and a dark force returned Emma to the courtyard behind Paris. She lay on her back, stunned but conscious, as the throbbing globe descended.

In the moment when her life might have flashed before her eyes, Emma remembered what Harry had said about the rogues turning on one another and realized that Blaise hadn't destroyed the priest and the fop. That would be some relief to Harry, if and when he figured out what had happened to her. When push came to shove, the rogues hadn't cooperated. They'd been distracted. They'd lost sight of the goal.

Em died when the globe touched her; there was no way she could have survived. She'd been incinerated. More than incinerated, she'd been stripped down to her atoms, even to her quarks and been reassembled, all in a single, blinding moment. She'd be as good as new once her vision cleared and it was already clearing. The wasteland came into focus around her—magenta sky, jagged dark walls, parched ground, and utter silence.

Emma hauled herself upright and took a slow walk around the empty courtyard.

Blaise was gone; the blond rogue was gone. Not a trace remained of them or their duel. Eleanor and her curses had disappeared, too—Emma examined every open, empty pit. Even the rogue corpses were gone. She had no idea who had won the duel. A double kill was a real possibility, as real as her own resurrection, as anything else in the wasteland.

Em heard a sound that could have been a footstep and turned around, full of hope. But it was only a bit of behind-Paris masonry tumbling to the ground. It signaled the start of a veritable rain of stone and mortar. Emma shouted Blaise's name one last time then ran from the courtyard as the whole construct came crashing down.

Billowing dust enveloped Emma from behind. She

coughed and choked and found herself on her living room floor with Nancy pounding hard between her shoulders. John handed her a wad of Kleenex. She hacked her lungs clear and took a glass of water from him as well.

"How long?"

Nancy answered, "About six hours. You reached out for me about four hours ago, but when I tried to bring you out of it, you pushed me away."

Six hours since she'd flipped the coin. Four hours, maybe, since the blond rogue had bounced her into a wall? It hadn't seemed that long, but it might have taken Emma a lot longer than she'd thought it had to pull herself together after the rogue's globe blasted her. If that were the case, then there was some small chance that Blaise was the one looking for survivors.

"Can you stand up?" John asked, offering his hand.

Em was stiff but otherwise undamaged and proved it by getting to her feet without help.

Nancy's scowling concern vanished, replaced by an excited smile. "Great!" She gave Em a big hug. "You did it! You pulled it off."

"I'm not so sure." Emma wriggled free. "I've got to talk to Harry first. There are some things I'm not sure of . . . a whole lot of things I don't understand."

"He's at the hospital," Nancy said with more glee than seemed appropriate. "Waiting for you."

John handed Em her coat. She took it, but didn't put it on.

"What happened while I was *gone*?"

"About an hour after you pushed me away—Harry called here: She's waking up, Emma. Eleanor's waking up! You did it. You set her free. I know he's dying to know what happened."

Em started to explain but Nance cut her off after a few words.

"No—wait 'til we get to the hospital. That's what he said. He doesn't want us asking you questions. He doesn't even want you to think about what happened until *he's* asking the questions."

That sounded like Harry, and as he obviously had secured the loyalty and cooperation of her closest friends, Emma shrugged into her coat and boots without an argument. There were a couple inches of snow on her walk, but the night sky was clear. John drove his car, Nancy drove Harry's rental, and Em sat in the passenger seat, staring out the window at the stars and trying to make sense out of a day that had begun a lifetime ago.

Jill was on duty at the hospital, all smiles and congratulations—Eleanor had focused her eyes. Eleanor had said a word. Eleanor had asked for Emma. Eleanor knew who'd stood by her.

Emma nodded but said nothing.

Whatever Eleanor had said or done a few hours ago, she was sound asleep when Emma walked into her room. Harry leapt up from a reclining chair whose comforts Em remembered all too well. His face was bruised, but the swelling was way down and he moved too easily for a man who'd been pulped less than twelve hours ago. Emma had suspicions that her stepfather's recovery was not quite natural, but kept them to herself when he embraced her.

"All's well that ends well, Emma," he whispered in her ear. "And you must have done very well, indeed."

"I had help," she whispered back. "Blaise Raponde was already there. The rogues did the hard work. He was in a duel with the last of them—unless Malerie—"

"We can worry about all that tomorrow—"

"I got stupid, Harry. I don't know what happened at the end. I wasn't there. I'd gotten myself killed—" The bill for the day suddenly came due; Emma began to tremble between Harry's arms. "Eleanor, the rogues, Blaise Raponde. No one was there behind Paris when it was over. Not even bodies. I was alone. The walls came tumbling down—"

Harry strengthened his embrace. "We'll talk about it.

You'll tell me *exactly* what happened. Don't borrow grief, Em. Eleanor's free. Take your victories where and when you find them." Harry let her go. He backed away and spoke for the others—Nancy, John, and a still-subdued Matt—to hear. "Yours was the first name out of her mouth. 'Where's Emma?' she wanted to know. I told her you'd get here as soon as you could. She wanted to talk to you, but she's weak as a kitten, and in quite a lot of discomfort, as you can imagine—"

Emma couldn't imagine. She forced herself to smile and say: "At least she didn't call me Merle Acalia."

She lifted Eleanor's hand and squeezed it gently, expecting her mother to wake up, but there was no response. Dr. Saha had roared back onto the scene, giving orders to everyone, even Harry Graves. Never mind that Eleanor had been in a coma for two months, Saha decreed that she needed sleep. If she awoke normally tomorrow morning—if she did, *then* they'd start physical therapy and schedule the procedure to remove her feeding tube.

"The good doctor thinks my wife will make a full recovery," Harry said with heavy sarcasm. "You know she will, Emma. You can be sure of it."

Emma nodded and tucked Eleanor's arm beneath the lightweight blanket. She and Eleanor still had a lifetime of unfinished business between them. Freeing Eleanor from a plague of curses and rogues would probably prove to have been one of the easier parts of their mother-daughter relationship.

A soft chime sounded in the corridor and a recorded message urged visitors to end their visits. John suggested a late supper; Harry said he wasn't hungry. The idea was dropped when Emma confessed that she wanted nothing more than to be left alone. Harry, Matt, John, and Nancy all wanted to give her a ride home. She had to accept someone's offer and, after promising the others that she'd call them in the morning, accepted Matt's.

"I'm sorry," Matt said as soon as they were in his battered car. "God, I'm so sorry. I don't believe what happened. What I did to Harry, to you. I'm so, so sorry, Emma."

Em patted him on the shoulder. "It wasn't your fault. If anything, I owe you the apology. If I weren't such an amateur at this curse-hunting business, I should have been able to put it together when you called on New Year's Eve."

"Sunday," he murmured, starting the car. "This all started last Sunday. It's all been a dream to me—a bad dream or a really bad movie. I can remember scenes, but most of it's empty places in my head until I was in that room, kicking the guts out of a man I didn't know. *Me*, Em, and I was kicking the crap out of him. Not a thought in my head. I didn't know who he was, or where, or why, but I'd have kept at it until he was dead."

"That wasn't you, Matt. It was her, Malerie—the rogue."

"Who was she, Em? I've been asking myself that. Whatever Harry says, she didn't just fall out of the sky. Is somebody sitting somewhere waiting for Malerie Dunbar to call home?"

Emma shuddered. "I hope not—I mean, I agree with you, Malerie Dunbar didn't just fall out of the sky. She had to have been born and maybe the police will match her up with someone, but honestly, I hope they don't come up with anything. People *do* disappear, Matt. Kids run away. They walk out of one life, into another, and sometimes they get forgotten. Sometimes they were forgotten before they left. They're never pretty stories. This one just happens to be uglier than most."

Matt said nothing while negotiating the maze of access roads that surrounded the hospital. When they were on the city streets, he asked: "Is that enough? We just close the book and keep going? That's what Harry said to me. 'Not to worry. No harm done.' Can you believe that?"

Em swallowed her reflexive, civilized response and said, "If I want to survive, I will—and you will, too. It's like a war, I guess. If you're smart—if you're smart and lucky, you don't think about what you've seen or done."

The light ahead turned red. They waited in silence until it turned green again, then Matt asked, "You want to hear the biggest joke of all?"

"A joke? There's a punchline to all this?"

"Yeah—the doctors are wondering if it was something in Mal's needle that woke Eleanor up. Like, if the poison didn't do it, maybe the shock did. That Dr. Saha, he was all excited. I could see the research paper in his eyes: 'The Effect of Near-Death Experiences on Comatose Women Who Aren't What They Appear to Be.'"

Emma wasn't tempted to laugh. "They'll calm down once they can't make any connections or patterns, Matt. Same as they did before. No pattern, no mystery, no interest."

"Then you'd better be careful."

"I'm not the one in the hospital."

"No, Em—you're the pattern. Strange patients get admitted to University Hospital, and funny thing, you're there to visit them."

She swore softly. "Maybe they'll pin it on you instead—the computer geek with a secret life. That's more of a cliché than the middle-aged librarian with a secret life."

Matt pondered that a moment, then asked: "Does that mean you're gonna give it up? Go back to being a librarian and nothing more than a librarian?"

"No," Emma admitted to herself and Matt together. "I don't think I could, if I wanted to. Harry said it was in my blood. He's right. He's a pompous blow-hard, but he's right, too. I'll let him teach me what I need to know and try not to get sucked in too deeply."

"You're still going to need a research assistant."

Em swallowed a lump. "I'd forgotten that. There's going to be fallout at the library from this. My assistant's not starting work on Monday."

"I meant with the curses and history," Matt corrected

quickly. "You need someone to help you dig up the facts and figures. Someone who doesn't have a life."

"Matt—it wasn't your fault. You were used. The rogue used you to get at me . . . and Eleanor and even Blaise Raponde. They hold grudges, I think."

"What you mean is that I'm too big a risk. You can't trust me 'cause there's no telling when I might get co-opted again and God knows what happens next time."

That was exactly what Em wanted to tell Matt, but she couldn't bring herself to say it, so she lied. "I didn't mean that at all. But, Matt—even if I can learn enough to keep you and Nancy and John and everyone around me perfectly safe, it's going to get *awkward*. Curse-hunting's ultimately a lonely life. A *long* lonely life, if you catch my drift."

Emma's thoughts slewed to the wasteland and the little shelter hidden in a little valley that looked like an orange section. She missed the start of Matt's reply.

"—And if she's your mother, how in hell old is Harry?"

"I have no idea, Matt. At least two hundred and fifty, probably three, probably more."

He whistled through his teeth. "Look, Em—let me help. Let me do something to make up for today."

They were nearing the Maisonettes. Emma was tired and willing to cut corners to end the conversation. "I'm going to need someone normal to talk to if I'm going to be dealing with the likes of Eleanor and Harry. You already know most of my so-called secrets. I can't imagine not keeping you informed, same as Nancy and John."

That lifted Matt's spirits. "We're your team, Em— Curse-Hunters Unlimited."

The words had the sound of prophecy. Em didn't argue or say another word about curses and rogues.

Once inside her home, she made a fuss over the cats. She cleaned up the kitchen and hauled all the Christmas boxes up from the basement—anything to avoid going to bed. Malerie would be waiting for her—the memories of

Malerie, anyway: Malerie sulking in Matt's office, Malerie taunting her at the restaurant, Malerie in a pool of blood, and Malerie in a crypt. Those images would haunt her no matter how long Emma lived, but what really kept her untrimming her Christmas tree in the wee hours of the morning was the fear that she'd seen the last of Blaise Raponde.

When the ornaments were boxed and loaded onto the basement shelves and her eyes were watering with exhaustion, Em finally gave in and turned out the lights. She was alone in the bathroom, alone in the bedroom, alone in the bed. Getting to the wasteland was no longer a challenge. Harry's silver coin was next to the answering machine where Nancy had left it, but Emma didn't need a real coin. She could imagine spinning it through the air. She could always catch an imaginary coin that always came up tails.

She could even land on her feet when she arrived in the wasteland, dressed in Mariana's blue gown and a pair of comfortable shoes. A shadow to her right marked the crescent-shaped hollow where she'd find her *place* in the wasteland, the shelter she'd created with Blaise Raponde's help.

Emma circled toward the shallow side of the hollow. When she saw a square of ordinary sunlight spilling onto the ground, she ran the rest of the way, but stopped short in the doorway, savoring what she saw.

Blaise Raponde sat in the upholstered chair, looking as solid and whole as he ever did and reading a letter—her letter, he said when he looked up.

Em protested, "I didn't write a letter," then she recalled the fragment of a dream.

"You wrote what would happen in your city of Bower, what would happen behind Paris. You were most precise." Blaise folded the letter and left it on the table. "I found no fault with your planning, and though nothing goes according to plan, in the end we each got what we wanted. I have had vengeance on the rogue who murdered me. You have your mother. Eleanor is herself, yes?"

"Yes—or she will be, soon." They were within arm's reach of each other, then closer, and Emma lost interest in her youthful mother. "When it was over and you weren't there, I thought I'd never see you again."

"I was there, Emma. I freed your mother and I waited for you until I was sure you would not come back to that place behind Paris, then I came here. This is our place. If you looked for me, I thought—hoped—that you would look for me here. I have been waiting a small while. I would have waited much longer. I have faith in you, Madame Mouse."

Emma laughed and closed the door.